Return
to
Love

Return to Love

a novel

Anita Stansfield

Covenant Communications, Inc.

Published by Covenant Communications, Inc.
American Fork, Utah

Printed in the United States of America
First Printing: August 1997

04 03 02 01 00 99 98 97   10 9 8 7 6 5 4 3

Library of Congress Cataloging-in-Publication Data

Stansfield, Anita, 1961-
    Return to love : a novel / Anita Stansfield.
        p.   cm.
    ISBN 1-57734-126-0
    I. Title
    PS3569.T33354R47 1997
    813'.54--dc21   97-23454
                                          CIP

To all those who have escaped their personal walls of Jericho.

And even more so, to those who have yet to find a way.

CHAPTER ONE
Provo, Utah

Colin Trevor wished he could melt into the crisp uphol-
stery and disappear. He pushed a tense hand through his wavy, sand-
colored hair and slid his lean frame as low in the chair as he could
possibly manage. He wiped sweating palms over his denimed thighs
as the bishop situated himself across the large, uncluttered desk. The
bishop's gentle smile did nothing to alleviate the knot forming somewhere between Colin's heart and stomach. He wanted to die. What
had he done to get into this position? Where had he gone wrong?

A warm hand slipped into Colin's, reminding him that he wasn't
alone. He turned to look at Janna. The slight tremor of her hand was the
only indication that she shared his anxiety. Her expression was dignified
without being prideful. Her green eyes met his, full of assurance and
hope. Colin cleared his throat and faced the bishop. He knew they could
get through this. As long as Janna was by his side, he could do anything.

"So," Bishop Bradshaw folded his hands on the desk, "what can
I do for you?"

Silence and a quick glance at Janna assured Colin that this was
up to him. "We need your help, Bishop." He fought to keep his voice
steady. "We . . . uh . . ." Colin cleared his throat again and Janna
squeezed his hand. "We've gotten into some trouble, Bishop, and we
can't get out of it without you."

If Bishop Bradshaw was surprised, he didn't show it. But how
could he not be? He was looking at the couple he'd often called the
finest example of youth in the ward.

"Go on," the bishop urged after a miserable silence.

Colin was vaguely aware of Janna as she pressed trembling fingers to her mouth. The last thing he'd ever wanted was to hurt her. But he had, and he knew it. If only to spare her any more grief, he had to get through this interview.

"Bishop," Colin straightened his back and went on, "I know you must be very disappointed in us . . . I mean me . . . being the stake president's son and all. I mean . . . he's not the stake president anymore, but he was until a few months ago. Of course, you already knew that. And that's irrelevant to this. But . . . the truth is, I haven't been doing everything I should, and it's caught up with me. This isn't Janna's fault, Bishop. I want you to understand that. None of this would have happened if—"

"Excuse me, Colin," Bishop Bradshaw interrupted gently. "I can see that you're upset, and I want to help you, but perhaps we would get further if I knew exactly what we're discussing."

Colin glanced down, embarrassed by his rambling. A warm chuckle from the bishop gave him the courage to go on. "Well, you see," he began again, "what happened is that . . ." Colin hesitated. Emotion rose in his throat. While he was trying to choke it back, Janna spoke with a trembling voice that tried to be strong.

"Bishop Bradshaw, Colin and I care for each other very much. You know we've been going together for more than two years now, and until a few months ago, we never had any trouble staying within proper boundaries. Still, it never really got out of hand until . . ." She bit her lip slightly and continued with a maturity far beyond her seventeen years. ". . . Until my mother died."

"She's not been gone a week, Janna," the bishop observed. "Are you saying that—"

"I'm saying that I fell apart when I lost her." Tears gathered in the rims of her eyes. "I lost all control. This is not Colin's fault. I was to blame for the—"

"That's not true and you know it!" Colin snapped. Janna threw him a sharp glance and he could see the hurt in her eyes. "I'm sorry," he added more softly, as if the bishop weren't present, "but I should have been the one to keep it in control. I should have been strong. I should have known better than to take advantage of you in a vulnerable moment when . . ." Recalling the bishop's presence, he hesitated.

"I'm still just assuming that this problem is what it appears to be," Bishop Bradshaw stated.

"Assume the worst, Bishop," Colin muttered. Janna squeezed her eyes shut and tears trailed over her cheeks. "What we have done is unforgivable."

"Unless the two of you have conspired to have someone murdered, I would not say it's unforgivable."

Colin just stared at the floor. Janna's eyes remained closed.

"Fornication is a serious thing, Brother Trevor," the bishop continued gently. Colin winced at the word being used in reference to him. Janna's hand tightened in his. "If that is what we're discussing, then the two of you have a difficult path of repentance ahead of you."

Colin took a moment to gather his words carefully. "That is why we are here, Bishop. Not only because you have the keys to help us, but because we can't make it through this alone."

For a few seconds Colin nearly expected Bishop Bradshaw to cry, but he gained his composure and offered a comforting smile. "I appreciate your faith in me, Colin, but I'd like to remind you—both of you—that it's only through Christ's atoning sacrifice that repentance is possible. That is where we need to look for the strength to make it through this." The bishop leaned back with an abundant sigh. "Now, I guess we should start at the beginning. I'm afraid I'll need to know exactly how this happened. I get the impression, Colin, from what you said earlier, that you feel other things have led up to this. Could you tell me what?"

Colin glanced at Janna, almost expecting an *I-told-you-so* expression. He well deserved one. But her eyes were full of love and acceptance. They always had been.

"Well, you see," Colin cleared his throat and straightened his back, "I haven't been doing so well with my church attendance, and I totally let my scripture study and daily prayer go. I don't know why. I guess I expected that all Brigham Young University students were good kids; but somehow I got pulled into a group that isn't. I mean, they don't really do anything bad, they're just . . . lazy, I guess." He met Janna's eyes. "Janna has been after me to straighten myself out. But like a fool, I didn't listen."

Janna's eyes darted away. Silence hung uncomfortably in the air until Bishop Bradshaw spoke again. "So, what you're trying to tell me is that you weren't doing what you needed to do to stay close to the Spirit."

Colin nodded feebly. "Then last week," he bit his lip and hesitated, "I saw an R-rated movie with some of the guys. I mean, I've seen one or two before, but I just wasn't prepared for . . . well," he swallowed hard, "for how bad it could really be." Colin's stomach began to smolder from the memory even now. "And then," his voice became unsteady, "when Janna lost her mother so unexpectedly like that, I just . . . I . . ." Emotion consumed him, and he was grateful when Janna took over.

"The day my mother had her stroke," she said carefully, "I was supposed to meet Colin for dinner. I was at the hospital until after she died, and . . . Colin took me home, and . . . I fell apart. I just cried and cried and . . ." She hesitated, and Colin shifted in his chair. "I asked Colin to stay with me. I was scared, but I didn't want to go to his house, being so upset and all. He insisted that I get some rest, but I didn't want to be alone. When I woke up in the middle of the night, he was there with me and . . ." her voice broke, "and . . . one thing . . . led to . . . another . . . and . . ."

After another miserable silence, the bishop asked quietly, "Did it happen more than once?"

"Twice," Colin stated with a bitter edge, "that same night." He hoped Janna knew the bitterness was directed toward himself.

"And since?" the bishop asked.

"Nothing," Colin said without hesitation. "The guilt set in quickly, Bishop. We've been very careful. We simply decided to get the funeral behind us and take a few days to . . ." he squeezed Janna's hand, "to get up the courage."

Colin was beginning to think the worst was over when the bishop asked some questions concerning specific details that were difficult, if not embarrassing, to answer. But Colin understood the gospel well. He knew the repentance process could not take place without the bishop knowing exactly what they were dealing with. As they discussed the situation in more detail, it became increasingly evident to Colin how gradual his fall had been. It was perhaps the most humbling moment of his life to have to admit that because of his lack of spirituality, he had been pressing boundaries of immorality with Janna for several weeks. It had become a source of contention between them, but he would never have dreamed it would come to this. Tears were shed, and the pain of regret was vivid. The probationary action for their sin was discussed carefully.

"Now," the bishop continued with a bright tone in his voice, "we must move forward with faith and not let this set the two of you back any more than absolutely necessary."

Colin felt hope in the squeeze of Janna's hand. He returned it with fervor.

"At this point, what are your plans for the future?" The bishop turned to Janna first.

"I'll be graduating from high school in a few months," she said. "My aunt will be staying with me until then. After that, I'll be moving to Arizona to live with her."

"Are you concerned about that?" Bishop Bradshaw asked gently.

"I'm not thrilled about it." Janna's tone remained light, but Colin wasn't fooled. She didn't like Aunt Phyllis and he knew it. "But she's the only relative I've got. I have nowhere else to go."

"Colin?" The bishop indicated it was his turn.

"I want to work toward a mission." He realized his hands were shaking. "I know it will take longer than I'd expected now, but . . . I still want to go, and . . . then I'm planning to get my degree in law here at BYU. I've already got nearly two years of credits behind me, and I'll just keep working toward my degree until I'm worthy to go on my mission."

"And do your plans for the future include each other?" the bishop asked.

"Of course!" Colin chuckled dryly. He couldn't believe anyone would think otherwise. "I love Janna very much, Bishop. I have every intention of marrying her—in the temple—after my mission."

"Of course you realize," the bishop said gravely, "there is the possibility of pregnancy. Then what?"

The question hung over the room like a dark cloud. As difficult as it was, Colin knew he was to blame for this mess, and he would take responsibility for it.

"Then we'll get married right away," Colin stated firmly.

Janna turned to him, gaping. "What about your mission? And

college? You can't just throw it all away to—"

"It would be hard, yes, but that may be the price I'll have to pay, Janna. We can go on a mission together one day, when our children are raised."

She looked at the floor. "Your family would be devastated if you didn't marry in the temple."

"My family would get over it when we are sealed. We're not the first Mormon kids to make a big mistake."

"You're right about that," the bishop piped in. "But obviously we will have to wait in order to determine whether or not there are results."

Colin nodded. Janna squeezed her eyes shut.

"In the meantime," the bishop continued, "I suggest the two of you take extreme precautions in the time you spend together. If you were not working toward sharing a future, I would recommend that you end the relationship now. But if the two of you are meant to be together, and it would seem you feel this is so, then you must be extremely careful. Satan will work very hard to pull you back down. These next weeks are critical. My suggestion is that you keep dates to a minimum. Spend time with each other in the presence of family members. Keep close contact by phone. For the present, concentrate on your schoolwork and keeping close to the scriptures."

Colin and Janna both nodded. The bishop went on with words of encouragement and suggestions. He spoke of the Savior's redeeming sacrifice, and tears fell again. They left the bishop's office holding hands. The months ahead would be difficult, but the first steps had been made and Colin felt a great burden lifted already. With Janna by his side, he could make it through anything.

"I'm so sorry, Janna," he said as they walked toward the car.

"Why do you keep apologizing when it's—"

"Because it *was* my fault," he insisted.

"So you keep saying, but I'll tell you again, Colin, I could have stopped at any given moment. But I didn't."

"You shouldn't have been put into a position where you had to stop it," he protested. "My father always told me that since guys get turned on easier, it's up to the guy to turn it off first."

"It takes two, Colin, to—"

"Don't say it." He held up a hand and opened the passenger

door for her. "Why won't you just admit that it was my fault and let it rest?"

Their eyes met, and she almost smiled for the first time since she had lost her mother—and her virtue.

"Why don't you stop talking and kiss me?" she asked.

"No!" He tried to keep from smiling. "Not until you admit it's my fault."

"All right, if it will make you feel better, it was all your fault, Colin." She touched his face and he kissed her quickly. "But it's up to both of us to keep it from happening again."

Colin nodded and helped her into the car. He closed the door and got in himself. Before he put the key in the ignition, Janna added, "I shouldn't have asked you to stay. We should have gone to your house where your parents were—"

"You just said it was all my fault."

"Only because you wanted me to."

"There's no good in speculating over should-have-beens now. It's over and done. We've just got to deal with it."

"I know," she said with a cracked voice.

"I love you, JannaLyn Hayne," he whispered with adoration, toying with the loose brown curls hanging over her shoulder.

"I love you, too, Colin. I would be nothing without you."

"No," he smiled, "it's the other way around."

"Stop talking and kiss me," she said. Colin smiled and filled her request. It was a common phrase between them, and he appreciated her using it now. They needed to feel a little normalcy in their relationship.

The weeks following that first interview were torturous for Colin. He followed Bishop Bradshaw's counsel to the letter, knowing it was the only thing that could save him. While he hated not seeing Janna every day, his thoughts were still too often absorbed with memories of their intimacy—memories that made the natural man in him want very badly for it to happen again.

They talked on the phone as often as possible, and their one date a week was with another couple, often Colin's older sister, Colette, and her fiance. On Sundays they attended church together and spent time with Colin's family. Their rare moments alone were tense and strained. Colin stayed close to the scriptures and prayed harder than he'd ever done in his life. Janna assured him she was doing the same, but there was a solemnity about her that he couldn't explain. When he questioned her, she simply told him this was not easy. He knew that to be true, but there was more. He prodded and questioned her and finally had to settle for the theory that women take things like this much more personally. That was understandable. On top of that, she had lost her mother and was now living under the formidable eye of her stone-faced Aunt Phyllis.

Colin dreaded Janna's graduation, knowing she would leave soon afterward for Arizona. The thought of separation was terrifying. She had been a part of his everyday life for more than two and a half years. But he was determined to marry her; miles and years would not keep him from that.

"Do you remember the first time we saw each other?" Colin asked late one Sunday afternoon while he and Janna sat together on his back lawn. His younger brothers were playing catch further down the huge yard. His mother sat close by, studying her Primary lesson for next week.

"I'll never forget it," she said, but there was an unexplainable sadness about her. "You changed my life, Colin." She lay back on the cool grass and closed her eyes while Colin meticulously painted her toenails a pale peach color. It was something he'd done often since the youth activity they'd attended where the girls got to paint the boys' toenails if they hadn't read their scriptures.

"How is that?" he chuckled dubiously, but her expression was serious.

Janna opened her eyes and gazed nostalgically toward the setting sun. She sat up and took his hand as he set his sister's nail polish aside. "You accepted me when no one else did."

Colin chuckled. "They're all a bunch of fools." He bent to kiss Janna quickly and caught a sly smile from his mother out of the corner of his eye.

Janna rubbed a gentle thumb over the white scar across the back of his left hand. "What made you seek me out, anyway," she asked, "when there were so many girls swooning at your feet—girls with much more to offer than me?"

"More what?" he laughed. "More makeup? More pomp and

circumstance? No, I don't think so." He touched the back of his fingers to her face. "You're not like those other girls. That's exactly why I sought you out. You're fresh and honest and vibrant. That's why I love you."

Janna glanced away, apparently embarrassed. She turned her attention back to the scar on his hand. "You never did tell me how you got this," she said in a light tone that defied the sadness filling her eyes.

"No one remembers," he stated. "With eight children, who could keep track?"

"You have a wonderful family," she reminded him.

"Yes," he glanced at his mother and agreed, "I do. And you will be a part of it, JannaLyn." She looked somehow doubtful and he couldn't understand why. He touched her chin to make her face him. "I swear by heaven and earth, Janna, you will be my wife. Nothing is going to change that. I know this is hard, but I'll make it up to you. I swear it."

For a moment he thought she was going to cry, but she chuckled instead. "You just get that mission behind you, Colin. There are people out there who need you more than I do right now."

"What's that supposed to mean?" he demanded, feeling uneasy.

Janna only smiled. "You will make a fine missionary, Colin. When you get back, life will fall into place for both of us."

Colin swallowed his concerns, but a nagging doubt smoldered in the pit of his stomach over the next several days. He made an appointment to speak with the bishop alone, wanting some advice on how to deal with Janna's emotions. Bishop Bradshaw listened with compassion, but he had no advice to give Colin that he hadn't already tried. Then he brought up something they'd discussed before that Colin had been trying to avoid.

"Have you talked to your parents about this yet?"

Colin sighed and pressed his forehead into his hand. "I don't know if I can, Bishop. I've prayed about it. I've tried to get up the nerve, but . . ."

"But?" the bishop urged.

"I think I could talk to my mother. But my dad and I . . ."
Colin couldn't find words to express the subtle estrangement that had

always existed between them.

"If your father hadn't been released as stake president, he would have to know."

"I'm aware of that," Colin said, inwardly grateful that this was no longer the case.

"I know it's difficult, Colin. I simply feel that talking to them about it would help you—and Janna—to get through this. You keep working on it, okay?"

Colin continued praying for help in following through on the bishop's challenge. He was contemplating the problem and ignoring the textbook in front of him when his mother knocked at the partially open door to his bedroom.

"May I come in?" Nancy Trevor asked.

"Sure, Mom." Colin stood abruptly as she entered the room.

"Can we talk?" she asked, sitting on the edge of the bed.

"Sure," Colin repeated, almost certain she had sensed that something was wrong. She'd always been far too perceptive to make him believe that she didn't have suspicions about the state of his life.

Colin sat back down, attempting to quell the sudden pounding of his heart. Was this the Spirit trying to give him a cue? Or was he just plain terrified? He'd grown a full head taller than his mother, but at the moment, he felt extremely small in her presence.

"Your father and I were talking about you last night," she began. Colin held his breath. He could feel it coming. "You're almost nineteen, Colin." She looked into his eyes, and it took great self-control to not turn away. He almost believed that she could read his mind. "You haven't said anything about a mission for a long time. We can't help being concerned, Colin." She paused and added gently, "Do you still want to go on a mission?"

"Yes, of course I do," he insisted.

"Good. Perhaps you should tell your father that."

Colin glanced away and sighed.

"I know you and your father have difficulty seeing eye to eye. But he has a right to know where your head is."

"I know," Colin said.

A growing silence made it evident that Nancy expected him to say something. His heart continued to pound. He had prayed for some help in putting things straight with his parents, and he'd never get a better opportunity than this. He turned to look at his mother's gentle countenance. She was patience personified; and of all her children, he knew he was the one who had tried her patience the most. She took his hand, but still she said nothing. As Colin attempted to form the words to tell her, the shame and guilt tightened his chest and made him sweat. *He was such a fool!*

Praying inwardly, Colin finally found the words to begin. "I want to go on a mission, Mom. I just . . . need some time. I haven't been living the way I should. I need to . . . get things in order."

"Okay," she drawled, and then she was silent again. He knew she wouldn't force him to tell her anything more, but she would make it terribly uncomfortable for him not to.

He took a deep breath and went on. "I don't have to tell you that my church attendance hasn't been real good. I mean, I've been doing better since . . . Janna's mother died, but . . . well . . . and I'm trying to get back on track with my scripture study and prayer . . . but . . . I've seen some movies I shouldn't have seen, and . . ."

"And?" she echoed when he hesitated. When he said nothing more, due to some unexplained strangulation of his vocal cords, she added, "I knew all of that, Colin. But I get the feeling there's something more. It's just one of those motherly things, I suppose. If you don't want to talk about it, I certainly can't force you. But I'm concerned, Colin." She leaned closer to him. "I'm your mother. If you're struggling, I want to help you. I just want you to know that I am here for you. I'm not going to pass any judgments or make it more difficult for you."

"I know *you* won't."

Nancy sighed. "I can't change the way things are between you and your father, Colin. But he's a good man, and I know he loves you." Through another grueling silence, Colin gathered his courage. He found it difficult to admit the full depth of his sins to his mother, but he finally managed to say, "I've had some immorality problems with JannaLyn."

Her expression didn't change. Her eyes didn't even flicker. "Is it bad?" she asked.

"Yeah, it's bad," he snarled with self-recrimination.

"So, what are you doing about it?" she asked.

"We've been to see the bishop. We're seeing him regularly, if you must know. We're almost never alone together. I'm reading my scriptures and praying more than I ever have in my life."

Nancy squeezed his hand. "That's good, then."

Colin took a deep breath and told her what she had a right to know. "I don't know when I'll be ready to go on a mission, Mom. I want to go; I'm doing everything in my power to get there. But it could be a while. I don't want to go without being absolutely certain that I'm worthy, and I'm ready. In the meantime, I'll keep working on my degree."

"I'm glad to hear that," she said. "I think your father would be glad to hear it, too."

Colin sighed. "Oh, come on, Mom. If I told Dad what I just told you, he'd fly through the roof."

"So, tell him what you feel like you can tell him, Colin. But don't shut him out completely." She touched his face and added, "He has a right to know where you are. He can't help wondering why your mission will be delayed."

Colin nodded, hating the way that knot of guilt and regret kept forming in his stomach. But he knew she was right.

"Is there anything else you want to tell me?" she asked.

Colin wondered if he should prepare her for the possibility that Janna might be pregnant. But he told himself he'd said enough for now. If he and Janna had to get married, his mother would obviously be one of the first to know that his goals would be severely altered. And she knew enough now that it wouldn't completely shock her. He shook his head firmly.

"Is there anything else you want to talk about?" she asked.

The full depth of his mother's support kicked in as he expressed his concern for Janna. She encouraged him to be patient and remember that she'd lost her mother. They talked for a long while about his relationship with Janna and the depth of his feelings for her. He was amazed at his mother's acceptance and encouragement. Before she left the room, she hugged him tightly, telling him in no uncertain terms how much she loved him, and that she was always there for him. With her hand on the doorknob, she turned back toward him and said, "JannaLyn is a wonderful girl, Colin. I was never very comfortable with the way the two of you fell in love at such a young age. But I've always loved her myself; I've always felt like you were meant to be together. I have every hope that it will work out." She lifted a finger and added, "But you keep your hands off of her until she is your wife, Colin. She's a daughter of God, and she deserves to be treated that way—especially by you. Don't hurt her again."

Colin barely managed to nod before his mother left the room and closed the door. He sat weakly on the edge of his bed. The knot in his throat pressed up into his head until he had no choice but to bury his face in his hands and cry. *He was such a fool!*

The following day, Colin sought out his father while he was reading the newspaper.

"Hey, Dad," he said, and Carl Trevor folded down the corner of the paper. "I just wanted you to know that I'm still working toward a mission. But there are some things I need to get in order first. I haven't been doing everything I should, but I'm doing my best to get my life on track. The bishop is helping me."

Colin's palms sweat while he could almost feel his father's head spinning with questions. But Carl finally said, "I appreciate knowing that. If there's anything I can do . . ."

"Thanks, Dad," he said and left the room. He didn't completely understand why it was so difficult to talk to his father. But for the first time in his life, he really wished that he could.

Colin told Janna over the phone about the things he'd told his parents. She didn't say much, and his concern for her deepened. There was a question he needed to ask her, but he didn't quite dare. The following day as their weekly bishop's interview commenced, Colin was relieved to have it approached head on.

"So," Bishop Bradshaw began, "it's been six weeks. We should know by now which direction should be taken." His eyes turned to Janna, but she was staring at her hands, folded in her lap.

"Janna," the bishop said gently, "is there any reason why Colin should not pursue his plans for working toward a mission?"

She didn't move. Colin's heart thudded into his throat. He knew it would be at least a year before he could go, but he wanted it so badly. He'd considered deeply what would happen if she was pregnant, and he was determined to take it on with faith and make the most of it. But oh, how he wanted to go on that mission, to start their lives out the right way! Would God allow a child to come into the picture now? It all hung on Janna's answer, but still she didn't move. Colin could almost hear the words ringing in his ears. Something inside told him a child had been conceived, but he didn't want to accept it; *wouldn't* accept it until he heard it from her.

"Janna," the bishop repeated and she looked up, startled, "is there any reason why Colin should—"

"No," she interrupted firmly, "there is no reason why Colin should not pursue his preparations for a mission."

Colin's sigh of relief nearly smothered his remaining doubts. He was grateful for the bishop's effort to clarify the situation.

"Janna," his brow furrowed with severity, "are you absolutely certain that you are not pregnant?"

"I am absolutely certain," she stated, and the interview continued as usual. But Colin was keenly aware of something different about Janna.

Once outside, he questioned her pointedly. "Are you all right, Janna?"

"I'm fine, why?"

"You just don't . . . seem like yourself. You haven't since—"

"I'm not!" she snapped. "Everything in my life has changed, Colin."

"The way I feel about you hasn't changed." He gently ignored her nerves, knowing they were warranted. "I will love you always."

"There are many years of uncertainty ahead, Colin. Don't make promises you can't keep."

"What's that supposed to mean?"

"Nothing." She walked away, but he grabbed her arm.

"If you said it, it deserves clarifying. What's it supposed to mean?"

"Exactly what I said. The future is always full of uncertainty. How can we know for sure what will happen?"

"I know you and I are meant to be together forever. And nothing can change that, Janna. Do you understand me? Nothing!"

Janna made no response. It was as if something had died inside her, but Colin felt helpless to fix it when he didn't understand it. In that moment, he feared she would never open up to him the way she always had before.

Weeks passing didn't narrow the distance between them. Was this the price of sin? he asked himself over and over until his head hurt. He dreaded the day she would leave for Arizona, but he was poorly prepared for the moment when it finally arrived.

Colin helped Janna pack the last of her things into the back of Phyllis's station wagon. Janna had only graduated last night, but Phyllis was more than ready to get her away from Provo, as if Utah were contaminated or something. He eyed the formidable aunt as she arranged her belongings in the back seat.

"Hurry along, Janna," she called, sticking her head out of the car. "We've got no time to waste. I've already spent three months of my life in this place. Enough is enough."

Colin didn't miss the dread emanating from Janna. But still, he wondered if she was dreading this separation as much as he. In his heart he believed there had to be an option, but Phyllis was unbendable. For a moment he almost wished Janna *was* pregnant; then he could marry her and take care of her, and she would never have to see Phyllis again. But as it was, Phyllis Gordon was Janna's only living relative—her mother's sister.

Diane Hayne had married young, and her husband left the family right after Janna's birth. She finally divorced him on grounds of abandonment, and Janna had only seen her father once, soon after her thirteenth birthday, when he returned and tried to get back into their lives. It wasn't long before Diane had sent him packing, and Janna spoke of the event as if it had been a nightmare. Diane's parents had died young. She and Phyllis were the only children, so the unmarried Aunt Phyllis was all Janna had left.

When everything was packed and Phyllis got into the car, Colin took Janna in his arms, wishing he could hold her forever. His gut instincts told him this was all wrong, but for the life of him he couldn't see how to change it.

"Write as soon as you get there," he insisted, trying not to cry, "and then I'll have your address. I'll write every day."

She nodded stoically. Her lip quivered. Colin felt tears gather in his eyes.

"Promise me you'll write," he babbled on. "The minute you get there, you must—"

"Stop talking and kiss me," she said, her voice barely steady.

Colin kissed her quickly, then hugged her tight. "I love you, Janna," he murmured, hating the desperation in his voice.

"I love you, too, Colin." She looked up at him briefly. Tears spilled over her face, then she held to him desperately. "Whatever happens, you must remember that."

"Come along, Janna," Phyllis called tersely. "You'll be eighteen in a couple of months, and then you can come back to this forsaken place if you choose."

"I have to go," she said with a little laugh that he knew was an attempt to keep from sobbing.

Not knowing when he would see her again, Colin momentarily disregarded all of Bishop Bradshaw's admonitions as he pulled her into his arms and kissed her. They'd not exchanged more than quick little pecks since the night Janna's mother died. But now, he kissed her as if he would die without her. In that moment, he almost believed he would. Janna clung to him and responded in a way that brought their intimacies rushing back to him. Oblivious to Phyllis's skeptical observance, Colin held her tighter, kissed her harder. He was terrified to let her go.

"I love you," Janna whispered against his lips. She pressed her tear-stained face to his throat. "I love you. I love you so much."

"I love you, too," he whispered. Phyllis tapped on the horn, and he gave Janna one more quick kiss before he let her slip away. In a matter of seconds she was in the car, and it was pulling away. Colin didn't know how long he stood there, feeling somehow dead inside, before he turned to gaze at the house, indulging himself in memories. He'd loved Diane Hayne almost as much as his own mother. If losing Diane hadn't been bad enough, now Janna was gone, too. And their home seemed as lifeless as Diane's body had looked in the casket. He turned to look at the *For Sale* sign on the lawn and resisted the urge to just tear it out of the grass and throw it into the street. When standing there became something close to torture, he forced himself to walk the two blocks home and face his life without Janna.

Colin watched the mailbox obsessively. His mother expressed

deep concern for him when nothing arrived from Janna and he became almost despondent. At first he was convinced that something had happened to her, but he checked with police departments and hospitals to no avail. He did everything he could think of. He tried to find Phyllis's address, but Janna had told him nothing more than "a town somewhere near Phoenix." Colin tried calling directory assistance for practically every town in Arizona, but either Phyllis didn't exist or she had an unlisted number. He would have gone to Arizona to hunt her down personally, but in his heart he knew he could never find her if she didn't want to be found.

Months after Janna left, Colin finally came to the conclusion that she needed time for some reason, and he had to let it go. It was the only possible conclusion. He worked zealously at putting college credits behind him. He went on his mission to Japan, certain that Janna would write when she was ready, and his mother could forward her letters. But the two years passed with a deep dread smoldering in him that made it difficult to be the kind of missionary he had hoped to be. In his heart he knew Janna was alive, and he knew she loved him. But something was wrong.

Colin returned home from his mission determined to find her, one way or another, if only to know *why* she had abandoned their relationship without so much as a letter. He advertised in newspapers in the Phoenix area, and received two responses. They both told him the same thing. Phyllis Gordon had passed away about two years after he had last seen Janna. Six months before her aunt's death, JannaLyn Hayne got married and moved away.

Colin felt sick. He might as well have been told that Janna was dead. Except that losing her to death might have been easier. At least he wouldn't have had to wonder. *Why?* He just didn't understand *why*. He had believed from the start that he and Janna were meant to be together.

It took weeks to deal with the shock, but once he did, Colin knew he had no choice but to make a life without her. He was on his way to becoming a lawyer, and he convinced himself that there were many wonderful women out there who could take away this ache. But every attempt he made at dating or developing a relationship always came up short. And deep inside, he knew he was fooling himself.

Years passing didn't alleviate the struggles for Colin. He could look back over his life and see that even though he'd repented and done his best to do the right thing, everything had gone steadily downhill since that incident with Janna. At least now, he had the sense to stay close to the Spirit. He believed it was the only thing that kept him on an even keel. There were moments when he wondered if his sanity was still intact. But a night came when the Spirit let him know that his feelings were not without warrant. He knew something was wrong with Janna; something was left undone. And only he could make it right. If he could just find her!

With fresh determination, Colin put the matter into the Lord's hands, concluding that he should have done it years ago. He believed that if Janna needed him, the Lord would lead her back into his life.

CHAPTER TWO

$\mathcal{J}$anna saw the change in her husband's eyes. After so many years, she could easily recognize the transformation from Jekyll to Hyde.

"You know, Russell," she said, taking a step back and attempting to hold her voice steady, "I simply haven't been well today. I tried to do what you asked, but I . . ."

Janna's voice faltered as Russell's narrowing eyes made it clear he'd stopped listening long ago. She knew that lowering herself to petty begging would make no difference. But after so many times, she wondered why she still had to be afraid. As Russell raised his hand to strike, Janna wondered once again what could make a man so heinous. She resisted the urge to raise her hands in protest, knowing it would only make him more angry. He backhanded her across the face with such force that she saw stars.

Janna attempted to steel herself for another blow, but the illness she'd fought with all day took hold. Her fear was swallowed by an enveloping relief. Everything went black.

Janna emerged into consciousness with a groan. She glanced around to take in her surroundings. At least he'd had the decency to move her to the bed this time. Trying to orient herself, Janna panicked.

"Matthew!" she whispered and sat up, then regretted it when her head swam and slammed back down on the pillow. Listening for any sign that he was all right, she felt immense relief to hear him digging in his closet where his favorite toys were kept. Like an answer to an unspoken prayer, he began to sing softly to himself and she knew he was fine. Russell had never hurt Matthew. The child was quiet and cooperative, and as long as he stayed out of Russell's way, there was never a problem. But one of Janna's deepest fears was the possibility that the situation would change. She dreaded the day when Matthew reached a new stage of independence, or an abrupt mood swing that was normal to a child's development. What if Russell didn't handle it well? What if he . . . No, she couldn't think of that. She just *couldn't!* She was barely clinging to the edge of sanity as it was.

Janna realized she'd drifted off again when Russell's voice in the hall startled her awake. She heard him say in a kind tone, "Hey, Mattie, your mother's resting; she's not feeling well. How about if we go get a hamburger?"

Matthew's response was not enthusiastic, but cooperative and respectful. Janna felt sure he wouldn't dare respond any other way. The incidents were not necessarily frequent, and Matthew had been carefully instructed to go to his room and stay there whenever Russell flew into one of his rages. But Janna worried about the emotional impact all this was having on the child. The effect of violent television on children was one thing; but what happened to children who experienced it in their own homes?

Hearing the car pull out of the garage, Janna sighed and relaxed. The effects of a head cold, combined with the recent blows to her face, made her wish for unconsciousness again. Now that she knew she was alone, she allowed the tears to come. Her crying always upset Matthew, and it made Russell angry. It was only in solitude that Janna dared to feel anything at all. For Matthew she had to be strong, and positive, and confident. For Russell she had to be perfect.

Just as she had a thousand times before, Janna asked herself how she'd ever come to be in this situation. She recalled a day when she had been young and strong, with her whole life ahead of her. Then it seemed that almost overnight her world had fallen apart. In these times of solitude, the events leading to this moment swirled endlessly in her head, with no sense of time or order. And in the midst of them all was Colin Trevor. As long as she could remember, there had only been one person—beyond her mother and her son—who had ever truly loved her. Her mother's death had been the beginning of this mess she'd created of her life. And her son was too young to understand. Colin was the single bright spot in her memories. But it was only in her mind that he existed now, and even that always brought her to the inevitable despair.

Still, she couldn't help herself. Thinking of him was almost like a compulsive addiction. Knowing she had some time, Janna allowed her mind to wander back to happier days. How clearly she could see Colin in her memory! The way he would look at her with his penetrating blue eyes—a blue so dark it was almost navy. And his smile always revealed deep dimples in both cheeks. A bare hint of a dimple occasionally showed in his chin, appearing at random as if it was a secret part of him.

She and Colin had loved each other. Their relationship was the kind that came along once in a lifetime, and she knew it. But she had betrayed him, and nothing had ever been right since. At the time, her reasons had seemed noble and good. But now it all faded into a blur, and she wasn't certain if she even had a clue about what was right anymore.

How clearly she recalled the last time she had seen Colin—the way he'd held her and kissed her, as if his life depended on her. Oh, how she longed to be held that way again—to just know that she was worthy of such affection.

Living in Arizona with her aunt Phyllis, following her mother's death, was every bit as miserable as Janna had expected it to be. Phyllis was cynical, ornery, and belligerent. And those were her good qualities. When Russell Clark came along, offering marriage, security, and an escape from Aunt Phyllis, Janna jumped at the chance, with no thought of the jagged rocks below. She often wondered if she should have prayed over the decision to marry him. But he had so thoroughly charmed her, she couldn't have possibly imagined him being anything but good to her. He'd had a job offer in the city she'd grown up in, and she'd longed to go back to Provo. No, Janna didn't pray about it, because she didn't want to know. She only wanted to get out, with the hope that Russell would somehow compensate for everything she had lost. And she had long since stopped praying, certain she was not worthy of *any* blessing from God. She had lied to and betrayed the love of her life, and she believed she had disappointed her mother before her spirit had even reached the other side.

And now, here she was. Janna got what she'd bargained for. She had a temple marriage. She had a fine home, nice clothes, financial security, and she certainly never went hungry. But the loving facade with which Russell Clark had lured her into marriage had fallen away, piece by piece. And now she went to church every Sunday with her husband and smiled, as if everything was perfect. Wherever Russell Clark went, he was a paragon of perfection. In the ward and neighborhood he was regarded as kind, honest, always willing to help. He was committed to his church callings, and always there to help a neighbor in need. At work, as a successful accountant, he was the one who always went the extra mile. His clients revered him as thorough, thoughtful, and generous. Janna was often told by outsiders how lucky she was to have such a dear husband. Around others, he treated her like a queen. He always complimented her, made sweet remarks, and showered her with gifts.

But Janna was nothing more than a prisoner, locked away behind walls as impenetrable as stone. She was bound to a lifestyle that demanded her full attention. If she gave even the slightest inkling of faltering in her responsibilities, there was a price to pay. And she had paid it well. But how long could she go on? There were times when she almost literally felt the walls closing in on her, as if they held her back from living a life that she wanted to believe she was meant to live. She was afraid to stay, and afraid to leave. She felt certain there was nowhere she could go where he wouldn't find her. And just the attempt at leaving would likely drive him to an anger so deep she believed he would kill her. If not for Matthew, she believed death would be preferable to living in her current circumstances—not to mention the fact that there was a perverse kind of pleasure in imagining Russell wasting away in prison for having committed murder. But Matthew was the most important thing. Janna had to survive, if only to see that he made it through this nightmare unscathed—if such a thing was possible.

As the room gradually dimmed with evening, Janna felt a darkness settle around her, deeper than any she'd experienced before. She knew in that moment that if something didn't change, she *would* die. Even if she physically survived Russell's abuse, she felt sure that her spirit could take no more. She would end up wasting away in some asylum, while Matthew . . . heaven only knew what might happen to Matthew.

Prompted by the deepest kind of desperation, Janna murmured toward the ceiling, "Please, God, if you're there . . . please help me.

Show me the way." Just saying it aloud somehow made her feel better. How many years had passed since she'd dared talk to God at all? Perhaps it was a step in the right direction. She doubted that anyone short of God himself could ever solve this problem.

Janna continued to pray aloud, at the same time allowing her mind to wander in search of any likely solution. But it always came to a dead end. She had no access to money that didn't have to be accounted for to the penny. She had no relatives; nowhere to go. She would even take living with Aunt Phyllis over this. But ironically, Phyllis had passed away not long after her marriage. If Janna had held out a few months longer, she would have had her freedom and a chance to make a fresh start. But there was no use stewing about that now.

Realizing that Russell and Matthew would be home soon, Janna felt a sudden urge to read out of the Bible. There had been a time when daily scripture study was as vital to her as brushing her teeth or eating. But she'd hardly opened the scriptures since she'd left Colin— as if the act of turning her back on him had in itself closed a door that she felt afraid to open.

Still praying in her mind, Janna thumbed carelessly through the book, feeling it was more a way to keep her hands busy than anything else. She wasn't expecting an answer, and when the book seemed to fall open to a particular page, her mind was wandering elsewhere. But when the words jumped out at her, emotion bubbled out so fast she barely had a chance to see them before her vision blurred. Frantically Janna wiped her tears, desperately needing validation that she'd not imagined it. Reading the words again, Janna gasped aloud. She couldn't explain it, but somehow she *knew* that God had given this passage to her as a sign that he had heard her prayer. It wasn't so much the words themselves as the feeling that had overcome her as she'd read them; as if it was an abstract kind of promise to give her hope. There it was in black and white, a single phrase. Hebrews chapter eleven, verse thirty. *By faith the walls of Jericho fell down.*

"Feeling better, I see."

Janna slammed the book closed, certain her expression betrayed the guilt she felt at contemplating any hope of being free of Russell. Matthew bounded onto the bed to hug her while Russell hovered in the doorway, looking as if he actually loved her.

"Did you have a good time?" Janna asked Matthew.

"I got a *kid's meal*," he announced, showing her the enclosed prize with childlike pleasure.

"That's great, sport." Janna smiled, ruffling his sandy-blond curls.

"You should get ready for bed now," Russell said in a tone of apparent kindness and caring. "If you hurry, I'll read you that new book I bought for you yesterday."

Matthew hesitated, and Janna recognized the glance he gave her. It happened every time the bruises showed up on her face. Matthew seemed to want to stay closer to Janna, as if he could somehow protect her or make it better. Janna smiled and touched his face, willing herself not to think about it. If she did it would break her heart. "You run along now," she insisted kindly. "Do what Daddy says. I'm sure I'll feel better tomorrow."

"I'm sure you will," Russell said. He smiled when he said it. His expression seemed to say that he was concerned for her well-being, but Janna knew better. What he really meant was, *I'm counting on everything being perfect and back to normal, or we could have more trouble.*

The following day, Janna *did* feel better. That in itself seemed an answer to her prayers. She contemplated over and over the scripture that had left such an impact on her. *By faith* . . . she thought over and over. The walls fell down *by faith*.

Russell came home with a dozen pink roses. She smiled and accepted his offering with a kiss, as if nothing in the world was wrong. She wondered what kind of madness could make him look her in the eye and say, as if he meant it, "I'm so sorry we quarreled, my love. I hope you can forgive me." The stark contrast in his behavior was the most frightening thing of all. But she tried to appreciate the way he coddled her, fighting to ignore the reality that this was only a predictable pattern in a never-ending cycle. At times there would be weeks between his outbursts, sometimes only hours. But inevitably they came.

Once the bruise on Janna's face had faded enough to be disguised with makeup, she was able to get out and confirm her suspicions. She was pregnant—again. She didn't even dare hope that it might actually go full term. And while a part of her ached for another baby, she had to wonder if it was just as well that they never made it. Would she really want another child to witness Russell's abuse?

Trying not to think about it, Janna concentrated on keeping everything in order. She began taking time to read the scriptures while Russell was at work, and her efforts at prayer were becoming easier. Inside she felt her hope growing, though at this point she could not see any possible means of escape. Still, she remembered that scripture. It didn't say that by money the walls of Jericho fell down. It was by *faith*, she reminded herself. And even if faith was something she struggled with, she felt as if God was hearing her prayers. She felt hope, and that was a step in the right direction.

While Janna struggled to keep the symptoms of her pregnancy from being noticed, she began to contemplate the idea of faith and works. Mulling it around in her mind, she came up with some things she could do to be prepared. She made some decisions, prayed, and felt good about them. Her first concern was for Matthew. She didn't quite dare admit outright to him that she would like to leave. While she knew he would say nothing to Russell, she felt certain he was too young to comprehend the full importance of keeping such a secret from his friends. And she could just imagine him telling his Primary teacher. If it got back to Russell . . . she couldn't even comprehend the gravity of the consequences she would suffer.

Still, Janna allowed the Spirit to help her prepare Matthew. A little at a time, they worked together to reorganize his room. They talked about what things were special to him or that he needed, and arranged them in a way that they could be packed in a hurry if the need arose. Janna told him stories about Jewish children escaping from Nazi Germany with practically nothing but their lives and their freedom. She told him about Lehi's family escaping from wicked Jerusalem, where Lehi would have been harmed if he'd stayed. Nearly every day, when Russell was gone, Matthew would ask her to tell him the stories.

While Matthew was gone to kindergarten, Janna did her regular chores with vigor, allowing her extra time to rearrange her own belongings. She went through the entire house, combing it carefully for anything that was of value to her. She rearranged her drawers and closet carefully so that she could pack quickly with the confidence that she had what really mattered. If she did get the chance to escape, she wanted to be able to run and never look back.

Janna also realized there were important papers she would need, and she felt as if she was on some secret mission as she carefully searched out insurance papers and other documents and made copies of them. In her search she came across cards, letters, and photographs that could almost make her believe she'd once shared a real relationship with her husband. The thought made her stomach churn.

When Janna realized there was nothing more she could do, dejection set in. She prayed specifically for something she could do to actively work toward escaping her personal walls of Jericho. The answer didn't come until she was sitting with her visiting teachers one morning. She'd canceled a previous appointment with them because of a visible bruise. Russell was generally considerate enough to keep the bruises where they wouldn't be seen; but occasionally, when his rage just seemed to come out of nowhere, he would strike her face and she was forced to stay secluded in order to avoid curiosity or embarrassment. If anyone questioned him, she would pay for it.

As her visiting teachers began giving the monthly message, Janna heard the words in her head: *Tell them.* Janna argued inwardly: *They'll never believe me.* But the voice urged her again, and she reminded herself to have faith. She was just wondering how to approach the subject when Edna, the older of the two, gave her the perfect opening.

"I saw your husband over pulling weeds at the church last night. I don't know how he manages to work full time and still do so much for others. He truly is a generous man."

"Yes," Karen agreed, "I'll never forget when I was so sick, and Russell came and shoveled us out from under that snowstorm."

"What I wouldn't give to have a husband that kind and generous," Edna continued. "Why, I can't hardly get Larry away from the T.V. You're a lucky woman, Janna."

"Well," Janna cleared her throat more loudly than she'd intended, "actually . . ." She squeezed her hands together to keep them from trembling. She'd never told *anyone.* "You see," she finally blurted out, "actually he flies into these horrible rages and . . . sometimes he hits me, and . . ."

Janna didn't know what she'd expected, but acting on a prompting from the Spirit as she had, she certainly wasn't prepared for the way Edna broke into laughter. Janna looked quickly to Karen, who appeared somehow alarmed and embarrassed, while Edna chuckled heartily, then elbowed her partner, saying lightly, "That's the funniest thing I've ever heard. Imagine, a man as good as Russell Clark beating his wife."

"Excuse me a minute," Janna stood up quickly, "I need to check something." She hurried into the kitchen and fought for composure, fearing she'd erupt into hysterics if she didn't get control of herself.

Janna returned to the front room to find both women looking upset. "Forgive me," Janna said. "Something's come up. I hate to hurry you along, but . . . well . . ."

Karen graciously hurried Edna out. The minute she was alone, Janna sat down and cried. She wondered how the Spirit could have prompted her to do something so utterly foolish.

Through the following days, Janna found it more difficult to pray and read her scriptures. She felt somehow betrayed, though a part of her wanted to believe there was some greater purpose to what had happened. But every time she thought about the incident, she turned warm with embarrassment all over again. What were Karen and Edna thinking of her now? Were they going to start gossip that would eventually get back to Russell's ears and catapult her into new depths of misery?

A week into summer vacation, nothing had happened to indicate that any problem had resulted from her impulsive outburst. Janna was trying very hard to focus on building her hope up again, when Russell flew into one of his rages because she'd suggested they go to the temple on Thursday instead of Wednesday so that she could go to homemaking meeting. He wanted to know what the women talked about at those meetings, and within minutes he'd thrown her to the floor and was kicking her. She heard Matthew's door close and knew he was all right, and thankfully the incident didn't last long. But in the night, she began to cramp and bleed. The following morning she miscarried. She took care of it on her own, just as she had once before, then she crawled into bed and cried, wondering how she was going to get things done to Russell's specifications when she didn't have the strength to get to the bathroom without feeling light-headed.

She was vaguely aware of a knock at the door, and heard Matthew answering it. Assuming it was one of his little friends coming to play, she shut it out and tried to find the gumption to get out of bed. The next thing she knew, Karen, her visiting teacher, was standing in the bedroom doorway.

"Forgive me," she said as Janna sat up abruptly. "Don't be upset with Matthew. He said you were resting, but I insisted he let me in. I need to talk to you, Janna, and I just had this undeniable feeling that you needed me today."

"Uh . . . come in . . . sit down." Janna motioned toward the edge of the bed. "Forgive me . . . I . . . uh . . ."

"Don't apologize. You have a right to be in bed if you don't feel well. Before we go any further, there's something I have to say to you that has been nagging at me for weeks—ever since our last visit."

Janna wasn't certain she wanted to hear this.

"I just want you to know, Janna, I believed you." Janna's eyes widened. "I apologize for Edna's reaction. Actually, she wanted me to tell you how sorry she is. I told her I thought you were serious, and she was horrified at the way she acted. But . . . well, truthfully . . . she doesn't want anything to do with it. She hasn't told a soul; she's almost afraid to. And I haven't told anyone, either. So you don't have to worry about that."

Janna sighed audibly. "I must admit that's a relief."

"Anyway," Karen went on quickly, as if she'd been memorizing this speech, "I've been praying for you, Janna, and I think the Lord wants me to be here—right now—today. I think you need me. I can't get Russell to stop hurting you. But I can be your friend; I want to be. And at least you can know you're not alone."

Janna couldn't hold the tears back. She understood now the reason for her prompting from the Spirit. And no harm had come from it. But here before her was a blessing she'd not been given since she'd lost Colin: a friend.

"So," Karen seemed suddenly uncomfortable, as if her speech had run out and she wasn't sure what to do next, "you're obviously not feeling well. Are you getting that bug that's going around, or—"

"Actually, I . . . I just miscarried a few hours ago."

Karen's eyes widened. "Well, you should go to the doctor and—"

"No," Janna insisted, "it's okay. It's happened before. I'll be all right. Russell didn't even know I was pregnant. I didn't want him to. I don't think he wants any more children. I'm sure I'll be fine. It's just that I feel so weak, and if I don't get the housework done, and dinner fixed, Russell will . . ." She couldn't bring herself to say it.

"Well, I told you the Lord let me know you needed me." Karen rubbed her hands together and came to her feet. "My kids are with my parents for the day, so I'm yours until about four o'clock. Where do you want me to start?"

While Matthew played outside, Janna sat on a chair in the kitchen and talked to Karen while she worked. She washed dishes, dried them, and put them away. She straightened cupboards according to Janna's instructions, marveling at the meticulous order of everything.

"That's the way it has to be," Janna explained. "If Russell finds something out of order, he lets me know."

Karen gave her a cautious glance before she asked, "Like . . . how?"

"Well . . ." Janna tried to think of an example. "Like the time he couldn't find a paring knife because the utensil drawer wasn't arranged the way he liked it. He slapped me and dumped out every drawer in the kitchen into one pile . . . then he told me to wash it all and put it away right before I went to bed." Janna briefly felt herself become lost in the past as the memory absorbed her. With a distant voice she finished, "It was one of the first times he'd screamed at me like that. I . . . I was terrified."

Janna shocked herself back to the present and turned to look at Karen. Her expression hovered somewhere between pity and horror. Janna couldn't believe she was telling someone these things. But it was evident that God had sent Karen to her. For a while they just sat and talked. Janna unburdened herself in a way she'd never thought possible, admitting that for years she had truly believed she somehow deserved Russell's treatment. She had been convinced that if she could just clean more, cook better, and try harder, he would be good to her. Then a day came when Janna realized the truth. No matter how imperfect she was, she didn't deserve to be treated so badly. Looking back, she wondered if it had been the Spirit helping her understand, in spite of her own lack of worthiness. The thought was very humbling.

Through their conversation, Janna learned that Karen had been divorced nearly a year, since her husband had left her for another woman. "If only I could be so lucky," Janna said, and they laughed together.

Before Karen left, the house was perfect, a casserole was in the oven, and a salad and dessert were in the fridge. Janna cautioned Matthew not to say anything about their visitor, or about Janna being in bed. He never talked to Russell anyway, but she always made certain things were very clear to Matthew.

The evening went relatively well, and Janna felt like it was another answer to a prayer that she had enough physical strength to fulfill her responsibilities. The next day, Karen came over again and followed the same routine. Her parents had offered to keep the children one more day. By the time Karen got her children back, Janna was feeling much better and was able to manage on her own. It was the first time in months that she hadn't felt like she was struggling just to avoid a beating.

With the evidence of prayers being answered, Janna renewed her faith and rededicated herself to study and prayer. The summer went relatively well. Her relationship with Russell seemed almost normal much of the time. She managed to keep up her responsibilities, and he showered her with gifts and charm. At times he treated her so well that she could almost pretend she was happy, were it not for the dark cloud of inevitability hanging over her. Eventually Russell would revert from Jekyll to Hyde, and her bubble of respite would burst.

Janna found a true friendship with Karen that helped get her through the down times. As she'd said at the start, Karen couldn't get Janna out of the situation. But Janna knew she was a blessing from heaven. Karen suggested more than once that perhaps Janna should find out about the local battered women's shelter. They had programs to get women and children out of such situations and keep them protected. Janna was admittedly interested, but fear held her back. She couldn't comprehend Russell not finding her, no matter how careful she was. Janna couldn't be certain if it was her lack of courage that kept her from looking into it, or if it just wasn't right for her. Either way, she let Karen know she appreciated the repeated suggestion. Then she filed it away as a future possibility and tried to forget about it, perhaps secretly hoping for a miracle but at the same time knowing she had to do her part. If only she knew what to do.

When school started again, Janna began to feel discouraged. The days were long with Matthew in first grade, and Karen had taken a full-time job now that her children were all in school. But Russell would not allow his wife to work outside the home beyond moderate work in the Church and the PTA. And Janna was hesitant to get too involved in those; Russell's interference somehow always made her look like a fool, while he came out looking like the sweet, tolerant husband.

While Janna tried to figure out something—anything—she could do to help the Lord get her out of this by helping herself, she came up empty. She felt helpless, and that resulted in dwindling hope. She often reminded herself to be patient, but her years with Russell already seemed like an eternity. Through much soul-searching, she knew that she'd made some bad choices, and she had allowed the Spirit to leave her life. Perhaps she deserved to be unhappy as a consequence of the things she'd done. But she certainly didn't deserve to live each day in fear of her own husband, wondering when the next time-bomb would go off. She'd come a long way since the time she'd believed that his behavior toward her was somehow her fault, and she now knew it was Russell who had the problem. She just didn't know how to fix it. Occasionally she considered calling for help from the women's shelter, but something held her back. She wondered again if there was a reason for it, or if Russell's abuse had affected her emotionally far more deeply than she had realized.

If the scriptures were true, then she had to believe it was never too late to start over, to make things right. There had to be an answer out there somewhere. She just had to find it, and she had to have the courage to act on it. *Faith*, she reminded herself. The walls fell down with faith.

* * * * *

A hot day in early September, Karen came by on her lunch hour to visit. Janna might have been glad to see her, if not for a minor incident with Russell the previous evening that made it difficult for her to walk without evidence of pain.

It only took Karen a minute to pick up on the obvious. "It happened again," she stated with certainty.

"Yes, well . . . at least he spared my face this time."

"Oh, how sweet of him," Karen retorted, her voice edged with sarcasm. Then her tone became cautious. "Janna, I've been thinking . . . maybe you should talk to the bishop. Tell him what's going on. Perhaps he could help you."

The very idea terrified Janna, but she had to admit, "The thought has crossed my mind a time or two, but . . ."

"But?"

"I guess I'm just concerned that it will only make things worse. The Russell he knows is a very different man."

Janna let the idea mull around in her head for several days. She prayed about it but couldn't feel anything one way or the other. Finally she gave in to Karen's plea to make an appointment. She knew the bishop was a good man, but she'd always found it difficult to relate to him for some reason. Perhaps it was just a personality clash, or maybe it was knowing that he really liked Russell. Of course; everyone did. And she could hardly blame them. She, of all people, knew how charming he could be. Still, as she gathered her courage to face the bishop and tell him the truth, she never imagined that he would politely dismiss her with diplomatic encouragement and patronizing reassurances. It wasn't until she was sitting in the car afterward that the reality of what had just happened became apparent: *He didn't believe her.* It was as simple as that. His advice had been—in a roundabout way—for her to work on improving her attitude toward her husband as the patriarch in the family, and to evaluate herself as a wife and homemaker.

As her conversation with the bishop pounded through her memory, Janna took hold of the steering wheel and a groan erupted from her tightening chest. She didn't even have to wonder what the repercussions of this might be. And two nerve-strained days later, her prediction became reality.

Janna willed herself not to show her nerves when she heard Russell come in from an elders quorum presidency meeting. Then she wondered what reason she had to be calm as she looked up from her sewing to see Russell's evil eyes fixed on her. There was no other way to describe that look. Plain and simple, it was *evil*.

Janna had barely sucked in her breath before he shouted, "I can't believe you'd have the nerve to lie about me that way to *anyone*, let alone the *bishop!*"

Any response Janna might have come up with was silenced by Russell's fist.

The following morning, Karen stopped by on her way to work, just a few minutes after Matthew had left for school. She came in without knocking, as she often did when she knew Russell wasn't home. Janna looked up from where she was sitting at the table with a cup of hot chocolate. She attempted to appear nonchalant as she glanced away, hoping to keep the bruised side of her face from Karen's view.

"Oh, not again!" Karen snarled. "What was it this time? Did you forget to buy toothpaste?"

Janna's hand trembled as she raised the cup to her lips and took a long sip. "The bishop told him what I said. He suggested to Russell that perhaps I could use some counseling, since I obviously have trouble seeing things realistically." Janna set the cup down and pushed a hand into her hair. "And of course, Russell assured the bishop that he was accustomed to dealing with my eccentricities. He told the bishop about . . . my dysfunctional upbringing, and . . ." Janna couldn't bring herself to go on. There was little point in it.

Karen had shown Janna many degrees of empathy through the course of their friendship, but all of it paled against the tears that fell down Karen's cheeks as she sat down carefully across the table. "I can't believe it," she murmured. "I . . . I don't know what to say."

"Well, that makes two of us."

Karen continued to cry as she spilled out her frustration toward the bishop. Finally, Janna reached across the table and took her hand.

"Listen," Janna said, "I know how you feel. The very same thoughts were going through my head last night. Needless to say, I had trouble sleeping. At first . . . I was so angry. But then . . . I thought of the way I had seen Russell before I married him. How can I fault someone for seeing him the same way I did? I just started to pray. I think I prayed half the night, just wanting to understand . . . to find some hope. And then . . . I just had this picture . . . kind of . . . appear in my mind. I could see Matthew. He was up to bat in a major league baseball game. That was it. And the words came to me: *He's out of his league.* Don't you see, Karen? I wouldn't be angry with Matthew if he struck out in a major league baseball game. Our bishop's a good man. He just has no idea what he's dealing with. And I'm not going to waste what little energy I have left holding a grudge against him."

It was several minutes before Karen spoke. "So," she finally said, "you apparently found some understanding. What about the hope?"

Janna squeezed her eyes shut and shook her head. "There is no hope."

"You have *got* to get out of here, Janna. Do you hear me? What are you afraid of? What could possibly be worse than living like this?"

"I'll tell you what could be worse," Janna snapped. "Living like some kind of fugitive; running—hiding. I have nowhere to turn, Karen. I have a son depending on me. I have nothing to offer him. How can I expect him to live like that?"

"Oh, but you expect him to live with *this*?" She motioned toward Janna's face.

"At least he has a roof over his head," Janna stated. "At least he's not some . . . *runaway*. There is no place I could go where Russell wouldn't find me."

"He'd never find you at that shelter, Janna. Its location is kept secret. You're not the first woman to be in this situation, you know. This kind of abuse is probably far more common than you or I could ever imagine. They'd help you, Janna. They know what they're doing. Nothing could be worse than living like this. *Nothing*."

Janna shook her head and rubbed her hands up and down her arms as a tangible fear chilled her through. At this moment, having enough faith and courage to get out of here seemed incomprehensible. Being safe from Russell was simply beyond her wildest imagination.

"Janna?" Karen said gently. "Are you hearing me?"

Janna turned to look at her. "I hear you, Karen. And I appreciate your concern. I really do. It's just that . . ."

"What?" she pressed when Janna didn't continue.

"I just don't know if I can do it. I mean . . . if I left, I'd have nothing. I would be completely alone with Matthew, and—"

"I'd do anything to help you, Janna."

"I know you would. But you'd be the first person on Russell's list when he came looking for me. And the last thing I want is to cause trouble for you."

"Okay, but there is always an option. *Always*. Listen to me, Janna." Karen leaned across the table and spoke firmly. "No one can get you out of this but you. There are people out there who can help, but you have to take those first steps. You can't give up."

Janna only stood and walked to the counter, attempting to ignore the pain. "Do you want some hot chocolate?" she asked.

Karen accepted the offer, and she didn't say anything more about getting away from Russell. What else could she say? Janna knew her friend was absolutely right: she was the only one who could do it. But she just didn't have the strength.

CHAPTER THREE

*F*eeling a desperate need to get out of the house, Janna carefully covered the remaining signs of her bruise with makeup, then gave Matthew careful instructions to stay in his room and keep quiet and busy. She put on the new sweater and earrings Russell had given her recently, made certain everything was in order, then approached him for the standard good-bye kiss.

"I'm leaving now." She bent over where he was reading the *Wall Street Journal* and pressed her lips quickly to his, smiling as if she enjoyed it. She knew from experience that any hint at dissatisfaction in her marriage would bring on his wrath.

"Back-to-school night, eh?" he asked. What he really meant was *I trust you will be at the school and nowhere else.* He had been even less trusting of her than usual since the incident with the bishop.

"That's right. I'll come straight home. Matthew's playing in his room."

"Very good," Russell said, then his face beamed with an apparently warm smile. "You look stunning, my dear." He took her hand and squeezed it as if he truly loved her. Perhaps, in his demented way, he did. "The sweater goes well with your coloring."

"Yes," she smiled in return, "you have good taste."

"Enjoy yourself," he said, moving his gaze back to the paper. From the condescending tone of his voice, she might have felt she was going to a movie with a girlfriend. Was back-to-school night such an indulgence?

It did feel good to be out, but it took great self-discipline to drive to the school and not head toward the mall or just go for a drive. Instead, she dutifully went to the meeting. She'd heard it all the year before, a month after Matthew had started kindergarten. Was first grade so different? Same rules. Same principal. It was just another layer of the drudgery of her life. But she tried to concentrate, reminding herself that this was for Matthew's benefit. He was, after all, the one bright spot in her life—her reason for living.

She was glad for the poor lighting in the school gymnasium. It made her less self-conscious about the fading bruise. There were a couple of women she'd worked with in PTA last year who gave her a congenial smile, and she saw a few ward members, but beyond that she knew no one. Karen was at a family birthday party this evening.

Janna settled into a chair on the aisle, reminding herself that she was quite accustomed to feeling like an outsider. It didn't matter where she was or who she was with, she always felt alone, always felt different. Beyond Karen and her mother, there was only one person who had ever made her feel at ease. But thoughts of Colin Trevor were something she was trying not to indulge in. They only added to her discontent, and she was trying so hard to be positive. Most of the time she felt as if she was barely managing to maintain her composure. If she thought too much about Colin, she would lose what little control she had.

No matter how she tried to listen, Janna's mind began to wander. The review of school policies faded into the background as thoughts of Matthew surfaced. As always, she felt concerned for him. What kind of life had she molded for her son? Would they ever find a way to be free of the oppression she felt? She didn't know how long she'd been praying for escape, but it seemed like forever. She thought about that women's shelter and wondered if maybe she *should* do it. She'd been praying for courage and strength, but it was difficult to feel either one.

When her thoughts became as tedious as the principal's oration, Janna pushed an idle hand through her hair and glanced around the crowded auditorium. Were all the parents as bored as she was?

Her eyes had barely moved when she caught sight of a familiar profile and her heart began to pound. For a moment, she almost believed she had seen Colin Trevor. But that was impossible. Wasn't it? Surely she was letting her imagination get out of hand. She tried not to stare at the uncanny resemblance. Of course, it had been years since she'd seen Colin. Would she recognize him if she *did* see him? When he turned just so, her pulse raced again. Could the similarity be just coincidence? Were her thoughts getting the better of her? Colin surely would not be here—not now! Any doubt was dispelled when he lifted his left hand to rub the side of his face. The scar she remembered so well was plainly visible. It *was* him! All these years, and there he sat—across the aisle, one row up, looking as normal as any parent. But he couldn't possibly have a child old enough to be in school, could he?

As the meeting droned on endlessly, Janna tried to convince herself to get up and walk out. But it was as if her seat had turned to lead. She didn't have the will to get up off that chair and move away. She speculated over Colin's reasons for being at the meeting in the first place. Perhaps if he had not gone on a mission, he could have a child in kindergarten by now. Or maybe he'd married someone with children from a previous marriage. The thought made her heartsick. A quick glance told her that he wore no wedding band.

Janna realized her palms were sweating, and the principal's voice was fading beneath the pulse beats in her ears. Colin glanced absently over his shoulder and Janna looked down quickly, not wanting him to see her. It would be too humiliating to admit to—or have him guess—what had become of her life. And how could she ever explain the way she had abandoned their relationship, leaving him to wait and wonder? Though he looked her way, he either didn't notice or didn't recognize her as he shifted in his chair and folded his arms over his chest. Janna took advantage of the change to study him. He looked older—no, more mature. Though still slender, his shoulders were broader, his features more defined. His hair was styled differently than she'd ever seen it, combed back off his face in thick waves that ended in a hint of curls hanging just over the top of his collar. He was wearing dark slacks with a white shirt, tie, and suspenders. She had to admit he wore them well. The fact was simple: Colin Trevor was more handsome than her memory could have ever done justice.

The reality of seeing him brought memories flooding into her mind. Janna became lost in the Sunday afternoons with his family, the high school games and dances they had shared, the Mutual activities, the long talks. Colin Trevor had taken her troubled soul and lifted it beyond its limits. He had believed in her, adored her, trusted her. Yes, he had trusted her—and she had deceived him, abandoned him, left him to wonder because she didn't have the courage to face him. He had loved her. He had sworn he would always love her. *He was looking at her.*

Janna snapped herself back to the present. She had been staring while her mind wandered, and now Colin Trevor was staring back.

A day never passed when Colin didn't think of Janna and wonder. But when he turned and saw her across the aisle, he had trouble convincing himself that this was not some kind of hallucination. He was so stunned he couldn't move, hardly breathed, wondered how to react. She was watching him, aware of him, but it was almost as if she was looking through him, not at him. While he was wondering what on earth she was doing here now, she apparently realized he was watching her and snapped her head the other direction as quickly as if she'd been struck.

It only took Colin a moment to realize that this was the answer to more than seven years of prayer. He was wondering how to get hold of her and have the chance to talk without making a scene, when the audience was dismissed to an open house with the teachers. She was sitting only three steps away, but by the time he stood, took a deep breath, and turned toward her, she was gone. All the years of aching pressed him to panic, and he pushed his way through the crowd, keeping his eye carefully tuned to her as she moved toward the door. But when Colin finally freed himself from the crush of people, she was nowhere to be seen. He cursed under his breath, grateful no one else was around when he looked heavenward and groaned aloud. All these years, and she was gone in an instant.

Janna pressed her back into the brick wall of the school building, pulling herself into the shadows. When Colin erupted through the door, he was so close she could almost reach out and touch him. She had to press a hand over her mouth to keep from crying out when he groaned toward the sky, a mournful sound that made her wonder what kind of torment she'd left him to suffer all these years.

She was relieved when he finally turned around and walked back inside, glancing over his shoulder more than once, as if he expected her to appear. How tempted she was to do just that. A part of her wanted to talk to him, to feel his arms around her. She wanted to get down on her knees and beg him to free her from this prison she had sentenced herself to. But how could she? Where would she ever begin to bridge the chasm of hurt she had opened between them?

Long after Colin left, Janna remained in the shadows, grateful that she briefly had the school yard to herself and no one could hear the occasional whimper escaping from her throat.

Janna fought to compose herself, then sneaked carefully into Matthew's classroom, grateful to see no sign of Colin. She heard the end of the teacher's oration and got copies of the necessary papers, then hurried out to the car before the meeting dismissed and sat in the parking lot for a few minutes, just trying to put her thoughts in order. She wondered for a moment if it was possible that Colin could be the answer to her prayers—and she had just run from him in fear. Fantasies of his rescuing her flitted briefly through her mind, but reality quickly squelched them. Karen's words came back to her: *No one can do this but you.* And Janna knew that was true.

Coming to the firm conclusion that Colin would not possibly help her out of this mess, even if he could, Janna convinced herself it was just as well that she'd escaped an inevitable interrogation from her high-school sweetheart. And what if someone had seen her talking to him, and mentioned it casually to Russell? She would certainly pay for that. Nothing made Russell more angry than anything remotely related to his unreasonable jealousy.

Janna walked into the house as if nothing was out of the ordinary. But it became increasingly difficult to keep her thoughts from wandering to Colin. She told herself it was a stupid resolve to try to keep from thinking about him, anyway. She'd *always* thought of Colin. He was her escape. She tried to imagine the life he might be leading, then tried to picture herself in it. It was a hopeless fantasy, she knew; but then, Karen had admitted to occasionally fantasizing about a date with Kevin Costner. At least Colin Trevor lived in the same town; but she felt certain the possibilities were equally remote.

Through the following days, as Matthew began to read and show a keen interest in his schoolwork, Janna found a worthy distraction in helping him learn. But he was beginning to make new friends, and the time he had for his mother was minimal. Still, she was glad to see him adjusting normally to life, especially under the circumstances.

In early October, Matthew requested permission to bring a friend home from school to play. His name was Brian, and Matthew talked endlessly of his fine qualities as a playmate. Janna told Matthew to get Brian's phone number so she could talk to his mother. It turned out that his mother, Cathy, had been on the PTA with Janna the year before, and they were vaguely acquainted. Cathy had gone back to school since her older children were either on their own or in high school, and her husband was often out of town. She was grateful for Janna's offer to pick Brian up after school and let him play with Matthew until she finished her classes.

Janna liked Cathy, and they talked for a few minutes when she came by to pick up Brian. She found it interesting that Brian was practically like an only child because his siblings were so much older. "Our little surprise," Cathy called him. Whatever he was, it gave Brian and Matthew something in common.

Russell came home while they were visiting, and he was his usual charming self for Cathy and Brian.

"I really appreciate this," Cathy said on her way out the door. "Tuesdays have been a challenge since school started."

"Why don't you let Janna pick up Brian every Tuesday?" Russell offered. "Matthew certainly likes him."

"That would be fine," Janna agreed, wishing she could have offered herself instead of feeling like Russell's puppet.

Through the evening, Russell was especially charming and sweet. He complimented her on dinner, and even helped clear the table. After Matthew had gone to bed, Russell found Janna in the kitchen and surprised her with a passionate kiss. For a moment, Janna almost became lost in it. He looked into her eyes, and she tried to comprehend the drastic contrasts in his character. At moments like this, it was easy to recall why she'd been so drawn to him. But now, her response was nothing more than a pretense for the sake of self-preservation. And the only way she could get through it was to allow her mind to wander.

"You are so beautiful," he whispered, easing her close while he pressed his lips alluringly to her throat.

While Russell slept with his arms around her, Janna asked herself for the millionth time if she was crazy. She was beyond hoping that a romantic interlude meant he would never hurt her again, but at times it could be so confusing. She eased away from him and cried silent tears, wondering how, for the sake of avoiding a beating, she could allow herself to endure something that had become so utterly repulsive. Had it come down to this?

Janna spent the remainder of the night sorting through her feelings—not wondering what she *should* be feeling, but confronting the real truth of what was going on inside her. Just before dawn, she came to the conclusion that if she couldn't find the courage to leave him because of the physical abuse, perhaps she could find the strength to free herself from this prostitution she was forced to endure. She felt quite certain God would not condone it—whether she was married or not.

The following Tuesday, Janna picked up Brian and Matthew after school, then stopped at the store to buy a few things. The boys each chose a snack, then had a little picnic on the back lawn while Janna prepared dinner. The boys played together so well that she hardly knew they were there. It didn't take long to see that Brian was a good boy. He always helped clean up without being told, and he did whatever Janna asked.

Cathy called about four-thirty to tell Janna that her husband was flying in earlier than expected, and she needed to go to the airport to get him. "Would you mind if Brian stayed a little longer this evening? I hate to put you out, but I don't know what else to do. I've just talked to my brother, and he said he could pick Brian up a little after six."

"That should be fine," Janna said. "The boys have been very good, and my husband just called to say he'd be late tonight anyway. It's no problem."

Not sure when Russell would arrive, Janna made certain the house was in order and kept a close eye on dinner, hoping it would stay warm in the oven without making it less appetizing. Russell was fussy about the way his meals were served.

At ten minutes after six, the doorbell rang. Janna was washing a pan and asked Matthew to answer it, knowing it was likely Brian's uncle. She heard the boys bounding to the door, then muffled conversation. Brian ran to gather his things as Janna dried her hands, walked into the front room, and stopped cold. Colin Trevor was standing with his hands in his pockets, staring at the family portrait above the cedar chest.

"What are *you* doing here?" she snapped before she even took a moment to consider the circumstances. Colin, Cathy's brother? Of course; she knew he had older siblings who had married and moved out of state before she and Colin had ever met. The connection was incredible.

Colin turned slowly to look at her. His eyes glistened with a hint of moisture. He turned back to the portrait and gazed at it. Unmasked pain filled his expression. She wished the boys would hurry back and announce that Brian was ready to go. But she could hear them giggling and knew they'd been distracted from their errand.

"You know," Colin said, his eyes still riveted on the picture, "I've been praying for years that I could find you. I don't know why, really. Maybe I just wanted to know for certain you were alive." He looked at her with eyes that could have turned her to stone. Motioning toward her with a gesture that seethed with sarcasm, he added coolly, "And here you are."

Colin's tone of voice changed as he glanced around. "I told my sister I'd be happy to pick up Brian; no problem. Just a simple little errand—and here you are."

"Quite a coincidence." Janna's voice was monotone.

"I don't believe in coincidences, JannaLyn."

Janna rubbed a chill from her arms. No one had called her that since she'd left Provo the day after her high school graduation. "You shouldn't be here."

"I'm picking up Brian. Apparently he's not ready to go yet."

"I'll get him," she offered and moved away, but he grabbed her arm. Janna glanced down at his hand, wondering why she could literally feel heat from his touch. She gathered the courage to meet his eyes. He was so close she could feel his breath.

"You owe me an explanation, Janna. And I'm not leaving you in peace until I get one."

"Please, Colin. Not here. Not now."

He glanced down at his hand, then slowly let her go. She took a quick step backward to put distance between them.

"I've waited a long time. I can wait a little longer."

Janna told herself to turn and walk away, but it was as if he held her in a trance. Memories came rushing back in torrents. She felt helpless to resist when he lifted a hand to touch her face, then her hair, as if he had a right to do so.

"You cut your hair," he said in a whisper, his eyes absorbing her almost intimately.

"I haven't worn it long since . . . since I married Russell." Just saying his name snapped her back to reality.

"I'll get Brian," she said and hurried down the hall. She returned with his jacket and backpack to report that he was using the bathroom. Matthew followed her back to the front room, and Janna trembled as Colin looked at the child, then at her.

"This is my son, Matthew," she said, wishing her voice hadn't quivered.

Colin's brow furrowed for a moment, then he said with a smile, "Hello, Matthew. It's a pleasure to meet you."

"Hi," Matthew said and ran back down the hall.

Janna was relieved that Colin hadn't said anything to Matthew about their prior connections. But something painful knotted inside her when he said, "Matthew's my middle name."

Janna avoided his gaze. "Yes, I know." She could almost feel his mind racing with questions she had no desire to answer.

"So, how are you, Janna?" Colin said quietly.

"I'm . . . okay." She forced a smile. "How are you?"

While Colin was trying to adjust to the fact that they were standing in the same room talking, a distinct uneasiness crept over him. Something wasn't right, and he knew it. "I'm okay," he replied, wishing he knew how to really talk to her. "How long have you lived here? I had no idea that—"

"Good heavens," she interrupted frantically at the same time he heard a car in the driveway. "My husband is home," she stated tonelessly, but there was no mistaking the fear in her eyes. "Please don't tell him that we were once . . . well, you know."

Before Colin could question her, she rushed down the hall, smoothing her hair. She appeared moments later looking calm and in perfect control, escorting Brian to the door at the same time a well-dressed businessman entered.

"Hello, Russell," Janna smiled. She reached up to kiss her husband's cheek while Colin wondered why he felt he was observing some kind of playacting.

"Hello, my darling," Russell replied with warmth while his cautious eyes took in Colin.

"This is Brian's uncle," Janna explained quietly as Russell tightened an arm around her. "Cathy had to go to the airport unexpectedly." Janna added to Brian, "Perhaps the two of you can play again tomorrow."

"Can I go to Brian's house tomorrow?" Matthew tugged at Janna's hand. "He's got a Hungry Hippo game, and—"

"I don't know, Mattie. We'll have to see."

"I'll be picking Brian up from school," Colin offered. "I'd be happy to get Matthew as well." He looked to the grinning Matthew. "And then your mother can pick you up before dinner."

Janna tried to pretend that she didn't know this man as she smiled and said nonchalantly, "I'll call Cathy in the morning and discuss it with her."

"Thank you for letting Brian play, Mrs. uh . . ."

"Clark," Russell provided.

"Ah, yes," Colin tried to smile. "It was a pleasure meeting you, Mrs. Clark. And you," he nodded toward Russell.

Janna wanted to collapse with relief when Colin and Brian finally left. But she managed to appear nonchalant and unruffled as she served dinner and went about her usual evening routine. She tried to convince herself that nothing had changed, but she couldn't help wondering about the things Colin had said. He'd told her he'd prayed to find her. Was this an answer to his prayers? Or hers? From the emotion she'd sensed in him, she wondered if her leaving him had affected him so deeply. He'd said she owed him an explanation; he was probably right, but she certainly had no desire to give him one. She wondered if he could possibly be the answer to her prayers. Even if he hated her for what she'd done to him, would he be willing to help her? And how could she go about asking without opening a huge can of worms?

Janna finally forced herself to stop thinking about it, convinced that she must put it in the Lord's hands and just keep having faith. Not even Colin Trevor could get her out of this mess. It was just as Karen had said. No one could do it but her.

* * * * *

Colin sat at the kitchen table, books open, eyes fixed to the wall. Cathy's hand over his startled him.

"Are you all right?" his sister asked gently.

It took him a moment to answer. "No. I don't think I am."

"Did something happen today or—"

"Yes," he interrupted, realizing he needed to talk, "something happened."

"Do you want to talk about it?"

"I was hoping you'd say that." He managed a smile, but it was gone quickly. Colin turned his gaze back to the wall and began, "You wouldn't remember much about my high school years. You were living back east at the time, already a mother. But I'm sure you knew I had a girlfriend—a girl I cared for very much."

"I seem to recall bits and pieces about her in Mother's letters," Cathy responded.

Colin chuckled, albeit sadly. "We were teased about puppy love. But Cathy," he turned to look at her, his eyes blazing, "I'm telling you, it was more. I loved her with all my heart and soul. I *knew* we were supposed to be together."

"What happened?"

Colin put his forearms on the table. "Her mother died the spring before she graduated." Associated memories caught him off guard, and he didn't continue until his sister nudged him. "Right after graduation, she left to live with her aunt in Arizona. She promised to write, but I never heard from her again. I had no way of finding her."

"Do you think something happened to her? I mean, if she were in an accident or something, wouldn't that explain—"

"Oh, I thought of that. I thought through every possibility. But . . ." he hesitated, trying to find the right words to explain, "but somehow . . . I *knew* nothing had happened. It sounds funny, but our spirits had always been so close that I believe I would have felt different if she had died."

"So, you're saying she just abandoned the relationship, with no explanation?"

"Exactly."

"And you were obviously greatly affected by this."

Colin nodded bitterly. "I tried to get her out of my head. All through my mission I prayed and fasted to be free of thoughts of her and get on with my life, but I could never do it. Finally one day I told the Lord, 'All right, if you're not going to help me forget about her, you're going to have to help me find her.'" Colin looked at his sister skeptically. She was a righteous woman with a great deal of faith, but they didn't always get along, and he'd never told anyone these things aloud before. It had always seemed so strange that he feared having it treated lightly.

"What?" she urged, apparently curious over his intensity.

"Cathy, almost instantly I felt an undeniable peace, as if the Lord was saying, 'Together we'll find her.' It sounded crazy. Even as much as I wanted to find her, it seemed preposterous. After my mission I immersed myself in my studies, but I also diligently tried to find her. I advertised in papers in the area I knew she'd moved to. I got two responses that told me the same thing. Her aunt had died, and she had married and moved elsewhere, but they didn't know where."

Colin closed his eyes. Even now, the memory of that moment left him heartsick—to think of her married to another man. And today he had seen the reality of that. *They had a child.* But hope filled him as he recalled another memory. "I became so discouraged. On one hand, I felt I was supposed to find her, on the other hand it seemed futile. I often wondered if the only reason I wanted to find her was to simply ask her why she'd left me that way. But there was more." He shook his head slightly. "It was as if the Spirit was telling me that something was left undone; there was something I needed to fix."

"Go on," Cathy urged when he hesitated.

"At that point, I tried to open my mind to finding someone else and settling down. I persisted for a couple of years, but nothing felt right. I couldn't get her out of my mind, and then when I hit a real low,

I had this dream. At first I thought it was just another pointless dream, but after many weeks I realized that the memory of it was very vivid. I believe the Lord was speaking to me through that dream, Cathy."

"Tell me about it." His sister seemed caught up in his story.

Colin's brow furrowed as he tried to put it into words. "I saw myself walking into a school with small desks; a children's school. She was in a room all by herself, seated in the center, just staring at an open book in front of her, looking baffled and frustrated. She looked up when she saw me come in, and she simply said, 'I need help with my math, Colin. Will you help me?' I took her hand and told her I would. She started to cry and buried her face in her hands, muttering something like, 'I'm so sorry I didn't let you see my picture. I couldn't have drawn it without you, and I should have let you see it. I'm so sorry.' Then I put my arm around her and told her that I would like to see her picture now. She looked up and the tears were dry. Her face looked hard, her eyes sad. She said, 'You'll have to scrape off the black paint, Colin. You can't see the picture until you scrape off the black paint.' She turned the page in her book that was lying open on the desk, and it was covered with many layers of black paint. I tried to scrape it off, but she wouldn't let me. She seemed to want me to, and yet she didn't. When I finally got to the picture, she started to cry again, but this time her tears were happy, as if she was at peace."

After a long silence Cathy said, "That's incredible. How long since you had this dream?"

"I'm not sure. A year or so, at least."

"Did you see the picture?" she asked.

Colin nodded, feeling hesitant.

"Well, what was it?" she prodded.

"It was me, as a child."

"So, what do you think it means?"

"If only I knew," he chuckled dubiously. "I assume the picture symbolizes my part in our relationship. All that black paint stuff leaves me baffled. I heard somewhere that school dreams mean there's something to be learned, but now I believe it was more literal than that."

"Now?" Cathy echoed.

"I saw her," he admitted, and Cathy's eyes widened. "At the school."

"Which school?"

"The elementary school."

"When were you—"

"Back-to-school night."

"And?" Cathy pressed when he said nothing more.

"She got away before I could talk to her. But I felt as if the Lord had led me to her. It was obvious she lived close by, but it still could have taken a long time to find her. I didn't know her last name or . . ." He hesitated.

"But you said something happened today."

"Cathy," he looked directly at her, "she is Matthew's mother."

Cathy was momentarily stunned. "You mean . . . Brian's little friend, Matthew Clark?"

Colin nodded. "He wants to come and play here tomorrow."

Cathy leaned back and chuckled. "I don't believe it. You're talking about Janna Clark."

Colin nodded, not liking that last name.

"But Colin, I know Janna. We worked together in the PTA last year." She chuckled as if this was all suddenly amusing. "I can't believe it. Janna Clark is your high-school sweetheart."

"Have you been listening to me?" Colin didn't see the humor. "There's a lot more to it than that."

Cathy sobered quickly. "I don't know what you're getting at, Colin, but Janna is a happily married woman. She's got a life without you. As difficult as that may be, you've got to face it."

"Then why the dream, Cathy? Why the feelings all these years? Can you really believe it's a coincidence that I found her where I did today? How can I possibly doubt that the Lord has brought us back together . . . for something?"

"What?" Cathy questioned cynically. Her intrigue with his story was obviously gone now that she knew it was Janna. Colin felt betrayed. He'd never dared share these feelings with anyone, and now he wished he hadn't.

"I don't know. But I believe there's something wrong. I don't think her life is as perfect as it appears to be."

"I didn't say her life was perfect, Colin. I said she was happily married. You can't just show up after all these years and expect her to drop everything and—"

"I never said I did," he pointed out. "But I'm going to find out what's wrong."

"What makes you so sure something is wrong?"

"I can feel it." He clenched a fist and gritted his teeth. "I've felt it since the day she left—no, before that. Something is not right with her, and it's up to me to fix it. I don't understand why I know that, I just know it."

"Why don't you just call her? Talk it through. Ask her why she left. Ask her if she's all right. Then you can get on with your life."

"Okay," he stood up, "I will."

"Not right now," she protested.

"Why not?"

"Her husband is probably home. I'm sure she doesn't want some old boyfriend calling her up and—"

"And what?" he interrupted. "If it's such a fine marriage, a little phone call from an old friend shouldn't cause any problems. They're happily married, remember."

Cathy said nothing. But something inside Colin told him the marriage was not so happy. Janna's fear of her husband knowing they were friends was not a subtle sign. It was like a flashing red light. The way she changed so drastically in Russell's presence was another. And on top of that, there was no mistaking the hollow quality of her eyes. Something wasn't right, and he was going to get to the bottom of it— the same way he'd scraped off that black paint in his dream.

Cathy gave him the phone number and stood by the phone with her arms folded. He dialed and willed his heart to slow down as it rang.

"Hello," Janna's voice came through so clear he had difficulty believing it.

"Hello, Janna," he stated.

She gave no response.

"It's Colin. I want to talk to you. Can you—"

"I'm sorry," she interrupted, "you have the wrong number."

She hung up abruptly, leaving him dazed. Cathy looked puzzled.

"She told me I had the wrong number. But I know it was her. Something is wrong, Cathy. I'm telling you, she's—"

"She doesn't want to be pestered," Cathy insisted. "Now why don't you just leave it alone?"

"I've been searching for her for years. I'm not going to leave it alone."

"I'm telling you she's happy."

"How do you know?"

"I can just tell," she nearly shouted.

"Well, I don't believe it," he snapped.

"Really, Colin. It's been so long since you've seen her. I don't think you have any idea what you're talking about. She's . . . well, to be quite frank, she can be kind of flaky. How do you know she isn't just . . . weird?"

"What do you mean by that?" he insisted.

"Oh, Colin," she began as if she had great gossip, "you can't believe how many times she's committed to something, then backed out at the last minute. No woman gets sick that much, on such short notice. Sometimes I really think she's a little off. I don't know, Colin; I'd say you're better off without her. She really can be flaky at times."

"You're doing a great job of making my day," he said with sarcasm.

The following morning, Colin was grateful to find his work slow. He had no motivation. His mind was absorbed with Janna. He'd found her! It was almost impossible to believe. But now what?

Cathy called him early afternoon and said she'd talked to Janna. He was supposed to pick Matthew and Brian up after school and watch them until she got home. Colin enjoyed the two little boys and observed Matthew closely as they played. He tried to comprehend that this was Janna's son. The reality that she was sharing a bed with another man unnerved him more than he wanted to admit.

Cathy called to say she'd be late and asked him to get some meat out of the freezer and thaw it in the microwave. "And be kind to Janna when she picks up Matthew," she added snidely before hanging up.

He had to admit he liked this arrangement of staying with his sister so that he could get out of debt faster, and she could get to her classes when her husband, Mark, wasn't available to watch Brian. But there were moments when she really got on his nerves.

The doorbell rang right on time. Colin answered it with a dramatic, "Hello, Mrs. Clark." Then he realized her husband was standing there with her. The uneasiness in her eyes seemed to pass quickly, but Colin sensed the way she seemed to want to disappear as she smiled and said nonchalantly, "Is Matthew ready to go?"

"Come in, I'll get him." Colin motioned them inside and walked down the hall. "He's coming," Colin announced when he returned. Following a long, silent moment where he found it difficult to keep his eyes off Janna, Colin turned to Russell, attempting to make conversation. "So, what do you do?"

"I'm an accountant," Russell smiled. "If you ever need one, look me up."

"Thank you, I'll keep that in mind," Colin replied. Matthew appeared, ready to go, and hugged his mother in greeting.

"Hi there, sport," Russell said to Matthew. He certainly *seemed* like a nice guy.

"Hi, Dad," Matthew said, then turned to Colin. "Thank you for letting me come and play, Colin."

"You're welcome, Matthew," Colin said, finding his eyes drawn back to Janna. Though she was obviously trying to appear relaxed, he knew she was extremely tense.

"Thanks again," Janna said and hurried out the door, ushering Matthew ahead of her.

"Yes, thank you." Russell smiled and closed the door behind them.

Colin stood there for several minutes, attempting to figure out what had just transpired. He didn't know what kind of relationship Janna and Russell had, but his instincts told him it wasn't the one he had just seen. With a prayer in his heart, Colin made up his mind to be patient and take this one day at a time.

CHAPTER FOUR

*J*anna was cleaning up dinner when the doorbell rang. Russell answered it and called toward the kitchen, "It's for you, my love."

Janna came to the front room where Russell was visiting congenially with Cathy.

"Oh, hi," Cathy said warmly to Janna. "I just wanted to stop by and thank you again for helping with Brian. My husband's schedule will change next week, and it shouldn't be so difficult. Anyway, I've brought you some cookies. It's so nice to have someone I can count on to see that Brian's taken care of during those in-between times."

Russell took the cookies with a gracious smile. "Why, thank you. That was very thoughtful of you."

"It was really no trouble," Janna said, trying to keep her voice steady. Did Cathy know that she and Colin knew each other, and would she say something? If she did, the results would be devastating. Janna couldn't even comprehend Russell's potential rage over such a turn of events.

"Well, I was wondering," Cathy went on, "if you would like to go to lunch with me tomorrow. Since our sons seem to have hit it off, I'd like to get to know you better."

Janna wondered if this had anything to do with Colin. Either way, she wasn't comfortable with it.

"Well, I don't know," Janna said hesitantly. "I've got some things that I need to—"

"I'm sure whatever it is can be worked around," Russell interjected. Janna wished she could hit *him* once in a while. "It would be good for you to get out, sweetheart." He smiled warmly at her.

"You're too hard on yourself."

Janna swallowed and tried to smile at Cathy. If she went against what Russell had said, she'd be asking for trouble. "That sounds nice," Janna said.

"Good, I'll pick you up . . . shall we say eleven-thirty?"

"I'll be ready," Janna said.

She was relieved when Cathy left, but Russell's demeanor changed so drastically in her absence that Janna felt certain he was upset.

"Is something bothering you?" she asked, wondering if she was supposed to notice this time, or ignore it.

"We'll talk about it after Matthew goes to bed," he said and huffed back to his newspaper.

Janna fought the urge to scream and run. She knew she was in trouble. Why hadn't she gone to that women's shelter months ago? If not for Matthew, she'd be tempted to sneak out the back door and leave this very minute. Steeling herself for the inevitable, she returned to the kitchen, wondering how she was ever going to make it through tomorrow. Old feelings welled up, threatening to strangle her. How could she forget the countless times she'd wondered what she'd done to provoke him? How many times had she apologized to him for being less than perfect, and begged him to give her another chance?

While she finished up the dishes, Janna contemplated her circumstances and the fear she was feeling. She tried to find a grain of hope inside her, but it seemed futile. In her mind she prayed with everything she had that she could get away from this place, away from this animal who claimed to be a husband to her. Then she reminded herself that she didn't deserve to be treated this way. Russell was a sick man. His problems had nothing to do with her.

Only a few minutes after Janna tucked Matthew into bed, she heard Russell call her from the front room.

"Did you need something?" she asked.

"I've had a thought that's been troubling me," he said, his nose still buried in the paper. Janna sighed. It was a common preamble for telling her that she wasn't performing up to his expectations.

"And what is that?" she asked. If she tried to avoid the conversation, it would only kindle his anger.

Russell methodically folded his paper and set it aside. He

straightened the stack of newspapers on the end table with his thumb and forefinger so the edges were all lined up perfectly. Then he folded his hands in his lap and looked up at her as if she was a child who had just come home with a bad report card.

Janna honestly had no idea what he was upset about. But she was not surprised when he said, "I noticed that you seem awfully nervous whenever little Brian's uncle is around."

Janna swallowed but didn't allow her expression to change.

"And how could I possibly not notice the way he looked at you?" Russell asked, a familiar venom seeping into his voice.

"Am I to be held accountable for someone else's behavior?" she asked straightly.

Russell lifted a brow and chuckled like the villain in a melodrama. "My, aren't we bold this evening." He stood before her and put his hands behind his back. That evil look came into his eyes.

"I simply asked a question," she stated. "Surely I deserve an answer."

"A man does not look at a woman like that without good reason," Russell snarled. "What have you done to make him look at you like that?"

"Nothing," she insisted.

"Why were you so nervous?" he demanded.

Janna swallowed. "Maybe I was concerned that you would misinterpret his interest in me, and take it out on me."

"So, you *did* sense his interest," he stated as if she were on trial.

Janna drew back her shoulders and looked him straight in the eye. She'd not stood up for herself in years. But she already knew he was going to hit her. Even if he was angered by her declarations, perhaps she needed to say them for her own benefit.

"I have done nothing wrong. I work night and day to please you. If it's not good enough, that's your problem. You have no right to treat me the way you do."

Janna barely got the last word out before he backhanded her across the face. "I will treat you any way I please." His voice picked up a deep, animal-like quality that always came out when he behaved this way. "You were nothing but a penniless little tramp when I found you. I made you what you are!"

"You made me what you wanted me to be!" she shouted back. "Your perfect little puppet, bouncing around on your strings for fear of being beaten. I will not—"

Russell hit her again, accompanying the blow with a string of profanities that made her skin crawl. She fell against the wall and slid to the floor, her head spinning. Russell took her by the shoulders and lifted her up, slamming her against the wall.

"It's him, isn't it!" he hissed. It was not a question.

"I don't know what you're talking about!" she snapped, tasting blood in her mouth.

"You've never *dared* talk back to me. But your old lover waltzes back into your life, and you just think you can do whatever you damn well please."

"I don't know what you're talking about," she repeated, but she feared her eyes had betrayed her. How had he found out? How could he possibly have known?

"You know *exactly* what I'm talking about." He slammed her against the wall again, and she could hardly breathe. "Do you think I don't remember your sweet confessions when I asked you to marry me? Did you think I would just forget that another man once had you? No, my love, I wouldn't forget. Of course, you never told me his name. But I find it interesting that Matthew's middle name is Colin. And it's startling the resemblance this Colin bears to *your son!*"

Janna slumped in defeat as he hit her again and again. He had won. No matter how she tried to play his games by his rules, he always caught her. He always won. She kept expecting it to end. She couldn't ever remember it being this bad. She wished for unconsciousness, but it wouldn't come. When she began wishing he would just kill her and get it over with, he finally left her alone.

Somewhere on the edge of coherency, Janna tried to orient herself to her predicament. What would she do now? If Russell knew the truth about Colin, and Colin kept popping up, there would be no living in peace. She had only two choices: she either had to convince Colin to stay away for good, or she had to get out. But one seemed as impossible as the other. If this was the answer to her prayers, she would rather just die. She finally drifted off to sleep with the thought that if she knew Matthew would be cared for, death would be the easiest way out. Perhaps Colin would take care of him. Perhaps that was the answer to her prayers.

Russell made certain Janna was up and dressed to fix him breakfast before he left for work. The moment he was gone, she collapsed on the couch and cried. She'd never hurt so badly in her life. That's what she got for sticking up for herself. That's what she got for praying.

Janna's tears gradually merged into a familiar numbness. She knew it was time to wake Matthew, and the thought of facing the day seemed more than she could bear. Seeking the strength to just get up and face the inevitable, Janna squeezed her eyes shut and prayed with all the fervency she could muster. *Please, dear Father, just help me get through this day.* She thought it over and over, hardly aware of the words shifting until she stopped to really hear what was going on in her head. *Just help me get out of here,* she prayed. And then the thought appeared in her mind, as if it was the most natural thing in the world. *No one can do it but you, Janna.*

Janna's eyes flew open as the thought startled her. She wasn't certain if she'd finally found the courage she'd been praying for, or if her desperation had just pushed her to the edge. Whatever it was, she knew what the Spirit was telling her to do. And she was surprised at how ready she felt.

"Matthew." She gently nudged him awake, feeling something inside her come to life that almost outweighed the fear pounding in her heart.

When Matthew finally became coherent enough to see Janna's face, he cried hysterically. It took several minutes to calm him down enough to get him to listen to what she had to say. Holding his shoulders firmly, she looked him in the eye and spoke with fortitude. "You're not going to school today, Matthew. I need you to help me. We're going to pack our suitcases, and we're going to leave here."

Janna took a deep breath and studied her son's expression. She'd said it out loud now; there was no backing down. She was grateful that Matthew didn't question where they were going or what they would do, because she wasn't certain yet. She just figured she'd get out of the house, and then she could get Karen to meet her somewhere and help her get to that women's shelter.

Janna was amazed at how Matthew flew into action. She'd never seen him get dressed and eat breakfast so quickly. He helped her drag the suitcases up the stairs and packed his things as efficiently as a child ten years older. Janna quickly thought everything through as she packed her own bags, grateful for the adrenalin that eased the pain of every movement. She was so absorbed in her thoughts that she didn't know Russell was in the house until he slammed the bedroom door. She gasped and took a step back as their eyes met.

"I had a feeling you might try something stupid," he said with an evil sneer.

That word *stupid* hovered in Janna's head as she wondered if she'd ever get out of this room alive. Russell's eyes shifted blatantly to the half-packed suitcases, then back to her face.

"Running away with your old lover?" he asked as if it were all very funny.

"This has nothing to do with him," she insisted.

"Well, I'm sure he would be as relieved as I am to hear that. I'm certain that once he realized what kind of woman you really are, he'd want nothing to do with you. And beyond that, it wouldn't take him long to realize that you're mine, Janna—forever! No man would be willing to pay the price of taking you away from me. No woman is worth a man's life—especially not you, my dear. So whatever you're thinking, you can forget it."

Russell moved toward her and she stepped back, willing her heart to slow down. He flung one of her suitcases onto the floor and the contents went flying. "You're mine!" he shouted, hurling her against the wall. She slumped to the floor as every nerve in her body reacted to the pain of last night's incident. She felt certain he would strike her, but he only lifted a finger toward her, adding through clenched teeth, "And if I can't have you, no man will." Moving closer, he finished in a voice more intense than she had ever heard. "I would kill you, my love, before I would ever let that happen."

Janna stayed as she was, literally paralyzed with fear, long after Russell left to take Matthew to school on his way back to work. He paused only long enough to inform her that he was taking all of the car keys with him, and he'd be expecting all of the suitcases to be unpacked when he got home.

Remembering her lunch appointment with Cathy startled Janna to her senses. Knowing she would have to call and make her excuses, she attempted to gather her courage. She was sick to death of making excuses, of lying and pretending, of being punished for Russell's insanity. She turned to look at her belongings scattered on the floor, then she picked up the suitcase and held it. For a long moment her darkest fears battled with each other, until a single spark of pure light pushed its way through, attempting to convince her that she was worth more than this. And from that light came the words—a concept she'd been taught over and over in her youth, but that had somehow become lost in these hellish years. First it was a thought, and then she was saying it aloud, as it came with such force there was no holding it back. "I am a daughter of my Heavenly Father who loves me!" She said it over and over, gaining momentum as she gathered her belongings and stuffed them back into the suitcase. Recalling that she had no keys to the car, she tried to call Karen at work, but they told her she had gone to Salt Lake for a meeting and they didn't know when she would be back. For a moment, Janna almost reconsidered. If Karen didn't get back before Russell showed up again, what would she do? Then those words returned to her mind with even more strength. If Karen couldn't help her, she'd call that women's shelter herself, and she'd get out of here—somehow. She'd get Matthew from school, and just take it one minute at a time. She didn't know where she was going. She didn't know what she would do. But she knew that God was on her side. And no matter what difficulties might lie ahead, this was the right thing to do *now*. She was putting herself into the Lord's hands, and she would not back down.

* * * * *

Colin got up just past dawn, with practically no sleep behind him. He wondered how much sleep he'd gone without through the years, wondering and worrying about Janna. While he'd prayed and pondered through the night, Colin had begun to put a few puzzle pieces together. He didn't understand why she'd left him, or why she would have married a man like Russell Clark. But he did know that something was wrong.

Staring out the window, Colin prayed for guidance in helping Janna. He kept thinking of her behavior when she'd been here, at

Cathy's house, with Russell. It reminded him of something, but he couldn't quite pinpoint it. Then, just as the sun began to peer over the distant mountains, Colin recalled a woman he'd been acquainted with on his mission. Janna was behaving much like that woman.

They had been teaching the discussions to a young couple with three small children. As they spent more time with the family, evidence of problems began to surface. The husband had admitted to being manic-depressive, but declared he had it under control and no longer needed his medication. But his wife was like a scared rabbit, and she and the children occasionally had visible bruises. They never did join the Church, but with the help of the mission president, the missionaries were able to get the family away from this man's abuse.

Colin got a sick knot in his stomach, wondering if his involvement in that incident had somehow been meant to help him understand what was happening now. Maybe he was jumping to conclusions. Maybe he wasn't.

While he showered, Colin tried to recall more details of that situation in the mission field. One thing stood out clearly in his mind: the woman had more than once begged them to stay away, mind their business, and pretend they didn't know. But when it was all over, she admitted her need for them. It was her fear of more abuse that kept her from accepting their help.

Feeling the pieces fall together, Colin believed the Spirit was with him, helping him understand. He felt determination and impatience to get to the bottom of this, but reminded himself to listen to the Spirit and not get ahead of himself.

Colin's thoughts stayed with him as he went to work and attempted to concentrate. He returned home mid-morning when an appointment was canceled due to illness, and he realized he'd left some important papers on his bed. He walked through the door and heard the phone ringing.

"Hello," he answered just as Cathy emerged from the bathroom, putting on an earring.

There was a moment of silence.

"Hello?" he repeated.

"Is Cathy at home?" There was no mistaking Janna's voice.

"Yes," he drawled, then hesitated. "Is everything all right?" he asked.

"I appreciate your concern, Colin," Janna said coldly, "but I'm fine."

Everything inside of Colin wanted to scream and demand that she tell him the truth, but he resigned himself to doing this the Lord's way, in the Lord's time. It could take months.

"Okay, Janna, but I need to talk to you. The least you could do is tell me why you never wrote to me. You left me without a trace. You at least owe me that."

After a long silence she answered, "Yes, I probably do. I'll call you later and we'll talk. But not now."

Colin could only hope she meant it. "I'll get Cathy," he said and handed his sister the phone.

While Cathy talked, Colin folded his arms and leaned against the counter.

"I understand," Cathy finished and hung up the phone. "I don't understand," she added to Colin.

"What?"

"She backed out. Says she's not feeling well. I offered to bring some lunch over and visit. She got awfully defensive."

Colin didn't dare tell Cathy what he *really* thought of all this, so he said nothing. He was relieved when she went on.

"Colin, looking back I wonder if you might not be right." Colin's eyes widened. "I mean, I always just assumed she was happy because he's adoring and sweet toward her, but . . . last night when I stopped by their house, I . . . well, I guess what you said made me look a little closer, and she seemed so . . . phony."

"Exactly!" Colin pointed a finger at her.

"But what could it mean?" Cathy asked. "Maybe she's got a terminal illness or something and—"

"Maybe," he interrupted, "but I don't think so."

"What *do* you think?"

"I'll tell you later, but right now I'm going over there. I think something's wrong. If my assumption is correct, she's not going to want to see me at all."

Colin forced himself to drive the speed limit, and tried not to appear too anxious as he approached the front door and knocked. There was no response. That wasn't a surprise. He knocked again. Still nothing.

"Come on, Janna," he called, hoping the neighbors would mind their own business. "I know you're in there, and I know something's wrong. Now open this door before I do it myself and—"

"Please, Colin," her voice came softly from the other side of the door. "I appreciate your concern . . . I really do. But . . . you have to trust me when I tell you that it would be better for both of us if you just turn around and walk away and pretend you never found me."

"I can't do that, Janna. Just open the door and let me see that you're all right. Then I'll leave, if that's what you really want."

He knew, she thought with certainty. Why else would he be so insistent about seeing her? Janna's mind raced in circles. Could it be possible that Colin was the means God had sent to get her out of here? A part of her ached to just tell him everything and beg him to take her away. But something held her back. It was as if Russell had some invisible leash around her throat that she was powerless to break. She thought of Russell's threats, uttered just this morning. How could she possibly expect Colin to get involved in this? He could never comprehend what a complicated mess he had stumbled into.

"JannaLyn," he said in a voice that warmed her, "you have to trust *me* when I tell you that I know I'm supposed to help you."

How could Janna possibly question that? Had she not just been praying for a way to get out of this house before Russell showed up again? Putting her pride in check, she took a deep breath and gripped the doorknob.

Colin's heart quickened as the door slowly opened, just enough for him to slip inside. He hesitated until he heard her say, "Come in."

Colin stepped in and tried to adjust his eyes to the dimly lit room. He noticed several suitcases lined up on the floor just as he heard the door close behind him and turned to see Janna leaning against it in the shadows. With the drapes closed, he could barely make out the shadow of her features.

"I really don't want you to see me like this," she said. "But the truth is, I need some help. I've been praying too long and too hard to let pride stop me now. But I don't want you involved any more than absolutely necessary—for your sake, as well as mine. If you're willing to help me, I am more than willing to accept it. But you have to know what we're dealing with."

"What *are* we dealing with, JannaLyn?" he asked. She didn't answer right away, and he motioned toward the suitcases. "You're leaving, I take it?"

"Yes, I'm leaving."

Colin was startled by the way his heart began to pound. When he had first found her, he hadn't dared hope for anything beyond an explanation. He'd convinced himself she was a married woman and that would never change. But now there was evidence that he still might have a chance to share a future with her. Could it really be possible? When she said nothing more, he repeated his first question. "What are we dealing with?"

As Janna attempted to gather the words to tell him, the reality rushed up in a wave of emotion. "He's a madman," she croaked, stepping into the light.

"Oh, dear God," Colin murmured when her face came into view. For a moment he found it difficult to breathe.

Janna saw Colin squeeze his eyes shut briefly. When he opened them, they were brimming with moisture. After all these years, it was difficult to comprehend that he would cry for her. She attempted to turn away as shame and humiliation seized her, but he took her arm with one hand and gently touched her chin with the other, forcing her to look at him.

"What has he done to you?" he whispered, wishing it were some kind of horrible hallucination. Both her eyes were black with bruises that spread onto her cheekbones. Her cheeks were swollen and discolored, predominantly the right side.

Janna watched his eyes absorbing the damage on her face and tried again to turn away. No one but Matthew had ever seen her this way; even Karen had never seen anything beyond a single bruise. She wondered how she had managed to hide it all these years and not appear an utter fool. Or perhaps she had. Realizing he wasn't going to let her go, Janna stared helplessly up at him, not knowing what to say.

Consumed with shock and empathy, Colin gingerly lifted a trembling hand to touch her face, as if he could heal it. Janna closed her eyes and her breathing became sharp.

"There's nothing to be afraid of, Janna," he whispered. "Everything's going to be all right."

"If he found us here like this, he'd kill us both."

"He's not here now, Janna. It's just you and me, and I'm not going to let anything happen to you."

He gently pressed her face to his chest, and Janna allowed the relief to flood into her and temper the fear. "You're the answer to my prayers." Her words erupted on a sob as saying it aloud confirmed its truth. He *was* the answer to her prayers. The timing alone was too incredible to question.

"No," he whispered as tears burned into his eyes, "it is *my* prayers that have been answered."

Janna didn't stop to ponder what he might mean. She was suddenly more concerned with the probability of Russell checking up on her again. "He's a madman," she repeated, stepping back to put distance between them.

"You're afraid," he said.

"Leaving is perhaps more frightening than staying."

"Then why are you leaving?"

Janna was surprised at how easily the answer came, and how firmly she was able to say it. "Because it's the right thing to do—for me, as well as for my son."

"Tell me what you need me to do—anything, and I'll do it!"

"Why?"

Colin knew there were a hundred ways to answer that question, but he settled for simply saying, "Because I know it's the right thing to do." While he was tempted to just take her in his arms and bawl like a baby, he put his emotions on hold and added, "Now, tell me what you need."

"I just need to get out of here . . . and to get Matthew from school. I'm almost packed, but . . . he took the car keys and I have no money . . . I have nothing. A friend told me there's a shelter for people like me—some kind of crisis center—but I can't get hold of her. I just need to get out of here before he comes back. Then I'll call her later, and she can help me."

"Okay," he opened his arms, "let's go."

"There's a suitcase in my room that I can't lift. Will you—"

"Lead the way," he said and watched her walk ahead of him down the hall. By the way she moved, there was obviously a lot more hurting than her face. While she put a few more things into the suit-case and closed it, Colin studied his surroundings. He couldn't help noticing how beautiful they were. Everything was high quality, exquisitely decorated, and in perfect order. And Janna was leaving with practically nothing.

"What?" Colin asked when she stopped what she was doing and panic rose in her eyes.

"If anyone notices me leaving in your car, they could tell him, and he'd trace it, and . . ." Her voice trembled. "He'll find me, Colin. I know he will. And he would kill me, or Matthew, or—"

"It's all right." Colin took hold of her shoulders and looked her in the eye. "We'll figure out a way." He thought quickly, at the same time praying for guidance. "What if I rent a car . . . or borrow one? No one will be able to connect it to you."

Janna thought about it a second, then nodded. "Please hurry," was all she said.

"Do you need help with anything else before I go?"

"No, just hurry. I'll leave the garage open. Pull in so we can load the luggage without being seen."

Colin smiled. "Good thinking. I'll be back to get you."

Janna nodded stoutly but seemed hesitant to let him go. He touched her face. "I'll be back in less than an hour. Hurry now, and don't worry. Everything will be all right."

She nodded again and he walked nonchalantly out to the car. As he drove, Colin prayed in his mind, needing to be certain they left no room for Janna to fear. He considered renting a car, but he knew it would require picture I.D. and a credit card. Then he recalled a casual acquaintance, a mechanic who worked at a garage close by where Colin had occasionally gone for car repairs. They had a couple of cars they loaned out while vehicles were being repaired. Colin uttered a quick prayer and was amazed at how easily he was given keys to a nondescript car for the afternoon, while the oil would be changed in his own car. With that done, he decided it would be better if he didn't pick Janna up himself.

"Cathy!" He ran through the front door, shouting her name.

"What?" She appeared from the kitchen, an alarmed expression on her face.

"I need you to go pick up Janna, right now, hurry. But put on a hat or something, and some sunglasses."

"What are you talking about?" she questioned.

Colin sat his sister on the couch and took her hand. "He's been beating her, Cathy."

Cathy put a hand over her mouth.

"Her face is a mess. She couldn't go out today because she didn't want to be seen. I don't know any more than that. But she's packed, and I told her I'd pick her up. I borrowed a car so the neighbors wouldn't recognize it. But I think you should pick her up. Pull into the garage and help her load the luggage, then drive away slowly and calmly. Take her to Mother's house. I'll take your car and meet you there."

"But what if—"

"Just do it. I'll call Janna and tell her you're coming, and then I'll call Mom."

Cathy nodded and hurried to find a hat, sunglasses and a jacket, and she was on her way. Janna was hesitant about having Cathy come, but Colin was gently convincing.

"Janna, the secrets are over. My family will help you, but you have to trust us. I'll meet you at my parents' house, and then we'll decide what to do next."

Janna was so full of gratitude she couldn't speak. She tried not to think about the fear.

Colin called his mother and prayed aloud that she would be home. "Hi, Mom," he said eagerly when she answered, the relief evident in his voice.

"Are you all right?" Nancy Trevor questioned.

"I'm fine, but I have a huge favor to ask you, Mother. Will you help me?"

"If I can."

"Mother, do you remember JannaLyn Hayne?"

"Of course."

"I found her."

"Where? How? I can't believe it." He knew she was not unaware of his feelings.

"I'll explain it all later, Mother, but right now . . . we have to help her. Can I bring her there? Can she stay there for a while?"

"Well . . . of course, but . . . what's wrong, Colin? You sound upset."

"Mother, it's too incredible to believe—how I came to find her, and to discover what was happening, but . . . her husband . . . he's been beating her, and . . ."

Nancy gasped. "Oh, no. Is she all right?"

"She will be, I think. But she has to get out. And he musn't find her. Cathy's going to get her right now, in a car I borrowed, kind of disguised and—"

"This sounds like something out of a movie."

"No, it's worse, Mother."

"Well, by all means, bring her here. She's more than welcome. We'll do all we can."

"I knew you'd say that. You're always so good to me."

"Janna's a wonderful girl, Colin."

"I know, Mother. I know. Oh, and Mom, she has a son. Matthew. He's five or six, I think. He'll be coming, too."

"Of course. It'll be a pleasure. I'll get the spare room aired out."

"Thank you. I'll see you in a few minutes." He hung up the phone and added in a whisper, "Thank you, God. Now, please, just help us get through this."

CHAPTER FIVE

*J*anna tried again to call Karen, but she still hadn't returned. She prowled through the house like a caged animal, frantically trying to be certain she had everything she needed. There would be no coming back. A twinge of sadness caught her—certainly not for Russell, but for her home. She had worked hard here, raised Matthew. Then she reminded herself of how her home had become a prison. With renewed determination, she removed the ring from her finger and laid it on Russell's dresser. A moment later she heard a car pull into the garage. Panic assailed her as she wondered if Russell had come back.

"Janna?" Cathy called from the garage, and she let out a slow breath of relief. She closed the garage door and dragged a suitcase out the door as Cathy got out of the car.

"Are you okay?" Cathy asked with a gentle smile.

Janna nodded, trying not to feel embarrassed. "Thank you for your help," she said as Cathy loaded the luggage with no trouble.

"I just need a minute," Janna added. She walked quickly through the house once more, then locked it up without taking any keys. She had no desire or need to ever return here.

Little was said as Cathy drove the car to Janna's old neighborhood in Oak Hills, on the east bench of Provo, and into the driveway of the home she remembered so well. She couldn't count the hours she'd spent here with Colin. Very little had changed, and she felt hope already.

Colin was pacing the driveway when the car pulled in. He rushed to the passenger door to help Janna out. She wore a scarf tied beneath her chin and dark glasses. She seemed guarded and tense, and it was difficult for her to get to her feet.

"Are you all right?"

"I will be." She smiled slightly, then bit her lip.

"Come inside and relax. I'll get the luggage out of the car in a few minutes."

Janna nodded and allowed him to guide her into the house. She was unaccustomed to having any help at all when she was in this condition, and she didn't know whether to feel embarrassed or somehow guilty for being treated so well. Reminding herself that embarrassment was not the issue, Janna paused a moment inside the door to absorb the memories. Some of the decor looked different, but the overall familiarity of the home rushed over her with an abstract kind of comfort.

"You look exhausted, Janna," Colin said. "Why don't you stay here tonight. Mother said that you and Matthew are more than welcome."

"Thank you, but . . ." Janna stopped her protest as the warmth and familiarity of her surroundings seemed to beckon her. She didn't want to bring any trouble to Colin's family, but she figured one night couldn't hurt.

"But?" he echoed when she hesitated.

"Thank you. That would be nice."

Colin smiled. "Can I get you something?" he asked hoarsely. "Are you hungry, or—"

"I'm all right, but . . ."

"What?" He sensed the concern in her voice.

"I'm worried about Matthew." She combed her hands through her unruly curls. "Will you—"

"Cathy's picking the boys up after school. She said she would go right into the classroom to get them before it lets out—just in case."

Janna nodded, seeming relieved. Colin felt certain she'd contemplated what her husband might do if he'd already discovered she was gone.

"Come along," he said. "I think you should lie down."

Janna followed Colin down the stairs and through the family room where she and Colin had spent endless hours as teenagers.

"Mother thought this room would suit your purpose." Colin opened the door and Janna pulled off her dark glasses. There were two twin beds with fluffy matching comforters, a large dresser, and a door that she could see opened into a small bathroom. "They use it when grandchildren come to stay from out of town," Colin explained. "But they all either live too close or too far away now. It only gets used about once a year."

"It's lovely," Janna said. "Thank you."

Their eyes met for a long moment, until Janna unintentionally cleared her throat and glanced away.

Colin tried to swallow the emotion beginning to get hold of him. "Why don't you rest while I get your things."

"Thank you." Now that the adrenalin of getting out of the house had settled, she had to admit that she was really hurting. Colin helped her to the edge of one of the beds and left her alone.

He hurried upstairs, but instead of going out to the car, he went into the bathroom and leaned wearily against the closed door. When he'd first seen Janna's condition, he'd directed his focus to seeing that she was safe. Now she was. His back slid down the door until he was sitting on the floor, his face buried in his hands. Doing his best to remain quiet and not draw his mother's attention, Colin allowed the emotion to bubble up from his chest like a volcano. He cried just enough to release the knots in his head and throat, then he forced himself to calm down and see to Janna's needs. He splashed cold water on his face and blotted it dry; then, feeling the emotion threaten again, he pressed the towel to his face and swallowed hard. Uttering a quick prayer, Colin thanked the Lord for helping him find her, and for knowing she was now in his care. Then he asked for help and guidance in facing what lay ahead. He prayed that Janna would be comforted and continue to trust him and his family.

Taking a deep breath, Colin hurried out to the car. Cathy had unloaded the luggage and Colin brought it in the house, trying to comprehend that Janna's whole life was now contained in six pieces of luggage—and that included Matthew's things, as well.

Colin's mother left to take Cathy home and discreetly return the car, while he took the luggage down to Janna's room and set it quietly by the closet. She appeared to be sleeping. When the chore was finished, he quietly watched her, losing track of the time. He was surprised when she turned to look at him, and he felt like a child caught with his hand in the cookie jar.

"I thought you were asleep," he said.

"Sleep can be hard to come by at times," she replied.

That wretched emotion threatened to bubble up again, and Colin coughed to hold it back.

"Janna," Colin said carefully, "we need to talk."

She looked disoriented and uncertain.

Colin cleared his throat and continued. "You're safe now, but we've got to be careful. We need to do everything possible to insure that you and Matthew *remain* safe."

Janna felt a little uneasy at the way he'd used that word *we*. "I'm certain that once I get to the women's shelter, everything will be just fine."

Colin took a deep breath and blurted out what he was thinking. "That's just it, Janna. Maybe it would be better if you stay here until—"

"Now, wait a minute," she protested. "I didn't ask for your help so I could become a burden to your family, and—"

"Listen to me, JannaLyn. You were practically a part of this family for years. I've searched long and hard for you, and you would *never* be a burden to me."

"I don't think you have any idea what kind of a mess you're getting yourself into."

"In my opinion, that's irrelevant. I *know* I'm supposed to help you, Janna, but I can't do that if you're—"

"You have no idea what you're talking about, Colin. It's only a matter of time before he finds me, and that means trouble for you. He told me many times that if I ever left him, he'd kill me."

"We'll find a way, Janna," he said with determination.

"I have nothing, Colin. I have no money—nothing of any value that's mine."

Colin took her shoulders into his hands and looked at her deeply. "It doesn't matter, Janna. Do you remember how Nephi said that he went forth, not knowing beforehand the things he should do? If he could do it, so can we."

"We?" she retorted. "I appreciate the concept, Colin, but you can't just breeze back into my life and pick up where we left off. I'm a married woman with some very complicated problems."

Colin glanced guiltily toward the floor and clarified, "By *we*, I meant my family."

"Well, perhaps you should let your parents speak for themselves."

"Fine," he said, throwing his hands in the air. It was becoming more and more apparent that this was not the JannaLyn he had once known. "But I can assure you that my mother would be delighted to have you and Matthew in her care."

"But what if—" She began to protest, but Colin's mother appeared in the doorway. Beyond a subtle deepening of the lines in her face, she looked no different. She'd always had a youngish way about her, and at the moment she was wearing jeans and a sweatshirt.

Janna stared up at her, and Colin sensed her embarrassment. He quickly attempted to ease it. "Janna, you remember my mother."

"Hello, Mrs. Trevor," she said, a subtle quiver in her voice. "I can't tell you how much I appreciate your letting us come here, and—"

"Don't you even think twice about it." The older woman moved toward the bed. "And you must call me Nancy." She turned to Colin and added, "I returned the car. It's all taken care of. Cathy's getting the boys after school."

"Thank you, Mother," he said. "You're wonderful, as always."

Nancy winked at her son and sat beside Janna, taking her hand gently. "Colin's absolutely right, you know," she said. "We would be delighted to have you stay with us as long as you need to."

Janna felt torn. While a part of her wanted to stay here where she'd once felt so at home, she was terrified at what the repercussions might be for Colin and his family.

"Thank you, but I . . . I need to think about it. I just want to do what's best for all of us."

"That's what we all want, Janna. You take all the time you need. But for the moment, I'll bet you're hungry. It's well past lunch time. I've got some soup heating upstairs; why don't we all have a bite to eat, then we can talk things through."

Janna nodded and came carefully to her feet. She tried to ignore the pain as she moved, not wanting to draw attention to herself. But she had to admit she was grateful for Colin's support as he took hold of her arm at the foot of the stairs. Their eyes met briefly, and Janna's mind flashed back to the closeness they had once shared. Quelling a sudden trembling, she concentrated on getting to the kitchen.

Nancy Trevor set a bowl of hot, homemade soup in front of her. Beyond Karen's friendship, Janna couldn't remember the last time anyone had done anything for her. "Thank you," she said. "It smells wonderful." Colin got the breadsticks out of the oven where they were warming and set them on the table. He sat across from Janna and offered a blessing.

Then the silence set in. Colin was just wondering how to handle it when his mother rescued him. He was amazed at the way she asked Janna simple questions about her plans and her feelings. She assured Janna that if going to the women's shelter was what she felt was best, they would support her in it. Then she offered an alternative. "I want you to know, Janna," Nancy said gently, "that we are here for you. It's good to know that a means is provided for those who have nowhere to go. But you *do* have a place to go."

While Janna was attempting to put words to her fears, Nancy asked more questions that made it easy to say what she needed to. She expressed her concerns about Russell finding her and causing trouble. She managed to tell them the threats he had made without bringing Colin into it specifically.

"Janna," Nancy said, "forgive me if I'm being presumptuous, and you feel free to speak up and set me straight. But right after Colin called me, I got down on my knees and asked the Lord if bringing you into our home was the right thing. I certainly didn't hear any thunder cracking, but I don't have any doubt that you're supposed to be here with us. I called Carl at work and talked to him about it, and he agreed with me completely. Now, you need to make your own decision, but that's how we feel. If the Lord wants you to be here, I'm certain he will make it possible for us to deal with whatever might come up. We can do a little research and find out what should be done to keep you safe, then take it on the best we can. You think about it and let us know. Whatever you decide, we'll do our best to help you."

Janna didn't know what to say. How could she possibly refuse? There was no describing her relief in knowing that someone was behind her, willing to help her through this. When the Spirit had let her know that Colin was the answer to her prayers, she hadn't comprehended that he was the link to providing so much. But the reality of divorce, and her fear associated with it, made her tremble.

Janna finally let out a little chuckle, if only to avoid crying. "I don't have to think about it," she said. "I would love to stay. I just . . . don't know what to say."

"You don't need to say anything, my dear. You just need to work on putting your life back together." Janna nodded and Nancy went on. "Perhaps we should discuss what needs to be done to insure your safety."

The ensuing silence made Janna realize she should be saying something. "I . . . I don't know where to start," she admitted. "My biggest concern right now is for Matthew. I'm almost afraid to send him to school. What if Russell picks him up there, or—"

"It's a legitimate concern," Nancy said. "So, let's talk about the options."

Janna nodded, seeming at ease, and Colin was grateful for his mother's matter-of-fact approach. He wondered if he was too emotionally involved to think straight.

"We could transfer him to the elementary school just down the street," Nancy suggested. "Or, if you feel uncomfortable with that, we could teach him here at home for a while."

Janna looked up at Nancy, feeling a sudden sense of awe. Perhaps it was the way she'd used that word *home.*

"I taught a couple of my children at home for short periods of time when they were struggling," Nancy said. "I could help you, if that's what you want to do."

Janna leaned back and quickly thought it through. "I have to admit it would alleviate much of my fear to know he was right here with me."

"Well, then," Nancy said as if she was really enjoying this, "I'll see about getting some materials tomorrow."

A new thought occurred to Janna. Her voice was laced with alarm as she declared, "I don't have any money, Mrs. Trevor. But when I get back on my feet, I'll find a way to pay you back and—"

"I won't hear of it," Nancy interrupted. "You were practically a part of the family for years. And even if you weren't, we are here on this earth to help each other, are we not? I can assure you that you and your son will not bring any burden upon this household."

Janna glanced down at the napkin on her lap and fidgeted with it for a moment. "I . . . I don't know what to say. I . . . just can't believe it. You're an answer to my prayers."

"Well, that explains everything, now, doesn't it? And I told you to call me Nancy. So," she continued with an easy smile, "we'll keep Matthew here at the house. We have plenty to keep him busy, I think. And we can have Brian come over a lot and keep him company. Now that Matthew's settled, let's talk about you, my dear."

Janna glanced at Colin as if he might rescue her, but his expression was determined, almost stern. She glanced down at her napkin again. Silence fell once more, but Janna said nothing. She was relieved when Colin spoke up, until the reality of his words sank in.

"You need to see a doctor, Janna," he said firmly.

"I'm sure I'll be fine," she insisted. "It's not the first time I've had some bruises." She didn't bother mentioning that it had never been quite this bad. "I'll heal soon enough, and then—"

"Janna," he interrupted, leaning closer to her, "do you want to spend the rest of your life hiding—afraid for your life?"

Janna's eyes widened, wondering if he'd read her mind.

"Listen to me, JannaLyn. He's out there, and he's going to be very angry. You told me that yourself. He's broken the law, and justice needs to be met. When justice is met, you will be safe from him. But we can't do that if we don't have evidence. We need a doctor's report and—" Colin stopped when her eyes filled with a terror that chilled him. He was wondering how to approach it when Nancy rescued him again.

"Janna, dear," she said gently, "I understand that this must be very difficult for you. You're in the habit of keeping this a secret, and we understand why. You've had no choice. But you have a choice now, and we want you to be safe and well. Let me take you to a doctor, so that we can make certain everything's all right."

Janna tried to think of an excuse, but she knew there wasn't one. She nodded in agreement, knowing they were right.

"That's good, then," Nancy said. "I'll make a call as soon as we eat. Let me reheat that soup for you, dear," she added warmly, taking Janna's bowl to the microwave. "You need your strength."

Janna forced herself to eat, knowing Nancy was right. It tasted wonderful, and it did make her feel a little better. But as she began to think all of this through, the fears began piling up again.

"If something is bothering you," Colin said, observing her closely, "then let's talk about it."

"I . . . I don't know where to start," she said, feeling like a broken record.

"What's bothering you most?" Nancy asked.

She thought for a moment. "I'm not so concerned about seeing a doctor as . . . well, I don't want to go out in public looking this way, and—"

"I'll just ask if we can bring you in the rear entrance," Nancy said. "Our doctor is also a family friend. I'm certain he'll accommodate us, and do everything he can to help."

Janna nodded, feeling some relief.

"What else?" Colin prodded gently.

She glanced at him briefly, then back to her soup as she stirred it methodically. "I'm going to need legal help, and as I said before, I have no money. I have nothing. He wouldn't let me get my hands on a penny without . . ."

Janna noticed a sly glance pass between Colin and his mother. "What?" she asked, wondering if she'd said something wrong.

"Colin can help you," Nancy stated.

Janna turned to him in question, and he took her hand across the table. Looking into her eyes, he said quietly, "My personal involvement with you makes it impossible for me to take the case, Janna. But I know one of my colleagues will take the case, and I can help. They're all good, and I can work something out to take care of the cost, whatever it may be."

Janna's eyes widened and he smiled. "You did it," she said, putting the memories together with the present.

"Yeah," he said a little sheepishly, "I'm a lawyer." His voice deepened as he added, "I've had little worth doing these last few years *except* go to school. I got through quickly."

Janna wondered by his tone if he was implying something personal. She ignored the implication and said, "That's wonderful."

Janna smiled completely for the first time since she'd come back into Colin's life. Her enthusiasm over his success didn't seem to fit with the concerns she had in her life, but he passed it off.

"He's done very well," Nancy said, "in spite of the struggles."

Janna's eyes narrowed on him, as if to ask, *what struggles?* Two implications were difficult to ignore. But his expression made her somehow uncomfortable, and she looked away. She finished her soup, grateful the conversation was dropped. Nancy offered her a second helping and she accepted.

When they were finished, Nancy went in the other room to use the phone while Colin cleared the table. He was putting the dishes in the dishwasher when she asked, "What struggles?"

Colin glanced toward her, then stopped what he was doing. He leaned a hand onto the counter with a heavy sigh.

"You don't have to tell me if you don't want to," she said, almost wishing she hadn't brought it up. "It's just that . . . I always imagined you doing so well."

Colin resisted the urge to just let it all out and tell her *exactly* how he'd been doing all these years. But this wasn't the time. He simply stated, "I haven't done well since you drove away with your aunt Phyllis and never looked back."

It took a moment for Janna to realize his implication. He was telling her that *she* was the reason for his struggles. The reality of that made her feel suddenly sick. She was glad to have remembered where the bathroom was as she hurried there and lost her lunch.

Hoping to avoid any more conversation for the time being, Janna quietly went to her room and began to unpack. The closet and drawers were empty, and she enjoyed putting their things away. A warmth settled around her that verified what she already knew: staying here was the right thing to do. The little bathroom was supplied with basic toiletries and clean towels. There were even tooth-brushes and razors still packaged, and Janna realized it was equipped to handle impromptu guests. Well, she certainly was that. But she *did* have their toothbrushes.

Janna glanced at the clock on the small table between the two beds and realized Matthew would be out of school in an hour or so. She'd feel much better once she knew he was safe. She wondered if Russell had tried to call her from work. If she hadn't answered, he would have gone home again. She couldn't even fathom the rage he would fly into when he discovered her gone. Warding off a sudden chill, she tried to think of other things. She focused on the future, allowing her mind to wander into the fantasies of freedom and safety that had helped her cope through these terrible years. She thought of Matthew as she put his things away. He would likely feel more at home if he arrived to see his toys and things already a part of the room.

A knock at the partially open door startled her. Janna turned to see Nancy.

"I'm sorry if I frightened you, my dear."

"It's all right." Janna chuckled tensely. "I'm just a little jumpy."

"That's understandable. Anyway, I've got you an appointment at 5:15 with the doctor. I'll go with you, if you like."

"I would appreciate that," Janna admitted, thinking for a moment how different everything would be if her own mother was still alive.

"Now," Nancy said, closing the door softly behind her, "since we're alone, and we can talk—woman to woman—is there anything you need? Anything at all?"

"I really can't think of anything," Janna admitted. "But I appreciate your concern—more than you can imagine."

Nancy looked at her, empathy glowing in her eyes, and for a moment Janna wondered if she was going to cry. But she smiled and put a motherly arm around Janna. "I'm glad we're here for you, Janna; more than *you* can imagine." She pulled back and met her eyes. "If there's anything you need, don't hesitate to ask. I mean that."

"Thank you." Janna smiled, then hesitated to tell Nancy what she had just realized a day or two ago. But she felt it was important. "There is one thing you should know." She paused and just said it. "I think I'm pregnant."

It was difficult to know what Nancy was thinking as she gave Janna a compassionate smile. "Well, then, you'd best take care of yourself. I'll be here if you need me. Now, why don't you rest? Cathy should have your son here before too long."

Janna nodded and Nancy left the room. Janna continued to unpack, feeling a need to be settled in, if only to give Matthew some security. She rested for a few minutes here and there, and took something for the pain when it began to worsen. She had to admit some relief at being able to see a doctor and be frank about her situation.

Her memories were clear of the first time this had happened, and how badly she had wanted to get some medical attention and be certain she was all right. But it hadn't taken long to realize the consequences she risked if she even attempted to draw attention to her abuse.

Janna felt immense relief when Cathy arrived with Matthew and Brian. Colin was nowhere around. Janna showed Matthew the room they would share and explained what was happening. She was glad that he seemed relieved and unconcerned. He was, in fact, anxious to finish their talk so he could play with Brian. Janna followed him into the family room, where Brian was digging into his grandmother's toy closet. She barely overheard Matthew's quiet response to something Brian had asked him.

"Somebody hit her," Matthew explained. "But we're going to stay here now, and he's not going to hurt her anymore."

Janna swallowed her emotion and watched them playing. Nancy came down the stairs, saying right off, "You must be Matthew."

Matthew looked up and said "Hi" politely before resuming his play. Janna saw some kind of emotion rise in Nancy's eyes before they turned slowly to meet hers with a gaze that seemed to see into her soul. Janna was wondering what to say when Nancy excused herself and hurried away.

The doctor's visit went as smoothly as could be expected. Nancy was kind and compassionate, staying with her every minute except when she was examined, and while some X-rays were taken. Dr. Reynolds felt that any risk to her pregnancy was outweighed by the risk of internal injuries. He asked many questions, but he was gentle and compassionate. Though she understood the need, she felt uncomfortable when he took pictures of her face from every angle. He gave her some prescription samples and some instructions, then he sent her home in Nancy's care.

"Carl's home," Nancy said as they pulled into the driveway, but Janna didn't see Colin's car. For some reason, facing Colin's father made her uneasy. "Don't worry," Nancy added, as if she knew what Janna was thinking. "He'll be as glad to see you as I was."

Janna wondered briefly why these people should be so glad to see her. What was she but a ghost out of their son's past, come back into their lives with a big bundle of problems that would undoubtedly affect their household?

She was hoping to get to her room and refresh herself a little before seeing Carl Trevor again, but he met them at the door.

"Hello, my dear." He smiled at Nancy and kissed her quickly. "And how are you, JannaLyn?" He took her hand and squeezed it, looking into her eyes as if nothing in the world was wrong. The way these people treated her, she could almost forget that her face was a mass of bruises.

"I'm better now," she admitted quietly.

"That's good, then." He ushered them into the house, explaining briefly, "Colin told me all about what happened, young lady. And I want you to know that he has my full support in bringing you here. We'll see that you're cared for; no matter how long it takes."

"Thank you," Janna said humbly. "You're all being so good to me, I don't know what to say."

"You just take care of yourself," Carl added in a gently booming voice that brought memories rushing back. Janna had always been in awe of Colin's father. He'd been kind to her, but in the years they'd been dating, he was serving as stake president until just prior to her mother's death. He'd been gone a lot, and often quiet when he was around. When he did talk, his voice had power and carried well. She couldn't remember him ever saying an unkind word, but his stature and manner somehow made her feel small. She realized now that Colin resembled his father a great deal.

"Why don't you get some rest while I fix dinner?" Nancy suggested.

"I'm all right," she replied. "Can I help, or—"

"Right now you need to recover from your ordeal," Nancy smiled warmly. "When you get feeling better, you're welcome to help as much as you like."

Janna tried to smile as Carl and Nancy left her in the front room. She wondered where Matthew was as she went down the stairs. The family room was quiet, but she could see Matthew sitting in front of the T.V., playing a video game.

"Hi, sport," she said. "How are you doing?"

"Hi, Mom." He glanced over briefly. "Uncle Colin taught me how to play this game. It's real cool."

"*Uncle* Colin?" she asked.

"That's what Brian calls him," Matthew explained, his attention remaining on the screen. "I asked Colin if it was okay, and he said it was. I really like him."

Janna was quiet a moment, reflecting on the ironies of her situation. She was glad, at least, to see Matthew preoccupied enough with his new surroundings that he was spared from the trauma of leaving his home. "You be good now," she said. "And remember to be polite."

"I will, Mom," he said.

Janna wondered where Colin was as she went to her room and lay down. But she drifted peacefully to sleep before she thought about it too long.

* * * * *

Colin sat down across the desk from Dr. Reynolds. He'd been the family's doctor as long as Colin could remember, and he'd become a friend of Carl's through the stake high council. But Colin never would have imagined discussing something like this with the doctor. Colin's head was still spinning from the whole thing.

"Your mother told me you needed a good case against this guy," Dr. Reynolds began. "That won't be a problem as far as I can see. Of course I will file a police report, and I'll certainly be willing to testify if I'm needed." There was an edge of anger in the doctor's voice that heightened Colin's dread.

"Is she going to be all right?" Colin asked, more concerned for her welfare at the moment.

Dr. Reynolds shifted in his overstuffed chair and rubbed his face with his hand. His distress was evident. "Eventually," he stated.

"Tell me."

"Well," the doctor threw the file on his desk, "beyond the obvious contusions on her face, which are apparently the result of at least four strong blows, she is . . . well," he shook his head, "I've seen car accident victims look better."

Colin briefly closed his eyes and swallowed hard.

"She didn't talk much, but from what she said and the evidence I saw, I would guess he not only hit her several times, but he kicked her around pretty good and slammed her against the wall a few times."

Colin put a hand over his mouth, fighting sudden nausea.

"The X-rays showed that nothing is broken, but . . . there is clear evidence that her right cheekbone has been cracked sometime in the past, more than once. And there is similar evidence in her ribs."

Colin shook his head, trying to absorb what that meant.

"And . . . ," the doctor drawled.

"There's more?"

"Colin," he said gravely, "I asked her some specific questions about . . . well, she didn't really want to talk about it. But there's no question that he . . ." He cleared his throat and looked up. "I really hate this. Colin, she told me that sexual assault was common."

Colin stared incredulously. "What are you saying?"

"He frequently raped her."

Colin couldn't speak for fear of falling apart.

"I will get a detailed report together." The doctor's voice turned hard. "I'll do everything I can to help get this guy behind bars, Colin. I think Janna just needs time to heal. I gave your mother instructions to see that she soaks in a hot bath frequently and takes it easy."

Colin nodded.

"And there's no question that she needs some counseling—and the boy, too. They must have been through hell. I've never heard of physical abuse without a lot of intimidation and manipulation. The scars inside could take years to heal."

Colin nodded distantly, lost in a whirlwind of thoughts.

"How exactly do you know this woman?" Dr. Reynolds asked.

"Uh . . ." Colin tried to snap himself into the present. "She was, uh . . . we dated in high school. Then she, uh . . . she moved, and we lost touch." Colin tried to control his stammering. "It's hard to say exactly how we came back together. I'm still trying to figure it out."

"Somebody must have been praying," the doctor suggested.

Colin chuckled without humor. "That's the only possibility."

Afterward, Colin sat in his car for more than half an hour, just trying to find the motivation to turn the key in the ignition. A month ago, he didn't have any idea where Janna was. Yesterday, he had only speculations and hope. Today she was in his care, depending on him to help her begin a new life of peace and security. But she wasn't just some client, for heaven's sake. He loved her. He'd *always* loved her. His prayers had been answered. He'd found her, and he was in a position to help her. But could he do it? Was he capable of lifting a mother and child from the depths of hell and insuring they'd never have to go back? And beyond that, was there any possibility of having a relationship with her again? Dr. Reynolds had suggested she likely had scars that ran deep. Colin felt sure she did. But somewhere beneath all the pain, did she still have any feelings for him?

Colin pressed his head to the steering wheel and prayed. He begged for the help and guidance he needed to get them through this. Then he finally turned the key and started home, with only one resolve firm in his mind. He'd just have to take it one day at a time, and do the best he could.

He walked into his parents' home just as they were finishing dinner. Janna and Matthew were there at the table, as if it was the most natural thing in the world.

"Uncle Colin!" Matthew jumped off his chair and flung himself into Colin's arms. Colin laughed and hugged him. He tried to imagine how starved the child was for a loving father figure, when a game of checkers and some video game instructions had already won such approval.

"How are you, buddy?" Colin asked and planted him back in his chair.

"I got past the first level on *Sonic*," he replied. "Will you help me with the next part?"

"Eat your dinner and we'll work on it for a while," he said, aware that he was being closely observed by Janna and his parents. He met Janna's eyes. "And how are you?"

"I'm being treated like a queen." She smiled timidly toward Nancy.

"If the shoe fits . . ." Colin smiled.

"I set a place for you," Nancy said, motioning to an empty chair. "You must be hungry."

"Actually," he admitted, "I'm not. Thank you, anyway." Colin couldn't even think of eating. The doctor's report was still smoldering in his stomach.

He went to the sink and began washing pans while they finished eating. Janna rose from the table and offered to help, but Nancy sent her along with strict orders to soak in a hot tub. "We'll keep Matthew busy," she said as if it would be a pleasure. "Take your time."

"Thank you," Janna said and went downstairs. In her bathroom she found everything the doctor had suggested to help ease her ailments. With a healthy amount of Epsom salts in the tub, Janna eased carefully into the water, letting the tension gradually relax out of her muscles. She wondered what Russell was doing now, but forced her thoughts away from him. Instead, she concentrated on the moment. She was safe and warm and comfortable. Matthew seemed happy and content. Her prayers were being answered.

* * * * *

"So, how are you?" Nancy asked Colin as they worked together to load the dishwasher.

"It's hard to say," he replied. He could hear his father's booming voice dramatically reading a story to Matthew in the other room. "I guess I'm kind of in shock."

"That's understandable."

"I'm really grateful for your help, Mother. She needs someone like you. You always know what to say and do. And . . . well, you're a woman, and—"

"Mothers usually are," she said lightly.

Colin smiled. "And you have a sense of humor."

"She'll be all right, Colin," Nancy said as if she had read his thoughts.

"I believe she will," he agreed. "But I wonder how long it will take."

"However long it takes, you need to be patient."

Colin looked at her in surprise. "Patient?"

"It's obvious you're still hopelessly in love with her, son. You're entitled to your feelings, but how you act on them could cause more harm than good if you don't give her time to heal properly. She was always a sensitive girl, and what she's been through is no small thing. I don't know if you want my advice right now or not, but I'm going to give it to you anyway."

Colin sighed and folded his arms, leaning against the counter. "I'll take all the advice I can get right now."

"For now, let your father and me be her shoulders to lean on. You concentrate on the child. He likes you, and he needs some male companionship. After what he's seen his mother go through, the very fact that he seems to trust you is a good sign. Janna is obviously drained emotionally; you can ease her stress by being there for Matthew. As far as Janna is concerned, you can be her friend—to a point. Be available, but don't push. For the most part, stick to supporting her through the legal process. You'll have to follow your own feelings, but just keep that in mind. She's still a married woman, and until that divorce is final, you remember where it stands. She's another man's wife, and you have no business entertaining romantic thoughts. Perhaps by the time she is single, both of you will be more prepared to see if you want to pursue a relationship." She took a deep breath and softly repeated her original advice. "Be patient, son— with yourself as well as her. You have your own healing to do."

Colin sighed again. "Yes, I suppose I do."

Matthew bounded into the kitchen, his story finished, asking Colin to come and help him play *Sonic*. "I'm coming," he smiled down at the child. Then he said more quietly to his mother, "Thank you . . . for everything."

Nancy touched his face quickly and went back to her work.

CHAPTER SIX

*A*fter her bath, Janna urged Matthew away from the T.V.—and *Uncle* Colin—to get ready for bed. They looked over the school papers in his backpack, read together, and she helped him with a page of homework. Then she tucked him into his new bed and sat on the edge to talk to him.

"Do you like it here?" she asked.

"Yeah, I do," he said eagerly.

"What do you like best?" she asked, wondering if it would be the video games or Uncle Colin.

Matthew surprised her with a mature response. "I like not having to hide from Russell and wonder if he's going to hurt you." Matthew had only called him *Dad* in Russell's presence.

"That's what I like best, too," she said. "It's going to take some time, but we're going to find a new life together, Mattie. Mr. and Mrs. Trevor are going to let us stay here until Russell and I are divorced, and we know he won't hurt me anymore. But for now, we have to be very careful. We don't want him to find us. Do you understand why?" Matthew nodded emphatically. "And one of the things I'm worried about is having him try to take you away from school." His eyes widened fearfully. "I think he knows that if he had you, he could get me to come back, because he knows how much I love you. What would you think about having school here at home with me and Mrs. Trevor for a while?"

Janna expected him to be disappointed about not seeing his friends and teacher every day, but instead he seemed to like the idea. Perhaps the fear involved with going to school made it easier.

"And you can play with Brian a lot since this is his grandparents' home," Janna said. This brightened his spirits further, and they talked about all they would do together to continue his learning and keep him busy, even though he couldn't leave the house very often. Janna also went over some basic household rules. She told him to always ask Mr. or Mrs. Trevor before using anything, and to always be polite. But she wasn't worried about his behavior. Russell had made him afraid to even breathe wrong for fear of the verbal rage that resulted.

Matthew finally drifted off to sleep, but Janna remained close to him, trying to imagine the future she'd always wanted for him. "Thank you, God," she whispered aloud. Her prayers had truly been answered.

* * * * *

It was nearly ten o'clock before Colin found the nerve to seek out Janna alone. After she and Matthew had gone to their room, he'd wandered out into the yard, thinking through his mother's advice very carefully. He could see the wisdom in it, but he knew that in order to help Janna fully—both as her friend and with his legal connections—the air needed to be cleared between them, at least to a point. And he knew he'd never get any sleep tonight without crossing that first bridge.

He knocked lightly at the partially opened door of her room, then peered in. She glanced up briefly but made no response.

"May I come in?" he asked quietly. Still she said nothing. He glanced at Matthew, sleeping soundly in one of the two beds, the light from the bathroom flickering over his face. "He finally gave up, eh?"

After a moment's silence, Janna said, "He was exhausted."

"Would it be all right if we talk?" Colin asked, as nervous as he must have been on their first date.

Janna didn't look at him. This was the moment she'd been dreading. Even more than facing the doctor or worrying over Matthew's reaction to all of this, she didn't want to talk to Colin. That alone made going to the women's shelter terribly appealing at the moment. But she knew she was supposed to be here, and she knew this had to be done. She owed Colin that much.

She stood resolutely and moved into the family room, where she sat carefully on the couch. Colin sat down beside her, then turned to face her.

"I don't know where to start." He chuckled tensely and glanced down.

"Well, if you're wondering whether or not I want your help legally—as much as possible—the answer is yes."

Colin was taken off guard. "Well, I hadn't really thought about that too much, but I'm glad to know you trust me enough to get someone to handle the case."

"Do you think this someone can handle *losing* the case?" she asked. Colin narrowed his eyes in question and she clarified, "It's not an easy case, Colin. I don't want you to get your hopes up and—"

"We have a very strong case, Janna. The doctor's report alone will put him away."

Janna chuckled dubiously. "You don't know Russell."

Colin wanted to ask about Russell, but they'd have plenty of opportunities to discuss such things in the days ahead. Right now, there were other more important things he needed to know. But the conversation had started off in the wrong direction, and he didn't know how to get it back.

"Janna," he finally said, "I want to help you through this. I . . . want to be your friend, to be here for you. But there are some things I need to know." He sensed her tension rising, but he continued carefully, knowing the subject had to be broached. "Janna, I have been searching for you for years; I've been praying that I could find you—if only to know what happened. Well, my prayers have been answered. I've found you. But I have to know . . . why didn't you write to me, Janna? Why did you just . . . leave me like that?" Hearing the emotion in his own voice, Colin was reminded of how deeply that one incident had affected his life.

While Janna wondered what to say, she realized she'd answered this question in her mind a thousand times. But it never sounded quite right, never made the sense that she felt it had when she'd decided to break contact with him. Sensing his impatience, she looked Colin in the eye and stated without emotion, "At the time, I believed you would be better off without me."

Colin was stunned. "That's it?" he questioned, his voice rising a pitch. He'd expected something dramatic—some long, detailed explanation of unforeseen complications that had come up. He'd perhaps expected to hear how Aunt Phyllis had manipulated her into something against her will. But all he got was *this*?

"That's it," she stated, as cold as ice.

"You believed *I* would be better off without you?" he repeated, perhaps hoping he'd interpreted it wrong.

"That's right."

"Are you sure you didn't mean that *you* would be better off without *me*?"

"I'm positive," she replied, not looking at him.

"What gave you the right to decide what was best for *me*? Couldn't you have at least *asked*? Couldn't you have taken a minute to *tell* me you didn't want anything to do with me?"

"It's not that I didn't want anything to do with you, Colin. I said you would be better off without me. It's as simple as that. I would have just held you back."

Colin came abruptly to his feet. It was the only way to respond to his anger without causing a scene or shattering what little trust he had developed with Janna.

Janna felt a sudden rush of guilt. Colin's anger was justified, and she knew it.

"I'm sorry, Colin." The softness of her voice caught his attention, and he turned toward her. He sensed her need to speak, though she seemed nervous. Attempting to swallow his anger, he sat back down and leaned his elbows on his thighs, hoping for some kind of explanation—something that would help this make sense.

Janna clasped her hands together in an attempt to keep them from trembling. She cleared her throat and began quietly. "At the time, I really believed it was the right thing to do. I know now that I was wrong. You can't imagine how many times I've regretted it. And whether or not you forgive me is up to you."

Colin pressed his head into his hands. It still made no sense to him. "I don't think forgiveness is the issue right now, Janna. How can I just put it away when I don't even understand why it happened? Do you have *any* idea how much sleep I've lost, just wondering *why*? It doesn't make sense to me, Janna. I just don't understand."

Janna fought to control the smoldering anxiety in her stomach.

She felt cornered. But there were things she just couldn't talk about; not yet. The silence grew miserable until she couldn't fight the nausea any longer.

"I'm sorry," she snapped and hurried toward her room. "That's all I can say."

Colin heard the bathroom door close and wondered if she was sick again. He fought the urge to wait for her to come out. But he suspected that pressing the issue too hard right now would only drive a wedge between them. Turning off the family room lights, he went upstairs to tell his parents good night. He found his mother sitting at the kitchen table with a plate of cookies, drinking a cup of hot chocolate. A cup and the chocolate mix were sitting by an empty chair.

"I figured you'd come up here sooner or later," she said quietly, motioning for him to sit down.

"And how much *later* were you intending to sit there?" he asked, wondering how she always knew when he needed a shoulder.

"As long as it took," she replied with a little smile. "Have some cocoa," she urged, but he didn't feel the motivation to do anything more than slump into the chair. Nancy poured hot water into his cup and stirred the mix into it, all the while watching him carefully, as if trying to read his thoughts.

"It's not easy," she stated, sliding the cup toward him.

"No, it's not easy," he replied.

"I have a feeling it will get a lot worse before it gets better," Nancy added.

"Oh, that cheers me up," he said with sarcasm.

"I don't think anything could cheer you up right now, Colin. But I'm here for you if you need to talk. It's better that you look at this realistically . . . don't you think?"

"Yes, I'm sure you're right. You always are."

"No," she sighed, "not always." She put a hand over his. "What's bothering you most, son?"

He thought about it a minute. "Well, when I think about the way that . . . *jerk* has treated her, it makes me sick to my stomach. But at least she's away from him. I know it will take time for everything to work out, but . . ."

"But something else is bothering you," she guessed.

"I just don't understand why she left me in the first place, Mother. All these years, I just wanted to know. I wanted to see her again so I could just *ask* her."

"Did you ask her?"

"Yes."

"And what did she say?"

"She said she believed at the time I would be better off without her. She told me she thought she would hold me back." Colin threw his hands up in exasperation. "What kind of reason is that? What right did she have to make that decision for *me*? I just don't get it."

"Then there must be more to it than that," Nancy stated firmly. "But maybe she's not ready to tell you yet."

Colin shook his head as if it could make him see more clearly. "I just don't understand."

"You're right about that. You can't possibly understand what prompted her to make that decision. And you can't understand the things in her heart that might have led up to making it. You can't begin to understand the kind of hell she's been through, living with a madman all these years."

"What's your point, Mother?" Colin was trying not to feel irritated. At times her straightforward manner could be hard to take.

"My point is simple, Colin. Don't expect to understand it; at least not yet. And don't try to tell her that you *do* understand. Give her the time she needs to trust you enough to share her feelings with you. Then she can help you understand—but only if she wants to."

While Colin tried to make that register in his brain, he realized he was just plain weary. "I think I need some sleep." He rose from his chair and kissed his mother's cheek.

"But you didn't even touch your cocoa," she protested.

"I haven't got much appetite," he replied and walked away. He paused for a moment and added, "Thank you, Mother." Colin opened the front door and called to his father, who was watching the news, "Good night, Dad."

"Good night, son," he called back. "Drive carefully."

Colin's numbness dissipated slightly as he drove in solitude. Tears leaked from his eyes as he tried to comprehend the enormity of Janna's suffering. He sat in the driveway for several minutes before going inside, knowing that Cathy would demand to know what had happened in her absence. He told her the bare necessities, thanked her for her help, and dragged into his room. Though he felt exhausted, Colin lay staring at the ceiling far into the night. Twenty-four hours ago, he could not have comprehended the changes that would suddenly occur in his life. But he had a feeling, as his mother had said, that it was likely to get a lot worse before it got better.

The next day, Colin went straight to his parents' home after work. Things at the office had been hectic as he'd attempted to make up for his absence yesterday and put some things into motion on Janna's behalf. He walked into the dining room to find his mother and Janna sitting with Matthew between them, looking at some schoolbooks.

"Uncle Colin!" Matthew bounded into Colin's arms. Colin laughed and hugged him.

"How are you today, buddy?" he asked, noticing that Janna's face was a little less swollen today, though she wouldn't look at him.

Matthew showed Colin the new schoolbooks Nancy had picked up that morning, and expressed his enthusiasm for the prospect of school at home.

"Why don't you run along and play," Nancy urged Matthew. "We'll start working on them tomorrow."

"Will you come play with me, Colin?" Matthew asked.

"In a little while." Colin smiled and touched the child's face. "I need to talk to your mother first."

Matthew reluctantly went downstairs, and Colin sat down. Janna shifted in her chair but still didn't look at him.

"Do you want me to leave?" Nancy asked.

"No," Colin said firmly, then his attention turned directly to Janna. "You and Matthew have been reported missing."

Janna looked at him then. "How do you know?"

"I have my sources. But that's not important. Your dear Russell has filed a police report that his home was broken into, and his wife and son are missing."

Janna swallowed hard and glanced down. "That's not surprising." She turned her eyes back to Colin's, wishing she could look at him without feeling either guilty or scared. "So, what now?"

"The police have been informed that you are not missing, and Russell has been notified that you are filing for divorce and pressing criminal charges, and he can communicate through legal channels."

Janna took a deep breath. "Thank you," was all she could think to say. Colin went on to explain that a protective order had been filed, and she would have custody of the child until the whole thing was settled. Her head swam with details that made no sense. She was amazed by his knowledge, and humbled by the reality that God would send him back into her life this way. If not for Colin, she felt certain that she'd have been blessed with other means to have her prayers answered, the same way Karen had come into her life. But she couldn't help feeling grateful for Colin's efforts on her behalf, in spite of all that was left unsettled between them.

"When you get feeling a little better," Colin said more softly, "I'll have you talk with Robert Taylor, an attorney with my firm, who will handle your divorce. He specializes in divorce and domestic violence. I've given him enough information to get him started on the paperwork."

Janna nodded gratefully. Silence ensued.

"As long as we're on the subject," Nancy said, "perhaps this would be a good time to bring up a few things I've discovered that might help. Let's just say I've been doing a little research. I've made some phone calls and talked to several people, and I've come up with some good information. First of all, there are some basic things we can do to insure your safety."

Janna was once again amazed at this fresh evidence of answers to prayer. She didn't know who Nancy had talked to, but she explained the typical behavior of this kind of abusive personality as if she had known Russell herself. She talked of methods such abusers might use to find the runaway wife, and precautions they could take to make it more difficult to be found. Again, Janna's head swam with all the details, and she was relieved that Nancy was thorough and levelheaded.

They decided to get Janna a wig that she could wear when it was necessary to go into public, and they even talked about coloring Matthew's hair to make him more difficult to recognize. Nancy felt certain that it would be almost impossible for Russell to connect her to the Trevor family, but Janna felt otherwise. Without getting into the specifics of what Russell had surmised about Colin, she told them that Cathy and Colin might be one of the first leads he would follow. This made Janna question her decision to stay here, but Nancy assured her that they all knew it was the right thing. She would call Cathy and warn her to be prepared and careful. They would all be certain they weren't being followed before even getting close to the neighborhood where Janna was hiding.

Together they agreed that Matthew should remain in the house or the backyard, since it was common for children to be abducted in order to get to the mother. It would be difficult, but Janna felt certain that Matthew's fear of Russell would motivate him to observe such rules.

Nancy cautiously mentioned that everyone she had talked to strongly recommended that both Janna and Matthew get some counseling right away. While Janna had mixed feelings about the idea, she knew it would be beneficial. She simply said that she'd like to get feeling a little better physically and let her face heal before she crossed another bridge.

When the conversation finally ran down, a tense silence hovered until Nancy said to Colin, "Are you staying for dinner?"

Colin glanced at Janna, then at his mother. "Thanks, I'd love to." He stood up and slid his chair under the table. "I think I'll see what Matthew's up to."

Janna sighed audibly when Colin had left the room. "It's not easy," Nancy said.

"What?" Janna wondered at times if Nancy could read her mind.

"Having your high-school sweetheart around while you're coping with something like this."

"No," Janna agreed, "it's not easy. But I don't know what I'd have done without him—or you," she added with a little smile.

"Why don't you go get some rest while I start dinner?"

"Why don't you let me help you?" Janna asked, coming to her feet.

"Janna," Nancy looked her in the eye, "I know you're accustomed to being busy, and this is hard for you. But Dr. Reynolds made me promise to see that you got plenty of rest. It's no extra work to cook for you and Matthew. You take it easy a few days, and then we'll go over some menus together and you can work into helping as you get feeling better, all right?"

Janna nodded gratefully. Though she felt a bit guilty for doing nothing while being treated so well, she had to admit it was nice to be able to rest her aching body, instead of pushing it to keep going.

The following day, Cathy called to tell Nancy that Russell had visited her the previous evening. Nancy put Janna on the extension, and the three of them talked for nearly two hours. Janna felt that Cathy had handled Russell very well by insisting firmly that she had no idea where Janna was, and she couldn't understand why he would even think she had anything to do with it. They were all disgusted by Russell's apparent broken heart over the situation. And it was validating for Janna to hear Cathy's amazement at how a man who could inflict such abuse could be so thoroughly charming. Nancy reminded Cathy to be careful when coming to visit, and Cathy felt confident that she could handle it. She said more than once that she would gladly do anything to help keep Janna safe. Again, Janna felt humbled by the evidence of her blessings.

Janna thought several times of calling Karen, but something told her to wait. She felt certain that Russell would contact her, as he had Cathy. And while she loved Karen dearly, she wasn't nearly as good a liar as Cathy was. If Karen was able to tell Russell that she honestly had no idea what was going on, then it might be better for all of them. For that reason, Janna realized it was likely good that Karen hadn't been the one to help her get away.

Janna expressed some concern for all the dishonesty, but Nancy answered with a firm, "My dear JannaLyn, when we are dealing with such circumstances, honesty is not black and white. The Lord wants you and your son to be safe and well, and it should be evident that he is with you in this." Janna certainly couldn't deny that.

On her third night in the Trevors' home, she found it impossible to sleep. As the darkness seemed to close in around her, she felt lonely and afraid. She thought of Colin, marveling at the way he'd come back into her life. The fantasies she'd indulged in for years suddenly seemed too close for comfort. How could she contemplate romantic thoughts of Colin when he was suddenly so much a part of her life, if only indirectly? She forced her thoughts away from Colin, and they wandered into the good moments she'd shared with Russell. She thought of the way he would hold her and love her when his abusive nature seemed magically absent. The loneliness inside her almost ached. She began to wonder what he was doing now, wishing that it might be possible to go back to him and know that he would never hurt her again. Then, like a flash of hot light, the fear seized her. How could she forget so quickly the pain he'd inflicted? Could the crumbs of charisma that he occasionally brushed toward her possibly compensate for the horrible reality of her life with him? As the night deepened and her thoughts snowballed, Janna began to wonder if she should just go back to him. Of course he would be angry. But once his rage was released, he would hold her and tell her how much he'd missed her, and how he could never live without her. Was the occasional abuse really so bad to live with? Was it worse than running and hiding in fear?

Janna finally drifted into a restless sleep, and awoke with her troubled thoughts still hovering. Nancy noticed her mood and questioned her pointedly. Janna felt hesitant to talk about it, but Nancy had a way of making it difficult to hold her feelings inside. She spilled the full truth of her thoughts, then felt silly for the obvious contradictions.

"How can I be so afraid of him and actually even consider going back?" Janna cried. "I just don't understand. I don't know what to do. Maybe I've made a mistake. Maybe I should just go back and . . . oh, I don't know." She pressed her face into her hands and groaned.

"Janna," Nancy said gently, "may I share something with you?"

Janna looked up and wiped at her face. "Of course."

"I have a good friend who went through similar things in her first marriage. I talked to her the other day, and she gave me some interesting insights. Actually, from what she told me about her own experience, what you're saying isn't so surprising."

"Really?" Janna couldn't quite believe that what she was feeling might make any kind of sense.

"She told me that she left her first husband three times before she finally found the courage to stay away. Apparently it's typical for these kinds of abusers to be very charismatic and charming. It's also very typical of them to use intimidation and isolation to convince the abused spouse that they can't survive in the outside world; that's how they instill a fear of leaving. She recalled reading somewhere that the average victim of domestic violence goes back eight times."

"Eight!" Janna cried as she focused on the reality of what going back would mean. What little bit of tenderness he might show her could never compensate for the hurt he would inflict. "But how could . . ." She couldn't quite put her thoughts into words.

"I also believe," Nancy went on, "that your confusion has a lot to do with the mind games these people play with their victims. Don't expect to understand it all at once, dear. Just hang on and keep praying. I'm certain everything will be all right."

Janna felt certain the things Nancy's friend had told her were an answer to her prayers. With some time it began to settle in, and she was able to focus more realistically on her relationship with Russell. At moments, however, it could still be confusing.

As the bruises began to turn yellowish and fade, Janna gratefully realized that she was not living in daily fear of Russell's rage. She quickly grew to love Nancy Trevor all over again. This woman was kind and gentle—and perceptive. Nothing got by her. And though that worried Janna at moments, she quickly realized that Nancy also respected her privacy and feelings.

Matthew had no trouble adjusting. He loved his studies, and he seemed perfectly content in the Trevors' home. Colin came every day, saying little but the bare necessities to Janna, but spending considerable time with Matthew. While Janna knew it would take time to get through the divorce, she tried not to even think about it. In the present, there was only one real source of concern, and she knew it couldn't be ignored much longer. She had told Nancy she was pregnant, and they had discussed it with Dr. Reynolds, but she felt certain that Nancy would leave it up to her to tell Colin. Even though he was keeping his distance from her, he was involved and he had a right to know. She was almost relieved when she walked in on Nancy and Colin talking about her, though they weren't aware of her presence.

"I'm worried about her, Mother. I don't think I've been here when she hasn't been throwing up. I hate to even say it, but do you think she could be anorexic, or—"

"She's not thin enough to be anorexic, Colin. I don't think there's a need for concern."

"How can you possibly tell how thin she is? With the baggy clothes she wears, you'd think . . ." He stopped when Nancy glanced over her shoulder, as if she sensed they were not alone. Janna was tempted to feel embarrassed for not announcing her presence, but she'd come beyond embarrassment with these people.

"I can assure you I'm not anorexic," Janna stated firmly. "I know I have a lot that needs to be worked out, but you can cross that off the list."

Colin stuffed his hands in his back pockets and looked sheepishly toward the floor. "And as for my wardrobe, Mr. Trevor." She spoke his name in a tone that made him feel like he had never been anything more to her than a lawyer, and she disliked him as that. "My husband would not have approved of my wearing anything in public that would even hint that I might be a woman. He was afraid I might draw the eye of some innocent man who would try to steal me away from him. I can't count the times he hit me because I was given a compliment in public. But that's getting out on an unnecessary limb, now isn't it? As for my throwing up, which you seem to have taken so much interest in, it's perfectly normal in my condition."

Colin's brows went up abruptly. "Your condition?"

"That's right," she clarified, "I'm pregnant. I'm surprised Dr. Reynolds didn't tell you."

"So am I," Colin said, sitting down a little unsteadily.

"I'm certain he figured you would tell him yourself, when you were ready," Nancy said and walked into the kitchen as if they'd just discussed what to have for dinner.

"Is there anything else you want to know?" Janna asked Colin with an increasingly familiar cold edge in her voice.

"Actually, there's a great deal I'd like to know, but I'm not sure you'd tell me."

"It's too bad you can't be my attorney. Then I would *have* to tell you."

"I was once your best friend. Have things changed so much that you couldn't just *talk* to me?"

"Apparently things have changed a great deal, Colin."

"Just talk to me, Janna." His voice lowered to a gentle plea. "I know this is tough for you. Let me be your friend."

She fidgeted with her hands and looked away. "What did you want to talk about?"

"Sit down," he urged, and she did. But she remained at the edge of her seat. "When did you find out you were pregnant?"

"The nausea started just a few days before you walked through my front door."

Colin took a deep breath. "And how do you feel about it?"

"What difference does it make?" she snapped.

"It makes a lot of difference. It's a baby, Janna."

"No, Colin, it's a pregnancy. Until I feel it move inside of me, it's just a pregnancy. And I can't afford to feel anything at all."

Colin narrowed his eyes on her, trying to figure where she was coming from. When he couldn't, he had to admit, "I don't understand."

Janna felt the urge to just tell him to mind his own business. But he was trying to help her, and he was being kind. Convincing herself there was no reason not to tell him, she drew back her shoulders and spoke in a voice that didn't allow her to feel the reality. "I've had three miscarriages since Matthew was born," she stated.

Colin leaned back and pressed his knuckles to his mouth.

"I only felt one of them move. That was the hard one to lose. I convinced myself the others were just pregnancies. I had to detach myself in order to cope."

Colin knew he could never comprehend her pain. But she was talking, and he didn't want her to stop. "Do the doctors know why . . . I mean, why it keeps happening?"

Janna leaned back and crossed her legs abruptly. She tapped her fingers nervously on the arm of the couch. "I only went to the hospital for the one I lost at five months. I didn't tell the doctor about the others. I just took care of it at home."

Colin was momentarily speechless. In this day of modern, thorough medical care, he couldn't fathom such a thing. "Why?" was all he could manage to say. She turned to look at him as if he was somehow stupid, and he wished the question hadn't sounded so incredulous.

"Because with the one Russell knew about, he told me I could handle it. And when Russell told me I could handle it, there was no disputing the issue. If I had been bleeding to death, he might have called an ambulance. Otherwise, I had things to do."

Colin heard his breathing turn rapid, but he fought to maintain a composed expression. If he let out his emotions now, she might never talk to him again. "So, what did the doctor say about the one that happened at the hospital?"

"He concluded it was obviously a result of falling down the basement stairs."

This time Colin couldn't even get the question out. He was relieved when she answered it anyway.

"No, I did not fall down the stairs. That was how Russell explained the bruises while he was standing at my bedside with tears in his eyes."

Colin shot to his feet and his fists clenched unwillingly. He would never have believed a person could feel so much hatred and frustration.

His obvious anger left Janna unnerved. In her heart she knew he would never act on his feelings the way Russell had, but she couldn't deny the tightening in her chest and head that accompanied being in the same room with an angry man. When he said nothing more, she excused herself and hurried away.

Janna awoke the next morning and realized it was Saturday. Matthew immediately informed her that it had snowed. Once she was dressed, they went upstairs to find Nancy and Carl looking out the front window.

"Why doesn't he just get out the snowblower?" Carl asked his wife.

"That wouldn't accomplish his purpose," Nancy stated.

"And what purpose is that?" Carl asked. Then he noticed Janna. "Well, good morning, my dear. How are you feeling today?"

"Better, I believe, thank you," she smiled.

"I love snow," Matthew declared, his nose pressed to the window, his eyes reflecting the early snowfall. "Can I go outside and play in the snow, Mom?" he asked.

"As soon as you have some breakfast and—"

"Oh, he's already eaten," Carl said. "We had some Cheerios together." He ruffled the boy's hair, and Matthew looked up at him with a sparkle in his eyes. "But I told him he couldn't go out until he asked you."

"It's fine, of course," Janna said, "as long as you stay in the backyard. Let's go find your snow clothes."

In the search, Janna discovered she'd not packed his snow hat.

But Nancy pulled a bag out of the closet with over a dozen winter hats in different colors and sizes. Janna drank a cup of cocoa and watched out the back window as Matthew went up and down the patio with a child-sized snow shovel Carl had produced from a corner of the garage. Then she wandered back to the front window, where Nancy was watching her own son shoveling a driveway across the street.

"Matthew really is a sweet child," Nancy said, startling Janna briefly.

"Yes, he is," she agreed. "And I see that Colin is working hard—as always."

"He does like to work up a sweat," Nancy chuckled softly. "He's been here shoveling since dawn. I think he's done most of the neighborhood."

Janna felt pieces come together in her mind as she recalled Colin's habits as a teenager. She had a good idea why he had so much energy. He was releasing his tension. "I seem to recall," she said to Nancy, "that he told me you'd taught him to work when he was angry or frustrated."

"Yes, well . . . it took him a few years to get the idea. He had a short fuse as a child, but after losing privileges several times for hitting his brother or breaking something, he learned to divert it into work. He keeps things maintained very well around here."

"He spends a lot of time here, I assume."

"More since he finally graduated and passed the bar."

"So, why is he living with Cathy?"

"A few years ago, he and Carl had a little falling out. At the time, Cathy had just decided to go back to school. Mark works out of town a lot, and Colin didn't want to pay high rent. He wanted to avoid debt as much as possible in getting his education. So he moved in with Cathy to help out with Brian some so she could go to classes. They adjusted their schedules to complement each other, and it's worked out well."

Janna nodded. She understood now why Colin was at back-to-school night, and his reason for picking Brian up at her home. Could it possibly be a coincidence?

"Of course," Nancy continued, "it didn't take long for things to mend between him and Carl. And your being here has smoothed over the rough edges from the incident."

"Me?" Janna asked, unable to hide her surprise. "What have I got to do with it?"

Nancy took a long sip of her cocoa as if they were discussing the weather. "You were the biggest reason they couldn't get along."

Janna felt stunned. When nothing more was said, she realized Nancy had no intention of explaining further—at least not without prodding. And Janna simply didn't have the fortitude to push anything at the moment.

The tension was broken when Nancy noticed Colin heading for the backyard. She moved to the back window and Janna followed. They both laughed as Matthew threw a snowball at Colin. Then Colin tossed his shovel into a snowbank, chased Matthew down, and threw him gently into the snow. Matthew came up laughing and threw another snowball at Colin. Colin pretended to be knocked over, and Matthew took full advantage of it.

"In some ways, they never grow up," Nancy said almost to herself. She smiled at Janna and added, "And I must admit I'm glad for that."

Janna was grateful when the weekend was over and Colin went back to work. While she had spent Saturday and Sunday mostly resting, at Nancy's insistence, Colin hardly sat down. His nervous energy nearly drove her to distraction. But at least he kept Matthew occupied, and she enjoyed watching them together, wondering what it might have been like if she'd not been such a fool. She didn't quite dare hope that they might have a future together; at this point, she simply couldn't bring herself to think beyond the divorce. The uncertainty was too frightening. And the cool distance Colin kept much of the time made her certain that whatever he might have felt for her once had simply changed too much.

On Monday, Janna worked out a simple schedule with Nancy. They set aside specific hours of the day for Matthew's schoolwork. Nancy felt the time structure was important for him so he would be able to handle going back to a normal school day when the time came. Janna felt confident about helping him with some subjects, and Nancy was more than eager to help with others.

While Matthew was having "recess," Nancy had Janna help her plan some menus. She encouraged Janna to tell her the foods she enjoyed cooking and what she and Matthew liked to eat. They talked a little bit about the housework and meal preparation, and Janna appreciated Nancy's willingness to let her help. Janna would keep the basement clean and in order, since that was where they spent most of their time, and she would cook three dinners a week and help with breakfasts. They would alternate planning Sunday meals, but help each other out.

Colin called in the afternoon to tell her that Russell's attorney had contacted Robert Taylor, Janna's attorney, for some negotiations. Russell had been willing to supply her with a monthly allowance for her needs until the divorce was settled. Janna was surprised—until she realized that Russell would want to appear to be agreeable and supportive. She was pleased to know that she would not have to depend on the Trevors for every little need. She discussed the money with Nancy, admitting that Russell had never let her have any control of financial matters, and she wondered about the best way to budget it. She appreciated Nancy's easy manner as they talked over their prospective needs and made a list. And though Janna suspected that feeding two extra mouths was not a burden for the Trevors, Nancy graciously accepted Janna's monthly donation to the grocery bill. Perhaps she sensed Janna's need to not feel like a charity case, and this small offering allowed her to maintain some dignity in helping care for herself and her son.

Colin brought a check from Russell the next day and handed it to Janna, saying nothing.

"Thank you," she said quietly. "Did you see him?"

"Thankfully, no," he replied. "The transactions are all being handled through his attorney."

Janna nodded.

"He did send a message," Colin added, his voice hard.

"Dare I ask?"

"His lawyer told Robert that your dear husband is devastated by your leaving. He can't possibly understand why you would want to walk out on him, when your relationship was so special. He wants you to come home and work it out, and forget about this divorce business."

The naked emotion that rose into Janna's eyes tempted Colin to cry. Her hand hinted at trembling as she pressed it over her face where the bruises were fading. "Did he say anything else?" she asked.

"No."

Janna looked at him. "And what did Robert tell Russell's lawyer?"

Colin sighed and glanced away. "My mother has a rule against using profanity in her home."

Colin walked away, and Janna wished she had some idea of what he was thinking.

The snow melted quickly and was replaced by a long spell of beautiful fall weather. Janna soon developed a comfortable routine, fitting into the Trevors' lives as if she somehow belonged there. By his own doing, Matthew began calling them Grandma and Grandpa, and they seemed to enjoy it. Janna grew to love and respect Carl and Nancy in a way she had not been able to fully appreciate as a young woman in their home. When Colin was around, he spent his time with Matthew. He barely acknowledged Janna at all. She felt that was just as well, though she couldn't help wondering why he seemed to avoid her. She asked Nancy about it, but she simply said, "I don't know. You'll have to ask him."

Inspired by Nancy's straightforward manner, Janna decided to do just that. She went downstairs where she knew he was watching T.V. with Matthew. She gasped when he started up the stairs and nearly bumped into her. "I'm sorry," he mumbled as he stepped back and motioned for her to pass.

"Actually, I was looking for you."

Colin glanced comically over his shoulder, as if she couldn't possibly be talking to him. "Oh, me," he said with exaggerated enlightenment. "Did you have a message for Russell?"

"No." She resisted the urge to get defensive. "I wanted to talk to *you*. Is there a problem with that?"

"No," his voice softened. She was actually promoting conversation with him. He reminded himself not to blow it before they even started.

"Can we sit down?" she asked.

He glanced toward the family room where Matthew was watching T.V. He was wondering how private she wanted this when she motioned him into her bedroom, but left the door open. She sat down on the edge of one bed and he sat on the other, facing her. It

was the first time he'd looked closely at her in several days, and he
noticed the bruises were barely visible. He couldn't help thinking how
beautiful she was; she always had been. It surprised him how quickly
his mind conjured up an accurate memory of how it felt to kiss her. A
quiver erupted somewhere inside him, and he forced himself to look
away and clear his head.

"I guess I'll get right to the point," Janna said, trying to ignore
the sudden rush of nerves she felt inside. If she hadn't already been
facing him, she'd have forgotten the whole thing.

"Okay," he urged when she hesitated.

"Your mother has been wonderful, Colin. She's been very frank
with me, and she's helped me see that it's a good thing to be up front
and open, which is something I've never been very good at. So,
forgive me if I fumble a little, but I thought it would be good for us
to clear the air a little, or at least get started on it, or . . ."

Her sentence faded, but Colin nodded as if he understood. *So
far so good*, she thought and cleared her throat to continue. "I can
understand why you're angry with me, Colin. I know that abandoning our relationship like that was wrong. I know it doesn't make
sense to you, but . . . well, maybe it will one day. Anyway, I want to
say that I'm truly sorry for the hurt I've caused you. And, well . . . as I
said, I know why you're angry, but . . . I have to ask you . . . well, I
just want to know why you . . . dislike me so much."

"*Dislike* you?" he echoed. She only stared at him. Colin sighed
and folded his arms. "You know, Janna, your assuming my feelings
and jumping to conclusions is what started this whole mess."

Janna looked away and reminded herself to stay calm. He had a
right to feel this way. She'd just told him he did. And he wasn't going
to hit her if she said something he didn't like. "So, I'm asking," she
said. "I get the feeling you dislike me, and I want to know why."

In the ensuing silence, Janna began to imagine his possible
responses. He would tell her that she'd hurt him too deeply. Or that
too much time had passed. Or that they just weren't right for each
other after all.

"Janna," he said softly, touching her chin to make her look at
him, "let me make something perfectly clear. A lot has happened in
our lives since you graduated from high school, and it's going to take

time and hard work to put it all in order. I admit I have some feelings to deal with, and a lot I need to understand. But don't think for a minute that it changes the way I feel about you."

Janna was taken so off guard she couldn't speak. His eyes bored into hers, as if they were trying to echo what he'd just told her. She knew that look well. But she had difficulty believing it could be true after all these years—after what she'd done to him.

"I don't understand," she finally said, certain she was reading him wrong.

Colin cupped her shoulders with his hands and leaned toward her. "Then let me make it perfectly clear, so there's no question about where I stand. What you are interpreting as *dislike* is nothing but a futile effort to keep my distance. I *have* to keep my distance, Janna, because you are still another man's wife, and I have no business thinking about you the way I do." Janna caught her breath and held it as he continued, his voice low and hoarse. "I love you, JannaLyn. Are you hearing me? I said that I love you. I've never stopped loving you. And when this is all over, I'm going to marry you, like I should have done as soon as your mother died. Then I could have taken care of you, and you never would have left with your aunt. And we could have been spending these years together. We can't change the past, but by heaven and earth, we will have a future—together. The three of us. I am going to raise Matthew as my own son, and this baby," he lightly pressed a hand to her belly, "is as good as mine. And I will not settle for anything less. Any questions?"

Janna didn't answer. She couldn't even move.

"Janna?" Colin questioned, suddenly fearing she would take his confessions and throw them back at him. He let go of her and leaned back. "Of course, if you don't care for me, then—"

"It's not that at all, Colin. It's just that . . ."

"Be honest with me, Janna. We're getting too old to be playing games with our lives. If it's just not there anymore, I'd rather know now, and—"

"I do care for you, Colin." A glisten of moisture rose in her eyes. "It's just that I thought you were so angry with me, and—"

"I *am* angry," he admitted. "And I'm frustrated. And scared. Like I said, it's going to take time. But that doesn't change the way I feel about *you*."

Colin saw her eyes narrow intently, as if she felt confused or distraught. "Is something wrong?"

"I don't know." She shook her head slightly then pressed a hand over her eyes. "It's just that . . . sometimes I wonder if I even have the sense to know truth when I hear it. You see," she met his eyes again, "Russell told me he loved me."

Colin looked away, his jaw tight. He didn't like having his expressions of affection compared to those of an *animal*. But he knew she needed to say it, and he was grateful that she was talking.

"He treated me like a queen, Colin. And there were times when he . . . was so good to me. How can I get over these fears and . . . *know* that what you're telling me is true?"

Colin was surprised at how easily he was able to answer that question. "Time, Janna. Just stick around long enough to give me a chance to prove it. That's all I ask."

Janna nodded slightly, which he took as an agreement. Impulsively he moved to the other bed and put his arms around her. He reminded himself he was her friend—only a friend, for now. At first she felt guarded and stiff, but gradually she relaxed in his embrace. She reached her arms around him and pressed her head to his shoulder.

"Oh, Janna," he whispered, "do you know how I've longed to just hold you in my arms and make all the pain go away?"

Janna pressed her hands against his back, feeling suddenly desperate to never let him go. She'd forgotten how it felt to be replenished and rejuvenated from an embrace. Holding Colin, the memories of all he'd given her came rushing back, and she let them come, losing track of the time she clung to him, oblivious to her surroundings, her face buried in his sweater.

Colin uttered a silent prayer of gratitude as he held Janna and felt the evidence of her need for him. He marveled at the miracles that had brought them back together. That in itself gave him hope in facing the enormity of what lay ahead. *One day at a time*, he reminded himself and just held her.

"Are you all right?" he asked, feeling her tremble.

"For the moment, everything is just fine," she replied softly.

Colin lifted her chin with his finger and looked into her eyes. It took every ounce of self-control to keep from kissing her. He forced himself to remember that she was a married woman, and in spite of the circumstances, he had no business even holding her this way. Instead, he simply touched her face. The gesture was tentative but full of promise. One day she would be his again. But this time he was going to do it right.

CHAPTER SEVEN

*O*nce Janna's face had healed, Nancy invited her to go to church with them. Janna was a little nervous over the prospect. This was the ward she'd grown up in, and she didn't want people wondering over details of why she was staying with the Trevors now. But Nancy talked to her about it, allowing her to express her concerns. Nancy assured her that all of Janna's peers from her youth were long gone, and the ward boundaries had been significantly changed recently. They had already decided that she would use an assumed name with everyone beyond family. And Nancy had bought a wig for Janna, which she actually liked. Thinking it through, Janna had to admit that she had a desire to go to church. She felt so much gratitude for the help God had sent into her life, and she missed having the opportunity when she couldn't go out.

Janna enjoyed her first day at church with Carl and Nancy. Matthew seemed to do well in Primary, and it helped to have Colin attending Cathy's ward. People were friendly and accepting without any apparent speculation. Sitting in the chapel, she thought how nice it was to not be with Russell, feeling as if his hypocrisy might smother her.

Later that day, she called Karen for the first time since she'd left home.

"Oh, my gosh," Karen said right off, "are you all right? I've been wondering about you ever since Russell told me you'd left."

"He told you?"

"Told me? He sat here in my front room for nearly three hours, crying his heart out. If I hadn't seen the evidence of what he'd done to you, I'd never believe it. The man's insane."

"Well, I'll agree with you there."

"And then," Karen added, "he got up in testimony meeting and announced that the two of you were separated, but you were trying to work it out."

It took Janna a minute to absorb this. "Oh, really?"

Janna quickly explained what was going on. She warned Karen to be extremely careful, and went over the precautions they were taking to insure her safety. Karen exclaimed several times how wonderful it was that she'd been able to get away. She then went on to tell Janna that Russell was still in the elders quorum presidency, and he'd been at the temple on ward temple night. The thought made Janna's skin crawl. But she maneuvered the conversation to more positive things, and actually enjoyed telling Karen a little about her relationship with Colin in high school. Not wanting to be on the phone too long, she told Karen she'd keep in touch and finally said good-bye. She was still sitting there, lost in thought, when Colin startled her.

"Something wrong?" he asked.

"Oh, no . . . not really. I was just talking to Karen, a friend of mine. She was my visiting teacher, actually." She told him briefly about how Karen had answered her prayers, and what a good friend she'd become.

Colin watched Janna's eyes become distant as she finished her explanation. "Did she have some bad news, or—"

"What?" Janna looked surprised.

"You look so . . . depressed." He sat down on the couch beside her.

Janna felt a little unnerved by his ability to read her so easily, but she simply said, "She was just telling me how Russell stood up in testimony meeting and declared with sorrow that he and I were separated, but we were trying to work it out. She said she saw him at the temple, and—"

"You're joking, right?"

"No." Janna was surprised by the intensity of his reaction.

"Whoa," he leaned back and took a deep breath. "I hadn't imagined him being active in the Church." He shook his head. "I guess that teaches me something about judgment."

"Actually, he's a counselor in the elders quorum presidency."

Colin attempted to swallow a sudden rush of anger as if he was swallowing a peach pit. He tried to comprehend how such a thing would affect Janna. "That must be tough for you," he said.

Janna looked into his eyes, briefly absorbing his genuine concern. "Yes," she admitted.

"Well . . . did you ever talk to your bishop about this, or—"

"Yes, Colin, I did," she interrupted, not really wanting to talk about it.

"And?" he drawled.

Janna took a deep breath. "He told me that *I* was the only one who believed Russell was violent."

It took Colin a full minute to absorb the meaning behind that statement. He finally retorted, "Well, who *else* is he going to be violent with?"

"That's what I asked him." Janna went on to explain the situation further so he wouldn't be left with the wrong impression. She explained the way Russell had been so perfectly charming when she'd met him. And she told Colin how the Spirit had helped her understand where the bishop was coming from, and how she'd finally made her peace with it.

As she finished, Janna was surprised to turn and find Colin's eyes glowing with admiration. "You're an incredible woman," he said. Janna just looked away, trying not to be embarrassed. He added gently, "All that judgment and misunderstanding must be difficult for you. Yet you handle it so well."

"I don't know about that," she laughed softly. "I'm not really bothered by what those people in my old ward might think of me. I have no intention of ever going anywhere near that neighborhood again. It's just the hypocrisy of the whole thing. When I think of him going to the temple as if . . ."

Her words faded and her eyes became distant again. Colin watched a subtle scowl crease her brow and wondered where her thoughts were. "As if?" he questioned gently.

"I don't understand how a man can take his wife to the temple, then take her home and call her a—" She stopped so abruptly Colin was startled.

"You can talk to me, Janna. I'm not going to think less of you for telling me how bad it was."

She straightened her back and sighed. "If only it were so easy. I'm not sure I *could* talk about it, even though I know I probably should. But if I were to tell you the things I'd heard and experienced in my marriage, it would be like an R-rated movie. And I don't want to subject anybody to that."

Colin leaned his forearms on his thighs and hung his head. What could he say? The sickness smoldered in his stomach. The anger knotted in his chest. The helplessness hovered in his throat. And then he realized that *Matthew* had also been subjected to whatever his mother had endured.

"I didn't intend to upset you. I'm sorry."

Colin glanced up, wondering if his emotions were so transparent. "Don't be sorry. Let's just say it's a learning experience for me. I've spent a lot of time learning about truth and justice. But I'm not certain I've ever fully comprehended before now the inability of justice to be fully satisfied in a world like ours. If I were to act on my emotions and take justice into my own hands, then I would spend time behind bars. If justice is met as it should be by the law, then Russell will spend time behind bars. But where is the justice in that? What does that do but temporarily pull the criminal from society? Does it heal the wounds? Soothe the hurts? Does it bring back lost innocence, or replace broken years?

"I've thought a lot, through my years of schooling, about my reasons for becoming an attorney. It was your mother who first suggested I consider a career in law. Her work as a legal secretary always fascinated me, and she knew it. The more I got into it, the more I realized that I had some very deep feelings about this business; that maybe this was really what I was *meant* to do—that I could make a difference in people's lives. I'm certain that every lawyer has his own personal reasons for doing what he does, and some of them are not especially concerned about honor and values. But I thought very hard about *why* I was doing this. I wanted to have a defined goal. And then one night, it came to me: safety and justice. I wanted to understand the law so that I could empower safety and justice."

Colin resisted the urge to touch Janna's face and shook his head slowly. "Putting Russell behind bars won't ever begin to meet justice, in my opinion. But it will get him excommunicated and end the hypocrisy. And it will make you safe. That's the most important thing."

Matthew came into the room and the conversation ended there. But Colin's vision of safety and justice stayed with Janna. However it turned out, she felt somehow awed by Colin's part in this. His willingness to help her and the emotion behind it brought to mind a knight on a white steed, charging the dragon head on to save the damsel in distress, who was being held captive within walls of stone. *The walls of Jericho.* She had managed to escape those walls, for the time being. And with Colin at her side, and enough faith, maybe they would yet fall and make her completely free.

The following morning, Janna was folding some laundry on the family room floor when Colin came down the stairs, obviously dressed for work.

"Is this a special occasion?" she asked.

He sat on the couch nearby and leaned toward her. "I needed to talk to you, and I didn't want it to be over the phone."

Janna sat up straight and ignored the laundry. "It must be serious," she said. "Is this business, or—"

"You have a hearing the day after tomorrow. Perhaps I should have told you sooner, but I didn't want you to worry about it any longer than necessary. You should be there."

Janna glanced down at her hands, feeling suddenly unnerved. "Will Russell be there?"

"Most likely," Colin stated.

Janna nodded resolutely, then listened as Colin explained the procedure and everything she needed to know. When he was finished, Janna met his eyes with a panicked expression.

"Everything will be all right, Janna." He took her hand.

Janna wanted to believe him, but the reality couldn't be denied. She knew how Russell's mind worked, and she felt certain this was not going to be easy, by any means.

The following morning, Nancy surprised her at breakfast with a simple announcement. "I think we should go shopping, Janna. I've asked Cathy if she would come over and watch Matthew for a couple of hours."

"Shopping?" Janna questioned. "I don't know if—"

"Oh, I know you don't really *need* anything, and I know it's difficult for you to go out. But it won't take long, and we'll be careful. I just wanted to buy you a new dress for the hearing tomorrow."

Before Janna could question her motives, Nancy explained. "You mustn't worry, Janna. You're going to do great, but sometimes a woman just needs the perfect thing to wear to give her a little confidence. When you walk into that courtroom, looking brilliant and courageous, you'll feel like you can take on the world."

Janna chuckled shyly. "Do you really think a dress could make that much difference?"

"I'm absolutely certain of it."

Janna enjoyed getting out, and soon relaxed as she convinced herself that the likelihood of running into Russell was too small to consider. She tried on several dresses, but nothing felt quite right. She trusted Nancy's taste, but Nancy kept saying that it just had to make her feel good when she looked at herself in the mirror.

It took some time to get used to looking at herself as a blonde, and she had to remember that she wouldn't be wearing the wig when she went to court. Janna began to wonder if the problem was with *her*—until she tried on a navy blue suit. Just looking at her reflection made Janna want to stand a little straighter and hold her chin higher. It had a straight skirt that hung below the knee, and a double-breasted jacket with a little peplum.

"What do you think?" Janna asked Nancy.

"I think you look incredible," Nancy laughed with obvious pleasure.

Janna tried to protest when she looked at the price tag, but Nancy was insistent. She then bought her some navy-colored pumps and an exquisite white blouse.

Janna could hardly sleep that night for fear of facing Russell. But she turned her mind to prayer and finally drifted off, imagining herself with confidence, wearing that new suit. The next morning, she was barely ready when Colin came to pick her up. She was just putting in the silver teardrop earrings Nancy had loaned her when he walked through the front door. She wondered for a moment what was wrong when he just stood there, saying nothing. Then she realized he was looking at her.

Colin reminded himself to breathe when his chest tightened. He'd not seen Janna in anything but baggy shirts and sweaters since she'd come back into his life. And this was not the skinny little teenager he'd fallen in love with. This was a sumptuous woman who had given birth and experienced real life. She wore the extra pounds well, with soft, full curves that made him long to get this divorce behind them.

"You look magnificent," he managed to say, thinking it sounded trite.

"Do you really think so?" she asked as if she truly didn't believe him.

"I'm absolutely certain of it," he said, and saw Nancy wink at him from behind Janna.

"I'm scared," Janna said as they drove toward the courthouse.

"That's understandable. But remember, you're not going to be alone with him. And anything he does or says can be held against him."

"That's just it," she said. "He's so smooth, I can just imagine what it will be like."

"Tell me," he said.

"He'll look like a lovesick puppy, with big sad eyes, as if he can't possibly imagine why I would leave him. Somehow he'll find a way to become the victim, and make me end up looking like a fool."

Colin wished he knew what to say. He didn't want to admit that he was scared, too. They agreed that Colin should keep his distance while Russell was anywhere around, to avoid having him make any connection.

Janna told herself to be confident as she walked into the courtroom, and it wasn't as difficult as she'd expected it to be. She just avoided looking at Russell at all. But she felt his eyes on her almost constantly. His outward expression was exactly what she'd expected, but she could almost feel his thoughts churning, trying to find a way to undo her. She was relieved to have it over, and she felt some confidence in seeing how well Colin had prepared her for this. At least he knew this business.

"Are you all right?" Colin asked when they met discreetly back at the car.

"I don't know," she admitted.

They drove toward home for several minutes in silence before Colin asked, "Do you want to talk about it?"

"If he finds me, he'll kill me," she said. "That restraining order isn't going to stop him."

Colin tried to comprehend the implications of her statement. "You're serious," he said.

"Yes," she turned to him, her eyes nearly burning through him, "I'm absolutely serious. If he finds me, he will *kill* me."

Colin cleared his throat. "Well, while he's serving time for aggravated assault, you can have a chance to put your life together."

"And then what?" she asked.

"We'll just have to make sure he never finds you," Colin said firmly, hoping she didn't sense his own concern.

Janna gave a dubious chuckle. "Maybe *I* should have killed *him*," she said. "I seriously considered it a few times. There were moments when life in a prison cell seemed a far better option than living with him." When Colin said nothing, she added, "It was Matthew who kept me sane. I had to survive . . . for him."

"And you need to *keep* surviving, Janna . . . for both of us."

Janna met his eyes and realized he meant it. She looked out the window and added something that she felt needed to be voiced. "You should know, Colin . . . he told me more than once that he would kill any man who tried to take me away from him."

Colin's brow went up. "Are you saying I'm in danger, as well?"

"There's no telling what he's capable of." When nothing more was said, she added, "Maybe you should just take me to that women's shelter and wash your hands of the whole thing before you get any more involved."

Following a moment of silence, Colin said, "Maybe you should just get used to the idea that you and I are meant to be together, and no threat or manipulation is going to keep me from being a part of your life."

"But what if—"

"I'll be careful, Janna. It's in the Lord's hands."

Janna said nothing more. The future was so uncertain that she hardly dared think about it. But at least she knew that if anything happened to her now, Colin and his family would see that Matthew was cared for. There was some peace in that. She only hoped that they would all remain safe from the complications she had brought into their lives.

Through the following day, Janna noticed a vague cramping settling in. By the time she went to bed, she knew she was miscarrying again. She hoped it would take care of itself in the night and avoid drawing any attention to her. But lying alone in the dark, with the pain setting in hard, she felt suddenly tired of being alone.

She was absorbed in silent prayer when Matthew's voice came through the darkness. "What's the matter, Mommy?" He sounded upset, and she realized her whimpering must have awakened him.

"It's all right, sport. Mom's just feeling kind of sick. I'll be okay." A minute later she heard Matthew scurry from the room. While she didn't want to bother Nancy, she couldn't deny the relief when Matthew returned with her a few minutes later.

"What is it, my dear?" Nancy made her way to the bed by the light emitting from the family room. "Are you ill?"

"I'm miscarrying," she explained, then bit her lip to keep from crying out as the pain intensified.

"Good heavens, we should get you to the hospital."

"No . . . it'll be all right. It would be harder on me to have to move right now. I just don't want to be alone. I'm glad you came. Stay with me, please."

A few minutes later, Carl appeared in the doorway, wearing a long bathrobe. "Is everything all right?" he asked.

"She's losing the baby," Nancy explained, nodding discreetly toward Matthew, who was looking frightened and upset. She added more softly, "She doesn't want to go to the hospital, but perhaps she could use a blessing."

Carl nodded and ushered Matthew out of the room. "Come along," he urged gently. "Your mother will be fine. Why don't we go read a story while Grandma stays with her."

"Thank you," Janna managed to say to Nancy. "It's never been quite this bad before."

"How many times has this happened?" Nancy asked gently.

"At home . . . this is three. I lost one at five months, and Russell took me to the hospital for that."

"Bless your heart," Nancy whispered, gently pushing the hair back off Janna's face with her fingers. "Don't you worry, now. We'll see that everything's all right. If it doesn't get better soon, I'm taking you to the hospital, whether you want to go or not."

Janna nodded and willed her body to get this over with.

* * * * *

Colin heard a phone ring somewhere in the distance, but he knew Cathy would get it and he drifted back to sleep. The next thing he knew, Cathy was nudging him awake. "Get up," she insisted. "Dad's on the phone. He wants to talk to you."

"What time is it?" he asked groggily, trying to focus his eyes as he lumbered toward the door.

"It's nearly three. I wonder what on earth could be wrong."

Colin's heart began to pound before he got to the phone. "What is it?" he asked right off.

"Sorry to wake you, son, but JannaLyn is in need of a blessing. I can't do it alone."

"Why? What's wrong?" he demanded.

"Just get here, and we'll talk about it."

Colin dropped the phone in his attempt to hang it up. Cathy fixed it for him and followed him back to his room. "What did he say? What's wrong?"

"It's Janna," he stated, motioning for her to turn her back so he could get dressed. "He just said she needs a blessing." Colin slipped out of his pajama pants, pulled on his jeans and buttoned them. "Okay, I'm decent. Hand me that shirt. He didn't tell me why. I'm sure you'll get all the juicy details later."

Cathy sighed in frustration and stood there looking agitated, as if her mind was spinning with the possibilities. "You just can't stand not knowing everything, can you?" Colin asked lightly while he tied his shoes.

"I'm going back to bed," she said, handing him his coat. "Be careful and call me at seven."

Colin didn't bother driving the speed limit through the deserted streets. He pulled into the driveway and ran through the front door, wishing he had some idea of what to expect. His father met him at the door.

"Stay quiet," Carl cautioned softly. "I just got Matthew back to sleep, and it took me four and a half stories."

"What's wrong?" Colin demanded, closing the door quietly behind him.

"She's losing the baby," Carl explained, "and she's having a hard time of it."

"Shouldn't she go to the hospital?" Colin asked, trying not to sound upset.

"We can take her to the doctor when it's over and make certain everything's all right. We called Reynolds, and he said it's just as well she stay put for now. He told us what to be concerned about. So far, she's not in any danger. She's just hurting badly."

Carl motioned Colin down the stairs. He could hear evidence of Janna's pain as they approached her bedroom door. His heart beat mercilessly as he took in the scene. Janna was curled up in the center of the bed, a sheet spread over her, moaning and writhing as if the pain was unbearable. Nancy sat at the head of the bed, one hand holding Janna's tightly, the other pressing a cool cloth to Janna's face. He saw his concern mirrored in his mother's eyes. He wanted to ask if Janna was okay, but he knew it was a stupid question.

Carl motioned Colin toward the bed. Nancy spoke quietly to Janna, "Carl and Colin are going to give you a blessing, my dear."

Janna's eyes shot open at the mention of Colin's name. Their eyes met for an instant before she became lost in the pain again. But she didn't seem terribly pleased to have him there.

Colin felt a little unnerved when his father made it clear that he wanted Colin to speak the blessing. Trying hard to shut out his own emotions and open his mind to inspiration, he put his hands on Janna's head, along with his father's, and blessed Janna that this ordeal would soon be over and that her body would recover completely from the effects of her struggles. Colin heard himself telling her that God was mindful of her suffering and her sins were forgiven. He promised her that with time she would find peace and safety in her life, and that Matthew would have brothers and sisters to grow up with.

When the blessing was finished, Colin stepped back. He felt a little disoriented, trying to comprehend the source of those words. He realized Janna seemed a little more relaxed. But before he and his father had a chance to leave the room, she cried out in apparent agony. Nancy hurried them out and closed the door. Carl said he was going to check on Matthew and try to get a little sleep before he had to go to work. Colin attempted to relax on the couch. An agonizing forty-five minutes later, Nancy came into the family room and declared that it was over, and Janna was fine.

"That was a beautiful blessing you gave her, Colin." Nancy sat beside him and took his hand.

"It wasn't me talking," he admitted, glancing briefly heavenward.

"I know," she smiled serenely.

"Are you sure she's all right?" Colin glanced toward the bedroom.

"She's fine. I'll take her to see Dr. Reynolds in the morning to make certain everything's in order."

"Why was she in so much pain?" he asked at the risk of sounding completely ignorant.

"Even though the baby was too small to even be recognizable as a fetus, the uterus has to contract almost as hard as with a full-term birth in order to get it out. It's not a pleasant experience. I lost a couple of babies myself."

"Janna told me she's lost others."

"Yes, we talked about that before the pain became too intense."

"Why do you think she's lost so many? Do you think something's wrong or . . . I mean, she had Matthew all right, obviously."

"I don't think Russell was kicking her in the stomach when she was pregnant with Matthew." Nancy's words hung thick in the air as Colin felt too queasy to respond. "It makes you angry," she stated.

"Angry?" he echoed with a bitter edge. "It makes me want to kill him with my bare hands."

"Russell will meet his justice in a courtroom. And you'd better keep your fists out of it." She paused and gave him one of her *you'd-better-listen-to-this-good* looks. "You're too much of a man to lower yourself to physical violence in response to your anger."

"Thanks to you," he uttered.

Nancy smiled and touched his face. "You were always a good boy, Colin."

"Not always," he said sadly.

"I know you've had some struggles, Colin. But we all make mistakes. It's how we respond to them that builds our character and makes us strong."

Colin thought about that a minute and knew it was true.

"I'm going up to bed," Nancy said. "Why don't you stay here on the couch, so you can be close by if Janna needs something."

Colin nodded, feeling a little apprehensive at being put in charge of such a sensitive situation. He settled down on the couch with a pillow and blanket, but he was barely comfortable when he heard Janna calling quietly for Nancy. He felt his way to her bedside, guided only by a dim light from the stairs. Not knowing what to say, he just slipped his hand into hers and squeezed it gently.

"Oh, you're so sweet," she said. Her voice betrayed the strain of her ordeal. "I'm sorry to be such a bother. I just . . . don't want to be alone."

Colin could tell she was crying, and he wondered if her pain was emotional or physical

"It's all right," he whispered.

Janna jumped at the sound of his voice. "Colin? I thought . . ."

"Mother's gone up to bed. She left me in charge." As he said it, Colin wondered if Nancy had done this on purpose. But why would his mother force them to spend more time together when she'd been so adamant about him keeping his distance? Janna said nothing and he added, "If you're not comfortable with me here, I can go get her and—"

"No, that's all right. I'm fine. There's no need for you to be here if—"

"You just said you didn't want to be alone. Or is it that you would rather be alone than be with me?"

Janna wondered if it was simply pride that made having him here difficult. But as questions swirled around in her head with her raw emotions, the feelings ruled out.

"Don't leave me," she whispered.

"I'm here," he assured her, sitting on the floor beside the bed.

Janna eased her head closer to Colin, where she could see the outline of his shoulder. She felt his fingers press gently over her brow, and she couldn't hold the tears back.

"Are you in pain?" he asked.

"A little, but it's not too bad."

"Then why are you crying?" His voice was gentle.

Janna found it difficult to answer. "I suppose I should be glad that I don't have to deal with the complications of having Russell's baby. And in a way I am, but . . ."

"But?" he pressed when she stopped abruptly.

"It was a part of me," she whimpered.

Colin smoothed a hand over her face. "Just like the others you lost."

He felt her nod. "He . . . he . . ." She seemed to want to say something, but her increasing emotion made it difficult.

"He what, Janna?"

She tightened her grip on his hand. "He . . . killed my babies."

Colin felt something in his heart break as she mourned the death of yet another child. She'd tried to tell him it was only a pregnancy, but he could see clearly that in her heart it was much more than that.

"It's okay," he whispered. "Go ahead and cry. You've earned the right to cry, JannaLyn."

Janna eased her face against his shoulder and cried helplessly. Colin tangled his fingers in her hair and whispered soothing words near her ear. She finally became still, and he thought she was asleep, until she began to shiver.

"Are you cold?" he asked.

"Yes," she said through chattering teeth. Colin went to the couch and came back with the extra blanket. He tucked it carefully over her and sat on the edge of the bed.

"Is that better?" he asked. She nodded but continued to shiver for several minutes. Concerned only for her welfare, Colin impulsively slid beneath the blanket, lying on top of the other bedding. He eased close to her back and put his arms around her. He wondered briefly if she would protest, but she seemed drawn to his warmth, and within a few minutes her shivering ceased.

As Colin began to relax, he tried to imagine how Janna might be feeling. He wondered if her distress was in not wanting to have Russell's child, when he had caused her so much pain. But she loved Matthew. He wondered if the baby had been conceived by force. The thought made bile rise into his throat, but he swallowed it and tried to bring his mind back to the present. The baby was gone, and though the trauma was not easy, he felt certain that in the long run she would be relieved. Then Colin wondered if he should feel guilty for being relieved. The thought of her carrying Russell's baby was unnerving. But he was committed to having a future with Janna, and he would take on whatever came along with her. He had no trouble caring for Matthew, and assumed it would be just as easy to feel warmth toward this baby, had it survived. But for both of them, getting through this divorce and starting over would not be easy. Not having to deal with a pregnancy would make it much less complicated.

Janna shifted in his arms, reminding him of her closeness. He felt relaxed but not sleepy, and forced his mind from troubling thoughts. He just wanted to enjoy feeling her in his arms.

Now that Janna felt warm and secure, she became consciously aware that Colin Trevor was lying beside her, holding her close. There was too much bedding between them for her to feel it was even remotely intimate. But she could feel his breathing behind her ear, and was keenly aware of his presence surrounding her. She couldn't deny the security she felt, having him so close. For the first time in years, she truly felt safe.

Feeling an ache in her lower back, Janna turned carefully in an attempt to ease it.

"Are you okay?" Colin asked.

"Yes, thank you," she said, settling her head near his shoulder. Colin could feel her breath against his throat, and he concentrated on the sensation. After all his years of searching for her, it was still difficult to comprehend that she was here. He felt a certain security in her apparent need for him, and instinctively he wanted to care for her. He felt her tremble slightly and asked, "Are you cold again?"

"No," she replied.

Colin pondered the other possibilities. "Are you afraid?"

"No," she said again.

"Then why are you—" She cut his words short by pressing her fingers to his lips.

"Stop talking and kiss me," she whispered.

Her words brought so many memories rushing back that Colin hardly dared breathe for fear of losing this feeling. It was easy to press his lips to hers, taking care to hold his passion back where it belonged. The clarity of his memories increased, and he heard himself moan against her lips. A formless desperation rose up from somewhere inside him and he kissed her harder, as if he feared he might never have the chance again. He felt her soften in his arms, sensed her need that matched his own. Then abruptly everything changed. He heard her whimper, felt her stiffen and ease back.

"I'm sorry, Janna," he uttered. "I didn't mean to—"

"It's okay. It's just that . . ."

"What?" he questioned, hearing emotion in her voice.

"It just . . . reminded me of . . . the night my mother died."

Colin sat bolt upright and put his feet on the floor. He pushed his head into his hands and groaned in self-punishment.

"I'm so sorry, Janna. My intention was not to—"

"It's okay, Colin," she assured him, but she couldn't think of anything else to say. While the memory of what their intimacy that night had triggered in her life was frightening, his nearness had sparked something in her that she had believed was dead. In spite of the loss she had just suffered, she couldn't deny feeling some hope in the evidence of Colin's affection for her.

She heard Colin move to Matthew's bed and settle into it. "I'm here if you need me, Janna," he said. "But I think I'll just keep my distance for the time being."

Colin rolled over and tried to go to sleep, but his thoughts and emotions kept him wide awake until he heard his mother upstairs fixing breakfast. He left Janna sleeping soundly and tried to concentrate on making it through the day.

Within a few days, Janna felt quite well physically. But a darkness hovered around her that she couldn't break free of. She prayed to understand it, but the harder she tried, the more confused she became. The events of her life that had led her to this point swirled together until she felt as if she was a ball of tangled knots. The past confused her. The future frightened her. And the present was just plain difficult as Colin drifted in and out of her days. At moments, she believed he still loved her as much as he ever had. But he remained distant and guarded, and there were times when she could almost feel an angry frustration brewing inside him. Knowing she was the reason for it, she wondered if she could ever have the courage to face up to resolving all that stood between them.

"Janna, are you listening to me?" Colin's voice startled her from her thoughts, and she looked up to see him watching her across the dinner table. Carl and Matthew had already finished eating and had gone out to the garage to look for something. Janna glanced at her supper. She'd hardly touched it.

"I'm sorry," she said. "I didn't realize you were talking to me."

She noticed a concerned glance pass between Colin and his mother.

"Janna, my dear," Nancy said, taking her hand across the table, "we're concerned for you. We understand that you have a great deal weighing on you, and we wondered if . . . well . . ."

Janna couldn't recall ever seeing Nancy Trevor at a loss for words. She turned to Colin as he took over. "I'll get right to the point. A few weeks ago, we discussed your getting some counseling. Now that you're feeling better, and you've had some time to settle in, perhaps you should get on with it."

The idea of counseling didn't appeal to Janna, but she conceded that maybe someone who understood this kind of thing could help her sort it out. She had to admit some relief in having someone else bring it up.

"There's one person I'd be willing to talk to," she said quietly. "He was a friend of my mother's. If he's still in the area, I'd like to talk to him."

"Okay," Colin said, feeling immense relief. For some reason, he'd expected her to protest the idea when confronted with it directly.

Nancy handed Janna the phone book. Within a minute she turned it toward Colin with her finger pointing to a bold listing. *Sean O'Hara, Ph.D., Family Counseling.*

"He helped me work through some things before I met you," she stated. "Will you call tomorrow and make me an appointment?"

Colin nodded, trying to absorb the idea that Janna had needed counseling as a young teenager. She'd simply never told him.

"I'm available for taxi service if you need me," he said.

"I appreciate that," she said, not wanting to go out alone.

Through the evening, Janna couldn't stop thinking about the implications of approaching her abuse through counseling. She felt downright scared to start pulling out all the things inside that she'd rather not look at. She kept wishing that Colin could go with her—

not just to drive her there, but to help her get started. But it sounded so preposterous.

While Matthew drifted to sleep in his bed, Janna sat close by, praying and pondering the situation. It was past ten o'clock when the thought appeared in her mind that she should just come right out and ask Colin if he would go. Without thinking it through any further, she hurried up the stairs, fearing he'd already left for the night. She stopped and gasped when she entered the dining room to find him standing on a chair, replacing a light bulb.

"Something wrong?" he asked, screwing the light fixture back into place.

"No. I just . . . wanted to ask you something. I was afraid you'd already left, but . . ." Feeling suddenly unprepared, she wanted to say that it could wait. But it couldn't. Instinctively she wanted a future with Colin, and she wanted to do it right. She felt like this might be a good place to start, but she didn't know how to approach it.

"I'm still here." He stepped down from the chair and slid it under the edge of the table. He pushed his hands into his back pockets and watched her expectantly.

Wanting privacy and a minute to think, she said, "Can we go downstairs?"

"Sure," Colin said and followed her to the family room.

By the time they sat down, Janna had made up her mind to just come right out and ask. As he'd once told her, they were too old to be playing games. Without looking at him, she said, "I was just wondering if you really meant what you said a while back . . . about you and me . . . working things out together . . . eventually."

"You can bet your life on it," he said.

Their eyes met, and Janna felt some relief from his genuine smile. She sighed and continued toward her point. "I was just wondering, because . . . well, it's about this counseling thing. Do you think it would be strange if I asked you to go with me—just to help me get started? And who knows? Maybe it would help *us* in the long run."

Janna was surprised when Colin laughed gently and gave her a quick hug. "What was that for?" she asked.

"You read my mind," he said. "I've been racking my brain to come up with a way to ask if I could go without sounding like an idiot."

"Do you need counseling too, Colin?" she asked facetiously.

But Colin was quite serious when he answered. "Actually, I don't think it would hurt me a bit. Since our struggles seem to be all tangled up, maybe it would be a good idea to start working them out together."

In spite of Colin's support, Janna was visibly nervous as they walked together into Sean O'Hara's office on the third floor of a professional building. She caught Colin looking at her with a little smirk. "What?" she probed quietly.

"I'm just trying to get used to you as a blonde. You do look adorable, but I think I prefer the real you."

"That makes two of us," she said, and Colin turned to speak to the receptionist.

"How are we going to pay for this?" she asked Colin under her breath while they were sitting in the waiting room.

"I can pay for it, Janna," he said without moving his eyes from the magazine he was thumbing through.

"You shouldn't have to," she replied. "I hate feeling like some charity case."

Colin looked over at her and set the magazine down tersely. "You are *not* some charity case. You are the woman I love."

Janna looked at him as if she didn't believe him, then she said nothing more for several minutes. Colin was looking through the magazine again when she said, "I doubt he'll even remember me. It's been a long time."

"Then we'll remind him," he said.

A minute later, they were led down a hall into a small but nicely decorated room with a window, three comfortable chairs, and a small table with a drawer in it and a box of tissues on top. On one wall was a large painting of a lion lying peaceably with a lamb. On the opposite wall, next to a floral wreath, was a family portrait of Sean, his wife, and four young children, all wearing plaid flannel shirts.

They'd barely sat down when Sean O'Hara walked through the door. They came to their feet as Sean extended a hand to Janna. She was briefly caught off guard by the memories that just seeing him brought back. He'd hardly changed at all. He looked at her face, then smiled, holding her hand in his.

"I know you," he said. "You're . . . wait, don't tell me. You're . . . uh . . ." He chuckled at himself. "I know! You're Diane Hayne's daughter." He gave her a brief hug, then added, "My first client."

"I didn't think you'd remember," she admitted.

"I'm not always good with names," Sean said. "But I never forget a face." He turned to Colin and shook his hand. "And this must be your husband. You made the appointment. Colin, right?"

"Colin Trevor," he said, then added, "I'm not her husband yet, but I have high hopes."

"Well, it's a pleasure to meet you, Colin." He sat down easily and crossed his legs, motioning to the other chairs. "Make yourselves comfortable, and please call me Sean." They both nodded and he went on, "So, tell me a little bit about what's going on in your lives."

Sean pulled a yellow note pad and pencil out of the drawer and jotted down a few notes as he listened quietly, occasionally asking a question. Colin did most of the talking as he briefly explained the course of their relationship. He left out the part about their intimacy as teenagers, and simply said that Janna had been in an abusive marriage and he'd helped her get away. Sean asked Janna if she had anything to add, and she shook her head solemnly.

"So," Sean said, "as I understand it, the two of you are here to just talk through some feelings and sort out the things that have occurred since you separated several years ago."

"I guess that sums it up," Janna said.

"Does that make us strange or . . ." Colin's voice faded.

Sean chuckled softly. "You know, talking to a counselor doesn't have the stigma that it used to. Actually, I don't believe there's a human being who doesn't have some kind of personal struggle through the course of a lifetime. There's nothing shameful or abnormal about talking it through with someone who has the training to understand human nature and help you make sense of it."

"I can go along with that," Colin said.

"And, personally, I wish more couples would work things out *before* they get married. It's good for the two of you to realize there are some tough things to deal with here as you work toward building a relationship again."

Colin met Janna's eyes and found some assurance in her subtle smile. Then she glanced down, wringing her hands as she said, "I know I need some help dealing with the abuse, and that has nothing to do with Colin, but . . ."

When she hesitated, Sean interjected, "I'm certain we'll need some time alone, Janna. But often a third party can help keep the objective clear. We'll just take it one step at a time.

"Okay," Sean crossed his legs the other direction, "before we get into anything, I want to commend you for being here. It takes courage to admit that you can't always do it alone, and I want you to know that I am committed to doing everything I can to help you work it through. I can listen. I can mediate. I can help you understand certain things. I can make suggestions. It's up to you to take what I give you and work with it. Are you with me?"

They both nodded.

"Now, I need to know that both of you are committed to being completely honest with me. It's as simple as that. You can consider what is said in this room as good as being under oath in a courtroom. If you're not comfortable with answering a question, or saying something, just say you're not comfortable with it. Understood?"

They both nodded again.

"So, the next thing is that we clear the air. I need to know if there is anything between the two of you that you might consider 'sacred ground,' so to speak. In other words, are there any topics that might bring out unnecessary tension, or be offensive?"

Janna felt momentarily uncomfortable. She knew things that would make Colin angry. But she felt it was inevitable that he find out eventually, and it was just as well that it came out here.

"There are no secrets between us, as far as I know," Colin said easily. "At one time, we were very open with each other."

"I don't have a problem with talking things out," Janna said.

Sean looked more directly at Janna and added, "When I worked with you before, we discussed some sensitive issues. Do you have a problem with any of that coming up now?"

"As far as I can remember, Colin knows everything. I'm fine with that."

"Good." Sean leaned back. "We have just accomplished what it takes some couples four sessions to accomplish. Now we can get started."

This made Janna feel a little better. Perhaps she wasn't so dysfunctional after all.

Sean began by going over some basic communication skills that would help their sessions together go more smoothly. He encouraged them to practice these skills with each other regularly in order to make the communication between them more effective. He then started asking questions about their relationship as teenagers. They actually laughed a little as they reminisced, and Colin intuitively took hold of Janna's hand.

"Everything was fine until my mother died," Janna said.

Sean looked up at her, his eyes wide. "I didn't know," he said quietly. "She was so young. What happened?"

"The doctors said it was a stroke. It all happened very fast." Janna felt pain gathering between her eyes and put her fingers there in an effort to suppress it.

"Her death must have been very difficult for you," Sean said with a gentle voice. "You implied that something went wrong between you and Colin when your mother died. Why don't you tell me about it?"

Janna glanced at Colin, hoping he would rescue her. Colin cleared his throat and looked at Sean. "The night Janna lost her mother, I stayed with her because she was terribly upset. With all the emotion and everything, we kind of just . . . got carried away."

"Are you talking about sexual intimacy?" Sean asked with no sign of shock or disgust.

"That's right," Colin said.

Sean asked questions about how they'd dealt with Diane's death, and the course their relationship had taken after that. When they came to Janna's leaving for Arizona, Colin became agitated.

"Are you having a hard time with this, Colin?" Sean asked.

"I just don't understand why she left like that. All these years I've struggled with it. I guess that's what's hardest for me."

"Janna?" Sean turned to her in question. "What can you tell Colin about this that might help him understand?"

Janna could feel a tangible pain develop in her chest. "I'm not comfortable talking about that right now," she said.

"Do you think we can reach a point where you will be able to talk about it, and help Colin understand?"

Janna hesitated, then said firmly, "Yes, I do."

"I can see that this is tough for you," Sean said to Colin, "but do you think you can be patient in working on other things until she's ready?"

"I can live with that," he said.

"Okay," Sean said, "why don't we jump ahead and talk about how the two of you came back together."

Colin quickly explained what had happened. Sean briefly discussed how confusing such abuse could be to the victim, then he asked Janna some questions about her relationship with Russell, which she answered readily.

"You know," Sean said, "it sounds like—from what little you've told me—that in many ways Russell is quite typical. This type of abusive personality tends to be well-liked and respected on the surface. In fact, there can often be aspects of the abuser's personality that are rather alluring—even to the abused spouse."

Colin listened in amazement as Janna explained the intensity of her confusion in the early years of her relationship with Russell. He began to feel a little sick as she alluded to a part of their relationship that had once been pleasurable for her. She glanced at him warily, as if she'd just remembered that he was there. While Sean explained something about the intimidation and manipulation that were associated with physical abuse, Colin's mind wandered to the reality that Janna had shared a lengthy intimate relationship with this Mr. Hyde creature who had nearly destroyed her. He had to briefly put a hand over his mouth to consciously will down a rush of nausea.

Colin focused on what Sean was saying as he encouraged Janna by telling her that once she'd walked out that door and left the abuse behind, she was no longer a victim, but a survivor. He summed up their session by telling them that sorting out what Janna had been through would take some time, but he felt confident that he could help her. He wanted to start by seeing Janna alone twice a week, and he mentioned that she could likely get some help with the cost through a program set up to help displaced abuse victims. He said that he would like to see them together occasionally, and with time their joint sessions would be more frequent. Sean also said that he

would like to have Matthew involved in a counseling program specifically for children from abusive homes. They made arrangements for
their appointments and drove home in silence.

"You okay?" Colin asked Janna as they pulled into the driveway.

"Yes," she said, but he didn't believe her.

Colin remembered Sean's advice to be patient. *One day at time*,
he told himself as he gently squeezed Janna's hand before they went
into the house.

CHAPTER EIGHT

*W*hile Matthew and Brian played in the backyard, Janna put the finishing touches on the meal she had prepared. Carl had gone with Nancy for her yearly physical, and Colin said he would come to dinner. It was gradually becoming easier for Janna to feel completely at home here, and it felt good to be working in the kitchen. Her sessions with Sean had been difficult, but his feedback was validating, and she could already feel some hope that she would be able to put the abuse behind her with time. She'd had one more session with Colin, which made it easier to feel comfortable with him. The progress increased her hope that the bridges left between them would not be impossible to cross.

The timer on the stove rang, and she hurried to pull the lasagna out of the oven. Unaware that the pot holder was wet, she wasn't prepared for the steam generated when it came in contact with the hot pan. Startled from the burn, she dropped the casserole dish. The closing of the front door was lost in the crash as the dish shattered over the floor.

Colin rushed toward the sound of Janna's cry. He came around the corner into the kitchen just as she was about to step back in bare feet, with broken glass and hot food splattered all around her. "Janna!" he called and took a step toward her. In an instant, her expression went from distress over the accident to complete, unmasked fear. He reached for her arm to keep her from stepping into the glass and hot lasagna, and her arms curled protectively over her face as she cried out. He grabbed her before she fell and carried her to the safety of a bar stool, ignoring the lasagna on his shoes.

When Janna recovered from the shock, she realized what she'd just done and willed her heart to stop pounding.

"Are you okay?" Colin asked gently.

She nodded, but he could see tears pooling in her eyes.

"I'm sorry if I startled you," he said. "I just didn't want you to hurt your feet, and . . ." She nodded again and put her hand over her eyes. Her chin quivered, and he realized what had just happened. "You thought I was going to hit you," he guessed with a degree of confidence. She nodded again and moved her hand over her mouth.

Colin groaned in empathy. "It's all right, Janna. I would never hurt you."

"I know," she whimpered, unable to hold the tears back any longer. "I was just startled and . . . I reacted."

"It's okay," he assured her.

Janna sniffled and took a deep breath, then turned to look at the mess she'd made. "Oh," she moaned, "look what I've done." Her voice picked up an unnatural edge. "I'm so sorry, Colin." She scrambled to get off the bar stool. "I'll clean it up. And I'll hurry and fix something else. I won't let it happen again, and—"

"Janna!" He put her back on the stool. "Will you please stay put so you don't hurt yourself? I am not upset. It was an accident."

"I know," she admitted sheepishly. "I just . . ."

Colin felt one of those sick knots in his stomach as the picture became even more clear. If Russell had walked in to find the same situation, he would have punished her for it.

He quickly decided a change of subject would be in order. "Hey, it's okay. You go get something on your feet, and I'll help you clean it up. We'll order a pizza."

Janna did as she was told, wondering why she felt somehow guilty for having such a disaster resolved so easily. She put on socks and shoes and quickly checked on the boys before going back to the kitchen. Colin had scooped the whole hot mess into a metal bucket with a dustpan and a spatula.

"After it cools, I'll throw it all away and clean the bucket," he informed her. "If you'll hand me some stuff from the hall closet, we'll get this mopped up in no time."

Janna fixed mop water, then took Colin's shoes to clean them while he finished up the floor. He ordered a pizza, then they sat down together on the couch.

"Thank you, Colin. I feel so stupid."

"Why should you feel stupid? It was an accident."

"I know."

"What happened, anyway?"

"I guess the pot holder was wet, and the steam burned my hand," she explained.

Colin looked at the palm of her hand and found the distinctive pink burn. "Why didn't you say something?" he asked, hurrying to the kitchen. He returned with some ice wrapped in a dish towel, which he placed in her palm.

"Thank you," she said. He smiled.

Carl and Nancy came home a few minutes before dinner was delivered. The pizza went well with the salad and dessert Janna had made, but she realized it was difficult for her to sort out the way she'd reacted to the accident. She marveled at Colin's acceptance and willingness to help. He met her eyes across the table and smiled. He really did love her, she reasoned; but she made a mental note to discuss the incident with Sean.

The following morning, Colin had a quick breakfast with Cathy then went out to his car, only to find all four tires slashed and the windshield severely cracked. It took him most of the morning to arrange for the car to be towed, get a rental car, and file a police report—all the while fuming inside. The police would blame it on delinquent teenagers, and of course they would find nothing to prove otherwise. But Colin's gut instinct told him differently. The job seemed a little too smooth and calculated. He *knew* who had done it, and he also knew there was nothing he could do about it. For that reason and many others, he decided not to tell Janna. Cathy agreed that it would only worry her, and she promised not to say a word. Later, when Janna asked why he had a different car, he simply told her his car was in for repairs.

Colin knew it wouldn't be too difficult for anyone to figure out where he lived and which car he drove, although he was always careful to be certain he wasn't followed to his parents' neighborhood. But he couldn't imagine how Russell Clark would connect him to

Janna. It simply made no sense, and they'd been so careful. He was tempted to ask Janna, but knew he couldn't without having her suspect that something had happened. Colin had little choice but to get the car repaired and try not to think about it. Still, the whole thing made him uneasy.

Later that evening, Colin told Janna that Robert Taylor would like her to come to the office to be certain he had everything in order to proceed with the divorce. Janna dreaded it, but knew it had to be done. She'd been able to handle everything on the phone so far. She liked Robert, but she wondered how much he and Colin discussed her case. There were things she simply didn't feel ready to face yet.

"Do you feel okay about coming to the office?" he asked.

Janna thought about it. She'd become less concerned about coming across Russell in a city this size, and she had to admit, "It would be nice to get out for something besides counseling appointments."

"You're welcome to use the car," Nancy offered, "and I can watch Matthew. I have plenty to do here at home."

"All right," Janna agreed.

"And maybe you could have lunch with me when you're finished," Colin said with a little wink. "We usually have it brought into the office."

"It sounds wonderful," Janna admitted. She went to bed feeling almost a childlike excitement. It was difficult to sleep as anticipation whirled around in her mind. Then, like a rock thrown into still waters, reality rippled around her. It was only a matter of time before Colin became aware of certain technicalities concerning this divorce—specifically, Matthew. And there would be no hiding the truth. She was amazed that she'd been able to avoid it this long. Of all she'd been through, it was the moment she dreaded most.

Janna arrived at Colin's office late morning. She felt an unexpected emotion as she noticed the shiny metal plate by the door: *Colin Trevor, Attorney at Law.* Then a bolt of irony shocked her as she recalled her anxiety. She attempted to keep her nervousness hidden as Colin first showed her his office, then took her down the hall and introduced her to Robert. She'd heard his soothing voice many times on the phone, but she was surprised to see he was stout and balding—nothing like what she'd expected. Colin left them to go over some papers together, and Robert said right off, "Colin has told me a great deal about the situation, and of course, you and I have talked on the phone quite a bit. But we need to clarify everything and be certain it's accurate."

"All right," she said.

"I asked you this once before, but I'm asking again. I assume that you don't have a problem with my discussing any of this with Colin."

Janna wished she could say *everything but Matthew*, but she just smiled weakly and said, "That's fine."

Robert asked her a lot of questions about Russell. Some were more difficult to answer than others. He asked details about how they had met, what their relationship was like in the beginning, and when she had begun to realize he was abusive.

Janna kept thinking of Robert repeating all of this to Colin. How could Matthew not come up? "Is all of this really necessary?" she asked.

"If I'm going to give the judge an accurate picture of the situation you were in, yes, it is necessary."

At Janna's obvious distress, Robert put down his pen and leaned back, saying gently, "Just a few more questions, and then you can go; we'll finish on the phone. This is tough for you, I know."

Janna tried to smile, and was grateful when he declared they were finished. "I'm . . . having lunch with Colin," she said as they moved toward the door.

"I'll walk you to his office," Robert offered, and she followed him into the hall. She really did like him, and she felt Colin had done well in choosing him to represent her.

They walked into Colin's office and he rose from behind his desk, smiling to see her. That dimple in his chin appeared for a second.

"How's it going?" Colin asked, and Robert began to give him a brief summary. Feeling uncomfortable, Janna excused herself to use the ladies' room.

"So," Colin said to Robert when they were alone, "how does it stand with the child custody thing?"

"What child custody thing?" Robert asked.

"I just wondered, with the criminal charges pending, what exactly you were pushing for concerning Janna's son."

"Child custody is not one of my main concerns here," Robert said. While Colin was trying to understand this, he added, "Since the boy was a year old when she married the man, it's not so difficult to defend his right to be with his mother. Of course, Russell's been supporting the child, and he still might attempt to get some visitation, if only to manipulate the mother, but with the criminal charges, I'm not terribly concerned about that."

Colin forced a steady expression, not wanting to appear ridiculously ignorant. "Of course," he managed, and Robert excused himself to go to lunch.

Janna returned a minute later, seeming nervous for some reason. Did she know Robert Taylor knew something he didn't? Not wanting to react impulsively, he asked, "So, how did it go?"

"Good, I think," she said. "It's hard to talk about, but I know it has to be done."

Colin nodded and said nothing more about it as they shared a lunch at his desk that had been brought in from a deli. While they were eating, Janna admired Colin's certificates on the wall, and they talked about his education and settling into the dream he'd always had of practicing law. Colin tried not to think about how she should have been by his side while he'd achieved his dream.

He hesitated bringing it up, but what Robert had said about Matthew wouldn't leave his mind. By the time he was finished eating, Colin knew it couldn't be ignored. He leaned back in his chair and tapped a pen against the desk. "You know, in the back of my head I've been concerned about the child custody thing with your divorce. If something went wrong with the criminal charges, I would hate to see Russell have rights concerning Matthew."

Colin watched Janna closely. Something akin to guilt rose in her eyes so quickly it nearly smothered her. Colin's heart began to pound. She was hiding something, and he knew it. *But what?*

Janna took a deep breath. As much as she'd tried to be prepared for this moment, she attempted to elude the truth without lying. "I'm not concerned about that. Russell cares nothing for Matthew. He never has. I doubt he will make any attempt to see him."

"How can you be so sure?" he asked, as any good lawyer would.

"I just know," she said emphatically, wondering by the intensity in his voice if he already knew.

"Does it have anything to do with the fact that Matthew was a year old when you married Russell?"

Janna quickly reminded herself it was dishonesty that got her into this mess in the first place. As much as she dreaded it, he had to know. They could not begin to have any real life together if he didn't. "Yes, I suppose it does."

"Matthew is not Russell's son," Colin said. It wasn't a question.

"No, he's not."

"I see." Colin couldn't deny a degree of relief that the little boy he had grown to care for had no biological connection to Russell Clark. He wondered if she had intended to keep this from him, or if he'd just assumed something because there was no cause to question it. Seeing Janna's apparent agitation, he wondered what had happened to her in the time between leaving for Arizona and her marriage to Russell. Could Matthew's birth have something to do with the reason she never wrote to him? Now was as good a time as any to find out what he'd been aching to know.

"Did you fall in love with someone else, Janna? Is that why you didn't write?"

She glared at him sharply. "No," she snapped, then her voice softened. "I've never loved anyone but you."

Colin didn't want to ask it, but he had to. "Were you raped, or—"

"No, I was not raped," she snapped.

Her defensiveness triggered all of Colin's subdued emotion related to her abandoning him. "Well, then, what happened?" Colin stood and leaned over the desk. "I have to know, Janna! You told me you would write. You never did. I've spent the last seven and a half years of my life wondering, and searching, and dying inside. Now you tell me you had a child before you were married. What happened?" he finished through clenched teeth.

Janna told herself to remain calm. He had a right to be angry, and he wasn't going to hurt her. She prayed for courage and took a deep breath. "Did you say seven and a half years?" she asked quietly.

"That's right. What's your point?" he asked tersely.

"Matthew will be seven next month," she stated.

It took Colin a long moment to figure why Matthew's age had anything to do with this. Then he sat down. Janna saw the realization begin to seep into his eyes, but he said nothing.

"That's right," she finally said when she couldn't bear the silence another second. "I was three months pregnant the last time I saw you."

Instantly, every unanswered question fell tidily into place. And with it came the pain. A tightness developed in Colin's chest from the air trapped in his lungs. He willed himself to breathe, but it came sharp and sporadic. His heart pounded painfully, and pressing both hands over it didn't alleviate the pressure. Through a blur of emotion he was aware of Janna sitting across the desk, looking almost cold. He couldn't begin to think what to say, even if he could find the strength to speak. All the wondering, and hurting, and searching, came back to him now with one harsh realization: *He had a son.*

"I can't believe it," he finally muttered, his voice barely audible.

The words seemed to release the memories with perfect clarity. Anger seeped into every nerve of his body. In an effort to subdue it, Colin shot out of his chair and turned his back to Janna. He swallowed hard and tried to think rationally. This was not the time or the place to blow up. But oh, how that anger consumed him!

"You lied to me." His words were harsh, but he couldn't say it any other way. She gave no response. "You lied to me!" he growled, turning to kick his chair in one swift movement.

Janna gasped and recoiled, then willed herself to stay calm. Colin looked into her eyes and found them cold and hard. How could she be so callous?

"You walked out of my life and never looked back." He pointed a finger at her and spoke in heated spurts. "You walked away from me without a word of explanation, and you *knew* . . . you *knew* you were going to have my baby. *My* baby, Janna. I went on a mission when I should have been changing diapers. I . . . I . . . spent all these years . . . alone . . . while you were raising *my* child under the same roof with a raving maniac. A day didn't go by when I didn't wonder and ache. And you *knew* before you even left."

Janna said nothing, didn't move. Her apparent indifference infuriated him, and he growled at her, "Can't you say anything?"

A tear trickled down each cheek as she murmured hoarsely, "I'm so sorry, Colin. I'm so sorry."

Colin collapsed into his chair. He watched her closely, wanting to tell her she'd brought all this misery on herself, that she couldn't comprehend the hell she'd put him through. But her simple apology said it all. She already knew. Every time Russell Clark hurt her, she surely would have regretted what she'd done. In the same instant, Colin wanted to throw anything he could get his hands on, and take her in his arms and hold her until he died. Instead, he pressed his head into his hands and slumped onto the desk. An anguished sob erupted from somewhere deep in his chest, followed by another, until he cried helplessly, oblivious to anything but the pain. When he finally looked up again, Janna was gone.

Colin panicked as feelings of abandonment came rushing back to him. He hurried out of his office, absently saying to the secretary, "I won't be back in today."

As he got in his car and started it, he tried to figure where Janna would go. She didn't like to be in public, for fear of Russell finding her in spite of her efforts at disguise. He hurried to his parents' home, while his anger battled inside with the wondrous realization that he was a father.

Colin sighed with relief to see the car in the driveway. He ran through the front door, and his mother looked up from her reading with wide eyes.

"Where's Janna?" he demanded

"I believe she's in her room. Is something wrong?"

"Where's Matthew?"

"He's playing at Cathy's until—"

"It's just as well," he said more to himself than to Nancy as he hurried down the stairs.

Colin could hear Janna crying before he threw open her bedroom door to see her tossing clothes into a suitcase. What little control he'd managed to maintain crumbled beneath the fear of losing her all over again.

"Don't you *dare* walk out on me again!" He flung her suitcase to the floor and its contents went flying. Janna backed toward the wall, trying to convince herself that he would not hurt her the way Russell had. But the fury in his eyes told her otherwise. She'd been hit by an angry man too many times; her heart beat into her throat and her stomach tightened into knots. Colin took hold of her shoulders and pressed her against the wall. She whimpered and tried to look away, but he wouldn't let her.

"You're not going to run out on me again, JannaLyn! Do you hear me? *You're not!*" He shouted the last two words and she slid to the floor, covering her head with her arms.

"Colin!" Nancy bellowed from behind him, startling them both. "For heaven's sake, calm down!"

"I'm *not* going to calm down!" he yelled, and kicked the suitcase across the floor. Janna whimpered and pressed a hand to her mouth.

Nancy took hold of Colin's shoulders and shook him. "Now you listen to me, young man," she said with the strength of a woman twice her size. "Whatever is wrong is not going to get solved with you shouting and kicking things. Janna's had to live in fear of one man. Do you think she wants to live in fear of you?"

Colin glanced toward Janna, who was cowering in the corner like a frightened animal. He squeezed his eyes shut in self-recrimination.

"Now, you go upstairs and do whatever it takes to calm down. I'm going to talk to Janna, and then I'll be up."

"Don't you let her leave!" he said firmly.

"She's not going anywhere," Nancy assured him.

Colin glanced again at Janna, then reluctantly went upstairs. He paced the kitchen floor, his strides gaining momentum as the reality came back to him all over again. He kicked over a kitchen chair, then kicked it again and sent it sliding across the floor.

Janna winced and looked toward the ceiling as she heard the thudding above her.

"Believe it or not, he'll calm down," Nancy said, putting a soothing arm around Janna's shoulders. She eased the younger woman to the edge of the bed and sat close beside her. "Take a deep breath, Janna." Her voice was gentle and had a calming effect. "Just breathe deeply. Nobody's going to hurt you. It'll be all right."

Janna did as she was told and gradually felt her heart rate slow down. She pulled off the wig and tossed it, nervously fluffing her hair with both hands. She glanced toward the ceiling as they heard another thud, then the continuing squeak of floor boards as Colin apparently paced the kitchen.

"Now," Nancy said, "what can I do to help?"

"I'm not sure there's anything anyone can do," Janna said, leaning gratefully on Nancy's shoulder. "I've messed everything up so badly. I don't know how he could ever forgive me. I think it would just be better to leave and—"

"Janna," Nancy interrupted firmly, "leaving is not going to solve the problem. You know that, don't you?" Janna nodded. If she'd learned anything at all, she knew that running from Colin had not done her life any good.

"When the divorce is settled," Nancy continued, "what you do is up to you. But for now, I'm going to see that you stay safe and do all you can to work things out. Don't you think it would be better for everyone if you at least try to work this out?"

Janna thought about it and nodded resolutely.

"I understand that Colin's anger is way out of line, but can you understand how he must feel to think of you leaving again? He loves you, Janna. His years without you have been very difficult. Do you see where his anger is coming from?"

Janna nodded again.

"The two of you have got to talk it through, whatever it is."

Janna's eyes widened with fear. They heard another thud through the ceiling. "We can't work this out alone," Janna insisted. "I can't talk to him like this." Tears bubbled out again, and Janna wiped frantically at her face.

"Do you want me to call Dr. O'Hara?" Nancy asked.

Janna nodded firmly. Nancy stood right up and went to the family room phone. Janna could see her thumbing through the phone book, then dialing the number.

"Please let him be available," Janna prayed aloud, hearing another thud upstairs. She wondered what condition the kitchen was in by now.

Nancy came back a few minutes later and announced. "He's nearly finished with his last appointment for the day. His receptionist told me that he has some time because there's been a cancellation."

"Thank you, God," Janna muttered under her breath.

"He'll call as soon as he's finished. In the meantime, I'm going to call Cathy and see if she'll keep Matthew until things settle down."

Janna nodded in appreciation. She heard another thud. Nancy went upstairs, and Janna could hear Colin shouting again, though she couldn't tell what he was saying. Janna closed her eyes and prayed, counting the minutes, waiting for the phone to ring.

* * * * *

"Shouting will not solve anything," Nancy said calmly.

"Well, I don't know what else to do!" Colin shouted.

"Do you want to tell me what all of this is about?"

"No!" he shouted louder.

Nancy just folded her arms and gave him an *I've-got-as-long-as-it-takes* look. Colin squeezed his eyes shut and a groan of disbelief came through his lips. He still couldn't believe it.

"Where's Janna?" he asked as panic seized him again.

"She promised me she would stay and talk about it. But she's not coming out until you calm down."

Colin thought of Matthew and shook his head. He was still having trouble swallowing this. He couldn't imagine how his family would react to knowing the truth. But they had to know eventually; there was little choice.

"Maybe you'd better sit down," he said.

"I will if you will," she replied calmly.

Colin took a deep breath and picked up the chairs and put them in place, albeit tersely. He willed his heart to slow down and sat on the edge of a chair, wondering how he was ever going to deal with these emotions.

Nancy sat and reached across the table for his hand. "Okay. I'm sitting."

"Well," he said, deciding to get right to the point, "I found out today that Matthew is my son."

Colin expected her to gasp or shriek. But Nancy's eyes didn't even flicker. "I know," she said softly.

It took a full minute for Colin to digest what his mother just said. "You *know?*" he finally muttered. "What do you mean, *you know*? Are you trying to say she told you about this, and neither of you had the decency to tell *me* that I—"

Nancy put her fingers over Colin's lips. "She didn't tell me anything, Colin." His eyes widened, and she moved her hand to his cheek. "You told me yourself—before your mission—that you and Janna had struggled with—"

"Yes, but you didn't know that we—"

"I suspected," she interrupted, penetrating him with her eyes. "Do you think I didn't notice the hours you were keeping during that period of time? Did you expect me to not see the frame of mind you were in when Janna's mother died? Or the way both of you changed after that? Of course, I was never sure . . . until I saw Matthew. Just seeing his little face took me back in time, Colin. He's so much like you. There are some things a mother never forgets." When Colin made no response, she added quietly, "Of course I noticed, Colin. He's my grandson." Colin squeezed his eyes shut as she continued. "I know there are many bridges to mend between you and JannaLyn, and how you go about it is none of my business. But *nothing* is more important than doing everything in your power to put your family back together and keep it that way. Don't expect it to be easy, and don't expect to be able to do it all by yourself. The consequences you're facing are severe; the scars run deep. Take time. Be patient with her. And for heaven's sake, keep your temper under control, or you'll scare her away for good."

Every grain of logic told Colin to remain calm. But his emotions felt as if they were locked inside a pressure cooker. All this time, his mother had known. Was he so blind? Was he so *stupid*?

"Does Dad know?" he asked, making no effort to hide the fact that he was upset.

"I didn't tell him," she replied. "If he figured it out, he never said anything to me."

Colin shook his head in disbelief. The whole thing just made him so *angry*.

The phone ringing startled Colin. Nancy got up to answer it, then she stretched the cord into the bathroom and closed the door.

"Thank you for calling back so quickly," she said into the phone.

"No problem," Sean O'Hara said as if he meant it. "What can I do for you? I was told that it's urgent."

"Something's erupted here between Janna and Colin. I would describe it as a volatile situation. But I'm not sure I could get them to come in or—"

"I can be there in five minutes," he assured her. "Emergencies are a part of the business. Can you give me an idea of what to expect in a nutshell?"

"Colin just found out that Matthew is his son."

"Oh, my," Sean said through a heavy sigh.

"Colin is understandably angry. But he's . . ." She heard a thud from the kitchen and knew he was having it out with the chairs again. "He keeps flying out of control. And Janna is understandably terrified."

"Okay," he said, as if that was all he needed to hear, "I'm on my way."

Nancy hung up the phone and left Colin to his anger. She found Janna curled up on the bed, crying uncontrollably.

"Dr. O'Hara is on his way over," Nancy said, pressing a soothing hand to her shoulder. "I told him what was going on."

"Thank you," Janna managed. "I just don't know how Colin could ever forgive me. I . . . I . . . should just leave. I can't stay here and—"

"You're frightened, I know," Nancy said. "But we'll get past this. It will take time for Colin to come to terms with this, but I believe he will."

Janna wished she could believe her. A minute later she heard the doorbell. Nancy ran to answer it while Janna went into the bathroom to wash her face and attempt to calm down.

Colin heard the doorbell and hurried to set the chairs in order. He continued to pace the kitchen, out of sight from the door. A traveling salesman or some other company—just what they needed at the moment.

"Colin," his mother said and he turned around, "there's someone here to see you."

Before Colin could ask, Sean O'Hara appeared by Nancy's side. Colin gave an exasperated sigh.

"I didn't really expect you to be glad to see me," Sean said easily. "But I'm not leaving until we can work this out enough to cope."

Colin folded his arms and leaned against the counter. He wanted to just pile on more anger, but something inside him was relieved to know that Sean could help him sort this out and make sense of it.

"Can we sit down?" Sean asked, motioning toward the table. Nancy slipped away.

"Okay," Colin said, "but be careful. The chairs have been abused."

They sat in silence for a couple of minutes while Colin felt as if Sean was trying to read him. Finally he said, "Your mother told me that you found out today Matthew is your son."

Just hearing it spoken aloud made the anger rise again. Colin clenched his fists and shifted in his chair. "That's right."

"And how does that make you feel?"

"Like breaking something."

"So, you feel . . ." Sean left it open.

"Angry!" Colin growled.

"All right," Sean leaned an elbow on the table, "we've concluded that you're angry. So, let's try to get to the base of it, where we can work it out. Where is the anger coming from, Colin?"

Colin tried to come up with a suitable answer, but all he could see was the anger. "I'm just *angry!*" he said in exasperation.

"I understand that you're angry, but anger is a secondary emotion, Colin. There is *always* something beneath the anger. Think of it as a chocolate. The anger is the chocolate coating. It's what you taste first when you bite into the candy. But what's beneath it, Colin? What's the filling inside? We have to figure that out before we can talk about it."

Colin leaned his elbows on the table and pushed his head into his hands. He was trying to make sense of the theory when Sean continued. "Are you frustrated, hurt, scared?"

"All of the above," Colin admitted.

"Okay, we're getting somewhere. You're scared. What are you afraid of?"

That was easy. "I'm afraid she'll run away again, and I'll spend the rest of my life wondering about her, just like I've spent the last seven years. I can't live like that anymore."

Sean continued asking questions, reminding Colin as he answered them that God had led him back to Janna, and he believed they were meant to be together. They talked about faith overriding fear, and Sean challenged Colin to pray for the ability to build his faith that Janna would be able and willing to make their relationship work. When Colin agreed that they had dealt with the fear, Sean moved on to frustration. Colin felt his agitation rise again as he was asked to define his feelings.

"It just frustrates me to no end," Colin sputtered, "when I think of the years we've lost. To think that all this time she was raising *my* son without me—that she would have the nerve to do such a thing without even telling me. She didn't even give me a choice. She lied to me, turned her back on me. She *betrayed* me. I thought she loved me more than that. I thought she had more character than that."

"And could I make a guess and say that's where the hurt comes in?"

"Yes," Colin said sadly, "that's where the hurt comes in." Colin pressed a hand over his eyes as tears brimmed with no warning.

"There's no need to hide the tears, Colin. That's your anger, finally coming out where it's supposed to."

Colin folded his arms and looked toward the window. He closed his eyes and the tears trickled over his face. "I just don't understand," he said. "How could she do that to me?"

"I don't know. Do you want to ask her?"

Colin looked at Sean and wiped away his tears.

"Do you think you're calm enough to talk to her now?"

Colin nodded. Sean hesitated a moment, as if to be certain, then he stood up and left the room.

CHAPTER NINE

Janna felt as if the waiting would never end as she sat on the family room couch with Nancy, who had told her that Sean wanted to speak to Colin alone first. How she wished she could eavesdrop! She longed to know just where she stood. At this point, she was prepared to leave here; perhaps she could go to the women's shelter. If she had gone there a long time ago, she could have started her life over without ever having to face Colin Trevor again.

"Are you all right?" Nancy asked.

"No," she admitted.

"You know," Nancy said as if she had all the time in the world, "there's no reason for us to pretend that you weren't once practically a member of the family. We hardly ate Sunday dinner for years when you weren't at the table. So, now that you've settled in, I think it's time we start being completely honest with each other."

Janna became distracted from what was going on upstairs as Nancy continued. "Your leaving here was very difficult for Colin," she said. "He just didn't get over it."

Janna looked guiltily at the floor but said nothing.

"I believe I mentioned before that Carl and Colin had a little falling out. It was difficult for Carl to understand why Colin would pine away for a girl all those years. He was patient to a point, but a day came when he told Colin he had to just get on with his life. I think Colin needed to hear that, but it was hard for him. He did his best to move ahead, but I knew he was hurting. When he had been home from his mission a while and wasn't dating, Carl tried to talk to him about it. When Carl found out he was still not over losing you, he became angry. That's when Colin moved out. Of course, it worked out nicely for Cathy. And with some time, Colin and his father were able to agree that they disagreed, and they mended their bridges. But there was always a certain amount of tension there." Nancy turned and looked at her. "Until you came to live with us."

"I don't understand," Janna said.

"When Carl heard how Colin had found you, and the situation you were in, he could see that there had been a reason for Colin's feelings. Carl always liked you, Janna. He's truly enjoyed having you and Matthew in our home."

Nancy allowed Janna the time to absorb everything that had been said.

"I know Colin was an answer to my prayers," Janna said. "There's no question about that. It's just that I never would have believed that Colin's finding me was the answer to *his* prayers." Maybe that's why she hadn't felt right about going to that women's shelter, she thought.

"Did you think he would just forget about you so easily?"

"I suppose I did," she admitted.

Silence followed, and Janna knew she would get no better chance to tell Nancy what she had probably already guessed.

"Did Colin tell you why he's so upset?"

"Yes," she stated.

Janna shook her head and pressed a hand over her eyes as if it might stop the endless source of tears. "And you're still sitting here, being so sweet to me, as if it makes no difference at all."

"Janna," Nancy took her hand, "let me make something very clear to you. I knew that you and Colin were having some struggles with immorality around the time your mother died. I was concerned. But it did not change the way I felt about either of you. The moment I saw Matthew, I knew he was Colin's son."

"I suspected that you did," Janna admitted.

"But I knew you would tell us when you felt the time was right. I want to see you and Colin work things out, so you can be a family. I'm certain your reasons for leaving him seemed right to you at the time. And you've more than paid the price for your mistakes. It's not for me to inflict more misery on you because this is a difficult situation. I'm here for you, Janna—no matter what happens. But . . . somehow I believe that you and Colin are meant to be together, and this is all going to eventually work out."

The tears came again. "Do you have any idea what that means to me?" Janna rested her head on Nancy's shoulder. "Nothing's ever been right since my mother died. But you've almost made up for that since I've come back. I don't know what I'd have done without you."

"Well, you'll never have to wonder. Even if things don't work out for you and Colin, you're still the mother of my grandson, and that makes you a part of the family."

Janna accepted Nancy's motherly embrace and cried away some of the tension. When she had quieted down, she asked, "Does Carl know—about Matthew?"

"I don't know, Janna. I didn't tell him. He hasn't said anything. I suspect he doesn't. Men often don't see the obvious, because they're just not looking for it. It simply would have never occurred to Carl— or Colin—to look for a resemblance, because they assumed he was your husband's son."

Janna became briefly lost in thought until Sean came down the stairs. "JannaLyn?" His voice startled her. "Would you come join us now?" He reached out a hand toward her. Janna took a deep breath and rose to take it.

"Are you okay?" Sean asked as they walked slowly up the stairs.

"I don't know," she admitted. "Everything's such a big mess. Sometimes I wonder if it's worth it anymore."

"Eventually it's always worth it," he said easily. "You stick with it, and I'm certain everything will be all right."

Janna tried to smile, but they had arrived at the kitchen table and Colin wasn't looking very happy.

"Have a seat," Sean said, pulling out a chair for her. She sat down and folded her hands on the table, trying to avoid Colin's eyes.

The silence became unbearable, and Janna began praying that Sean would find a way to ease it.

"Colin?" he finally said. "Isn't there something you wanted to ask Janna?" Following more silence, he said, "She's here now, so why don't you go for it?"

Sean leaned back in his chair and folded his arms, clearly indicating it was up to them to get started, and he would likely wait forever.

"Uh . . ." The sound croaked out of Colin's mouth. "I . . . I just . . . I have to know, Janna . . . I mean . . . I just don't understand . . . why you left like that . . . when you were pregnant, and . . ." Colin cleared his throat. "That's what I wanted to ask you." He glanced toward Sean and received a slight nod of approval.

Janna looked at Sean a second later and received an equivalent nod, encouraging her to go on. "I just believed that—"

Sean interrupted. "Don't tell me," he said gently, and pointed to Colin. "Tell him. I'm just the referee."

Janna reluctantly met Colin's eyes. Just seeing the anguish in his expression made the tears threaten again. Determined to just get this over with, she took a deep breath and blurted it out. "I truly believed that I was doing you a favor, Colin." His eyes widened. His expression became cynical. But she ignored him and continued. "It's just that, from the moment I met you, I was always so in awe of you. You were always so confident, so full of life. I'd often imagined what a wonderful missionary you would be, and I thought about your dream to become a lawyer. And when I found out I was pregnant . . ." Janna paused to gain her composure enough to speak. "I thought of all the good you could do; of the lives you could touch. I truly believed I would be doing you a great disservice to hold you back just because you'd been in the wrong place at the wrong time and fell into the trap that got me pregnant."

Janna looked away to indicate she was finished. She heard Colin sigh heavily. He didn't sound pleased with her reasons.

"So," Sean said, leaning forward, "you have your answer, Colin. Is there anything you'd like to say?"

"I didn't fall into any *trap*, Janna. I made my own choices—choices that affected *both* of us. And I was prepared to take responsibility for them. I *wanted* to marry you. I knew something wasn't right before you even left for Arizona. But I couldn't fix it because I didn't know what it was. You *lied* to me."

When he was apparently finished, Sean said, "Janna? Is Colin—"

"He's absolutely right," she murmured, tears streaming over her face. "What else can I say?"

Sean turned to Colin. "How do you feel now?"

"Angry," he stated. His tone made Janna wince.

"What's beneath the anger, Colin? Do you feel—"

"I feel *angry*, dammit!" He shot to his feet and kicked the chair over. Janna recoiled and forced back the impulse to run. She understood now what had caused all those thuds.

"Okay," Sean said, apparently unruffled, "you feel angry. So, get it out of your system."

Colin kicked the chair. Janna flinched. While he paced with clenched fists, Sean turned to Janna as if nothing were out of the ordinary.

"You seem upset by his anger," Sean said. "Are you concerned that he's going to hurt you?"

Janna wondered how he'd hit the nail on the head so quickly, but she didn't quite dare admit it. "I . . . I don't know."

"Well, who is he angry with?" Sean asked.

"Me," she croaked.

"Do you think he will take it out on you?" Sean asked.

From the corner of her eye, Janna was aware of Colin becoming still. She glanced at him, then looked at Sean.

"Well?" Sean pressed. "Do you think Colin will take his anger out on you and hurt you?"

"I don't know," she cried. "He's never hurt me before, but . . . Russell didn't hurt me until . . ."

She was relieved when Sean didn't ask her to finish the sentence. This conversation had nothing to do with Russell. Sean turned to Colin and motioned toward the chair. "Do you want to join us now?"

Colin tersely put the chair back in its place and sat on it.

"Janna seems to believe that you might hurt her when you get angry with her. Is that true?"

"No," he said directly to Janna. In a softened voice he clarified, "I know I have a short fuse, and I know I act like a child sometimes. But I would never, *ever* hurt you."

"Do you believe him?" Sean asked Janna.

"I want to, but . . ."

Sean spoke to Colin as if Janna weren't there. "I can understand where your anger is coming from, Colin. And I want you to understand how your anger is perceived by Janna. She grew up without knowing her father, Colin, beyond that one incident. And I don't need to tell you what her marriage was like. You're the only other man she's ever had any real interaction with. If you react with such behavior toward her, she will believe that all men are violent, because she has nothing else to gauge it by. Do you understand what I'm saying?"

Colin sighed and nodded, wishing he'd understood it before he'd blown up—twice—and terrified Janna. He felt nearly sick to think how it must have affected her.

"Okay," Sean went on, "so what do you think we should do about it?"

"I don't know," Colin admitted, pressing his head into his hands. "Why don't you help me out here, Sean."

"All right. We could take a lot of time learning about anger and how to deal with it, but we can get into that some other time. For now, I have a suggestion. If you feel so angry that you just have to let it out, then go outside and find a way to get it out of your system without allowing it to affect the people you care about. Is that reasonable?"

Colin nodded firmly. Sean turned back to Janna. "You told me you want to believe that Colin would never hurt you, but I can understand why that would be difficult for you. I have a suggestion, if you want to hear it."

Janna nodded and he went on, leaning close to her. "While you're deciding whether or not you believe him—even if it takes months—you don't ever have to be alone with him if you don't want to. Would you feel safe if you knew that Colin's mother or father was in the house with you?"

A part of Janna knew her fear was unreasonable. But she had committed herself to being completely honest with Sean. She nodded resolutely.

"Is that all right with you?" Sean asked Colin. He nodded. They were almost never in the house alone anyway.

"Okay." Sean turned back to Janna and spoke to her as if Colin was not present. "Now, Janna, you need to understand something. Colin is in mourning right now." Janna glanced toward Colin, but he was obviously as baffled as she was. "You see, when a human being has a loss, whatever it may be, it is necessary to mourn that loss. If we don't mourn properly, the hurt just festers down inside of us and becomes toxic. Colin said that he has a short fuse, and it's good that he can admit that. But I think you'll see that once he lets the fuse burn, he's able to get past the anger. You see, Janna, anger is one of the first phases of mourning. What Colin is feeling right now could be compared to how he might feel to have just discovered that a loved one was killed in a senseless accident. He's in shock, and he's angry. What Colin has lost here is time. For him, I'm assuming he feels that he has senselessly lost these years with you and his son."

Sean turned to Colin as if to verify his statement. Colin nodded in agreement, feeling the anger melt into a certain awe at Sean's insight, and his ability to put it into words so easily.

"He needs to grieve that loss, Janna," Sean continued. "Once he gets past the anger, he just plain has to grieve. The more he talks about it, cries over it, and just feels it, the faster he will heal and be able to forgive you. Do you want him to forgive you?"

"Yes, but I wouldn't blame him if he never did."

"Janna," Sean put a hand over hers, "Colin's a good man. My guess is that his goal in this is not to hold a grudge for the rest of his life. He knows enough about the gospel to know that such an attitude would not do any good to anyone. He simply has to get past the anger and the grief before he can forgive you fully, and for the right reasons. Are you with me?"

"I think so," Janna nodded.

"Good. Now, if you want to talk about this some more when it starts to jell in your mind, we can do that. Okay?"

Janna nodded, and Sean turned to Colin. "Are you understanding what I'm saying, Colin?"

"I believe so," he said, actually feeling calm.

"It's important that you don't try to forgive too soon. Forgiveness is vital, yes. But if you put it on the agenda too early, it's not complete. Feel the feelings. Talk it out. I'm available as much as you need me. I suggest that forgiveness be the goal we're working toward. How do you feel about that?"

"It feels right," Colin said.

"Janna?"

She nodded, but hardly dared hope that such a thing was even possible.

"Now, this works both ways," Sean added, his gaze shifting back to Colin. "In her own way, Janna is mourning the same loss. She made a bad choice, but no mistake warranted the treatment she has received these last several years. Janna has many layers of grief that need to be felt and worked through. She's not only lost years, she's lost her dignity, her identity . . . her babies."

Sean allowed Colin a minute to absorb the implication before he added, "Moving on . . . while Janna needs to understand that you are grieving, and there is much to be talked out and felt, it's important that you try to understand where her motives were coming from."

Sean was quiet for a moment, then said, "I'd like you to try something with me. It might feel strange at first, but humor me, okay?" They both nodded. "Okay, stand up. Trade chairs."

They both looked baffled but did as he asked. "Now," Sean said, "once you sit down, you need to imagine that you are the person who just got out of that chair." He motioned toward Janna and said, "You are Colin Trevor now. Try to put yourself into his mind and think how he might have felt when he realized you had abandoned your relationship with him. Try to imagine his feelings and thoughts. You may not be able to accomplish this quickly. I want you to think it through more between now and our next appointment." Sean's voice adopted a subtle change that made Janna realize he used a different manner of speaking to her than he did to Colin. He was speaking to her as though she *was* Colin. "Just to get you started, tell me, Colin," he said, even though he was speaking to Janna, "how did you feel to realize Janna had abandoned you?"

Janna tried very hard to do as Sean was asking. She looked at Colin as if she could somehow read his thoughts. The empathy rose in her so quickly she was almost startled. Tears pooled in her eyes as she tried to speak his feelings. "I felt . . . baffled. And . . . betrayed. And hurt."

"Okay, good." Sean patted her on the shoulder in a gesture common between men. Then he turned to Colin and looked at him in the gentle manner he had previously used with Janna. "So, tell me, Janna, what were your reasons for leaving Colin the way you did?"

Colin shook his head in an attempt to clear it, then tried to focus on this exercise. He found it very difficult, and wondered if he was so poor at empathizing.

"Take your time," Sean said and leaned back in his chair.

Colin uttered a silent prayer for help, knowing it would get him started on that road to forgiveness. He was surprised at how quickly it came to his mind once he got past his own emotions. He recalled Janna's seemingly pointless explanation when he'd first asked her this same question weeks ago. The answer made sense as he repeated it now. "I believed he would be better off without me."

With Colin's utterance, he felt the empathy rush from his heart into his throat, as if it were a tangible warmth. He leaned back and covered his mouth with his hand to keep from crying out. Sean said nothing for several minutes, as if he was allowing them time to absorb the feelings they'd just experienced.

When Sean finally spoke, his voice was quiet and kind. "I don't believe that Janna ever intended to hurt you, Colin. I get the impression that in her mind, what she did was a completely selfless sacrifice." He paused and added, "I believe she loved you very much, and I think that with some time and nurturing, she may realize that she loves you still.

"And, Janna," he turned to her, "I believe that Colin would not have spent these years praying and searching for you if he didn't love you very deeply. While you think through the things we've talked about, try to bear that in mind."

There was another silence until Sean spoke. "Do either of you have anything you feel should be covered now, in order to cope until we can meet together again?"

Janna thought about it and shook her head.

"Colin?" Sean asked when he said nothing.

"I think I can manage," he stated.

"Good," Sean smiled. "Anything else?"

"Uh . . ." Colin felt hesitant to bring this up, but knew it was important. "How do you think we should handle this with Matthew?"

Janna's sudden panic didn't go unnoticed by either man. "Do you have strong feelings about this?" Sean asked.

"I . . . don't know what to think," Janna said. "I'm just . . . concerned."

"Does Matthew believe that Russell is his father?" Sean asked.

"No," Janna insisted. "He called him *Dad*, because Russell

insisted on it. But he hated Russell. I told him a long time ago that . . ."
Janna turned to Colin. She could feel his gaze penetrating her. She was
tempted to abbreviate her explanation, but reminded herself that she
was committed to honesty, and it was Matthew's welfare that concerned
her most. If she told Colin something different than she'd told
Matthew, it would end up hurting both of them. "I told him often that
his father and I loved each other very much, but that circumstances
made it so we could not be together. I told him that his father did not
know about him, but if he did, he would love him very much."

Colin rubbed his eyes with a thumb and forefinger as a fresh
rush of emotion caught him off guard.

"Okay, then," Sean said, "you've been honest with Matthew.
That's good. He's not going to have any perceptions shattered, or feel
terribly disoriented. How do you feel about this, Colin?"

"I want him to know," Colin said firmly, in spite of the crack in
his voice. "But I want to handle it correctly."

"How is your relationship with Matthew?" Sean asked.

"We play together. I think he likes me," Colin said.

"He adores you," Janna interjected, almost smiling.

"Well," Sean said thoughtfully, "it's really up to the two of you,
but I don't see any obvious problems with telling him the truth as soon
as possible. Personally, I feel it would be better to tell him straight out
soon, rather than having him overhear it or figure it out later. Two
words of caution. One: Be completely honest with him. Kids are
smart. Don't try to pull anything over on him. And two: Tell him
together. This needs to be a mutual project, with complete agreement
between the two of you on how it is handled. That's my suggestion."

Colin nodded, feeling that his question had been answered
adequately.

"Anything else?" Sean asked. They both shook their heads.

"Now, don't expect this to be easy," Sean went on. "You've got
some big bridges to cross, and a lot to talk through. Take it one step
at a time, and don't be too hard on yourselves—or each other."

Following another brief silence, Sean came to his feet. "Well, I'll
be on my way, then. If you need me, don't hesitate to call. And I
mean that. Why don't you come in tomorrow at four. I'm sure it's
open. We'll see how you're doing."

"We'll be there." Colin rose and shook his hand. "Thank you, Sean. I'm glad someone can get me to see reason."

"You're doing just fine, kid," Sean smiled.

"Thank you, Sean," Janna said and hugged him.

"You hang in there." Sean touched her chin briefly and headed toward the door.

For an eternal minute, Colin and Janna stood at opposite sides of the table, watching each other tentatively.

"I'm truly sorry, Colin," Janna said, and tears threatened again. "I never imagined it would hurt you so deeply. If I could go back and do it again . . ." Her emotion made it impossible to go on. She looked away and pressed a trembling hand to her mouth.

Colin watched her and felt immense gratitude for Sean's helping him to get past his anger and begin to understand where she was coming from. He felt tears brim in his own eyes, but at least he understood them. He could now grieve for his losses and work toward putting them behind him. But as he watched Janna crying, one thing stood out clearly. The losses were mutual, and they shared the same grief. It had affected them differently, but the time they might have been together was still lost. As he opened his heart to try to understand, he felt a softening that prompted him to move around the table. She glanced up as he closed the space between them, and he heard her take a sharp breath. But the fear in her eyes quickly turned to relief as he lifted a hand to touch her face.

"Forgive me for my anger," he whispered and pressed a brief kiss to her brow. Then she was in his arms, holding to him desperately, crying against his shoulder.

"I'm so sorry," she murmured.

"It's all right." He pressed his lips into her hair. "We're together now, Janna. We'll work it out."

"I take it we're on the right track," Nancy said from behind, startling them both.

Janna pulled back and wiped at her face, embarrassed until she realized Colin was crying, too.

"Your father is home, Colin," Nancy added. "I think perhaps the two of you should talk to him before Matthew comes home."

Colin's heart began to pound. He met Janna's eyes and saw his own reluctance mirrored there.

"Are you all right?" he asked and took her hand into his. She nodded and he took a deep breath, glancing toward his mother. "I guess it's time to face the music."

Stoically they went into the front room and sat together on the couch. Nancy sat in the rocker near the window.

"Hi, Dad," Colin said, and Carl folded down the corner of his newspaper.

"Hello, son," he said. Then he glanced around the room and seemed to realize that something unusual was taking place.

"Can we talk to you?" he asked.

"Sure," he said and set his paper aside. Janna liked the way Carl's newspapers were always so disorderly. It distracted her briefly from the moment.

Colin felt Janna's hand tremble in his. He was reminded so much of their confession to the bishop that he briefly became lost in thought.

"Any time now, son," Carl said and startled him.

Colin took a deep breath. "This is some pretty heavy stuff, Dad. Are you still going to love me when we get this over with?"

Carl glanced dubiously toward Nancy, who just shrugged her shoulders. "You know I will always love you, Colin." His eyes shifted to Janna. "And I don't know what's coming, but the same applies to you, young lady. Somehow, I think you were meant to be a part of this family."

Janna tried to give him a smile, then she stared at the floor, feeling shame rise warmly into her face.

Colin tried not to think about the conflicts he'd had with his father in the past. He didn't question that Carl Trevor was a good man, but Colin had never felt completely trusted. It was as if his father had never quite believed that Colin might have the good judgment to make his own choices correctly. He knew from things his siblings had said that they all felt the same way to a degree. But for Colin it seemed more intense—as if his personality had been more prone to clash with his father's. Yet they all agreed they had been raised well by good parents, and overlooking their father's minimal faults was not a problem. At the moment, however, Colin suddenly felt like a naughty teenager, about to prove that his father had been absolutely right. In the ensuing silence, Colin reminded himself not to think about it too much. He just had to say it and get it over with.

"Well," Colin said, clearing his throat loudly, "you were aware that I had some struggles before my mission . . . and that's why it was delayed. You might have guessed that some of it had to do with Janna."

"I remember," Carl said.

"Well, I don't have to explain to you what's happened in the meantime. The thing is . . . that I just realized today . . . is . . . well . . ."

Just as when they'd confessed their sin to the bishop, Janna rescued Colin from his stammering. "Perhaps it would be better if I do this. It's my fault that it all happened this way. After my mother died, Colin and I had some problems with immorality. But while Colin was working very hard to put his life in order, I lied to him and left town, when I should have stayed and faced up to the consequences. You see, Colin had no idea that I was pregnant."

Carl's eyes narrowed. He lifted a finger and opened his mouth, but nothing came out.

"What we're trying to tell you, Dad, is that Matthew is . . ." Colin's voice caught. "He's my son." He glanced at Janna. "*Our* son."

Carl said nothing. He didn't move. His eyes focused on Colin, then shifted to Janna, then back again. The silence grew painful. Colin saw the muscles in his father's face tighten as he leaned back and crossed his legs. He wiped a hand briefly over his eyes as if it might help him see this clearly.

When Colin could bear it no longer, he said, "Well, don't you have anything to say?"

"I'm not certain I understand this," Carl stated curtly.

"What don't you understand?" Colin asked in the same tone.

"Are you trying to tell me that you served a mission unworthily?"

Colin took a deep breath and reminded himself to stay calm. "No, Dad, that's not what I'm saying at all. We went to the bishop right away. I completed the repentance process. I just didn't *know* Janna was pregnant."

"That was my fault," Janna interjected. Colin could feel her hand trembling, but her voice didn't betray it.

"That's irrelevant right now, I think," Carl said to her. "It's evident

that my son wasn't behaving the way he was taught." Carl turned to face
Colin with eyes that pierced him through. "You always were a little
headstrong. Should I say that this doesn't surprise me, or—"

"Is this an attempt to say 'I told you so'?" Colin interrupted.
"Because if it is, I don't need to hear it. It always seemed that you
expected me to mess up somewhere. I never walked out the door
without feeling like you expected me to do something wrong if you
weren't there to hold my hand. Well, you know," Colin's voice picked
up a subtle sarcasm, "they say that people eventually become what's
expected of them. It would seem that I'm the loser you expected me
to be. And I've got the illegitimate son to prove it. If you—"

"That's enough!" Carl said, and Janna winced visibly. She could
see now that there was a lot more between father and son than she
had ever realized before. She didn't understand it, but it was making
their problem all the more complicated, and she hated it.

"It would seem," Carl went on, "that you want me to just smile
and accept the fact that you have an illegitimate son, as if it were no
big deal."

"It *is* a big deal," Colin stated, barely maintaining his composure, "and I—"

"Yes, it certainly is," Carl interrupted angrily, "and if you think
that—"

"Carl," Nancy stopped him with a voice so calm and firm that
the room became still. "Colin is a grown man. He's not a boy. He's
not a loser by any means, and he doesn't need our permission or our
approval for *anything*. As I see it, Colin and Janna are both well aware
of the price of sin, and I'm certain that by the time this is all sorted
out, they'll have paid it many times over. Colin has served a worthy
mission. Janna's been through the temple. The mistake is in the past.
It's not for us to criticize and condemn. It is for us to accept Matthew
unquestionably as our grandson, and to support Colin and his *family*
as they work through all of this."

Carl sighed with apparent frustration and pushed a hand into
his thinning hair. "Okay," he said, his voice surprisingly genuine.
"Your mother's right. I'm sorry."

Janna was amazed at the way Nancy Trevor had just calmly
corrected her husband without embarrassing him. And she was even

more amazed at the way Carl humbly accepted it and admitted he'd been wrong.

"Thank you," Colin said with a sigh. "I only ask that you treat Matthew no differently. You've been good to him, and he needs you. He needs to know that he's accepted and loved unconditionally. None of this is his fault; he's already been through more than any kid deserves."

Colin glanced at Janna, not surprised by the tears in her eyes. He put an arm around her and urged her head to his shoulder. At least it seemed they were on the same side now.

"One thing." Carl pointed at his son. "In my opinion, you'd do well to see that she gets that divorce so you can marry her and make it right."

"We're working on that, Dad," Colin assured him.

"Good," Carl said. He looked at them both again and added, "I appreciate your being honest with me. We'll just take it on the best we can, eh?"

Colin nodded, feeling a little helpless. In spite of his differences with his father, he had to admit he was in awe of his parents' love and acceptance.

"Does the boy know?" Carl asked.

"Not yet," Colin said, "but we're going to tell him soon."

"Good. If there's anything I can do to help, let me know." He looked at Janna and added, "He's a wonderful boy. It's been a pleasure to have him around."

"I think being here is the best thing that ever happened to him," Janna admitted. "I can't tell you how grateful I am for your acceptance and all you've given us."

"Don't think a thing of it," Carl added. "You're family."

Janna wanted to remind him that he didn't know there was a blood connection when they'd first moved in. But Carl picked up his newspaper and Nancy disappeared into the kitchen as if they'd just announced they were going to the prom. She only hoped that telling Matthew would go well.

Janna was just wondering what to do with herself when Colin urged her downstairs, her hand still firmly in his. He led her into the bedroom and closed the door. For a moment she felt nervous, wondering if he was here to vent more anger. She hardly dared breathe when he went to his knees, saying quietly, "Pray with me, Janna. We need all the help we can get."

Janna knelt to face Colin, and he took both her hands into his. She couldn't hold the tears back as he verbally prayed for forgiveness for the mistakes they'd made that had brought them to this difficult point in their lives. He prayed for help in controlling his anger, and he prayed that Janna would forgive him for his weaknesses that had hurt her. He prayed that they would be able to get beyond this divorce, heal the wounds, and begin a new life together as a family. He told the Lord that he wanted to take Janna and Matthew to the temple and be with them forever. He prayed that they would be guided in discussing this delicate situation with Matthew, and he prayed that Matthew would be able to understand these events and feel secure and safe. He thanked the Lord for Sean O'Hara, for his insight and knowledge, and for his parents and their acceptance and understanding. When the prayer was finished, they both remained quietly holding hands for several minutes.

"I should go get Matthew," Colin finally said, coming to his feet. He knew that Janna would not even ride in the car to Cathy's house; it was too close to her old neighborhood. "We can talk to him after dinner."

Janna nodded and Colin opened the door. "Thank you for the prayer, Colin," she said, amazed at how far they had come in the last several hours.

"If there's one thing I've learned through these years, it's that I can't do it alone." Colin's emotion rose unexpectedly as he tried to comprehend the events of this day. He gave her a long, yearning gaze and pressed a hand into her hair. "Janna," he whispered as tears seemed to come out of nowhere. He urged her close and felt her crying against his chest.

"I'm so sorry, Colin," she murmured through a sob.

"I know," he cried and pressed his face into her hair and wept. When his emotion only gained momentum, he reminded himself of what Sean had said about needing to mourn. As if the thought alone gave him permission to feel what he was feeling, he held Janna tighter and cried harder. When he finally calmed down, Janna looked up at him and touched the tears on his face with trembling fingers. Colin closed his eyes and pressed his lips to her brow, trying to comprehend that she was the mother of his son. He kissed away the tears on her cheeks, then allowed his lips to linger there. Reminding himself of the harsh reality that she was another man's wife, he felt anger over their circumstances creeping back in. He abruptly took a step back and wiped his face dry with his sleeve.

"I should go get Matthew," he said tonelessly. "Do you want to come, or—"

"No," she insisted. He nodded and hurried out to the car before his emotions erupted all over again.

The few times Matthew had gone to Cathy's house since their escape, he had curled up on the floor of the car until they were safely in the garage. Then he stayed in the house, completely out of sight. Even though Janna had dyed Matthew's hair almost black, they weren't willing to risk having him seen. It was only the boy's desperate cabin fever that had prompted Nancy to get him out of the house once in a while. Matthew seemed to enjoy the secrecy for the most part, which made the whole thing a lot easier to cope with.

By the time Colin arrived at Cathy's home, he felt confident that he could maintain control and appear as if nothing was wrong. He pulled into the garage and closed the door, then he had to swallow hard and will back the tears when Matthew bounded out the door from the house before Colin was even out of the car.

"You ready to go?" Colin asked.

"Grandma called and said you were coming," Matthew said, jumping into Colin's arms in their usual greeting. Colin briefly closed his eyes to absorb the reality. *This child was his own flesh and blood.* If he had only known, what would he have thought that first time he'd picked him up from school and watched him playing with Brian? *The boys were cousins.* The whole thing still seemed too incredible to believe.

Matthew jumped in the backseat of the car and made himself comfortable on the floor with a couple of storybooks he kept hidden under the seat. Colin waved at Cathy as she peered out the door to be certain he had gotten Matthew. He opened the garage and backed out, then checked his rearview mirror frequently until he was long out of the area where Russell might be watching. The child chattered nonstop about all the things he'd done that day. Colin absorbed it all—as a father. He observed Matthew closely as they arrived and went in the house. It was difficult for him to see any obvious likeness to himself; but he had to admit, now that he was looking for it, there was a definite family resemblance in his features.

Carl and Nancy did well at keeping the tension from showing at the dinner table. While Janna and Colin hardly ate and fidgeted with their silverware, Carl kept Matthew talking about what he'd done at Cathy's house, and what he wanted to be when he grew up. When dinner was over, Nancy insisted on cleaning up. Carl said he'd help her. Matthew asked Colin if they could play a game.

"Maybe later, buddy. First, there's something your mother and I need to talk to you about. How about if we go downstairs?"

Matthew led the way and sat on the couch, not seeming concerned in the least. As soon as Colin sat beside him, he wished he had asked Janna earlier about how much Matthew already knew on certain matters. Now, he felt totally at a loss for words. He looked at Janna as she sat on the other side of Matthew, and was relieved when she seemed prepared.

"Matthew," she began, "do you remember how I told you that Colin and I were friends before I married Russell?"

"I remember," he said. "And that's why we get to stay here with his mom and dad."

"That's right," Janna said. "And do you remember how we've talked about why Russell is not your father?" Matthew nodded and she went on. "Will you tell me what you remember?"

"You said that Russell wasn't my dad. You said that my dad was somebody you loved a real lot before you married Russell."

Colin met Janna's eyes briefly. He still could hardly believe it.

"And you said that my dad didn't know about me," Matthew added. "But you said that if he knew about me, he would love me a lot."

"That's right," Janna said. "And now that we've been able to get away from Russell, and you're almost seven years old, it's time that you know more about your father. I want you to know that the reasons I didn't stay with your father and marry him were not right. I made a very big mistake, Matthew, and it's made life very hard for all of us. But we're doing our best to work it out so we can be a family again." Matthew looked a little lost, so Janna hastened to add, "Matthew, Colin is your father."

Colin held his breath as Matthew turned to look at him, his eyes narrowing. He looked back at his mother, then at Colin again. A little puzzled wrinkle developed at the top of his nose, then he said dramatically, "You mean . . . you guys actually . . ." He hesitated long enough for Colin to wonder how much this child knew about such things. Then Matthew finished abruptly. ". . . *kissed?*"

Colin chuckled with relief. "Yes, Matthew," he said, "we actually kissed. I fell in love with your mother when we were very young. We were best friends, and we wanted to get married, but some things happened that made it so we couldn't. But that's all in the past. Your mother and I have some things to work out, but no matter what happens, I'm still your father, and I'm always going to make certain that you and your mother are cared for."

"Okay," Matthew said. "Can we play a game now?"

Colin raised his brows and looked toward Janna. She seemed relieved and amused.

"All right, buddy, we can play a game now."

"Is it all right if I call you *Dad?*"

"Only if I can call you *son*," Colin said, feeling the emotion catch him again.

"Okay," Matthew said and hurried off to find what he wanted to play.

"Are you all right?" Colin asked Janna.

"I think I feel better than I have since the day I left you," she said quietly. "How about you?"

"Now that I've gotten past the shock," he took her hand and squeezed it, "I can't think of anything I'd rather be than Matthew's father—except perhaps your husband."

Janna glanced away. "One step at a time, Colin."

"Come on," he said, urging her off the couch. "What you need is a rousing game of *Chutes and Ladders.*"

Janna looked up at him as they walked the few steps to where Matthew was spreading the game on the floor. She wondered how she ever could have left him.

Colin arrived at Cathy's place late. He crept quietly inside and locked the door, wanting nothing but to crawl into bed and give his mind a chance to sort all of this out.

"You look awful," his sister said. He turned to see her looking up from a book.

"I thought you'd be asleep," he replied tonelessly.

"Mark went to bed a long time ago, but I just couldn't relax, so I thought I'd study."

"Well, I'm going to bed," Colin said before she could get into a conversation.

"I talked to Dad a while ago," she said as he started toward his room. Colin stopped and resisted the urge to call his sister a busybody and stomp off to bed. He turned slowly as she finished. "He said something was up, but I should wait and let you tell me."

"I'll tell you in the morning. I'm exhausted."

"I have classes in the morning," she said impatiently.

Colin sighed, moved to the sofa, and slumped onto it wearily.

"So, what is it?" she asked while he was trying to gather his thoughts.

Colin felt no inclination to get into any great explanations. Without preamble he announced, "I found out today that Matthew is my son."

Cathy gaped. Then she chuckled dubiously. "You're kidding, right?" she finally said.

"No, I'm not kidding," he stated.

Cathy shook her head in disbelief. "What you're saying, then, is that you slept with Janna . . . before your mission."

"That's what I'm saying," Colin said through a yawn.

"I can't believe it."

"Well, it's true." He stood up. "I'm going to bed. We can talk more when—"

"Wait a minute," she insisted and he sat back down. "How can you just yawn and walk away? This is serious."

"Yes, Cathy, it's serious. I have spent much of the day screaming or crying or in shock. Just because I've got it out of my system for the moment, and I'm too exhausted to think straight, doesn't mean I'm treating it lightly. I had no idea she was pregnant. She lied to me, okay? She left because she didn't want me to be burdened by this. She wanted me to go on a mission and become a lawyer, and she thought she would hold me back. I went through the full repentance process before my mission, but that doesn't make the facts go away. It makes me sick to my stomach to even think about it. While I was on the other side of the world, feeling like something wasn't right, she was raising my baby. What else do you want to know?"

Cathy looked at him as if he'd just announced he was going to become a monk. "I just can't believe it."

"What can't you believe?" he asked, feeling irritated.

"I always thought you were such a good kid."

Colin made a mental note to talk to Sean O'Hara about handling his frustrations with his sister—not to mention that this conversation was reminding him a little of his earlier encounter with his father. "For the most part, I *was* a good kid," he said in a patronizing tone, barely calm. "I made a couple of wrong turns and got carried away. We loved each other, Cathy. Her mother had just died. We didn't just jump into bed because we were bored and we'd heard sex was fun."

"You don't have to get so upset," she retorted.

"You don't have to make me feel like I'm on trial or something. I told you what was going on because you're my sister and you have a right to know. If you want to think less of me, fine. But don't you dare show anything less than perfect acceptance to Janna and Matthew. This is between me and Janna, and we will work it out." He stood up and walked away. "I'm going to bed."

Colin turned back briefly and added, "I'm going to stay at Mom's through the holidays, then I'm getting an apartment. Now that Mark's job has changed, I assume you can manage without me."

"You're hardly here anymore as it is," she said.

"It's just as well," he replied and went to his room.

As Colin lay in bed, attempting to relax, the whole thing hit him all over again. *Matthew was his son.* As he allowed the reality to sink in, the grief Sean had warned him about came with it. Alone in the darkness, Colin allowed—even encouraged—the tears to come. He cried for the years without Janna, the wondering and waiting. He cried for everything he'd missed through the early years of his son's life. He cried for all Janna had suffered during this time, and the hardships still ahead. And he cried for the loneliness and heartache associated with the whole thing. He tried to imagine what their lives might be like if she had told him the truth about the pregnancy. They would have married right away, and she never would have had to leave with her aunt Phyllis. He could well imagine having financial struggles, and getting his education might have taken longer. But his family would have helped, and he and Janna would have been together. They could have gone to the temple and had one or two more children by now.

Somewhere around three in the morning, Colin convinced himself that wallowing in the past would get him nowhere. He had to take on the future with enough determination to get Janna out of this mess she was in so he could marry her and she wouldn't have to live in fear. He finally drifted off to sleep from pure exhaustion, resolving to make the future bright. He was not about to make all of this even more difficult by holding a grudge or letting it eat at him. At least now he understood why Janna had left, and that in itself gave him a new sense of peace.

Colin woke up before his alarm clock went off. He lay there in the predawn light, orienting himself to the previous day's events. Then, all at once, he recalled the dream he'd had many months earlier. It had given him the hope that he could find Janna, and made him believe she needed him. But only now did he understand it. Warm goose bumps rushed down his back as it all made perfect sense—her apologies for not showing him the picture, the layers of black paint covering it, the image of himself as a child finally showing through.

Colin arrived at work early and plowed through everything that had to be done. When he knew Robert was alone in his office, he went to talk to him.

"How's Janna's case coming?" he asked.

"Good," he said, "but if this creep is typical, I'm sure he'll have some ace up his sleeve. It's difficult to feel too comfortable."

Colin nodded and sat down. "There's something you should be aware of. I don't know if it makes any difference or not, but . . . well, you know that Janna and I were high-school sweethearts."

"Yes," Robert drawled, looking over the top of his glasses.

"Well, until yesterday, I believed that Matthew was Russell Clark's son."

"Ah," Robert said. "I thought you seemed a little . . . disconcerted."

"Yes, well, the thing is . . . Matthew is *my* son."

Colin expected some severe reaction, but Robert only took off his glasses to look at Colin without them. Then he chuckled. "The rebelliousness of youth comes back to haunt the aspiring young attorney," he said. Then he chuckled again.

"Thanks for your understanding," Colin said with sarcasm. "I just wanted you to know the truth so you wouldn't be in for any surprises."

"I appreciate that," Robert said as Colin rose to open the door. "But even knowing the whole truth, we could still be in for some surprises."

"That's what I'm afraid of."

"Hey, Colin," Robert stopped him. "It's between you and me."

"Thank you."

"And just so you know, I'll do my best to take care of her the way you would . . . if you could."

Colin nodded. "I know she's in good hands."

Colin returned to his office, trying not to feel unsettled. If nothing else, knowing Matthew was his son made him all the more determined to do everything in his power to put their lives in order. He grabbed a quick lunch, then went to Cathy's and loaded most of his belongings into the car. Since he'd always considered his living arrangements with her to be temporary, he'd never settled in too deeply.

"What's up?" Nancy asked when she met him and a large box at the door.

"I'm moving back in. Is that okay?"

"Of course it's okay, but—"

"Just for the holidays," he added on his way down the hall to his old room. "I usually spend most of December here anyway. I'm getting an apartment after Christmas, though. Okay, Mom?"

"Okay," she said, holding the door for him while he deposited the box on the floor. "Are you and Cathy fighting again?"

"Let's just say there's . . . tension."

"And why is that?" Nancy asked, following him back out to the car.

"She's a busybody," he stated. "I love her, Mother, and I appreciate all she's done for me. But she's nosy."

Colin opened his trunk and handed his mother a bag. He picked up another box and followed her into the house. "Does this have something to do with Janna and Matthew?" Nancy asked.

"It didn't help any, I suppose," Colin admitted. "Let's just say she was rather . . . critical of my mistakes."

"She'll get over it," Nancy soothed as they set down their loads in the bedroom. "She's always been curious and outspoken—and you've always been short-tempered and impetuous."

"Impetuous?" he echoed. Then he looked down at the boxes at his feet and chuckled. "You mean like moving back home on the spur of the moment without even asking my mother?"

Nancy smiled. "You're always welcome here, Colin."

"Yes, I know. But my student loans are almost paid off, and I think it's time I started building a real life." He sat on the edge of the bed next to his mother. "I have a family now."

"So you do," Nancy said. "And how are you swallowing all of this?"

"I'm getting used to it, I think," he admitted. "I just want everything to be settled so I can take care of them—like I should have been doing the last seven years."

"I'm sure you'll make up for it in due time," Nancy said.

"I love her, Mother," he whispered. "And I love Matthew. Just as soon as possible, I'm going to marry her, and we're going to start over."

"That sounds great, Colin. But it might be a good idea to ask her first—after she's divorced, that is."

Colin nodded absently as he tried to comprehend just how wonderful that would be.

"So, you're almost out of debt, you say?" Nancy walked down the hall, and he followed her out to the car for another load.

"Well, actually, I have almost enough in savings to pay off all my student loans, but I thought I'd better keep some on hand for emergencies. Right now, I need to be sure Janna has what she needs."

Nancy nodded her approval. Colin handed her a box and then picked up the last one and headed into the house. "And is your car paid off yet?"

"Not quite, but almost," he answered. "Although I'm thinking of trading it in on something . . . different."

"Why?" She looked puzzled.

"Oh, I'm just . . . impetuous," he smirked.

They set the boxes down and Nancy put her hands on her hips.

"I shouldn't ask so many questions," she said. "You'll soon be calling me a busybody, like you do your sister."

Colin laughed and hugged her. "Being overtly curious is not your problem, Mother. I know you're just concerned."

"I think Cathy's just concerned, too, Colin. She just gets a little carried away."

Colin nodded in agreement. "We'll work it out," he assured her. "We always do." He looked around. "Where are Janna and Matthew, by the way?"

"Matthew made a friend next door; he went over there for a little while. I made them aware of the situation so they'll be careful. Janna was resting, last I checked."

"Thanks for your help, Mom." He kissed her cheek and hurried downstairs.

CHAPTER TEN

*C*olin leaned against the door frame of Janna's room just as she swung her legs over the edge of the bed. "Hello," he said and startled her. "Are you all right?" he added, moving toward her with his hands in his back pockets.

"I just didn't sleep very well last night."

"Must have been an epidemic," he said.

"And how are you?" Janna asked, hoping the questions wouldn't open a new can of worms.

"I'm actually doing pretty good," he said, then he glanced at his watch. "We have an appointment with Sean in less than half an hour."

Janna looked panicked and rushed into the bathroom. "I'll hurry," she called. "Ask your mother if she'll watch Matthew."

The session began with tension, but eventually became productive. They spent much of the time sitting in each other's chairs, working on understanding each other's feelings in more depth. Colin felt that the most difficult thing for him to deal with would be the betrayal. He wanted to be able to trust Janna, but he had to admit it wouldn't be easy. Sean reminded them that the issues between them were complicated, and emotional healing took a good deal of time and effort. Colin felt a new gratitude for having started out sharing some counseling with Janna. He couldn't comprehend facing this without Sean's help—a fact which he chalked up as one more piece of evidence that the Lord was blessing them.

They asked Sean how his work was going with Matthew. He reported that one of his associates, who specialized in what he called "play therapy," felt that Matthew was fairly well adjusted considering what he'd witnessed in his young life. Sean had spent some time with Matthew as well and agreed. But he added that they both were concerned that the child seemed guarded in some respects.

"Like what?" Colin asked.

"Well," Sean leaned forward, "with the play therapy, the child is given many different avenues to play with houses and people in family situations, so we can observe their perception of their home life. Matthew seems to have a clear understanding of what an appropriate family life entails, but there are areas where he seems . . . uncomfortable."

"I don't understand," Janna said, hating the uneasiness that crept down her spine. "What areas?"

"It's a little abstract, actually. We simply feel like he's holding something back. But just as I said before, healing takes time. We've given him some things to think about, and . . . *permission* to be able to speak his feelings. I believe with some time he'll open up more, and we can find out what's really going on inside his little head."

Sean answered a few more questions, then encouraged them not to get worried or uptight on Matthew's behalf. They both agreed that he was doing well and was in good hands.

"At least he has a father now," Janna said with a warmth in her voice that radiated through Colin.

On the drive home, Colin glanced toward Janna as she stared out the window, apparently lost in thought. He felt a little quiver inside as he tried again to comprehend that she was the mother of his son.

Colin spent some time with Matthew after dinner, while Janna helped with the dishes then immersed herself in a book. He watched the boy closely, trying to grasp the reality. Nancy came to check on them and commented quietly, "The resemblance is incredible."

Colin looked at her dubiously. "Personally, I don't see it."

"I believe such things are hard to see in oneself."

After Matthew had gone to bed, Nancy sat beside Colin on the couch and set a photo album on his lap. She opened it and pointed to a picture. Colin caught his breath.

"When I first saw Matthew," she said, "I hunted down this particular album. I guess I had to convince myself it wasn't my imagination. You were nearly eight here. It was the summer before you were baptized."

"I can't believe it," Colin admitted, lifting it closer to his face. "If it wasn't black and white, I would think it was Matthew."

"Amazing, isn't it?"

"What's amazing?" Janna asked, and they looked up to see her.

Colin motioned for her to sit beside him. He set the book on her lap, but said nothing. When Janna saw Colin's young face looking up at her from the page, something painful stirred inside her. She tried to swallow the emotion, then realized it wasn't going to go away. Meeting Colin's eyes, she hoped he understood the regret she felt. She didn't dare speak for fear of losing her composure. When her emotions began to melt, she abruptly put the book into Colin's hands and hurried to the bedroom.

Colin stood to follow, but Nancy stopped him with a hand on his arm. "Tread carefully, Colin," she whispered. "She may just need some time alone."

Colin nodded and moved away. He hesitated a moment before knocking lightly at Janna's bedroom door. She opened it a crack, and he could see she'd been crying.

"Are you okay?" he whispered, knowing Matthew was in bed.

She shook her head. "I'm sorry. I just . . ." She didn't finish.

"Do you want to be alone?" he asked outright.

Janna hesitated, then shook her head again. Colin held out his hand and she took it. She glanced back at Matthew, then slipped out the door. Colin led her to the couch. Nancy had gone upstairs and the family room was vacant. He sat close beside Janna and resisted the urge to put his arm around her. "Do you want to talk?" he asked quietly.

"Do you think we can without Sean?" she asked lightly, but he knew she meant it.

"We can try," he said.

Following a long silence, Janna admitted, "Sometimes I just hate myself for being so stupid. I never should have left you, Colin."

"Well, then," he said with a smile, "we agree on something."

Janna looked up at him with fresh tears showing. "I'm so sorry," she whispered.

"I know," he said gently.

Janna sighed. "Tell me what we would have done if you had known I was pregnant."

Colin took a deep breath. "You can't imagine how many times I wished that you were."

Janna leaned forward abruptly and looked at him in surprise.

"When I realized you were leaving with your aunt, I *wanted* you to be pregnant, Janna. I know that's far from the ideal way to start a marriage, but I wanted to marry you and take care of you. And when I didn't hear from you, I thought over and over that if I had married you, we would be together."

Janna put some distance between them and settled into the corner of the couch, trying not to think too hard about it. "Phyllis was furious when she found out I was pregnant. I can't say that I blame her, but she certainly had a way of making my life miserable. She sold my mother's house and took over all of her assets, but a day never passed when she didn't remind me that I was a burden to her. She ignored Matthew completely, as if he didn't exist. One time she told me if I didn't keep him out of her things, she would put us both out on the street. She never even used his name. She called him the . . ."

"What?" Colin insisted, trying to keep his emotions from erupting. She was talking, and he knew from Sean's guidance that talking led to healing.

Janna looked hesitant. She lowered her voice to a whisper and her chin quivered. "She called him the little bastard."

Colin cleared his throat vehemently and swallowed hard. But the anger he felt was directed toward the circumstances that had caused Janna so much misery. Thinking back on some of his feelings as he'd sat in her chair in Sean's office, Colin tried to comprehend the full spectrum of Janna's life. He listened with growing empathy.

"I met Russell at church. He treated me like a queen, and he seemed to enjoy Matthew. I knew I could never love him, at least not the way I'd loved you. But when he asked me to marry him, all I could see was a way out. He was moving back here, and I wanted to be here . . . as if it could somehow bring back my childhood. He had everything to offer—most especially an escape from Phyllis. It didn't take me long to realize what a mistake I'd made, especially when Phyllis died not long after we were married. I inherited everything she had. She wasn't rich, but it was a significant amount. Russell invested it or something; I never saw a penny of it. Things got steadily worse from there." She sighed again. "I should never have left you."

"I'm here now," he said.

They sat together in comfortable silence for a short while. Colin felt a strong urge to kiss her and abruptly eased to the edge of the couch.

"Is something wrong?" she asked.

"Yeah," he chuckled tensely, "you're married, and I have an impeccable memory."

It took Janna a moment to understand what he meant. Then she felt herself turn warm.

Colin stood and stuffed his hands in his pockets. "I think I'll go up to bed now," he said resolutely.

"*Up* to bed?" she asked.

"Oh, I forgot to tell you . . . I'm staying here through the holidays. Then I'm getting an apartment."

Janna nodded, wondering if she could bear having him under the same roof all the time, especially when her own mind was wandering where she knew it shouldn't.

Colin took a few steps before Janna stopped him.

"Colin," she said and he turned back, "do you regret that it happened? You know what I mean."

"I know what you mean," he said, then sighed. "Of course, if I had a chance to live life over again, I would have stayed on the straight and narrow. If I've learned anything from my mistakes, I know that no moment of pleasure is worth the price that must be paid. But . . . how can we possibly look back and separate the sin from all we learned through the struggles? And how could we separate it from the fact that Matthew exists, and that we love him?"

Janna smiled. "That's how I've felt, but I never knew quite how to say it."

Not wanting him to leave, but knowing they had to be careful, Janna steered toward a subject she'd often wondered about. "Where did you go on your mission, Colin? You never told me."

"Japan," he stated.

"Tell me about it," she requested.

Colin hesitated only a moment before he sat back down at a safe distance. At first he just answered her questions, but gradually his memories gained momentum, and he found himself telling her of experiences he'd almost forgotten. With Janna sitting beside him, caught up in his stories, Colin realized something that he'd missed before. He couldn't possibly regret his mission, any more than he could regret Matthew's existence. It was difficult to sort regrets in with the realities. He realized, as he crawled into bed around midnight, that he needed to appreciate the good things that had come out of these years and concentrate on the future. He drifted to sleep quickly, determined to make that future a good one—for all of them.

The following day, Colin came home early afternoon.

"What's the occasion?" Nancy asked when he walked into the kitchen.

"I just need to see Janna for a minute," he said.

"She's putting laundry in, I believe," his mother reported.

Colin found Janna pulling wet clothes out of the washer and throwing them into the dryer.

"Hello," he said and she jumped.

"Don't do that to me!" she insisted, and he chuckled.

"Sorry," he finally admitted when she glared at him. "I just wanted to give you these."

Colin pulled a dozen red roses out from behind his back. Janna gasped. "What on earth for?" she asked, hesitantly reaching out to take them.

Colin's expression became intense. "These are the flowers I would have brought to the hospital after you gave birth to my son."

He felt suddenly concerned when she looked away, obvious shame rising into her expression. "Hey," he lifted her chin with his finger, "my intention was not to upset you, Janna. I just wanted to let you know how grateful I am for everything you went through to give him life, and to see that he was cared for."

Colin smiled and decided to leave it at that. "Better late than never," he said and hurried out to the car, knowing there was much to do at the office.

Janna sat down on the laundry room floor and cried. But she had to admit that once the emotion subsided, the tears had been cleansing and she felt a little better. She inhaled the roses' sweet fragrance and took them upstairs to put them in water.

Since Colin would no longer be staying with his sister, he figured it was a good time to buy a different car and take some precautions to see that it couldn't be connected to Janna. He settled on a teal-blue convertible Mustang, and the trade left him without a car payment. When Janna and his parents questioned him on this sudden change, he simply said, "I've always wanted a convertible."

Colin and Janna's next session with Sean was the Monday after Thanksgiving, but the weather was more like September. Janna felt relaxed and at ease as they sat down and exchanged small talk. Then Sean got down to business.

"Janna," he began, "there is something I've been thinking about. I wonder if perhaps what happened with your father might have unconsciously affected the way you felt about yourself, and contributed to the decisions you made . . . both in leaving Colin, and in marrying Russell."

Janna nodded, but Colin felt lost. Sean went on. "Do you remember how we discussed that what your father did affected your self-perception, and how that affected your behavior and your choices?"

"I remember."

"And even though you dealt with the situation quite well at the time, do you think it's possible that perhaps losing your mother, and the way Phyllis treated you, brought back the low self-perception and made you feel somehow unworthy of Colin's love, or perhaps responsible for what happened between you?"

"You've lost me," Colin said, narrowing his eyes.

"I'm with you," Janna said and Colin leaned back, reminding himself to be patient. "I think I understand what you're saying. And actually, the thought has occurred to me before."

"I'm still lost," Colin repeated.

"What aren't you getting?" Sean asked easily.

"What's this about Janna's father?"

Sean looked at Janna just as the realization struck her. She felt suddenly nervous and shifted in her seat. "I'm sorry," she said to Sean, "I honestly thought he knew. I . . . I thought my mother had told him years ago."

"Told me what?" Colin asked impatiently.

For a long moment, Janna felt completely at a loss. She could see Sean trying to gather his thoughts, and hoped he could rescue her.

"Okay," he finally said, "it looks like we need to back up a little here."

Colin hated the uneasiness creeping up the back of his neck as he began to wonder over Janna's obvious distress.

"Janna," Sean said gently, "is there any reason why Colin shouldn't know about—"

"No," she interrupted, "I honestly thought he knew. It's not something I enjoy talking about, but . . . I think he needs to know . . . and you helped me deal with the worst of it years ago—I think." She stood abruptly and added, "I'm going to the ladies' room. I'll let you tell him."

When they were alone, Sean turned solemnly to Colin. "I think she wants you to know, but she doesn't want to say it."

"Well, I'm going to feel a lot better when I know what *it* is," Colin said curtly.

Sean leaned his elbows on his thighs and looked directly at Colin. "At the same time Janna's mother was helping my wife and me with a legal problem, she came to me and asked if I could talk to Janna. You know, of course, that Diane was a legal secretary."

"Yes, I know," Colin stated, suddenly missing her. "She was the reason I wanted to be a lawyer."

"Anyway, Diane didn't know what was bothering Janna, and hoped I could help. I was close to getting my master's degree, and I was more than willing to do what I could. Janna was very open, and we got to the problem quickly. You see . . . well, were you aware that Janna's father came back for a short time when she was thirteen?"

"Yes," Colin said, suddenly feeling a little sick as the severity in Sean's tone mixed with what Colin already knew. He was telling himself not to assume the worst, when Sean confirmed it concisely.

"He sexually abused her, Colin, using threats and manipulation to keep her quiet about it."

"Oh, dear heaven." Colin leaned back abruptly. He planted his forehead in his hand and realized his heart was pounding. Instantly, several unanswered questions fell into place. He'd always wondered over Janna's apparent lack of self-worth, and her vehement hatred toward her father, whom she had barely known. And something in the back of his memories concerning their intimacy had always

nagged at him. There had been something in the way she'd given in
so easily that didn't go along with what he knew of her character and
her values.

"I get the impression you're upset," Sean said, reminding Colin
that he wasn't alone.

Colin looked up and took a deep breath. "It's just . . . such a
shock, but . . ." He tried to briefly explain his thoughts to Sean,
grateful that Janna had not returned. Sean confirmed his assump-
tions, but Colin was left feeling especially uneasy over one point. "I
only wish I had known."

"Do you think it would have made a difference?" Sean asked.

"I don't know, but . . . I mean . . . maybe I would have been
more careful if I had known she was so . . . vulnerable."

"Are you talking about your physical intimacy?"

Colin nodded. He became lost in thought again when Sean said
nothing more. Looking back, he could see Janna as a sitting duck,
perfectly set up for the trap he had pulled her into by his lack of spiri-
tual conviction at the time. He felt a little sick.

"Are you okay?" Sean asked.

"Is it that obvious?" Colin tried to chuckle, but it came out
sounding more like an anguished moan.

"Maybe we should talk about it," Sean suggested.

Colin nodded, then tried to gather his words. "You said this
thing with her father may have affected her choosing to leave me. Do
you think it affected her reasons for becoming intimate with me?"

Sean was quiet a moment. "Well, we'd have to ask Janna, of
course. But I know it's common for victims of sexual abuse to be
more prone to immorality problems, because they already feel they've
been defiled. They also tend to equate sex with love. If her only
perception of any affection or love from her father was a brief sexual
encounter, perhaps the shock of losing her mother made her subcon-
sciously want a tangible validation that you loved her."

"That's what I was afraid you were going to say," Colin
admitted, marveling at how Sean could put his feelings into words.

"Why don't you tell me what's bothering you, Colin," Sean
suggested quietly.

"I just wish . . . that I hadn't been such a jerk and—" Emotion rose up to choke him as the memories came rushing back. "I wasn't living the way I was supposed to," he cried softly. "I lost sight of what really mattered . . . and all I wanted was to have her. I wasn't thinking of her; I didn't stop for a second to consider what might have been going through her head, or the long-term results of what I was doing. I was just . . ." He couldn't think how to put it.

"Consumed with passion?" Sean offered.

"That's putting it politely, I suppose," Colin said. "It's just that . . . if I could have foreseen the repercussions, I don't think I could have ever gone through with it."

After a minute, Sean said, "That's one of the characteristics of sin, Colin. We lose control of the outcome." A long moment later he added, "Can I share something personal with you?"

"Sure." Colin narrowed his eyes with interest.

"I was about nineteen when I moved in with a woman. It was before I joined the Church. Nevertheless, I knew it was wrong, but I didn't care. The long-range results of that relationship were filled with more pain and despair than I could ever have comprehended. But the struggles eventually led me to Mormonism, to the woman I married, and to the work I love. How can I wish it hadn't happened? Is it possible to pull out a thread of our lives and not have the whole tapestry become unraveled?

"It's okay to look back enough to understand and learn from our mistakes. But there is no place in this life for regrets, Colin. The past can't be changed; it can only help us make a better future. Janna is stronger than you think. *You* are stronger than you think. Satan has a way of putting pieces together to catch us in traps of tremendous complications. But God is always stronger, always there, always willing to help us out if we do our part. I know that with all my heart and soul. That's why I'm here where I am, with a beautiful family waiting at home for me. If you feel the need to clarify your feelings to Janna about this, by all means, do so. But don't think you have to dredge up the whole issue again just because you learned something you didn't know before. Both of you completed the repentance process for that sin a long time ago. You need to heal, not repent. You need to work toward forgiveness and understanding, and regrets don't fit in. Are you with me?"

Colin nodded and attempted to swallow his emotion. But his

voice cracked when he said, "Yes, thank you. You always manage to say what I need to hear."

Sean smiled subtly and leaned back. "Well, I try, but . . . I have to give credit where credit is due. Without the Lord's help, I'm not sure I'd do much good for anybody."

"Well, thanks anyway," Colin added. He glanced toward the door. "Do you think Janna got lost?"

"I think Janna's giving us some space," Sean said and walked into the hall. He brought her in from the waiting room.

Janna looked tentatively toward Colin as she sat down. She figured Sean would come and find her when they'd had a chance to say what needed to be said. But she wondered how the revelation might have affected Colin. Would he think less of her? Would he be disgusted by her upbringing? Would he realize that their fall had been very much her fault? She wasn't certain of his thoughts, but she didn't miss the warmth and acceptance in his eyes as he took her hand and squeezed it gently.

The three of them talked briefly about the effect of Janna's abuse on the choices she'd made that had led to the present circumstances. Sean stressed that the purpose of this discussion was not for Janna to have regrets, or to feel shame and guilt. It was only to help her understand that the steps of her life were connected to a situation that had not been her fault. Janna had to admit that over the past few weeks, each counseling session had made her feel a little better about herself as she gradually came to understand how the events of her life seemed to be connected.

Colin said nothing as they began the drive toward home. But she was surprised when he drove instead to a park and quietly helped her out of the car.

"Let's walk a few minutes," he said, taking her hand in his.

"There's something I want to say," he began after they'd ambled slowly for several minutes. "But it's not easy to say, so please be patient with me."

"Fair is fair," she said, knowing she'd often felt as he likely did now.

Following another minute of silence, he went on, "I guess I just want to say that I'm sorry . . . for what happened between us . . . when your mother died."

Janna looked up at him with a question in her eyes.

"Let me clarify this," he said quickly before she could misunderstand. "I don't want either of us to waste time regretting things that can't be changed, and I know we're both grateful for Matthew's existence. But what I mean is . . . I just want you to know that I think I'm finally beginning to understand something my father told me when I was sixteen." He paused to sort out his thoughts. "He sat me down one evening after a general priesthood meeting and told me that holding the priesthood was a great responsibility. Of course, I'd heard many times of the obligations that went along with it. But he said something I'd never considered before, and I wish I had thought it through more carefully at the time. He told me that a man who holds the priesthood has a special stewardship concerning the women in his life—to care for them, and look out for their well-being."

Colin looked skyward, silently asking for some divine help—not only in explaining this to Janna, but in dealing with the emotions bubbling up inside that he thought he'd dealt with a long time ago.

"What I'm trying to say, Janna, is that I had no idea how much my straying from the straight and narrow would affect you. I didn't know what had happened with your father, but it shouldn't have mattered. I should have had the respect for you that you deserved. I should have never put you in the position where you had to say yes or no. The bottom line is that I was doing things to drive the Spirit away, and it made me lose sight of the fact that you were a daughter of God who needed me, as the only priesthood holder in your life, to look out for your well-being. Instead, I let my passions take control of me, and all I could think of was having what I wanted, with no thought of the consequences." Colin swallowed hard and added firmly, "For that I am truly sorry, Janna, and I pray that one day you will find it in your heart to forgive me."

They walked for several minutes before Janna said, "I wanted it too, Colin. At the time, I wanted it more than I'd ever wanted anything in my life."

"I know," he said quietly. "But maybe you needed to feel loved and secure more than anything else. And I believe I could have found a better way to let you know that I would be there for you—that I loved you." He stopped walking and looked into her eyes. "That I would always love you." Colin pressed his fingers tenderly over her cheek. "Forgive me, Janna."

Janna tried to absorb the affection in Colin's eyes and the depth behind his words. Overcome with emotion, she buried her face against his shoulder. "Forgiving you is not a problem for me, Colin," she said without looking at him. "It's forgiving myself that I seem to have trouble with."

Colin urged her to a nearby bench and sat close beside her. "Tell me," he encouraged.

"It's just that . . . even though I understand what Sean means when he says that what my father did affected my choices, I wonder sometimes why I couldn't have been stronger." Emotion caught her voice and she glanced away. "Why couldn't I have stood up to him? Why did I let my father do that to me? Why did I let Phyllis treat me the way she did? Why was I stupid enough to leave you? And to marry Russell? And to let him hit me and . . ." Her words faded into tears and Colin put his arm around her shoulders. "And why didn't I . . . have the courage to tell you I was pregnant? Why couldn't I believe that I was worth more than that to you?"

Colin tightened his embrace. "And why didn't you just slap me and tell me to keep my hands to myself?" he asked, but his light tone didn't hide the gravity of what he meant. Janna nodded slightly against his shoulder. "Well, you shouldn't have had to. I should not have—"

"You already told me that, Colin," she interrupted. "Like you said, there's no good in regretting it. And I don't see any point in hashing out whose fault it was. I just want to understand why I've always been such a . . . *wimp.*"

Colin chuckled slightly, but she went on. "I don't want to be that way anymore, Colin. I want to be strong and confident . . . like you." She looked up at him, her eyes glowing with admiration.

"Whatever qualities I have that are worth having, I probably owe to my parents. Maybe you should talk to them."

"Maybe I will," Janna said, feeling something warm and peaceful swell inside of her.

Colin smiled and wished he could kiss her good and hard. Sensing a need to change the subject, he said with enthusiasm, "You know, JannaLyn, Christmas is coming. Maybe we should go shopping."

"Shopping?" she echoed.

Colin chuckled. "What do you think Santa should bring my son this year?"

Janna tried to comprehend what the prospect of spending Christmas with Matthew might mean to Colin. Then she marveled at the reality that they would be together through the holidays. They would almost be the family they should have been all these years. At the moment, Christmas seemed like a miraculous distraction from the difficulties of her life that still lay ahead. She came abruptly to her feet. "Shopping sounds absolutely wonderful," she said. "But first of all, I'm starving."

Colin laughed and they walked back toward the car. "I know the perfect place for a Christmas-planning lunch," he said. Janna laughed with him.

In spite of the nip in the air, Colin put the top down on the car. Janna wrapped her coat tightly around her and relished the wind in her hair. She felt alive and full of hope. It was difficult to comprehend in that moment that Russell Clark had ever been a part of her life.

* * * * *

Colin was going over some business at the desk in his bedroom when his father knocked at the door.

"Could I talk to you, son?" he asked.

"Sure, come in," Colin said, but he felt nervous as his father closed the door and sat on the edge of the bed.

"There's something I feel I need to say. But before I do, I want to clarify that I know what your mother said about you is true. You're a man now, Colin, and you have to make your own choices. And you're a good man. I know you want to do what's best for you, and for Janna and Matthew. That's why I think you should be aware that the Church does not approve of someone dating—at all—until a divorce is final."

"Dating?" Colin echoed. "Have Janna and I been *dating*?"

"You took her to lunch, shopping, and—"

"Dad," Colin said, willing himself to stay calm and not let this turn into an argument, "we're going to counseling together to work out all the garbage that's happened since high school. We have a common son. We went to pick out his Christmas together. I don't see where—"

"Hear me out, Colin, please. I'm not saying that you're doing anything wrong. These are extenuating circumstances; I understand that, and I believe the Lord does, too. But you and Janna got involved once when it wasn't right. She's vulnerable, Colin, and so are you. I've sat on many Church disciplinary councils, and I've seen sad, harsh evidence of how Satan uses vulnerability and weaknesses to set traps for good people with good intentions. I'm not trying to criticize or judge here. I'm just telling you to be careful. A man who is a recovered alcoholic should know better than to go into a bar to socialize. A lonely man who shares a son with a married woman should know better than to be alone with her."

Colin sighed and pushed a hand through his hair. He wanted to argue, but he couldn't deny the truth of it. His father was right. Still, he said, "Dad, we've never been alone in the house. In the rare moments when you or Mom aren't here, Matthew is always close by. I've made a point of seeing to that."

"I know, Colin. The situation is unique. I understand that. The only reason I brought this up at all is just because . . . because I love you, son. And I know how much you love her. It's got to be difficult to be around a woman you care for, day in and day out, and not have a complete relationship. Just stay mindful of it, and don't take for granted that you're strong enough to keep it from happening again. Don't hurt her twice, Colin."

While a part of Colin was tempted to become defensive, he reminded himself of what his father had started out saying: he was a man now. He could be man enough to accept his father's advice and concern without making a big deal of it. And as he allowed the thoughts to mull around in his head for a minute, he had to admit, "I know you're right, Dad. And I appreciate your talking to me about it. Sometimes the attraction is so . . . intense. But I keep imagining myself taking her to the temple when my thoughts get out of hand."

"That's good. Keep it up. And if there's anything I can do to help, just let me know."

Colin smiled. "Thanks, Dad. You and Mom just keep track of us, okay? You won't offend us by being good chaperones."

"Okay," Carl smiled and extended a hand toward his son. Colin shook it firmly as his father added, "And next time you go shopping or out to lunch, take your son, or your sister, or your mother . . . or even me. You know I'd rather dig a trench than go to the mall, but for *you* I would do it."

Colin chuckled and his father gave him a quick embrace. He lay awake far into the night thinking of their conversation, and he had to admit he was grateful for the reminder. He could see that he'd been bending the rules a little too far, and the last thing he wanted was to bring any more difficulties into their lives. He finally drifted to sleep, concentrating on that image of taking Janna to the temple, praying it would not be too long.

* * * * *

Colin pulled his car into the garage to get it out of the cold so he could change the oil. Matthew hovered close by, handing him tools and asking questions. Colin felt warmed by his son's personality. At moments he seemed so young and naive, and at others, almost like an adult, with perceptions and vocabulary that were surprising. He wondered if all children were this way, or if Matthew was unique.

"Dad," he said firmly while Colin was laying under the car, "can I ask you a question?"

"Of course, buddy."

"If you're my real father, did you hurt Mom the way Russell did?"

Colin slid out from under the car and sat up. This was not what he'd expected. He tried to think quickly of the best way to respond, knowing this was an opportunity for some very important communication. He wondered if Matthew's opening up this way was a result of the work the counselors had been doing with him. As he briefly contemplated the depth behind Matthew's question, he felt a little unnerved, recalling that Janna had described her marriage as an R-rated movie.

While Colin was trying to come up with an appropriate response, Matthew added, "Russell told me that what he did to Mom was the way a man was supposed to treat a woman, so I just have to know if you—"

"Come here, Matthew," Colin said gently, holding out a hand. As Matthew sat beside him on the garage floor, Colin wondered what kind of warped perception the child had about life, and love, and relationships. He put an arm around his son, praying inwardly for help. The silence grew long, but the child didn't seem impatient.

"Matthew," he began, "the relationship between a man and a woman is meant to be a beautiful, wonderful thing. Your mother and I loved each other very much; we still do. I made some stupid mistakes, but I have never hurt your mother. The way Russell treated your mother was wrong. He wasn't kind, and loving, and gentle. He was cruel and hurtful."

Matthew looked into his father's eyes, as if he was searching for sincerity. He asked pointedly, "Did you ever hit Mom?"

"No, Matthew—never."

"Did you ever call her bad names?"

"No, Matthew."

"Then why did she leave you?"

Colin took a deep breath. "It's a complicated thing, Matthew, but I think she was just afraid. She told me that—" He stopped when Janna came through the door from the house to check on Matthew.

"The two of you don't appear to be working very hard," she said with a smile.

"We've been talking . . . man to man," Colin informed her.

He was searching for a way to explain the topic delicately when Matthew interjected, "Mom, can I ask you a question?"

"Of course," she said. Colin attempted to warn her with his expression, but she was obviously not prepared.

"Mom, if Dad never hit you or called you bad names, then why did you leave him?"

Colin glanced up to see Janna turn pale. He shot to his feet and put an arm around her without touching her with his greasy hands. "Just answer the question, Janna," he whispered, feeling her lean into him for support. "You can react later."

Janna glanced up at him, grateful for his insight. "Because I was a fool, Matthew. I didn't want to keep your father from going on a mission, and going to college. I realize now that it wasn't fair of me to not tell him about you. I should have given him the opportunity to make his own choices."

Colin felt one giant step closer to putting all of this behind them as he looked deep into Janna's eyes. The regret was still there, but mingled with it was a warmth that increased when she added, "But with any luck, we'll all be together as a family before too long."

When Colin impulsively pulled Janna closer and kissed her, he wasn't thinking about the fact that she was still married, or that their son was watching. But when he turned to see Matthew's serene little smile, he was glad he'd done it. Perhaps it was the first step toward teaching Matthew by example what the relationship between a man and a woman was *really* supposed to be like.

Matthew acted as the perfect chaperone when he started talking about his upcoming birthday. Colin slid back under the car to finish the job, and Janna slipped quietly back into the house. After Matthew had gone to bed, Janna asked Colin about the things Matthew had said.

Janna couldn't help getting emotional as she thought of the impressions Russell had given Matthew, but she felt a little better when Colin reminded her that Sean was already working with Matthew, and with time he felt certain the boy would be able to deal with what he'd been subjected to in his young life.

The day Matthew turned seven was difficult for Colin. He smiled and tried to steer his mind to the gratitude he felt for having Matthew in his life now. But when the celebrations were complete and Matthew had finally gone to sleep, Colin went to his room and cried. As he thought of the years lost and the hellish environment his son had been exposed to through his most impressionable years, he couldn't hold down the anger and resentment. He cursed himself for being stupid enough to take what hadn't belonged to him outside of marriage. And he cursed Janna for being stupid enough to believe that she would hold him back by staying. He couldn't deny the sense of betrayal that still simmered inside him, and knew he still had a long way to go to reach his goal of forgiving her. He was grateful to be alone when the emotion gained momentum. A knock at the door sent him frantically wiping his face with his sleeve.

"Yeah?" he called, and Janna peered in.

"Are you all right?" she asked.

He hesitated, then shook his head.

"May I come in?" She entered and closed the door without waiting for a response. "I know I've said it before, and it sounds pathetically trite . . . and I know it can't replace what's been lost, but . . ." She bit her lip. "I'm so sorry, Colin. You should have been there for the last six birthdays, and it's my fault that you weren't. I just want you to know how deeply I regret that."

Warmth bathed Colin's emotions. He held out a hand toward her, and she stepped forward to take it. He knew they were making progress, and he believed in his heart that everything would be all right.

His belief was tested a few days later when he and Janna met with Sean following another of his appointments with Matthew.

Colin listened with growing dismay as Sean explained his concern over some things Matthew had repeated while recounting his conversations with Russell.

"Are you saying," Colin asked, aware of Janna's increasing pallor, "that these inappropriate discussions may have a deeper effect on Matthew than we think?"

"What I'm saying," Sean leaned forward, "is that such conversations are sometimes indicative of a bigger problem. This could well explain why he's been hesitant to open up during some of our sessions."

Colin looked over to see Janna press a trembling hand over her face. Her lips were almost white, and she took hold of his hand so hard it hurt. "What are you saying, Sean?" he asked.

"I'm not going to jump to conclusions, Colin, but I think we need to take some steps to get the full truth in the open. The only facts I have are that Matthew had practically *no* conversations with his stepfather when his mother was present. Yet Matthew reports long, detailed lectures about relationships and intimacy, things that no seven-year-old should know, given to him by his stepfather—in private."

Janna groaned, and Colin felt sick. Sean tried to give them some encouragement about discovering such things early and being able to work them through before they could get in the way of puberty and adulthood. He told them that he was required to file a police report if there was any evidence of abuse, and in this case he felt it was necessary. Even inappropriate conversation was considered to be a form of abuse. Sean and his associate would continue working with Matthew in the hope of getting him to open up completely so they could begin the healing process. He gave Janna and Colin some information on how to deal with young children and abuse, and encouraged them to read it and be prepared.

"If he comes to you with a confession," Sean said, "stay calm. Don't punish him for talking about it by making it a miserable experience. Let me know immediately, and then let me help him and you—*if* it's even there. Maybe it was just talk." Sean sighed. "Maybe it wasn't."

Sean's attention turned to Janna in the ensuing silence. "You don't appear to be doing well," he finally said to her. "Want to talk about it?"

While Colin felt numb, as if he was watching all of this from outside himself, Janna was trembling, breathing sharply, wringing her hands.

"Janna," Sean said, "is there anything I can do to help with—"

"Put a weapon in my hands," she seethed, "and just let me *kill* that man. If I had known then, I fear I might have done it. The only thing that kept me going was my belief that Matthew wasn't being harmed. If I had known . . ."

Colin put an arm around Janna and let her cry, whispering gently, "Maybe it's a good thing you didn't know."

Janna continued to struggle with her feelings through the following days. She wondered if she had ever prayed so hard in her life. Even her desperation to escape Russell's abuse somehow didn't compare to the possibility that he might have abused Matthew. She managed to put on a mask of normalcy, and she was grateful for Colin's level-headed attitude as they discussed it with his parents.

Colin said little, but she knew in her heart that he was going through his own personal hell. There was nothing in his attitude that even remotely indicated he was blaming her. But the bottom line was clear in her mind: if she'd not left Colin when she was pregnant, their son would never have been exposed to such horrors.

Janna began to wonder if they were being paranoid about all of this, and perhaps nothing horrible had happened beyond these "inappropriate conversations." But following Matthew's next appointment with Sean, the child approached Colin and Janna while they were sitting on the family room couch.

"Can I tell you something?" Matthew asked.

Colin put down the briefs he was studying, and Janna set aside her scriptures. She could almost feel it coming by the solemnity in her son's eyes.

"You can tell us anything, Matthew," Colin said.

"Do you promise not to get mad?" he asked.

"We promise." Colin passed a knowing glance to Janna. She could almost read his thoughts.

"Well, there was some stuff Russell told me not to tell anybody. But Sean told me I shouldn't keep secrets that were bad secrets."

"That's right," Colin said hoarsely.

Matthew got emotional then. "Russell hurt me, Mom," he said awkwardly.

While he was crying, Janna leaned forward, saying gently, "How did he hurt you, Matthew? What did he do?"

"He . . . He . . ." The child was crying so hard he couldn't get it out.

"Take a deep breath, son," Colin encouraged, putting an arm around him. "It's all right. You can tell us. We're not going to be angry. It's all right."

Matthew finally calmed down and began a detailed explanation concerning a number of incidents where Russell had hurt him when Janna had not been present. Accompanied by a great deal of verbal rage, Russell had hit Matthew a number of times, and more than once had shaken him. When Matthew apparently had no more to say, Colin and Janna exchanged a concerned glance. *Was there more?*

Janna was wondering how to approach the subject when Colin came right out and asked Matthew, in a straightforward but delicate manner, if Russell had ever touched him inappropriately. Everything inside of Janna wanted to collapse with relief when Matthew's genuine surprise and innocence became immediately evident. The child had no idea what he was talking about.

Colin calmly assured Matthew that he'd done nothing wrong, and they were proud of him for having the courage to talk about the way Russell had hurt him. He talked to Matthew about going to see Sean again, and the way he could help Matthew understand the wrong impressions Russell had given him. Janna just held her son in her arms and cried silent tears. It took every ounce of self-control to hold her emotion in check. While she was relieved by the evidence that her son had not been sexually abused, she couldn't free her mind of the images of Russell screaming at Matthew and hurting him phys-

ically. But the last thing she wanted now was to upset the child any
further by allowing this bubbling, aching turmoil inside her to erupt
in his presence.

When it seemed that nothing more would transpire, Janna took
the opportunity to slip away, knowing by the excruciating pounding
in her head that her willpower was wearing thin. She shifted Matthew
to his father's arms, touching his face in an effort to convey her love
and acceptance. Then she hurried into her room and closed the door.

In an effort to remain quiet, Janna pressed a hand over her
mouth as the first sob erupted. All this time, she had believed that in
spite of everything, she had kept Matthew safe. Where had she gone
wrong? How could she have been so stupid as to believe that Russell
wouldn't hurt Matthew, too? Emotions and questions rumbled
through her as she curled up in the dark and cried.

* * * * *

"What's the matter with Mom?" Matthew asked a few minutes
after Janna left the room.

"I'm certain she's upset about what happened to you, Matthew.
She knows it's not your fault, and she's very glad you told us. But I
know it makes her very sad."

When Matthew seemed to accept this explanation, Colin took
him upstairs, discreetly requesting that his parents distract the boy.
Then he went back down to Janna's room, trying to comprehend
what she must be going through. A light knock at her door brought
no response. He pushed it open and walked carefully into the dark-
ened room toward the sound of her uncontrollable weeping. His
heart ached to see her curled into the fetal position, oblivious to his
presence, even when he touched her face.

"Janna," he whispered as tears of empathy coursed down his
face. She only cried harder.

"I need to be alone," she managed. "Please . . . could you . . .
take Matthew and . . ."

The rest was unintelligible, but Colin nodded and said, "I'll put
him to bed upstairs. If you need me, you know where I am."

Colin pressed a kiss to her brow and covered her with the

comforter from the other bed. He found Matthew's pajamas and toothbrush and went upstairs.

It wasn't too difficult to ease Matthew's fears concerning his mother, and he fell asleep quickly in Colin's bed. Colin told his parents the things Matthew had said, and they both got a little emotional. Concerned for Janna, Colin went back to her room, where she was still lost in anguish. He left her alone as she'd asked, but left her door open slightly and sat in the dark on the family room couch, crying silent tears while he listened to Janna's heartbroken sobs echo his own misery.

CHAPTER ELEVEN

*L*ong after Colin left to put Matthew to bed, Janna's torment continued. She thought about her own abuse at the age of thirteen, and the way it had affected her life. She knew now how her mother must have felt when Sean had told her the truth. Janna had always wanted her mother to know, but she'd feared confronting her with it. Sean had helped them bring it into the open. And now, all these years later, Janna understood her mother's pain. While she felt immense relief that Matthew's abuse had not been the worst, the very idea that her son had been harmed at all seemed utterly unbearable. Had her mother felt this horrible helplessness, this intense guilt in wondering if she could have prevented it?

The clock on the bedside table read 3:28 a.m. when Janna finally calmed down enough to focus on the green numbers shining through the darkness. She forced herself to sit up and gain some equilibrium. She groped her way into the bathroom, then back to the bed, before she wondered where Matthew was. Just needing to see him and touch him, she hurried into the family room and switched on the light in order to see her way up the stairs. She gasped to see Colin sitting on the couch.

"How long have you been there?" she asked, her voice raspy.

"Who knows? Since ten or so, I think."

Their eyes met briefly, sharing a silent misery.

"Is Matthew—"

"He's asleep in my bed. He seemed okay."

Janna watched him another moment, then hurried upstairs. She flipped on the hall light and tiptoed to the edge of the bed where

Matthew was sleeping soundly. Fresh tears spilled as she pushed the curls back from his face and pressed a kiss to his forehead. She lost track of the time as she hovered close to him, trying to comprehend the horror of what she'd put her child through.

"Janna." Colin touched her shoulder and startled her. "You need to get some rest. Come along." He escorted her back to her room without her permission, and paused at the door. Following an awkward silence he asked, "Are you all right?"

"No, are you?"

"No."

Silence again.

"Colin," Janna said, "I . . . I don't know how . . . you could ever forgive me for putting your son . . . through this."

Colin's eyes widened in astonishment. "What exactly did *you* put him through?"

Janna glared at him as if to say it was obvious.

"Listen to me, Janna. There is only one thing I have to forgive you for. You told me you weren't pregnant, and you left me. That's where it ends. Don't think for a moment that I am even remotely blaming you for anything that happened to Matthew."

Janna's emotion bubbled out all over again, though she had to admit a great deal of relief in knowing that Colin wasn't holding it against her. But the pain of Matthew's confession haunted her relentlessly.

They all felt a little better after Matthew spent a long session with Sean. He explained to Janna and Colin that the boy seemed to have a strong spirit and good instincts. The fact that he had been very trusting of Colin right from the start was an example of this.

"Many children who have been exposed to domestic violence won't trust any men, and they're also very overprotective of their mothers. But Matthew has seemed to realize that Russell's behavior was not normal. I think Janna's influence on him, along with her honest approach to the problem, have helped him considerably."

Sean emphasized that he was absolutely certain there had been no sexual abuse beyond inappropriate conversation. He declared that the child was actually handling it pretty well, and his perception of Russell's mistreatment was basically healthy. "He knows that Russell is clearly out of his life, and he's more concerned about his mother."

Sean finished by looking directly at Janna. "I'm concerned about his mother, too."

"I'm all right," Janna lied.

"No, she's not," Colin insisted. "She hardly eats. She barely sleeps. She cries whenever Matthew's not looking." Colin expected Janna to glare at him for telling on her, but she only looked despondent.

"I think that's understandable," Sean said to Colin. "My guess is that Matthew's safety has been the one point in Janna's life that she felt some control over. It kept her sane; it kept her going when nothing else could. Her perception of that control has just been shattered."

Janna listened to Sean's explanation and had to admit that it made sense. She just didn't know how to deal with these feelings. Through the following days she prayed almost continually for the strength to endure, often recalling Sean's reassurance that Matthew was strong and would be all right. But it was difficult not to feel a fresh layer of anger and bitterness.

Colin's concern for Janna was deep, but he felt powerless. Pondering what he might do to help her—not to mention himself— he asked his mother, "Do you think it would be inappropriate for Janna and me to go to the temple?"

Nancy was briefly thoughtful. "I know it's difficult to comprehend at the moment, Colin, but she's still a married woman."

"That marriage is nothing but a farce. It was crime disguised by a gold ring."

"We all know that, Colin, but she's married nevertheless, and you must be careful."

"I know," Colin admitted, but he felt frustrated. He was trying to adjust to being a father to Matthew without being married to Matthew's mother. He knew that going to the temple would help him find the peace he was seeking, and he knew Janna hadn't been there since she'd left Russell. He believed it would help her, as well—if only to go there without Russell and his hypocrisy holding her hand in the celestial room.

"Hey," Nancy set a hand on his arm, "how about if I take Janna to the temple? And you can go with your father. We'll just ride together since we happen to be going to the same place."

Colin grinned. "You're a genius, Mother."

"Just mind your P's and Q's, Colin. You need the Lord's blessing in this, so do it right."

Janna seemed pleased with the idea when Colin mentioned it. She only requested that they not go to the Provo Temple, since that was where Russell had always taken her.

As they made their excursion to the Mt. Timpanogos Temple, Colin was humbly in awe. He keenly felt evidence of the Lord's blessing on their endeavor. He resisted holding Janna's hand, but just seeing her within temple walls was like a balm on his troubled heart.

"Why are you crying?" he asked Janna in a whisper while she stood facing one of the huge mirrors in the celestial room.

She looked up at him and smiled serenely. "I just feel better, that's all. Sean's right; Matthew's a tough kid. He has a wonderful father, wonderful grandparents, and a wonderful counselor. And I know it could have been so much worse. He's going to be fine."

"And he has a wonderful mother," Colin added, resisting the urge to touch her. She turned back to the mirror and he looked in the same direction. With the mirror on the opposite wall facing it, they could see an endless string of their images, side by side, in the reflection.

"Eternity," Colin whispered and felt peace. It was as simple as that. He knew that he and Janna were going to make it, and Matthew would be fine. By Janna's expression, he didn't even have to ask if she felt it, too. He only hoped the peace of this moment would carry them through.

Janna felt evidence of the gospel working in their lives as Matthew's abuse became something they were able to cope with and accept. With Sean's help and a great deal of prayer and study, Janna was surprised at how quickly she was able to come to terms with it. They knew the healing would take time, but they were doing everything they could for the moment, and she felt confident that eventually Matthew would be able to face his own future with a healthy perspective.

As Christmas drew closer, Janna became caught up in the preparations and thought less and less about the uncertainty of their future and the nightmare of their past. For now, she and Matthew were safe, and she was going to enjoy it.

Janna had forgotten about Colin's intense love of the Christmas season; or perhaps she'd never really comprehended how much he enjoyed it. She was amazed at the fervor with which he approached each holiday event. Together with Nancy and Carl, they decorated, shopped, baked, and wrapped gifts. Colin had Matthew close by in nearly everything he did when he was at home. And Janna felt an unfamiliar inner peace as she observed them together.

All things combined, Janna found herself feeling the spirit of the season in a way she never had before. Of course, Christmas had always been nice with her mother, but it had just been the two of them, except for the time Colin had spent with them during the holidays. And Christmas with Russell had always been formal and edged with the tension of his demanding that everything be perfect. He had been generous with his gifts for Janna and Matthew, but the lack of love had always been blatantly evident.

Now, being in the Trevors' home, with the opportunity to be a part of every aspect of the preparations, Janna felt a sense of belonging and giving she'd never experienced. She and Colin helped Nancy bake many kinds of Christmas goodies and prepare gifts for family members who lived too far away to come home for the holidays. Together they prepared Christmas packages for each of Colin's siblings and their families, except Cathy, and had them mailed before the middle of the month. When that was finished, Janna began wondering what gifts she might give to her new *family*. They had all done so much for her that she couldn't begin to think of something to express her true feelings, especially on her tight budget.

Janna continued to see Sean, as did Matthew, and occasionally she had a joint session with Colin. The sessions gradually became less tense as Janna could feel things beginning to make sense inside, and she felt she was at least on the road to healing. Sean reported that Matthew was doing as well as could be expected, and that he was a bright, well-adjusted child, especially considering what he'd experienced in his young life.

As time passed, Janna began to notice a new tension developing between her and Colin. It was evident every time she met his eyes. His unmasked desire stirred something in her that felt like a long-lost friend. Gradually, memories that had been too sensitive to dwell on before came back to her with increasing clarity. Occasionally she would catch her mind wandering to how it felt to be held and kissed by Colin Trevor—thoughts that no married woman should be thinking. To be sure, her marriage had been little more than a farce; Russell had done nothing to warrant her affection or loyalty. But she often reminded herself that she was still married. No matter how bad it had been, she was still legally Russell Clark's wife, and she felt certain God would not approve of her wandering mind.

Janna couldn't deny, however, the way her thoughts seemed to aid her healing to some degree. Her memories of her relationship with Colin were beginning to convince her of the true depth of Russell's dysfunction and the way it had affected her. Layer by layer, the reality was becoming more evident.

As Janna's feelings for Colin gradually became more and more a part of her everyday life, she began to wonder if a future with him might actually be possible. If not for Russell, she might be willing to believe in it. But her fear of his retribution still hung over her like a dark cloud that she chose to ignore much of the time. Their day in court was set for early in January; until then, there was nothing to be done. So she tried not to think about it, and concentrated instead on the present.

On a particularly cold afternoon, while Matthew was cutting and pasting a school project, Janna joined Nancy in the kitchen. Together they mixed fruitcake and shared small talk, mostly of Christmas and the weather. When they both lapsed into silence for several minutes, Janna felt it was a good time to get some advice.

"I just can't think of what to get Colin for Christmas," she admitted. "I've racked my brain over and over. Do you have any ideas?"

"That's a tough one," Nancy chuckled. "He's not too big on material possessions, so it should probably be something from the heart."

"Well, I agree," Janna said, "but that's easier said than done. I mean, ours must be one of the strangest relationships in history. Here we are, living under the same roof with a common child. We're going to *marriage* counseling together, but we're not married. What can I give him that will tell him how much I appreciate him . . . and care for him . . . but not be . . ."

"Too presumptuous?" Nancy guessed.

"I suppose that's it."

"Well, let me think a minute," Nancy said as she poured the candied fruit into the huge bowl of batter.

Janna turned to wash her sticky hands at the sink and noticed a light snow beginning to fall. Mormon Tabernacle Choir Christmas music drifted in from the front room. The scent of pine from the nearby Christmas tree subtly permeated the air. And the kitchen smelled of spices and a warm oven. The coziness made Janna long for life to always be this way. Would it ever be possible to have a home of her own, where she could live without fear and dread?

Janna was grateful when Nancy spoke and interrupted her thoughts. "I think that whatever you give him, it should be something you make. Of course, that's just a suggestion. You can take it or leave it." She paused, then added, "Is there anything you enjoy doing or—"

"Well, I can do just about anything on a sewing machine if I set my mind to it. But I had to leave all of that behind when—"

"You're welcome to use mine, of course," Nancy insisted.

Only then did Janna realize she'd missed the time she used to spend sewing to fill empty hours. It was the one creative thing she'd been able to do through her married years.

When the fruitcakes were in the oven, Nancy took Janna downstairs, to the other side of the family room, and opened a door into a well-equipped sewing room.

"Wow," Janna said, rummaging her hand through a pile of odd fabric scraps while her eyes took in the machine and a rack full of brightly colored spools of thread.

"You're welcome to use anything you can find in here," Nancy said. "It's all just a bunch of leftovers. The machine is pretty basic; I'm sure you wouldn't have any trouble with it."

Janna still didn't have any ideas for Colin's gift, but the next morning she put on her wig, borrowed Nancy's car, and picked up some fabric to make pajamas for Matthew. Nancy kept him busy while Janna cut them out and got started, then she worked on them late at night while he was sleeping. She began to look forward to her time in Nancy's sewing room, where she kept Christmas music playing on a little tape machine.

Just past midnight, nine days before Christmas, Janna felt restless and decided to hurry and finish up the hemming on Matthew's pajamas before she went to bed. The time factor concerned her, as she still hadn't come up with any ideas for Colin—not to mention the fact that she still had nothing for his parents. She'd found a good deal on the things she needed to make decorative wall hangings for Cathy and Karen. And thanks to Colin, they had more than enough for Matthew. But the rest had her stymied. She was stewing over it when she looked up to see him standing in the doorway.

"Still at it, eh?" Colin said. "Do you know what time it is?" he added, sauntering toward her.

"Yes," she admitted, "but I don't think I can sleep."

"Something wrong?" he asked, picking up the little flannel shirt, complete except for the buttons. Colin smiled at the little zoo animals on the fabric as he imagined Matthew wearing the new pajamas on Christmas Eve.

"No," Janna said, her concentration focused on her sewing, "I just don't know what to get your parents for Christmas."

Colin looked surprised. "You helped me pick out gifts for Mom and Dad last week when—"

"Those are from *you*, Colin. I need to—"

"Janna, they are from *both* of us. If you want to get them some other little thing, that's up to you. But what we got for them is from you and me and Matthew. And don't go spending a lot of money on them . . . or me. That's not what Christmas is about. Besides, you've got plenty of things you need to spend your money on."

"You don't let me spend it on anything," she retorted.

"You contribute more than enough to the household, Janna."

"But I've not contributed a dime to my doctor bills, or—"

"Janna," Colin knelt beside her and took her arm, forcing her to stop sewing, "I should have been taking care of you and Matthew years ago. What very little I am contributing to your needs now has not begun to make up for that. Please . . . let me do this. Let me take responsibility for you and my son. And don't begrudge it."

Janna could hardly argue with him. The look in his eyes alone melted every ounce of her pride. "You're too good to us, Colin," she said, turning her attention back to her sewing.

"Never," he whispered, aching to just hold her.

Janna began to feel self-conscious as he continued to watch her while she sewed. "What are you looking at?" she finally asked.

"The most beautiful woman in the world," he replied.

Janna gave him a dubious glance. "You need to get out more, Colin," she stated.

Colin chuckled. "I got out plenty in the last seven years, thank you very much. It only proved to me that I had the best to begin with."

Janna turned again to look at him, surprised by the sincerity in his eyes. "You really mean that, don't you."

"Yes," he said with conviction, "I do."

"But I . . ."

"What?" he urged when she hesitated.

Janna was grateful that she had quickly rediscovered the friendship she'd once shared with Colin. It was easy for her to admit, "I've never been able to lose those extra pounds after Matthew was born. I hate my hair like this, and I—"

"Janna," he interrupted, touching her chin to make her face him, "you are a beautiful woman. Everything about you is beautiful. Do whatever it takes to stay healthy and to feel good about yourself. Beyond that, nothing matters to me except that I have you in my life."

Janna turned back to her sewing, trying to absorb the depth of his compliment. Had Russell's constant belittling settled into her so deeply that she found it difficult to believe Colin meant what he'd just said?

"I love you, Janna," he said, resisting the urge to touch her face.

"You shouldn't be saying things like that to me," she reminded him. "I'm a married woman, and—"

"You don't need to remind me of that," he said, standing up straight and shoving his hands into the back pockets of his jeans. "No one is more aware of that than I am. I'm doing my best to mind my manners, but in the meantime, I'm not going to let you forget how I feel about you."

Janna stopped her work again and looked up at him. Impulsively she stood and pushed her arms around him, hugging him tightly. Colin responded by drawing her close and pressing his lips into her hair. A tingling erupted deep inside her and she forced herself to step back.

"We must be careful, Colin," she said.

"I know," he admitted sheepishly. "I feel guilty every time I think of how I kissed you the night you lost the baby, but—"

"Please don't apologize for something that's given me more comfort than you can possibly imagine."

"How's that?" Colin lifted a brow in surprise.

Janna glanced away and pretended to be busy examining the pajama shirt with her fingertips. "It . . . reminded me that . . . being kissed . . . and held by a man . . . could actually be a positive experience."

Janna noticed Colin take hold of the table as if to steady himself. She gathered the courage to look at him, then nearly wished she hadn't. She could see his chest rise with every breath he took. His eyes left nothing guarded. More than anything, she wanted to just press herself into his arms and give no thought to tomorrow. But they had done that once, and the resulting pain was still with them. She was relieved when he turned to leave, hesitating only long enough to say, "I'm going up to bed now."

Janna forced her mind back to her sewing and soon had the project finished and cleaned up. But when she crawled into bed, it was difficult not to think about Colin and the way he affected her.

Colin lay staring into the darkness. He felt a nearly tangible pain from wanting Janna. Knowing he couldn't handle this problem alone, Colin turned his mind to prayer, pouring his heart out and begging for help to get him through this without crossing lines that he knew from experience would only bring more pain. He finally drifted to sleep, imagining himself kneeling across a temple altar with Janna, being married to her for eternity.

Colin awoke with an idea that gave him a secret excitement. On his way to work he made a quick stop at the bank, then he anonymously mailed Janna a letter in care of Robert Taylor. He felt a growing excitement for the Christmas celebrations ahead—with Janna and Matthew—and it was easy to plow through his work with zeal. He was amazed at what he could accomplish when getting finished in order to be with them was his reward.

* * * * *

Janna was barely awake when she thought of something that made her sit up in bed with excitement. She knew now what she wanted to get Colin for Christmas, but thinking it through, she felt disheartened. How could she possibly manage?

Quickly she dressed and went upstairs, knowing Colin would have already left for work. She wasn't going to give up on the idea until she'd at least talked to Nancy about it.

"Good morning, dear," she smiled toward Janna. "Would you like some hot chocolate?"

"I'd love some. Thank you."

"Is Matthew still asleep?"

"Yes, I think he had trouble settling down last night. All he talks about is Christmas. I don't think I've ever seen him so excited."

Nancy chuckled and passed Janna a steaming cup. "Well, it's certainly fun for us to have a child in the house for Christmas. It's been a while."

"Nancy, I was thinking this morning about something I had considered giving Colin when we were dating, but I suppose I left before I got a chance."

"And you're thinking it might be right for Christmas?"

"Well, maybe. But it's just that I don't know how I could possibly manage. Still, perhaps it could get me brainstorming."

"Well, what is it, dear?"

"I wanted to make him a quilt."

Nancy smiled so quickly that Janna was surprised. "What?" she questioned.

"Oh, it's just that we've had a little running joke the last few years. I made him a quilt before his mission, and we actually shipped it to him so he could use it. But when he was nearly ready to come home, he felt prompted to give it to a family he'd helped convert. He wrote and asked if it was all right, and of course I gave him my blessing. I told him I'd make him another one. But honestly, I've just put it off. Occasionally he asks me when I'm going to do it."

"Well, then perhaps I shouldn't," Janna began. "I mean, maybe it would be better if you do it when—"

"On the contrary," Nancy said. "I think it would mean more to him if it came from you. I could help you, of course."

"But I wouldn't know where to begin," she admitted. "I helped my mother some, but that was a long time ago. And where would we put it without him knowing? And the materials would be expensive. I just think it will have to wait until—"

"Now, let's not throw it out before we look at the possibilities," Nancy said.

Janna felt a real desire to follow through on her idea as Nancy speculated over how they could do it. She managed to overcome Janna's every argument—except the money. Nancy offered to loan it to her, but Janna didn't feel comfortable with that. She wanted the gift to be from *her*.

After breakfast, Janna prayed about her dilemma, and in the afternoon she felt drawn to the pile of scraps in the sewing room. Recalling a method she'd once used for making some throw pillows, she began cutting and sewing them into a growing star pattern. She took time out to help Matthew with his schoolwork, but by the time she heard Colin come in from work, she had a fairly decent start. She hurried to hide the project in case he came downstairs, and had barely stuffed it into the scrap box when she looked up to see him standing in the doorway.

"This came for you today," he said, nonchalantly handing her an envelope.

"What is it?"

"How would I know?" he replied, walking away. "I told Matthew I'd help him with his reading. I'll see you later."

Janna sat there alone, staring at the envelope, feeling uneasy. It had no return address, and her name was typewritten, in care of her attorney. Who knew that Robert Taylor was her lawyer besides Russell? Karen? But she talked to Karen regularly; why would she send something like this?

Janna tore it open and gasped when she found nothing but a money order for two hundred dollars. She looked again at the envelope, as if she might figure it out. Then she hurried upstairs to show it to Nancy.

"If Karen doesn't have money to give away, maybe it's from one of your old ward members," Nancy suggested. "They could have gotten the lawyer's name from Karen. Or maybe it's even from Russell."

"I don't think Russell would have sent this. If he did send extra money, he would want me to know it was from him."

"Perhaps he told someone who your lawyer is."

"Perhaps," she said, feeling secretly thrilled to think of someone actually wanting to help her in this way. Nancy reminded her that it didn't matter who it was from. It was obviously someone who had listened to a prompting from the Lord; so, in essence, it came from him. Janna liked that theory, and she thought long and hard about how best to spend it. When she mentioned it to Colin, he just smiled and said it was nice.

The next morning, Janna took the car and cashed her money order. She set aside twenty dollars for tithing, and a little more for a fast-offering donation. Then she went to the fabric store and quickly found herself admiring a richly colored material that would set off the star pattern she had begun yesterday. She bought everything she needed for a queen-sized quilt, then hurried home, excited to show it to Nancy.

When Colin came in the door from work, Nancy called up from the family room, "We're down here!"

Colin bounded down the stairs, then stopped in surprise. "Whoa!" he chuckled. "What is this?"

Janna gave him a brief smile and continued to pull yarn through the tightly stretched fabric with a needle, and tie it off.

"It's a quilt, dear," Nancy stated as if he were inane.

"I can see that, but—"

"Don't get your hopes up," Nancy said dryly. "I'm very much aware that I still owe you a quilt. But I've got a mind to make you help me with it when I decide to get around to it."

"Well, I know you better than to think that you'd start a project like this less than a week before Christmas."

"It's Janna's project," Nancy announced. "I'm just helping out a little here and there."

"It's for a friend," Janna said with a deadpan expression. "I've just been racking my brain to think what I could get. I mean, what do you get for someone who does more for you than you could ever pay back? I told you about Karen, didn't I?"

"Yes, of course," he replied.

Janna was proud of herself for her straight face. She hadn't actually *told* him the quilt was for Karen; she had just mentioned her friend's name in the same paragraph.

Janna could almost sense Colin's disappointment as he moved closer to examine their work. "It's beautiful," he said.

"Janna made the center piece from some scraps," Nancy reported. "Then she just whipped the top together in no time at all."

"She *is* an incredible woman," Colin commented, winking at Janna, who shook her head dubiously.

Janna was amazed at how quickly the project was finished. Nancy helped some here and there, but mostly she kept Matthew occupied with schoolwork and Christmas projects. He had Christmas pictures and paper chains taped up all over the house.

On the twenty-second, Janna finished binding the quilt and wrapped it up. She hid it in the bottom of her closet. That same day she finished her gift for Karen, wrapped it up, and sent it with Cathy, who promised to deliver it.

"Quilt all done?" Colin asked when he came home.

"Yes," Janna replied. "I had Cathy deliver Karen's gift today."

Colin nodded.

"If you really want one that badly," Janna said, chuckling at his obvious disappointment, "I'll help your mother make one after Christmas. Maybe you can even help."

Colin smiled. "I'll look forward to it. If we do it after your divorce is final, maybe I could kiss you once in a while."

Janna tried to smile, but instead she turned away, not wanting him to see the dread she was suddenly feeling.

"What's wrong?" he asked, making it clear that he missed very little.

"I try not to think about it," she admitted, "but I can't help being scared when I do."

"The divorce or the prosecution?" he asked.

"Both," she said quietly.

"However the divorce settlement works out, you'll still be divorced, Janna. Then you can get on with your life. As far as the criminal prosecution goes, we just have to hope for the best. We're adding child abuse to the other charges. It's in the hands of the prosecutor, but

I really believe we'll win." Colin's confidence made Janna wonder if he really comprehended the full spectrum of Russell's character.

"I'm not so sure," she said. "I've told you what he's like."

"How can he dispute black and white evidence?"

"I don't know, but he'll find a way. I guarantee it."

Colin wanted to argue, but the last thing he wanted was to mar Christmas with tension over this. "At least it will be over soon," Colin said. "Let's just worry about it next year."

Janna nodded, then hurried to change the subject. "Would you mind taking me and Matthew to the mall after dinner?" she asked.

"No problem. Did you need something?"

"Well, Matthew keeps asking if he can go. Russell and I always took him to the mall to see the decorations and talk to Santa. He's kind of expecting it."

"Then, by all means," he said with obvious pleasure, "*his father* would be delighted to take him to the mall."

"Colin," Janna said and he sobered from the tone of her voice, "I love you."

Colin almost choked up. It was nice not to wonder.

"I just wanted you to know that."

"I love you, too," he said, wishing he could kiss her.

Aside from the continual caution they needed to use when going into public, the excursion to the mall felt like something off a Christmas card. Matthew told Santa what he wanted, all of which was already wrapped and hidden in the garage. Then he walked between his parents, holding their hands as they looked at all the decorations and bought some ice cream. Before they left, Janna asked if they could make one more stop. She led them to the back of a store where a number of small porcelain statues were displayed.

"I want that one," she said to Colin, pointing at a depiction of grandparents sitting on either side of a young boy.

"It's beautiful," Colin said.

"I want to give it to your parents," she announced. "But it can be from all of us."

"Whatever you want to do," Colin said. "If you want to—"

"My mind is made up," she said, and Colin took Matthew to look at some pictures while Janna paid for it and waited to have it wrapped.

The mall was closing when they finally left. On the way home, Matthew fell asleep in the back seat. Colin took Janna's hand into his as he drove.

"This is the way it should always be," he said.

Janna gave him a wan smile, then turned to look out her window.

"We will be together as a family, Janna. I swear it by all I hold dear. We will."

In her heart, Janna wanted to believe him, but the threat of Russell finding her hung over the future like a dark cloud. *Enjoy the present*, she reminded herself and squeezed Colin's hand. She hoped he knew how grateful she was for all he'd done for her.

* * * * *

Christmas Eve was a bustle of excitement. Carl and Colin both had the entire day off, and it seemed like a holiday already. That evening, Cathy's family came over for a traditional family dinner, along with a reading of the Christmas story by candlelight around the tree.

It was after nine when Cathy's family left. Janna let Matthew open his new pajamas, and he squealed with delight. He hurried to change for bed, but getting him to settle down wasn't so easy. Colin finally carried him downstairs after he'd hugged Grandma and Grandpa each three times. While being tucked into bed, Matthew reached his arms around Colin's neck. "I love you, Dad. This is the best Christmas I've ever had."

"But Christmas morning isn't even here yet," Colin chuckled.

"Whatever Santa brings me, it'll be great, 'cause we're together like a family, and me and Mom don't have to live with Russell anymore."

Colin held Matthew close for a long moment. "I love you too, Matthew. And this is my best Christmas ever, too. Being with you and your mother is the most wonderful thing in the world."

Colin agreed to read Matthew one brief story, then Janna came to kiss him good night, and they left his room together. Colin quietly led her to the Christmas tree, where they sat close beside it.

"What are we doing?" she asked.

"Killing time until the little bug goes to sleep," Colin said. He stretched out on the floor and relaxed.

"So," he said, looking up at her, "what do you want Santa to bring you, young lady?"

Janna chuckled softly. "I have everything I need for the moment," she insisted.

"But what do you *want*?" he asked.

"Isn't it a little late for putting in requests?" she asked. "I dare say he's already got the sleigh loaded."

"Just humor me," he said.

"What do *you* want?" she asked.

"I want to take you on a honeymoon to a quiet little hotel on a beach somewhere, and make up for the last seven and a half years."

Janna looked at the glistening tree lights, if only to avoid his gaze. "I want to be free," she said quietly. Then, more to herself, she whispered, "By faith the walls of Jericho fell down."

"What?" Colin leaned up on one elbow. "What did you say?" he asked again when she didn't answer.

"By faith the walls of Jericho fell down," she repeated.

"I don't understand."

"It's a long story."

"I'm not going anywhere, and I don't think Matthew will be falling asleep very soon."

Janna gazed up at the tree, absorbing the Christmas music floating from the stereo. "After I left you, I quit praying completely. I suppose I felt unworthy of even expecting God to listen to me after what I'd done. When I reached a point where I knew I couldn't take living with Russell anymore, I started to pray again. I felt so trapped, as if I was literally within prison walls. I could see no way out. But just a little while after I uttered that first prayer, I was thumbing through the Bible and that line jumped out at me." She repeated it wistfully, "By faith the walls of Jericho fell down."

Janna sighed, and Colin settled his head back on the floor. "I didn't know how it would ever happen," she continued, "but I knew God had let me know that he would help me. Even then, it was months before I finally found the courage to do it. And it still amazes me that you found me when I really needed some help. I know it was a miracle. Still, sometimes it's hard to believe that anything could make me completely free. I still feel these invisible walls around me, and I wonder . . ."

"You *will* be free, Janna. I promise you that. We will find a way."

"Even if we lose in court?" she asked.

"Yes," he insisted, "but I believe we'll win."

"Let's not talk about this right now."

"Okay, let's talk about what it will be like to go to the temple together, to be married forever. And we'll have Matthew sealed to us."

"I need a divorce first," she said. "Do you know any good lawyers?"

"I know a few lawyers," he replied lightly. "Whether or not they're any good remains to be seen, I suppose."

"And I'm going to need my sealing canceled," she said.

The thought was disconcerting to Colin, but he only said, "I hope it doesn't take too long."

They exchanged a smile, then Colin closed his eyes and sighed peacefully. He almost drifted to sleep, imagining a life that could always be this way. At the moment, the threat of Russell Clark seemed as distant as the moon.

"Oh, there you are," Nancy said, startling Colin. "I just checked on Matthew. He's asleep, and it's getting late. If you have work to do, maybe you'd better get started."

"Yes, Mother," he said facetiously and forced himself to his feet. "Come along, Mrs. Santa," he added, holding his hand out to help Janna up.

When everything was set out around the tree, and Matthew's stocking was filled, Janna slipped off to her room. She got all ready for bed, then studied the Book of Mormon until she knew everyone else had retired. Quietly she crept up the stairs with her gift for Colin, and carefully tucked it in a corner, behind the tree and out of sight. She returned to bed undetected and drifted to sleep, as excited as a child for morning to come.

When Matthew awakened Janna, it was still dark.

"Mom! I think Santa came! Wake up! Hurry! Hurry!"

"What time is it?"

"Five-four-nine!" He repeated the numbers on the clock.

Janna groaned. "Go wake your father. But you can't open your presents until Grandma and Grandpa wake up."

The next thing Janna knew, the light came on in her room. "Wake up, gorgeous!" Colin said far too jovially for six in the morning. She pulled the covers over her head and heard him laugh. An instant later, her bedding flew off and she was being scooped into his arms.

"Stop it!" she demanded. "Put me down!"

Colin just laughed and carried her up the stairs. By the time he got her to the couch, she was laughing. She was glad to be wearing heavy flannel pajamas.

"You're a scoundrel," she said as he sat beside her, out of breath.

"A scoundrel?" he echoed with exaggerated shock in his expression. He glanced toward Matthew, who was searching for all the gifts with his name on them while he waited for Nancy and Carl.

"Well," Colin added, eyeing Janna mischievously, "maybe I am." He leaned over to kiss her cheek quickly.

"Cut that out!" Nancy said as she came into the room, tying her bathrobe about her waist.

"It was just a little peck on the cheek, Mother. No different than I would kiss my sister."

"Well, you keep it that way," Carl said, albeit lightly.

They laughed and had a wonderful time as Matthew opened his gifts. Janna felt pure joy to observe him being so bubbly and full of life. Christmas mornings had always been so stifled and quiet with Russell. He couldn't tolerate the noise.

Matthew was almost as excited to give his gifts as he was to see what Santa had brought. Janna had helped him make a recipe holder for Nancy, and a pencil cup for Carl. He gave Colin a box filled with lots of goodies, some socks, and some of his favorite aftershave.

When Matthew didn't have any gifts left, he settled down to play with what he had, and the adults began opening their gifts. Nancy and Carl loved the gifts from Colin and Janna, and Colin opened several nice things from his parents. But Janna was surprised by the number of gifts she received. She said several times that they were spoiling her and she didn't deserve it. But they were gracious, and Janna had to admit she'd never felt so happy.

Nancy and Carl gave her a beautiful journal and some books—a couple of novels, and two books written for abuse victims that she could hardly wait to dig into. They also gave her a beautiful skirt, a sweater, and some earrings. Colin gave her a portable CD player for her room, along with three CDs. One was a collection of hits from the years they had dated in high school. Colin assumed they were pretty much finished when Carl pulled out the big, puffy package from the corner that had nearly become lost in the piles of wrappings and gifts.

"It's for you," Carl said, planting it on Colin's lap.

"Me?" Colin said as if he truly couldn't believe it.

Colin only had to touch the gift to realize it was soft and lightweight for its size. The tag read, *To Colin, with all my love, JannaLyn.* He met her eyes briefly as the words began to take hold in his mind. As he tore into the paper and the familiar fabric came into view, his vision suddenly blurred.

"I don't believe it," he murmured. He laughed to avoid crying. "It's beautiful." Colin leaned back and let the quilt fall over his lap. He looked at Janna and wished he could tell her what this meant to him. After all these years without her, to have something so beautiful, made by her own hands, was like a miracle to him.

Impulsively he pushed the quilt aside and moved to take her in his arms. "I love you," he murmured near her ear. "It's the most wonderful thing you could ever have given me, Janna. I love it. Thank you." He eased back to look at her face. Tears were brimming in her eyes. He hugged her again, trying to remember that he needed to treat her like a sister.

"I'm so glad you like it," she said.

Colin laughed and eased away. "You lied to me!" He pointed a finger at her and laughed again.

"No, she didn't," Nancy said. "I heard what she told you. She said it was for a friend who had done more for her than she could ever repay. She just happened to mention Karen right after that."

Colin laughed again and pressed his hand lovingly over the pieced star design in the center of the quilt. "One day," he mouthed more than said toward Janna. He held her hand and spread the quilt over their laps as they watched Carl and Nancy open their remaining gifts for each other.

While they were cleaning up the mess and sorting gifts, from out of nowhere Colin produced a large Christmas stocking, stuffed to overflowing. "Looks like Santa knew you were here," he said, handing it to Janna.

She was so surprised she hardly knew what to say. She couldn't thank Colin in front of Matthew, because it was supposed to be from Santa. She felt warmed by the evidence of her son's innocence and youth. In spite of the abuse, he could laugh and believe in the magic of Christmas.

"What's in it, Mom?" Matthew excitedly helped her dump its contents. There was lotion, bath gel, hair clips, gum, candy. She found a bookmark, some pens, a candle that smelled like peaches, and some odds and ends of makeup, actually the kind she used.

"Wow," she said, trying not to let her voice crack, "Santa must really love me, and he knows just what I like."

She discovered several bottles of nail polish in various colors, and said nonchalantly, "I wonder what this is for."

Colin smirked, and she knew this had something to do with the countless times he'd painted her toenails when they'd been dating.

Matthew quickly turned his interest back to his new toys. Colin whispered in Janna's ear, "Mother picked out most of it, I admit— except the nail polish." He lifted his brows comically. "I did that."

"You're all just too good to me, Colin. I feel guilty for even being here sometimes, when I think how—"

Colin put his fingers over her lips. "We're just making up for lost time."

Janna nodded and reminded herself to be gracious. She hugged Carl and Nancy and told them how much she appreciated everything. She was amazed at how they truly seemed to regard her as a member of the family.

They worked together to prepare a big breakfast of waffles and sausage and eggs. Then Colin and Matthew went out to the backyard to play catch with Matthew's new ball and glove. Janna wondered for a moment what Russell might be doing, then she realized that she didn't care.

The day went too fast, especially for Matthew. But he fell asleep quickly, then Colin and Janna sat on the family room floor with her new CD player and listened to her new music. Colin played her segments of the CDs he'd gotten her, explaining why he liked them and why he wanted her to have them. While they talked, he insisted on painting her toenails pink. Then they played every song on the CD from their high school years. The memories rushed back, making them laugh and talk far past midnight. Colin urged Janna to dance with him, and soon they were behaving far more silly than they ever would have dared at their high school dances.

The mood quickly sobered when a slow, sad song began. Colin eased her into a relaxed, easy dance step and she moved with him as naturally as breathing. He wondered how many times they had danced this way in their youth, with no inkling of what the future might hold. And how many times had it been to this song?

"Careful now," Janna said with a little smile. "Remember, we have to stay far enough apart to get a Book of Mormon between us."

Colin smirked, recalling the rules of their church dances. "Cheek to cheek, but not chest to chest," he added, and pressed his cheek to her brow, closing his eyes to absorb the reality.

"This is nice," she cooed.

"How is that?"

"I wonder if I've ever felt so loved and secure in all my life."

Colin looked at her in surprise. An unsettling thought struck him, but he felt prone to share it. "When your mother died, we should have danced all night." She looked confused, and he clarified, "You needed to feel loved and secure. We could have accomplished it with a dance."

Janna only sighed. "Maybe," was all she said, closing her eyes to become lost in the dance.

When the song ended, Colin took a step back to put distance between them. "I almost forgot," he said, reaching into his shirt pocket. "I have something else for you. I wanted to give it to you when we were alone."

"Really?" Janna smiled. "I have something else for you, too. But I wasn't sure if I should get it out yet or not."

Colin held out a tiny package. Janna held it a moment, baffled by the poor condition of the wrapping paper. It didn't look at all like it was for Christmas.

"I wrapped that two days after you left for Arizona," he said. "It was supposed to be your graduation gift, but it wasn't ready when you left. I was going to send it as soon as you wrote with your address, but . . ."

Janna met his eyes and swallowed hard. She looked back at the little package, feeling almost afraid to open it.

"Better late than never," Colin said in a tone that tempted her heart to break.

Janna's fingers trembled slightly as she tore carefully into the paper. Tears pooled in her eyes as she opened the little box, and she had to stop a moment and blink them back. Gingerly she pulled out the fine gold chain with a delicate locket hanging on it.

"Open it," Colin said, watching her face closely.

Janna popped the little locket open and squinted to read the inscription inside. *To JannaLyn, my forever love. Colin.* It was dated for her graduation, the day before she had left him. Staring at the words, Janna wanted to apologize all over again for being so stupid. But there was nothing she could say that hadn't already been said too many times. Instead, she just clutched the locket tightly and pushed her arms around his shoulders.

"It's beautiful," she whispered. "Thank you."

Colin just held her, relishing her closeness, trying to keep his mind where it belonged. He uttered a silent prayer for strength, and thanked God for bringing her and Matthew back to him.

"I have something for you," she said and quickly went to her room. In the drawer, beneath her nightclothes, were two identical books. She lifted one of them out and closed the drawer.

Colin gave her a questioning look as she held the book out toward him. He took it slowly and she sat beside him. Realizing it was a photo album, he felt suddenly hesitant.

"I always got double prints. I told Russell I was making an identical album to give Matthew when he grew up. But in my heart, it was always for you."

Colin took a deep breath and opened the cover. The first page had only a picture of Janna, her hair long and curly, looking very much as he'd remembered her, except that she was extremely pregnant. The picture was a side shot, and she was holding her dress beneath her belly, laughing.

"I forgot that was there," she chuckled with embarrassment and reached to turn the page. But Colin held it down, trying to absorb what he had missed. He wanted to tell her that he should have been there; he should have been the one behind the camera. But she already knew, and he would not ruin these moments with regret.

Colin couldn't help shedding a few stray tears as they went page by page through Matthew's life. Janna talked of the things he'd done and said as he'd grown. She told Colin about his first day at school, and his first stitches, when he'd fallen off a swing at the park. She talked about the times he'd been sick, and how he'd once spent a few days in the hospital with a respiratory infection.

The album ended with Matthew's first day of first grade. Janna closed the book and said quietly, "The rest aren't developed yet."

Colin turned to her and simply said, "Thank you." He put his arm around her and reminded himself that they were building a life together, and one day these missing years would seem insignificant. He prayed for that day to come quickly.

CHAPTER TWELVE

*O*nce Christmas was over, the court date approached far too quickly. Janna both dreaded it and wanted to have it over with. And while Colin seemed extremely confident that the case would put Russell away, she had to wonder if he had any idea what Russell was really like. Colin suggested that perhaps they should have Matthew testify of the things he'd heard and seen, since he was the only actual witness to Janna's abuse. But Janna simply didn't feel good about it. Matthew seemed to have forgotten all about Russell, and he was doing well. She didn't want to open up old wounds that were just beginning to heal. She knew Colin felt Matthew's testimony would make a big difference, but he didn't argue.

Nancy offered to buy Janna another new dress for the dreaded event, but Janna assured her the navy blue suit would serve the purpose just fine. She didn't want Russell to think she was spending the money he sent her on a new wardrobe.

Janna didn't sleep at all the night before her case went to court. By tomorrow evening she could either be free, or her imprisonment would only intensify. She prayed with all her heart and soul, but still she felt completely unprepared when it came time to go.

Nancy took Matthew to spend the morning with a neighbor, then she drove Janna to the courthouse. Colin met them, looking calm and confident. While Nancy and Colin were talking for a moment at the perimeter of the courtroom, nonchalantly keeping their distance from Janna, she unexpectedly caught Russell's eye. *Those evil eyes.* She glanced away quickly when his expression seemed to suggest that he had her right where he wanted her. She knew the look well.

Colin sat down with his mother on the front row of the court-room, just behind Janna and the prosecutor, waiting for the judge to arrive. He turned to look at Russell, surprised to find him staring. There was no question that Russell had connected him to Janna, and he wondered how, when they had been so careful. Russell had that lovesick look Janna had once described, but there was something evil lurking beneath it. Colin stared him down while images of the abuse inflicted on Janna and his son stormed through his mind. He was relieved when the judge entered and broke the tension. He wished he could handle the case personally; he felt pumped with adrenalin and more than ready to blow Russell Clark out of the water. However, they had no choice but to put it in the hands of the state and hope for the best.

Janna was grateful that everything got underway with very little delay. She avoided looking at Russell, but she was keenly aware of him looking solemn and discouraged, as if his heart had been broken. He might as well have worn a neck brace, she thought with disgust.

Janna was amazed as the prosecutor began to present a surpris-ingly accurate picture of her marriage to Russell. He told the judge about the horrors of her imprisonment and fear, and the effect it had had on the child. He put Dr. Reynolds and Sean O'Hara both on the stand, and she felt a little nauseated to hear the details of all that had happened to her and Matthew laid out on the table. But she knew it had to be this way; she was only grateful that Matthew didn't have to be a part of it.

Colin was called by the prosecution to testify concerning the condition he'd found Janna in the day she'd left Russell. Janna was pleased at his complete and absolute honesty, when she knew it would have been easy for him to embellish the story to make it sound better on her behalf.

When it was time, Janna walked with courage to the witness stand, and managed to keep her hands from trembling as she was questioned. In spite of her nerves, she was able to answer all the ques-tions with confidence, and she had to admit she felt good about it.

Janna was almost beginning to believe they might actually win this case—until Russell's attorney began presenting his defense. He lied as smoothly as the prosecutor had presented the truth. The reality

Janna had feared began to descend as Russell's fabrication came to light. With perfect finesse and polish, this man told the judge how Russell Clark had treated his wife like a queen. He talked of the way Russell had taken a woman who had nothing but a dysfunctional background and an illegitimate child, and had given her a life of ease and comfort. Character witnesses were brought forth to testify what a wonderful man Russell was and all the good he'd done. They were people Janna knew—some she'd gone to church with.

"How can a lawyer lie like that?" Janna whispered discreetly to Colin when the attorneys were both talking quietly with the judge.

"Maybe he's not lying," Colin answered. "Maybe he believes that everything Russell told him is true."

Janna sighed and resigned herself to the worst. She was reminded of when, not long after she'd married Russell, she began to realize that her husband was a madman. To this day, his shrewdness left her stunned.

She began to feel nauseated when Russell took the stand. With emotion in his voice, he told the judge of his love and devotion to Janna, and how he couldn't understand why she would want to leave him when he'd done so much for her.

"Well, actually," Russell said, "I believe I do understand."

"Could you clarify that, please?" his attorney asked.

"Late last summer, I began to notice a discontentment in Janna. In reality, she'd always seemed somewhat discontent. I often wondered if she still had feelings for Matthew's father, though she refused to talk about it. But it began to worsen, and I became concerned. Then I realized that she had somehow come in contact with Matthew's father again, and she was seeing him."

Colin used every ounce of self-control to maintain his composure. He knew that to react would only make him look more like the fool. He could see now where this was headed, and he felt sick knots forming in his stomach. He glanced briefly toward Janna; she looked pale and gaunt, as if she felt ill.

"And who exactly is Matthew's father?" the attorney asked.

"His name is Colin Trevor," Russell answered.

Colin felt the judge's eyes discreetly take in his presence all over again. Judge Beckett was a man Colin respected and looked up to. The possible ramifications of this disclosure were downright sickening.

Russell went on to explain the times he'd encountered Colin, and the obvious attraction he saw between Colin and Janna. He mentioned that he'd figured out who this was because Matthew's middle name was Colin, and the resemblance was striking.

"The next thing I know," Russell said indignantly, "I come home to find my house has been broken into, and my wife is gone. I was shocked when I heard she'd been beaten up like that. I felt sick." His voice caught with apparent emotion. "As close as I can figure, an intruder attacked and raped my wife, and she decided to take advantage of this to leave and put the blame on me."

Russell finished his testimony with another heartfelt plea concerning his love for Janna, and his shock at her doing something so devious. It was also implied that the child abuse charges were a fabrication, and that Colin and Janna had manipulated Matthew's confession. While Janna's head spun with the fear of what Russell might do to her now, she couldn't help feeling another layer of sickness over what this was doing to Colin. He was being slandered publicly.

Janna felt numb as the judge announced that the case was being dismissed. She couldn't quite fathom the reality that Russell Clark would walk away from these criminal charges unscathed.

Janna sank into her chair the moment court was adjourned. She felt Colin's hand on her shoulder at the same moment she saw Russell's hands come down on the table in front of her. She looked up to see his face close to hers.

"You should know," he said quietly, "that I always get what I want in the end." He turned toward Colin and added, "This is not over yet, Mr. Trevor. She's still mine."

"Are you making threats?" Colin asked in a calm voice that belied the fury building inside him.

Russell gave an expression of perfect innocence, then he chuckled as if this was all very amusing. "Of course not," he said, then he turned his eyes to Janna. "Janna knows that she will always hold a place in my heart." He touched her chin, but she jerked away and recoiled. Russell chuckled again and sauntered away, sharing a hearty laugh and a handshake with his attorney.

Feeling a sudden, desperate need to get out of the room, Janna stood and turned abruptly, searching for Nancy's face. "Where's your mother?" she asked Colin, hearing an edge of panic in her own voice that began to dissolve what little was left of her calm exterior.

"She had to get Matthew. I guess Mrs. Miller had an appointment. I told her I'd take you home," he said quietly.

"Then get me out of here," she rasped, her voice barely audible.

Alarmed by the tone of Janna's voice, Colin took notice of her increasing pallor. With a hand at her elbow, he guided her quickly out of the room and down the stairs.

"Are you okay?" he asked as they emerged into the bright, cold afternoon.

"No," she said with a shaky voice. "Just . . . just . . . take me home."

Colin wanted to die inside as he helped her into the car and noticed she was trembling. He wondered as he drove home if his overconfidence had left him unprepared for this. As much as Janna had warned him, he never could have comprehended or predicted this outcome. Not only was Janna left in fear of Russell finding her again, but Colin had to wonder how this would affect his career as a reputable attorney in this city. He'd just been publicly humiliated. In front of a judge he admired and respected, Russell had accused Colin of lying on the witness stand, manipulating a woman out of her marriage, and being the father of an illegitimate child. Well, he certainly couldn't deny that last one. But neither could he explain to the legal community the circumstances that had created this mess. And far worse, would Janna ever be able to live any kind of a normal life?

"Are you all right?" he asked, noticing the way she fidgeted and kept glancing in the rearview mirror.

She said nothing, but her breathing became so sharp he feared she'd hyperventilate. "Don't worry," he said, taking her hand, "I'll make sure no one follows us. I won't let him hurt you."

Colin's words seemed to shock Janna into full comprehension. With no warning she groaned, doubling over as if she was experiencing physical pain.

"Janna!" Colin panicked. "What is—"

"Just . . . take . . . me . . . take me . . . home!"

Colin was careful to make certain there were no cars behind

him before he started into their neighborhood. Janna walked blindly within his embrace into the house. He helped her to the couch, where she practically collapsed. As she curled up and moaned, Colin tried to comfort her. But she completely ignored him.

"Listen to me!" he insisted, taking hold of her shoulders. "Calm down, and let's talk about this."

Janna shook her head frantically. "He'll find me. He'll . . . He'll kill . . . me."

"I won't let him," Colin said, but she shook her head again and he wondered why she should believe him. He'd told her she would win the case, and that she wouldn't have to live in fear. If nothing else, he felt a deepening of empathy for what Janna had gone through, married to a man like that. It was a wonder she had survived at all.

"What's wrong?" Nancy asked, emerging from the bedroom in jeans and a sweatshirt.

Colin just shook his head in frustration while Janna seemed oblivious. Nancy motioned him out of the room and sat down next to Janna.

"It's all right, dear," Nancy said, putting an arm around her. "You just go ahead and get it out. Just cry it all out." As if all she needed was permission, Janna sobbed without control against Nancy's shoulder. Gradually, her emotion dissipated into a blanket of numbness.

"Do you want to talk about it?" Nancy asked quietly.

Janna shook her head.

A minute later, Nancy said, "Why don't you go and change your clothes, and I'll see that Matthew's got something to do."

Janna nodded and went slowly downstairs to her room. With mechanical motions, she changed her clothes and hung up the suit and blouse. Then she sat on the edge of her bed and stared at nothing, trying to comprehend the reality. But at the moment, she couldn't feel anything at all.

"Hi," Colin said, and she looked up to see him leaning against the door frame.

"Where is Matthew?" she asked, shifting her eyes back to a blank stare.

"Mother's going over his math with him."

Janna nodded.

"Mind if I sit down?" he asked, sauntering toward her.

Janna shrugged but said nothing.

"I'm truly sorry, Janna," Colin said, thinking his words sounded pathetically trite. "I keep wondering what I might have done differently."

"It was out of your hands, Colin."

"I know, but . . . maybe I didn't completely believe what you told me. It's obvious that I *did* underestimate him. I just . . . never dreamt someone could be so . . . low."

"It's not your fault," Janna said tonelessly. "I mean . . ." She finally turned to look at him, and the numbness faded slightly. "Your testimony was beautiful, Colin."

Colin rubbed his hands together. As he tried to think it all through, the full gamut of what had happened today came rushing up to hit him between the eyes. "I'm so sorry, Janna," he said, his voice cracking.

Janna turned to look at him just as tears spilled down his face. She took his hand into hers and squeezed it. "If nothing else, I have to admit that it's somewhat validating to know I'm not the only one Russell has been able to get the better of." Her voice lowered. "I only wish he hadn't said those things about you, and—"

"Don't worry about that," he said. Admittedly it bothered him, but his concern for Janna was far more important at the moment. "I'm not going to let that keep me from making it in this business."

Janna managed a smile.

"There's something I need to ask you," he said carefully. "I . . . don't want to bring it up, really . . . but I have to know."

"Go ahead."

"Russell said that he figured out Matthew was my son—that his middle name was . . ."

"Colin," she provided.

"I didn't know." He pressed his hands together tensely. "But how did he know, Janna? Did you tell him, or—"

"I briefly told him the situation before I married him. I never told him your name, or anything about you. But he's so shrewd, so . . . insidious. Apparently he sensed something . . . between you and me . . . and with the name . . . and the resemblance . . . he just . . ." Janna's voice faded with emotion as the memory of that night came back to her.

"He just what?" Colin insisted when she faltered.

Janna's gaze dropped to the floor. "That was the night before you brought me here."

Colin's chest tightened as the connection took place in his mind. *He* was the reason Russell Clark had beaten and raped his wife that night. How clearly he recalled Janna's insistence that her husband not know of their connection, but he'd never dreamed . . .

"I guess I wasn't a very good actor," he said, his voice unsteady.

Janna chuckled tensely. "I never was."

Through the following days, Janna tried to shut out the reality that Russell was free and clear. Until the divorce was final, she felt crippled to do anything else. She couldn't make it alone on the money she was getting. She felt almost as helpless and scared as she had before she'd ever escaped. Maybe more so.

Ironically, Robert pushed the divorce through quickly following the trial. She didn't know how he did it, but she was grateful to have it over. The divorce was granted, and Janna was given a generous one-time settlement, due mostly to the inheritance from her aunt that Russell had invested. Janna had told Robert she preferred it this way, rather than having any monthly connection to Russell.

Little was said between her and Colin as he drove her home from the hearing. While she had expected the divorce to somehow make her feel better, the reality that she had severed herself from Russell was frightening. She could almost feel his rage when she thought of how all of this would appear to him, how he would twist it in his mind and use it against her.

She walked numbly into the house with Colin. They found a note that said Nancy had taken Matthew with her to do some errands. Janna sat on the couch and Colin looked down at her, stuffing his hands into his pockets.

"You okay?" he asked.

Janna shook her head. Colin sat beside her and took her hand, but he didn't know what to say. He told himself they shouldn't be alone together this way. Their eyes met, and Colin felt all his concerns dissipate behind a single fact. *She was no longer married.* His hand almost trembled as he reached up to touch her face. It took no effort to kiss her. At first it was meek, as if he had trained himself to hold back for so long that it took a few seconds for his lips to get the message. At the first hint of response, Colin pressed his hand to the back of her neck, urging her closer. Their kiss turned warm and moist as he felt her hands come over his shoulders, clinging to him with the same urgency he felt within himself.

"I love you," he murmured against her mouth. Then he kissed her again, easing her closer, holding her tighter. When he felt certain he could take no more, he eased carefully back and met her eyes.

"I love you, too," she whispered. Tears pooled in her eyes as she added, "Whatever happens, you must remember that."

Her words triggered something in his memory. It took a moment for it to jell in his mind, and when it did, his emotions reacted immediately. "That's what you said just before you drove away with your aunt Phyllis." He couldn't avoid the curt tone.

Janna looked away abruptly.

"What are you thinking, Janna?" he demanded, hating the urgency in his voice. She didn't answer. "You can't just run out on me again. Do you hear me?" He took her by the shoulders and forced her to face him. "Talk to me!"

"What can I do?" she cried. "He'll find me! What kind of life is that for us? I can't possibly expect you to—"

"Whatever life we have, we will have it together. Do you hear me? We'll move out of state. I'll get a job somewhere else. We'll change our names. I don't care what it takes, Janna. I will *not* live without you and Matthew! Are you hearing me?"

"But you can't do that," she insisted. "How can you sacrifice being close to your family, your practice here, everything you've worked so hard to—"

"*You* are what I've worked so hard for, Janna. Don't you understand that? The rest means nothing without you. We'll pray about it. We'll find a way—together."

Janna pulled herself into his arms, wondering why it was so difficult to believe him. At the moment she felt so completely terrified, she couldn't comprehend a future at all, let alone a life with Colin.

"Janna," Colin felt a sudden desperation as he looked into her eyes, "marry me . . . soon. Even if we moved to Salt Lake or something, he couldn't trace us. We'll be careful. At least we can be together. Give me a chance to be Matthew's father—to make it right."

Janna was momentarily speechless. She hesitated saying the first thought that came to mind, but she felt it had to be voiced. "Don't be marrying me just to right an old wrong, Colin. You can be Matthew's father without—"

"I *love* you, Janna," he said angrily. "Why does that seem so difficult for you to believe?"

"I don't know," she admitted, looking away. "I think there are a lot of things I don't know." She turned back to his expectant gaze and admitted, "I need some time, Colin. I just have to . . . think things through. I can't start over until I cope with everything that's happened. Does that make any sense?"

Colin hesitated. He leaned back and nodded resolutely. It made sense, but he didn't want to hear it. He had to admit that his deepest fear was having her leave him again, and he would not rest easy until she was his wife.

As Colin lay awake far into the night, playing it all around in his head, he wondered if leaving town was the best answer. It would solve every problem—including the way he'd been slandered in the court-room. He went to work the next morning with a fresh resolve to find a position with a law firm somewhere else as quickly as possible. Then he could get Janna away from here and they could truly start over.

Colin had only been in his office a short time when he was told that Judge Beckett was on the phone. Colin took a deep breath before he picked up the receiver, wondering why the judge who had handled Janna's case would want to talk to *him*.

"Judge Beckett," Colin said with enthusiasm, hoping to cover his concern about what the judge might be thinking of him now. "What can I do for you?"

"I couldn't stop thinking about you the last few days," he said in a kind tone. "I'm certain that case was difficult for you."

Colin was momentarily speechless. This was not what he'd expected. "Yes," he finally managed.

"I just wanted to let you know that I'm pleased with the way you handled yourself, and I hope you won't let this set you back."

Colin couldn't think of anything to say, and was relieved when Judge Beckett went on.

"For some reason, you got me thinking back to the day when I first realized that some people really do lie under oath. And some people will go to great lengths to cover evil. It can be tough to swallow for a man who believes in truth and is committed to fighting for it. I would like to think that I've learned to discern truth through my years in this business. But sometimes it's difficult to know. Off the record, I wanted you to know that I regretted the verdict. There was simply too much reasonable doubt to put the man away. But between you and me, his story was just a little too perfectly portrayed to be true."

"Some of it was true," Colin admitted.

"I'm sure it was," the judge said easily. "I wish I could count the times I've seen a grain of truth transformed into a big shiny pearl of lies."

Colin wished he could tell this man how much his observation meant to him. But again, he was speechless.

"You're a good lawyer, Mr. Trevor," Judge Beckett said firmly. "This business is full of setbacks. Don't let it throw you off. Just find a way to learn something from it and forge ahead."

"Thank you, Judge. You can't imagine what it means to hear *you* say that to me."

"Maybe I can," he said quietly. "I was a struggling young lawyer once. Hang in there, young man. And if I were you, I'd get busy and marry that lovely young lady."

"I'm working on it," Colin admitted. "When it happens, you'll be one of the first to know."

"Good," the judge chuckled, "I'll count on it."

Colin stared at the phone for several minutes after he'd hung up. He couldn't believe it. It was as if his prayers, not yet spoken, had already been answered.

"Thank you, God," Colin muttered aloud and forced himself back to his work. He had no idea where to begin trying to put together a life for himself and Janna elsewhere, but he resigned himself to pray about it and put it in the Lord's hands, hoping deep inside that Janna wouldn't leave before he had a chance to get an answer.

* * * * *

Janna found it difficult to get out of bed. She had heard evidence from upstairs that both Carl and Colin had eaten breakfast and gone to work. Matthew had dressed himself and gone up more than an hour ago. She knew that Nancy had likely fed him and put him to work on some school project, and she felt guilty for not taking care of her son personally. But no matter how she tried, Janna just couldn't muster the motivation to face anything beyond the walls of her bedroom.

Janna was scared—plain and simple. No matter how she looked at it, she knew in her heart that she would *never* be free of Russell Clark. She couldn't explain it, but something inside told her it was only a matter of time before he found her. She knew his mind. She knew his determination. And she was scared.

"Are you feeling all right?" Nancy asked gently from the doorway, startling Janna slightly.

"Just lazy," Janna admitted, sitting up to lean against the head-board. "It's a good thing Matthew has you around, or—"

"Don't you think a thing of it." Nancy sat on the edge of the bed and crossed her legs. "He's no trouble at all, and these last several days have been tough for you, I know. I think you're entitled to be exhausted."

Janna attempted a smile, but it faded quickly into an unexpected surge of tears.

"Do you want to talk?" Nancy asked.

Janna said nothing for fear of sounding like a blubbering idiot.

"Are you afraid Russell will find you?" Nancy asked.

Janna nodded dejectedly.

"Then we need to do whatever it takes to be certain he won't."

"And what about Colin?" Janna managed. "Is it fair to expect him to run and hide for my sake?"

"JannaLyn," Nancy said firmly, "Colin *loves* you. Do you understand what that means? I'd wager everything I own that he would take you to the ends of the earth to keep you safe, if that's what it would take."

"She's absolutely right," Colin said from the doorway, startling them both.

Janna met the intensity in his eyes and could think of no logical reason not to believe him, but something in her just couldn't fathom *anyone* loving her that much.

"What are you doing here?" she snapped.

"I live here," he stated, "at least for the moment." He moved toward the bed and stuffed his hands in his pockets. "Actually, I think some prayers are being answered. Do you want to hear about it? Or should I go back to work and—"

"*I* want to hear about it," Nancy said.

Colin looked straight at Janna, obviously waiting for a response. "I'm sorry," she said. "Of course I want to hear about it."

"First of all," he said, "Judge Beckett called me earlier." Janna looked up in alarm. He briefly explained the conversation. Nancy and Janna both wiped at their tears.

"And," he went on, "with a few tips from some people in the office, and a few phone calls, I think we have some options that won't be terribly difficult."

"What do you mean?" Janna asked.

"I know of two, maybe three law firms in the Salt Lake area that are willing to consider taking me on. And I found a couple of available apartments; one is in the avenues."

While Janna was trying to figure out how to ask what he was getting at, Colin sat down on the opposite side of the bed from Nancy.

"Janna," he leaned toward her and pressed his fingers together, "it's a big city. We'll get lost there. He'll never find us. But it's not so far from family that we can't have some help and support."

So many protests erupted into Janna's mind that she didn't know where to start. When the silence became filled with tension, Nancy said quietly, "Maybe it's too much . . . too fast, Colin."

Colin took a deep breath and reached out for Janna's hand. "Listen," he said, "if I'm going too fast, all you have to do is say so. Tell me what you want to do, Janna, and we'll do it—anything." Still she said nothing, and he added, "Do you want to talk to Sean?"

Janna shook her head slightly. "I can't expect Sean to solve all my problems. I have to do this on my own."

"Okay," Colin said. "So tell me what I can do to help you, Janna, and I'll do it."

"Did you hear me, Colin? I said I have to do this on my own."

"Why?" Colin demanded, unable to help feeling panicked. His mother's gentle hand on his arm reminded him to stay calm. But his instincts were telling him that he needed to make Janna a part of his life and get her away from here. Still, he couldn't force her. "Janna," he said softly, "I'll give you all the space and time you need, but for the love of heaven, don't shut me out. All I ask is that you tell me how you feel, and don't leave me to wait and wonder."

"Tell me if I'm out of line," Nancy said, "but maybe a priesthood blessing would be in order here."

Colin looked hard at Janna, as if to echo his mother's statement.

"I'll think about it, thank you," Janna said.

Another grueling silence was broken by Matthew as he entered the room and crawled onto Colin's lap. "Hi, Dad. What are you doing home?"

"I just needed to hug you," Colin said as if nothing in the world was wrong.

Janna watched Colin with his son and felt hard pressed to keep from sobbing. At least they had each other, she thought. When Russell found her, Matthew would at least have his father.

Colin went back to work, and Janna soaked in the bathtub a long time, wishing she could make sense of her thoughts. Even her prayers seemed muddled and confusing. Her only recognizable course of action came from Nancy's suggestion. When Colin walked in the door late afternoon, she was waiting for him.

"Hello," he said, setting his briefcase down.

Janna nodded and blurted it out before she lost her courage. "Will you give me a blessing?"

Colin smiled and held out his hand, relieved when she took it without hesitation. "It would be an honor."

Right after supper was cleaned up, Carl assisted Colin in giving Janna a blessing. Colin felt nervous, and at first the words came slowly and stilted. But gradually he felt a warm peace settle over him, and the thoughts flowed through him unrestrained. He heard himself telling Janna of her great worth in the sight of God, and the good she could bring to others as she faced the layers of healing with courage and allowed those around her to help ease her burdens. Emotion accompanied his last statement before he closed the blessing. With a cracked voice he promised Janna that as she made her choices with faith and fortitude, setting her fears aside, the Lord would protect her and keep her safe.

Janna said nothing after the blessing beyond a sincere, "Thank you." She said little the following day, until Matthew had gone to bed. Colin looked up from the desk in his room to see her standing in the doorway.

"Hello," he said, holding out a hand. She hesitated a moment, then stepped forward to take it.

"There's something I need to tell you," she said. Colin moved to stand up, but she stopped him. "It will only take a minute."

"Okay," he said, willing his heart to be calm.

"I want to marry you, Colin, but . . ."

"But?" he echoed.

"I need some time."

Colin swallowed and cleared his throat. "Okay. And in the meantime?"

"I don't know." She turned away and folded her arms. "Maybe *I* should get an apartment, change my name. Maybe I just need to make it on my own for a while."

Colin forced himself to not start shouting protests. Sean had told him to expect this, but he still had trouble accepting it.

"And Matthew?" he asked.

"I don't know," she said. "I guess that would be up to him. Maybe it would be better if he stayed with you . . . for a while, at least, until I can . . ."

"Until you can what?" he pressed when she didn't finish.

"I don't know!" she snapped.

Colin held his breath and uttered a quick prayer for help. "Janna," he said a minute later, "I just want you to think about one thing. Are you acting out of fear or faith here? Think about what that blessing said. Do what you feel you have to, but do it for the right reasons. I'm here to help you, not hold you back. Do you understand?"

Janna nodded quickly and left the room.

Through the following days, Colin watched Janna slip further into a depression that he neither understood nor knew how to broach. He talked to Sean on the phone from his office, and tried to do as he'd recommended and just let her have some space. He suggested to his mother that perhaps he should move out as he'd planned originally, but she felt that he should be there, for Matthew if nothing else.

Colin felt voices of protest screaming in his head when Janna asked that he take her divorce settlement check and cash it. He offered to take her to open a checking account, but she feared having her social security number attached to something that would make it easier for Russell to find her. When she accused him of trying to control her life, he gave in to the request and gave her the cash. It was a little unnerving to think how far she could go, and how long she could live, on that much money.

Colin reminded himself that Janna was a free agent. He just had to have faith and be patient, and he only prayed that his patience would pay off. For him, life would be nothing without Janna and Matthew. If only he could convince Janna.

* * * * *

Janna woke up one morning a week after her divorce and actually felt better. She wasn't certain yet what she would do, but recalling that blessing, she had to admit that she needed Colin and his family. She told Colin so at breakfast, and he smiled as if she'd just given him the world. He reached over the table and quickly kissed her before he left, and she wondered if maybe she should just stop wallowing in her fear and marry him. He'd promised to take care of her, and to take the necessary precautions to keep her safe. What more could she ask?

Late morning, Nancy left to go to a Relief Society presidency meeting. Janna sat down with Matthew to go over some school papers. They were laughing together when the phone rang. Janna answered it with a cheerful "Hello," but her heart began to pound when only silence followed.

"Hello?" she repeated.

"Janna, my love." Russell's voice was unmistakable. "You can't know what good it does my heart to have finally found you."

Janna covered her mouth with her hand to keep from screaming. She swallowed carefully and forced a steady, firm voice. "You must have the wrong number," she stated and hung up the phone.

For a moment, fear paralyzed her. She couldn't move, couldn't breathe.

"What's the matter, Mom?" Matthew asked, startling her back to reality. She stared helplessly at her son, willing herself to stay calm for his sake. "Who was on the phone?" he demanded, much like his father would have.

"Honey," she said, pressing a trembling hand over her heart, "it was Russell. He's found us."

"You gotta call Dad!" he shouted. "You gotta—"

Janna nodded and managed to punch out the number. "Could I speak to Colin Trevor, please?"

"I'm sorry," the receptionist replied. "He's in a meeting now. Could I—"

"Thank you," she said and slammed down the phone. Frantically she tried to think what to do.

"Call 911," Matthew suggested firmly.

She *could* call the police, but to tell them what? That she'd gotten a phone call?

"That's a good idea," she said, "but there's nothing they can do about it right now." She took a deep breath. "Karen," she muttered and quickly punched the number, praying her friend would be there. Was this her day off? What were the chances?

"Oh, thank God," Janna muttered when Karen answered.

"Janna? What's wrong?"

"Will you come and get me? Right now?"

"I can, yes. Why? Is it—"

"Please, just come and get me. Don't let anybody follow you. Hurry."

"I'm on my way." Karen said and hung up. She'd only been to the Trevors' home once for a few minutes. Janna prayed she would remember how to get there.

Janna missed getting the phone on the hook, but Matthew picked it up and fixed it before he followed her down the stairs.

"Mom, are you—"

"I have to leave here for a while, Mattie," she said, frantically throwing things into her suitcases. She forced herself to take a deep breath and speak to Matthew as reasonably as possible. "You're a big boy now. You can go with me, or you can stay with your dad. But it wouldn't be fair for me to put your dad and grandma and grandpa in a bad situation. They've done so much for us already."

"But where are you going?" he asked, tears welling in his eyes.

"I don't know for sure."

"Will you come back?" he cried.

Janna wanted to tell him she would, but she couldn't bring herself to say it. "I don't know," she said, barely able to see what she was doing as hot tears burned into her eyes. When she finally managed to focus again, Matthew was packing his things just as haphazardly as she was.

"What are you doing?" she asked.

"I'm going with you!" he insisted.

While Janna couldn't help feeling grateful that he would still choose to be with her, she prayed that he would remain safe in her care. Perhaps she could arrange for Colin to get him later.

"Colin," she murmured under her breath. She couldn't leave with no explanation. He'd never forgive her.

While Karen was loading the luggage into her car, glancing both directions down the street every few seconds, Janna dialed Colin's office again. She was given the same answer.

"Could I connect you to Mr. Trevor's voice mail?"

"Yes, please," Janna said, thinking this would be better in the long run.

Listening to Colin's voice on the recorded message, Janna felt the reality of what she was doing flooding her mind and heart. The beep on the other end of the phone shocked her to action. She quickly gave the message, then let Matthew say something. Then she left, trying not to think too hard about what to do beyond the moment.

Janna made Karen drive around for nearly an hour before they found an obscure motel, and Karen went to the office to get a room. Confident that she had eluded Russell—at least for the moment— Janna relaxed and tried to gather her wits. She couldn't find the courage to call Colin and tell him where they were. But she told herself she would, just as soon as they got settled somewhere. In the meantime, she tried not to think about him kicking the kitchen chairs across the floor.

* * * * *

Colin walked into his office and tossed some papers on the desk. He loosened his tie and sat down to check his messages, making notes on the calls he needed to return. The fifth message sent his heart racing.

"Colin." Janna's voice was barely discernible through her obvious crying. "He found me."

"Dear God, no," he muttered, shooting out of his chair. Then he forced himself to hear out the remainder of the message.

"He called me here. Please . . . understand. I have to go. I love you, Colin," she cried. "Please forgive me. I'll always love you."

Then Matthew's voice could be heard in the background. "Let me talk to Dad. Let me talk." His emotion was equally evident.

"It's the voice mail," Janna said quietly. "Just leave him a message."

"I love you, Dad," Matthew cried. "We have to go now."

The phone clicked and Colin ran out to the car, knowing full well they were long gone. He cried and prayed aloud as he drove, hoping they were safe, wondering if he'd ever see them again.

Leaving the car door open, he sprinted into the house and down the stairs. He slowed as he entered the empty room. For a long moment he just stared at the open drawers, and the scattered belongings that hadn't quite made it to the suitcases in the frenzy. He sat unsteadily on the edge of Janna's bed, and the pain knotted somewhere between his chest and his stomach.

"No!" Colin howled toward the ceiling, then he pressed his head into his hands and sobbed.

An hour later, he was still sitting in the same place, his tears gone dry, his heart aching, his head numb. He heard his mother come in the house, but he made no effort to move.

"What happened?" Nancy asked frantically when she entered the room.

Colin cleared his throat, but his voice was hoarse. "I . . . uh . . . got this message . . . on my phone. Apparently . . . he found them. So they left, and . . ." Colin pressed his hand over his eyes, realizing the tears hadn't gone dry after all.

"Are they all right?" Nancy asked, sitting beside him.

"We can only hope. I don't know where they are, or . . ." He sniffed and wiped his face. "She told me at the breakfast table that she . . . she needed me, and . . ." He couldn't finish.

"Obviously, fear overruled the rest," Nancy said gently.

Colin nodded. "I know her fear is understandable, but . . ." He pressed his face to his mother's shoulder and cried like a baby. There was some comfort in knowing that she was crying, too.

CHAPTER THIRTEEN

*J*anna and Matthew rested peacefully at the motel that night, and the following afternoon Janna found an obscure two-bedroom apartment available in Springville. She borrowed Karen's car to make the deposit and get the keys, putting everything under the name *Jane Carlson*. She bought some groceries and a few things to get by on for a day or two, grateful she had the money from her divorce settlement to rely on. Realistically, she figured she could manage without working for another six months, and still have enough to get by with a small income for several months after that, if she needed to.

Late that evening, Karen drove her and Matthew to their new home. Janna had decided that she didn't want Matthew to know exactly where they were, for reasons she didn't fully understand. She justified it to Karen with a simple, "I'm paranoid, okay? Just humor me."

They drove around until Matthew fell asleep in the back seat, then she urged him inside where a bed was made for him on the floor. He quickly fell back to sleep. Janna hugged Karen at the door and locked it behind her when she left.

The next day, Janna took Matthew with her and Karen to buy a used car. Karen took care of the transactions and registered the car in her name, and Janna paid her back in cash. Then she took Matthew with her to pick out some furniture. They had lunch and bought some more things for the apartment.

That night while Matthew slept, Janna had to admit that it felt good to be on her own, caring for herself. But she still couldn't get rid of the fear that Russell would eventually find her. And while a part of her longed to call Colin, if only to let him know they were all right, she just didn't feel ready to face him. She wanted a future with him, and she believed it was by far the best thing for Matthew, but she just couldn't be sure if it was the right thing for *Colin*. Maybe she was doing him a favor in the long run. She felt certain if he stopped to look at the big picture, he would realize that the trouble she'd bring into his life would not be worth it.

Reasoning that she needed to at least let him know they were all right, she called her attorney and asked him to give Colin the message.

Janna answered Matthew's requests to call his father with the explanation that they didn't have a phone, grateful that he didn't realize there was a pay phone on the corner. When they finally had a phone installed, mostly for the sake of being able to call for help if they needed it, Matthew insisted on calling his father. Janna gently told him that if he really wanted to call him for a few minutes, it would be all right. But she explained that it was important for her to have some time on her own.

"Don't you like Dad?" he asked with perfect innocence.

Janna sighed. "Matthew, I love your father very much. I always have. But there is so much that's happened since . . . since you were born, that makes it difficult for me to be . . ."

"Safe?" he guessed.

"Yes. I need to be safe, and so do the people I love. If you decide you want to go live with your dad, then that's up to you. But for now, I just need to have some time by myself."

Matthew seemed to accept the explanation. He asked if he could just leave a message on Colin's voice mail at work. Janna complied, and after that Matthew stopped pestering her about contacting Colin. They stayed busy with schoolwork, often visiting the library and taking short trips to museums and galleries. And they went to church, using assumed names.

Karen kept in close touch by phone and occasionally came to visit, always making certain she wasn't followed. Janna felt ill at Karen's first report of seeing Russell at church, acting as if nothing had happened. He continued to hold a temple recommend and a church calling, and he was generally accepted by the ward as "the poor sweet man, abandoned by his dysfunctional wife and slandered by her lover." Karen also mentioned that he was dating, and Janna felt sick to think of another innocent woman falling into his trap.

Janna tried to force such thoughts out of her mind, as there was nothing she could do about the situation. Instead, she concentrated on the present; yet she couldn't deny the walls still surrounding her life. She'd come a long way, but her personal walls of Jericho were still intact. She wondered if *anything* could actually make them fall and set her free.

Gradually, Janna began to feel less afraid and more alive, though her struggle to have faith continued. And the more time that passed, the more she missed Colin. She only prayed that when she saw him again, he would find it in his heart to forgive her for leaving him— twice.

* * * * *

Colin didn't sleep at all the night after Janna left. He curled up in the quilt she had made for him, wishing it could make him feel closer to her. He had hoped she would at least let him know if they were all right, but she didn't. After much prayer, he felt certain in his heart that they had eluded Russell. But the very idea that she had fled without him was unsettling.

Colin called Sean from his office and left a message. Sean called back an hour later. "What's up?" he asked.

"Janna left," Colin stated.

"Whoa," Sean sighed. "Do you want to talk about it?"

"That's why I called."

Colin and Sean shared a long lunch, during which Colin repeated the details of Janna's departure and how it made him feel. Sean concluded that it really wasn't such a surprise, seeing that she had basically told him the week before that she was planning to be on her own for a while. "Russell's appearance just put that into motion a lot faster," Sean suggested. "Obviously her fear just overtook all her other emotions."

Sean paused and leaned a little closer. "I know this is hard for you, but the fact is, it's out of your hands for the time being. Even when abuse isn't present, divorce requires a time of renewal. People in difficult marriages lose themselves, and they have to find themselves again before they have anything to give. She loves you. I think when the time is right, she'll just. . . *pop up.*"

Colin pushed his hands through his hair. "And what if she doesn't?" he asked.

"You told me she said she wanted to marry you. She's the mother of your son. But she has to make her own choices, Colin. Don't jump into marriage too soon, for the wrong reasons, or you'll have a whole new can of worms to deal with. She's done well, admittedly, but trust me when I tell you there are many layers of healing left for her to discover—and some of them are going to be hell."

Colin leaned back and fought the urge to cry. "I guess I should stop feeling sorry for myself and remember what she's been through."

"Wouldn't hurt." Sean shrugged easily.

Colin chuckled dubiously. "Are you this way at home?"

"I drive my wife crazy," Sean chuckled.

Colin leaned his elbows on the table. "No, seriously, Sean. How do you handle the struggles in *your* relationships? Or don't you have any?"

Sean shook his head with a little laugh. He was quiet for a minute, as if lost in deep thought. "I'm going to tell you something, Colin. Maybe it will make a difference; maybe it won't. But if something I've learned from real life can help you, then it doesn't hurt to share it."

"I'm listening," Colin said, sensing that this *something* was close to Sean's heart. Colin doubted that he shared it with just anybody, and he couldn't help feeling warmed by his confidence.

"Colin, when I married Tara, she was pregnant from a rape."

Colin sighed and leaned back. "Wow. That's . . . tough."

"It was tough. But *she* was tough. She handled most of it really well, actually. I just tried to be there for her. I suggested options, then she made her own choices. I had to let her feel the pain, and not take it personally. And I had to accept the fact that all that pain wasn't going to go away all at once. Years after we placed the baby for adoption, Tara went through a whole new bout of struggling over it. Something she read in a book just . . . triggered a layer of emotion she hadn't dealt with. She just kind of . . . freaked out for a while. And I simply tried to be there for her."

"I think I get the point."

"Janna's a wonderful woman, Colin. But every man she's ever trusted has hurt her. And you were one of them. You left a seventeen-year-old girl with some tough choices. She didn't necessarily choose well, and beyond a point you had no control over it. But the facts still remain. And more important than the facts is how Janna *perceived* them. What I'm really trying to say, Colin, is that if you're determined to marry a woman who's been through hell, you'd better be committed to carrying her across some hot coals in bare feet. Because my bet is that one day she's going to punish you for what you did to her—and maybe even for things you *didn't* do to her. It won't be intentional, or even conscious, but it will happen just the same."

"Are you trying to cheer me up?"

"I'm trying to prepare you for every possibility. Decide what *you* can live with, then give Janna her choices and respect them. Support her in them. But don't try to fix her problems, and don't let her press your boundaries. When those things happen, you come up with a very nasty problem on top of all the other problems."

"And what is that?" Colin asked cynically.

"It's called codependency, and it's an easy trap to fall into when you love someone who's struggling. Janna's distance right now might be just as good for you as it is for her. When you do see her again, be prepared, and be careful. Your happiness is just as important as hers. And Matthew can't be happy if his parents aren't."

Sean leaned back. "Enough preaching. Forgive my intensity, but I must confess that you and Janna are close to my heart. I want to see you have a good life together, and I'm glad you trust me enough to let me help."

Colin shook his head. "We'd never make it without you, Sean. I thank God quite regularly for you and your know-how."

"Well, if I ever need a lawyer, I'll let you return the favor."

"It would be a pleasure." Colin smiled, then the sadness filled him again. "Do you really believe I'll see her again?"

"My opinion?" Sean smiled. "If God led you to her once, he'll help you find her again—when the time is right."

Colin had to admit that gave him some hope. And his bruised spirit was soothed slightly the next day when Robert peered into Colin's office.

"Janna called me with a message for you," he said.

"What?" Colin bolted out of his chair, wondering why she couldn't have called *him*. Or at least his voice mail.

"She said it was long distance and she couldn't hang on. She told me to tell you that they're safe and she loves you."

"That's it?" Colin demanded.

"That's it," Robert said with a sympathetic smile.

While the news contributed to Colin's frustration, he had to admit being grateful for some evidence that they were all right. But he still missed them. And as time dragged on, he realized how many years he'd spent paying for that one night of pleasure with Janna. He fasted and went to the temple more often, praying that he would find her. He made some effort, but quickly found it futile. However, he found some comfort in the thought that if he couldn't find her, Russell probably couldn't either.

He felt a little better when he got a message from Matthew on his voice mail. The boy didn't say much, but his words let Colin know that they were all right and verified what Sean had told him. It was evident from what little Matthew said that Janna needed some time and space.

Through the following weeks, Colin appreciated Sean's friendship as much as his parents' support. They insisted that he remain at home with them for the time being, and he was grateful to not be alone. They all knew that if Janna made contact, it would be to his parents' home; he just hoped it would happen before he lost his mind. He tried to keep busy, and he spent a lot of time contemplating the things Sean had told him. But he was lonely, plain and simple. It seemed he'd spent his entire adult life waiting and wondering about JannaLyn Hayne. And he felt just plain weary.

Seven weeks after Janna's disappearance, the phone rang while Colin was sharing the usual quiet dinner with his parents.

"I'll get it," he said as he stood. "Hello," he answered absently.

"Dad?" Matthew's young voice came through the phone as if he was afraid of being overheard.

"Matthew?" Colin questioned, feeling pulse beats in his ears. His mother stood and hurried toward him anxiously. Carl slid his chair back and observed with a furrowed brow. "Is that you, son? Is something wrong?"

"I just miss you, Dad." Colin could tell he was crying. "And I miss Grandma and Grandpa, too."

"We all miss you, too, buddy. Is your mother all right?"

"She's fine. I think she misses you, too. But she's afraid to come home. She's afraid Russell will find her, and he'll make things bad for you and Grandma and Grandpa, too. I wish Russell would just die so we could come home."

"I know how you feel, Matthew. I miss you so much I can hardly stand it."

"Mom said I could come live with you if I wanted to. But just between you and me, Dad," he said in a perfectly mature tone, "I think she needs me."

"I'm sure she does," Colin said, fighting back his emotion. Silence followed, and he hardly knew what to say. Did he dare ask where to find them? He had to at least try.

"Matthew," Colin began carefully, "do you think it would be all right if you told me where you are, so I can help you and your mom—just in case you need anything? Maybe I could come and visit you, just to make sure everything's okay. What do you think?"

"Okay," Matthew said.

"Where is your mother now?" Colin asked.

"She's in the bathtub. She thinks I'm playing with my *Star Wars* stuff."

"Do you know your address, Matthew?"

"Sure," he answered with confidence. "Mom had me learn it in case I get lost."

"That's great, son. I have a pencil now, and I'm going to write it down."

Matthew repeated the numbers perfectly, but Colin had one big question. "What city are you in, Matthew?"

He said nothing. "I'm not sure, but I know it's far away from where you are. It took us a long time to drive here."

Colin looked to his mother, who was obviously nervous. Uttering a quick, silent prayer, Colin persisted. "Has your mother told you the name of where you're living?"

"I think so, but I can't remember."

"Tell me about the places you've gone. Is there anything you've seen that might help me know where it is?"

"We've been to the library, and the grocery store."

Colin sighed and tried not to feel exasperated.

"There's mountains."

There were dozens of cities along the Wasatch mountains alone. It could be anywhere.

"We went to some places where we saw lots of pictures and things."

"Museums?"

"Yeah, museums."

Colin sighed. That didn't help any.

"Matthew," an idea occurred to him, "do you know your phone number?"

"I only know the first part," he said.

"That's good enough, buddy." Colin felt the hope seep into his voice.

"It's 4-8-9," he said proudly.

Colin wrote it down. That certainly narrowed it down. He'd just have to do some research to find out where that prefix came from. Then he wondered if it was in a different area code. Matthew had said they were very far away. Then something occurred to Colin, like a light coming on in his mind.

"Matthew, tell me what numbers you dialed to call me."

Matthew repeated the number.

"Did you dial a one, or any other numbers before you dialed my phone number?"

"No," he said as if he had no idea what his father was talking about.

Colin pointed to the phone book and Nancy grabbed it. "That's great, buddy. Just hold on a second here."

While Colin was thumbing frantically through the local cities, looking at the prefixes, Matthew said, "Gotta go." There was an immediate click.

"Wait, Matthew . . ." Colin felt distressed when he realized Matthew was gone, then he found himself looking at the Springville phone listings. All the numbers began with 4-8-9.

"I think our prayers have been answered," he said, absently hanging up the phone. Nancy hugged him and Carl leaned back with a sigh.

"What did he say?" Nancy insisted. "Did he sound okay?"

"He sounded fine. He said everything's all right. He's just lonely." Colin heard his voice crack and hugged his mother again.

"Now what do I do?" he asked, sitting down at the table again. "How is she going to react if I just show up at her door?"

"If you walk in there and demand to bring her home, it could be a problem," Carl said. "So, take it slow. Visit your son. Court her."

"*Court* her?"

"Let me explain it to you, son," Carl chuckled. Colin leaned his elbows on the table and tried to ignore the rush of butterflies in his stomach. He couldn't believe it. *He'd found them.* And this time he was going to do it right.

* * * * *

Janna was in the bathroom when she heard a knock at the door. Her heart quickened as it always did when she wondered if Russell had found her. She reminded herself that the door was securely locked, and Matthew had been strictly instructed never to open it, but to always wait for her. She washed her hands and stepped into the front room, wondering what Matthew was laughing about. She'd not heard him laugh like that since . . .

Janna couldn't help but gasp when she saw Colin standing by the door, with Matthew wrapped around his neck. A hundred questions shot through her mind, but she was speechless as their eyes met and the emotion of just seeing him made everything else momentarily insignificant. When she couldn't think what to say to him, she spoke to Matthew, lightly scolding him. "I thought I told you never to open the door without—"

"You told me not to open it unless I was absolutely sure it was someone we could trust, Mom."

Janna couldn't argue with that one. Colin slowly set Matthew down and produced a bouquet of pink roses from behind his back. He squatted down and handed them to Matthew.

"Give these to your mother," he said. Matthew dutifully handed the flowers to Janna. She briefly inhaled their fragrance, then met Colin's eyes again. Colin then pulled something out of his jacket pocket and handed it to Matthew. "Why don't you go try that out, buddy, while I talk to your mom for a few minutes."

"Look, Mom, it's a Millennium Falcon. Thanks, Dad!"

"You're welcome," Colin chuckled, then he nodded toward the hall and Matthew reluctantly slipped away.

Their eyes met again, but Janna still couldn't think where to begin. She became aware of the music she'd left playing—one of the CDs he had given her for Christmas.

"How are you?" Colin asked quietly.

"We're okay," she said. The silence set in again. "Uh . . ." She cleared her throat. "How did you find us?"

"Don't worry," he said, sensing the underlying fear in her question, "Matthew called me. I really don't think Russell will be able to find you."

"We can hope," she said, breathing an audible sigh.

"You won't be angry with Matthew, will you?" he asked. "He told me he was lonely, and . . ."

"Actually," Janna glanced down shyly, then showed a tentative smile, "I have to admit I'm glad to see you."

Colin chuckled with relief, but realized he was still feeling the nerves that had assaulted him as he'd approached her door. He glanced at his surroundings, noting that the tiny apartment was sparsely decorated, but clean and cozy.

"Your hair's grown," he said, thinking the loose brown curls looked nearly as long as they had been in high school. "I like it."

She smiled shyly. "Thank you for the flowers," she said, inhaling their aroma again. "They're beautiful." She glanced at him then turned away. "I think I'll put them in water. Would you lock the door?"

Colin turned the deadbolt and followed her into the kitchen, watching as she carefully arranged the roses in a juice pitcher.

"I hope you're not angry with me for leaving again," she said, knowing she'd never get her heart to slow down until she confronted the obvious questions. "I know it wasn't really fair, but . . . I was scared."

"I'll admit I was pretty upset at first." Colin sat down on a bar stool. He noticed there were no table and chairs. "But I talked it through with Sean. I think he helped me understand."

Janna chuckled tensely. "He seems to understand me better than I do."

"Yeah, I know how you feel," Colin added.

"So, what did Sean say about me?" Janna asked, still arranging roses.

"He said your fear of Russell overruled your other emotions. I can understand that." He paused and asked, "Is that true, Janna?"

She swallowed hard, but didn't look at him. "I suppose that's true," she admitted. "I hate it, but it's true."

"He also said you still loved me, but you needed some space— to find yourself again and know for certain what you wanted."

Janna stopped and placed her hands on the counter as his description seemed to wrap up her feelings so neatly. She felt Colin's breath close to her ear before she consciously realized he had stepped quietly behind her. Her heart quickened and her chest rose with each breath.

"Is it true, Janna?" he asked in a whisper, taking her shoulders into his hands. "Do you still love me?" When she hesitated, he began to ramble in an attempt to ease the silence. "You don't have to answer that now if you don't want to. Either way, I'm not going to force you to go home with me. If it's important for you to build a life of your own here, then I will respect that. All I ask for is the opportunity to spend some time with Matthew. I need him in my life, Janna. And I believe he needs me, too. My parents miss him dreadfully. They miss you, too, but they understand what you're struggling with. I'll give you all the time you need, Janna. Just let me be a father to Matthew, and let me be there for you. Let's start over, and do it right this time."

Janna turned so quickly to face Colin that it startled him. She looked up to meet his eyes, and a single tear rolled down her cheek. "Yes, it's true, Colin," she said.

It took Colin a moment to connect what she'd said to the question he'd asked. He was just about to ask her to clarify it when she lifted her lips to his and pushed her arms around his shoulders.

"I missed you so much," she cried softly and kissed him again. Colin pulled her as close as humanly possible, kissing her as if he might never have the chance again. Then he just held her, relishing her closeness and her apparent need for him. After being without her for so long, he felt as if he'd come home.

Colin stepped back in an attempt to keep his head where it should be, then he impulsively put a hand to her waist and urged her into a slow, simple dance. He closed his eyes to absorb the reality of her presence, wanting this moment to last forever.

"I don't think you could get a Book of Mormon between us," she said.

Colin chuckled and brushed his lips over her brow, tightening his fingers over hers. "I don't think you could get a piece of paper between us. But it's okay. We have a great chaperone in the other room."

Janna met his eyes and smiled. "Oh, I've missed you," he said. He kissed her quickly, then added, "I was wondering if you'd go out with me tomorrow night. Matthew's invited to spend the night at Grandma's house. I'd like to take you to dinner and a play, then I will see you safely home. I'll bring Matthew back Saturday afternoon, and that will give you some time to yourself. Then, if you'd like, I thought the three of us could go on a picnic or something."

Janna smiled. "Well, you seem to have everything planned out nicely."

"I've had a lot of time to think about it," he said a little too seriously.

Janna glanced down briefly. "I'd love to," she said. "It sounds wonderful."

Colin reminded himself not to overdo it. He stepped back and walked out of the kitchen, saying, "I'd better see what Matthew's up to."

Janna set the roses on the T.V. and admired them a moment. She smiled, feeling the warmth of Colin's presence, even from the other room where she could hear him playing with Matthew. While they were busy, she straightened up and looked in the fridge to see if there was anything she could fix for dinner that would be suitable to serve a guest. She had a casserole in the oven and a salad in the fridge before Colin appeared, Matthew hanging onto his back.

"It looks like the two of you are having a good time," Janna commented. She added, more to Colin, "He's been terribly bored and lonely."

"Dad said I get to sleep over at Grandma's tomorrow night, and stay and play on Saturday. Then we're going on a picnic, and you get to come, too, Mom. Isn't that great?"

"Yes, sport, it's great," she agreed.

Colin recalled his self-admonition to not move too quickly or push too hard. Reluctantly he said, "I really should be going. I've already—"

"Oh, don't go!" Matthew whined. "We rented *The Empire Strikes Back,* and we were gonna watch it. Stay and watch it with us, please! Can he, Mom? Can he?"

Janna had to admit she didn't want him to leave, but she didn't want to seem overbearing. "That's up to your father," she said. "Maybe he has other plans or—"

"Oh, I don't have any plans," Colin interjected. "I just didn't want to wear out my welcome."

Janna smiled. "I don't think that's possible." Colin grinned.

The evening went well, and Colin slipped reluctantly away after Matthew fell asleep. "You take care now," he said, kissing Janna good-bye at the door.

"You don't have to tell me to be careful," she admitted. "I'm so paranoid it's pathetic."

"Be careful, not scared, okay?"

"I'll try." She managed a smile. "Thank you, Colin. I'm looking forward to tomorrow."

"Me too," he agreed and slipped away. Janna locked the door and went to bed, feeling warm and happy for the first time since Christmas.

The following morning Janna took Matthew to the mall, where she bought herself a new dress for her date. They had a corn dog for lunch and went home to work on his school lessons. By the time Colin arrived to pick them up, Janna was so consumed with butter-flies that she could hardly bear it.

Matthew answered the door and she came out of the bedroom, putting silver loops into her earlobes.

"Wow," Colin said when he saw her. She felt his eyes drinking her in, provoking a whole new bout of butterflies.

"Wow what?" she asked, picking up her purse as Matthew dragged his overnight bag and pillow out the door.

Colin chuckled. "Just looking at you makes my heart beat faster. That's what." He gave her an endearing crooked smile. "Or maybe I shouldn't admit such things on a first date."

"First date?" she echoed with a laugh. "Our son is waiting for us."

Colin stepped toward Janna and lifted her chin with his fingers. Slowly, tentatively, he kissed her, whispering close to her face, "Let him wait."

He kissed her again, and Janna groaned from the intensity of the fluttering in her stomach.

"Is something wrong?" he asked, still holding her chin.

"Butterflies," she said shyly. "I seem to have an epidemic."

Colin smiled and ushered her out to the car. In the fifteen minutes it took to get to his parents' home, he listened as Matthew talked nonstop, mostly telling his father about their excursion to the mall earlier, as if it had been a high adventure.

"You went to the mall, I take it," he said to Janna during a rare quiet moment while Matthew was looking out the window.

"Whatever gave you that idea?" she asked, and he laughed.

"How did you get there?" he asked.

"I have a car."

Colin nodded. "That's good." He reached over and briefly rubbed the fabric of her skirt between his thumb and fingers. "Did you get *this* at the mall?"

She smiled and he took her hand. "Your mother told me that a new dress can give a woman that extra boost of confidence."

"Do you need that with *me?*" he asked lightly.

She smiled again. "I need all the help I can get."

"It *is* a nice dress," he said, "but all you have to do is be yourself, Janna, and I can't help but love you."

Matthew started talking again and they exchanged a warm glance. When they arrived at the Trevors' home, Nancy rushed out laughing and pulled Matthew into her arms. "Oh, Grandma missed you!" she exclaimed. "And I think you've gotten a little bigger."

"I missed you too, Grandma," he said, then ran to Carl, who had just come out the door.

"Janna," Nancy said as Colin helped her out of the car. "You can't imagine how I've missed you." She hugged Janna tightly, then pulled back with tears in her eyes. "This house just isn't the same without you."

Janna smiled and glanced down. "I've missed you, too," she said, then looked around quickly as if she was suddenly nervous.

Carl had a turn hugging Janna, then Colin took her hand. "This is all very quaint," he said, "but we have dinner reservations. It would seem that Matthew's not likely to notice we're gone for a while." He'd already disappeared into the house.

"Have a good time," Nancy called and waved as they backed out of the driveway.

"Do my parents make you nervous?" he asked after they'd traveled a few minutes in tense silence.

"Oh, no," she insisted, "of course not."

"Then what's the deal?"

"What do you mean?"

"You were nervous back there." He looked over at her. "You still look nervous."

Janna felt a little unnerved at his reading her so easily. But she reminded herself that Sean had taught them to be open and honest, even with things that might seem insignificant. She cleared her throat carefully and admitted, "Well, Russell knew I was staying there, and . . ."

"What?" he questioned. "You think he'd be staking out my parents' home with the hope that you'd show up this much later?"

Janna forced back her impulse to get defensive. "I don't know what he would do, Colin. But he tracked me down once, and I'm scared—plain and simple."

Colin wanted to remind her that the Lord had promised her in a blessing she would be protected if she didn't let fear rule her choices. But something told him it would only increase the tension between them. He tried to think how Sean would tell him to handle this.

"Okay," he finally said, "I can see that it would be difficult to not be afraid. But we're being careful. Let's try to put it in the Lord's hands, all right?"

She said nothing until they pulled into the parking lot of one of the finest restaurants in the valley.

"Colin," she said, "this place is expensive."

He smiled and unfastened his seat belt. "I'm an attorney."

"So business is going well, then?" she asked as they walked inside.

"Actually, yes, all things considered. Although," he added facetiously, "most rookie lawyers don't have the luxury of living with their parents. The rent's cheap."

"They love having you there," she said.

"So they tell me."

After they had ordered, Colin took Janna's hand across the table and resisted the urge to propose. Instead, he asked her questions about the things she and Matthew had been doing, and he talked a little about his work and what was going on with his family.

"There's something I want to ask you," she said as they drove to a community theater in Orem.

"Okay, I'm listening."

"I've been thinking about taking some classes, probably two or three evenings a week."

"That's great," he said eagerly.

"I was wondering if you would be willing to take Matthew while I go. I could bring him over and—"

"I'll do anything I can to help," he insisted. "It would be a pleasure to have Matthew."

"Thank you," she said, wondering why she felt somehow guilty for getting something she wanted so easily. Russell's probable interrogation over such a request stormed through her mind until she forced it away, turning her mind to the present. For the moment, everything was perfect.

CHAPTER FOURTEEN

*J*anna thoroughly enjoyed the play, and it was difficult to tell Colin good night. She slept in the following morning then took a long bath, enjoying a brief reprieve from having a seven-year-old as her constant companion. By the time Colin and Matthew came to pick her up, she felt rejuvenated and happy to see them.

"I like your Saturday attire," she said as he opened the car door for her.

"My *Saturday attire?*" he laughed.

"Oh, yes. You look marvelous in your *working* clothes. I especially like you in suspenders." She smiled mischievously. "But I love the way you look in jeans, Mr. Trevor." She touched his face. "And the way you don't shave on Saturdays."

Colin's mouth went dry as he admitted, "You're making my heart do that . . . racing thing."

"Good," she said, "then we're even."

Colin forced himself to keep his mind on the moment. He put the top down on the car, and Matthew laughed at the wind in his hair as they drove. Seeing Janna close her eyes and lift her face to the wind, he thought she'd never looked more beautiful.

Their afternoon together was filled with fun and laughter. It was a little windy for a picnic, but they managed anyway. Then they bought a kite and went back to the park to take advantage of the weather. Afternoon merged into evening, and they stopped on the way home to rent a movie and buy a pizza for dinner. Somewhere in the middle of *Return of the Jedi*, Janna laid her head on Colin's shoulder. While Matthew was enthralled with Luke Skywalker and

Darth Vader battling it out, Colin eased Janna closer and pressed his mouth over hers. He kissed her over and over, relishing her response.

Colin finally forced some distance between them, whispering lightly, "Why don't you slap me when I do that?"

Janna only smiled. When he couldn't keep himself from staring at her, he purposely slid all the way to the other end of the couch and she laughed softly. He felt some peace in the evidence of her healing. She seemed more like the Janna he'd fallen in love with than she ever had before the divorce. He couldn't deny being grateful for the time she'd had to "find herself," as Sean would say. It was obviously working.

Wanting desperately to touch her, but fearing his own desires, he reached over and tickled her for a second instead.

"Stop that!" she laughed and slapped his hand.

He looked at her with exaggerated innocence, and she laughed again. She pretended to be enthralled in the movie until he tickled her again. "What are you doing?" she demanded with a little squeal.

"I was just seeing if it still works." At her baffled expression he added, "I used to be pretty good at tickling you. Remember?"

"Oh, I remember all right," she chuckled and held up a finger in warning. "But I'm too old for that now."

"Never," he growled and eased a little closer.

"Colin," she drawled, then couldn't help laughing.

In one agile movement, Colin pulled her into his arms, tickling her ribs mercilessly, then her knees, then her ribs again. Matthew paused the movie and told them to be quiet, but he seemed to be enjoying their entertainment while Janna laughed and wiggled and hit Colin, trying to get him to stop.

"Okay, enough," she said breathlessly, but he started all over. "Stop it!" she demanded, then without warning her laughter turned instantly to a shriek of protest, hysterical with fear. Colin drew back as if he'd been slapped. At the same moment, he heard Matthew scurry away and close his bedroom door.

"What?" he asked while Janna stared at him as if he was some kind of rabid animal.

Janna tried frantically to think of a way to explain what had just happened. In trying to make sense of it, a combination of fear and embarrassment made her just want to disappear. She turned away and shook her head, covering her mouth as if she might scream again. She got up to leave, but Colin stopped her with a firm hand on her arm.

"If you're upset, fine. But don't walk out on me. Help me understand this, Janna."

She nodded glumly and sat down.

"I'm not going to hurt you, Janna," he said gently. "Do you believe me?"

She nodded again, but a whimper pressed through her lips. He realized she was breathing hard and fast. "Take a deep breath, Janna," he said, looking into her eyes. "Just slow it down. Come on."

She did as he asked, wrapping her arms around her middle and closing her eyes while she tried to think clearly.

"Now," he said, "what happened?"

"I . . . I don't know. It just . . . scared me."

Colin leaned back and sighed. It was evident they had a long way to go.

"Do you want to talk to Sean about it?"

Janna's brow furrowed. "Not really, but maybe we should."

"Is it all right if I make an appointment . . . for Monday, if he's available?"

Janna nodded.

"Why did Matthew leave like that?" he asked.

Janna bit her trembling lip, then answered without looking at him. "I taught him to do that when . . . when Russell was hurting me."

Colin rubbed a hand over his face, feeling a little sick. "Does he think . . . ?" He couldn't finish.

"I don't know," she said.

Colin took a deep breath and went to Matthew's bedroom. He knocked lightly on the door but got no response. He slowly pushed it open, and the sickness rose from his stomach into his throat. Matthew was sitting on the floor by his bed, his eyes squeezed shut, his hands over his ears, rocking slowly back and forth. Tears streamed down his face.

Colin knelt beside him and gently touched his shoulder. Matthew's eyes flew open in fear. Colin pulled the boy's hands away from his ears and said firmly, "I didn't hurt your mother, Matthew.

She just got scared for a minute. I would *never* hurt her, or you. Do you understand?"

Matthew nodded stoutly.

"Then why are you still crying?"

"I got scared, too," he said.

Colin pulled the child into his arms, grateful that he didn't resist. "I didn't mean to scare you, buddy. I'm so sorry."

A few minutes later Janna appeared, looking calm and happy. She soothed things over quickly with Matthew, assuring him that Colin had not hurt her. But her behavior reminded Colin a little of the way she'd pretended to be happy to see Russell when he came through the door from work. It was evident that she'd been well trained in putting up a perfect front.

Janna assured him everything was fine before he left, but the episode consumed his mind right up to the minute they walked into Sean's office.

"It's good to see the two of you together again," Sean said, lifting a brow quickly toward Colin as if to say, "I told you so."

"What's up?" Sean added.

Colin explained, from his perspective, what had happened Saturday evening. Janna stared at the floor, saying nothing. Sean asked them both a lot of questions, then sat thoughtfully for a few moments.

"Janna," he said, "I want to explain something to Colin. If I say anything that you don't agree with, speak up. All right?"

Janna nodded, but that frightened look rose into her eyes.

"Colin," Sean leaned his forearms on his thighs and looked directly at him, "I am getting the impression here that the solution is rather simple, but for complicated reasons. Janna simply needs to know that you respect her boundaries implicitly."

"I assume you're going to tell me the complicated reasons."

"I think it might help you understand."

"Well, I want to understand," Colin said, trying not to feel frustrated.

"Let's start with Janna's father. When he . . ." Sean stopped when Janna got up and walked out of the room, closing the door rather loudly.

"I think she's trying to tell us she's not comfortable with this," Sean said, looking concerned.

"It would seem that way."

Sean leaned back and sighed loudly. He then went into a detailed explanation of the helplessness Janna must have felt when her father abused her, using not only threats and manipulation, but his physical strength, to force her to act against her will. Then he focused on the hurt inflicted upon Janna by Russell's physical dominance.

Colin pressed his head into his hands and listened with growing revulsion. "And the point is?" he asked without looking up when Sean was apparently finished.

"Forgive the dramatics, Colin," he said. "But you need to understand the impact of what happened in that moment when Janna suddenly became powerless, for one reason only: You are bigger and stronger than she is."

"But I would *not* hurt her!" Colin insisted.

"*I* know that, and *you* know that. And deep inside, I think Janna knows that. But the bottom line is simple: When she says enough, when she says stop, that's what she *means*—and you'd better listen. She's been taught that a man's physical strength puts her in danger. You need to teach her that *your* physical strength will never be used to violate her boundaries. Every human being has the right to those boundaries. If you're tickling a child and they ask you to stop, you should stop. This tells the child, 'You have the right to declare what happens to your body, and I, as an adult, respect that right.' Am I making any sense?"

Colin leaned back and blew out a long breath. "Yes, I understand."

Sean changed the subject by asking how things were going otherwise, and Colin reported the positive things that had occurred in the last few days. He left the office feeling hopeful, but with his eyes opened to the enormity of the challenges ahead.

That hope carried Colin through the next several weeks. Janna started some classes at Utah Valley State College, and Matthew spent an increasing amount of time at his grandparents' home. Colin and Janna dated regularly, and he was careful to keep his distance, for a number of reasons. He did his best to let her know of his desires without invading her space or allowing those desires to get out of hand. And he was always careful to be certain he wasn't being followed when he went anywhere near Janna's apartment.

Matthew invited Colin to go to church with them, and Janna didn't seem to mind. It was then that Colin realized she was using an assumed name. He noticed later that her utility bills were also addressed to "Jane Carlson." While it was easy to forget about Russell and pretend he didn't exist, he had to admit that Janna's fears were justified, and he was glad to see her taking precautions. There was no comprehending what might happen if Russell *did* find her. It made him all the more anxious for them to have a life together, so he could be there for her and Matthew and help keep them safe.

Gradually Janna became more like herself, and with Sean's occasional input, Colin began to learn more about what she had been through. Perhaps equally important, he felt himself coming to terms with the way all of this had affected *him*. He found that he had healed enough to forgive Janna for abandoning him before his mission, and he was ready to put the past behind them. He told her so one Wednesday evening after they'd gone to a movie and Matthew had stayed at Grandma's. He explained how the feelings of betrayal still crept in occasionally, but they talked it out and he felt considerably better when they vowed to always be completely honest, no matter how difficult. He told her with emotion that it was forgiven, and he asked her forgiveness for the difficulties he had caused in her life because of *his* bad choices. She cried and clung to him, and Colin decided it was time to move forward.

The following evening, Colin brought Matthew home after work.

"Hey, Mom," Matthew announced when he walked in, "I've got something I have to ask you."

"Okay," she said, smiling when Colin winked at her as he walked in and closed the door.

"You have to sit down," Matthew said, urging his mother to the couch.

"All right. I'm sitting." She looked up at Colin's conspiratorial grin, wondering what they were up to.

"Okay, Dad," Matthew held out his hand, "let's have it."

Janna laughed at her son's adult behavior. Colin pulled something out of his jacket pocket and gave it to Matthew. He placed his hands casually on his hips and nodded an apparent go-ahead to the child.

Janna was momentarily preoccupied with the reality that Colin Trevor was truly a handsome man. She came back to the moment when Matthew cleared his throat elaborately, as if he was about to give some grand performance.

"Are you ready, Mom?"

"I'm ready," she said.

Matthew histrionically went down on one knee and held out a little box toward her, saying with a deep voice, "Mom, Dad wants to know if you'll marry him."

Janna took a sharp breath as Matthew opened the box and held it closer to her face. "See, it's a ring," he said.

"I can see that." Janna took the little box and lifted her eyes to meet Colin's. His unmasked vulnerability was so touching she could hardly speak.

"Try it on, Mom," Matthew insisted. "Try it on."

Colin hated the pounding of his heart as he watched Janna ease Matthew close to her and whisper something in his ear. He could almost imagine her trying to explain that he needed to go in the other room and let them talk—that she still wasn't ready. He wondered if he could take more waiting, while everything inside of him was aching to just have her in his life completely, to care for her and protect her.

Colin was startled from his thoughts when Matthew tugged on his arm. "I need to tell you a secret," he said. Colin squatted down and held his breath while Matthew moved close to his ear. "She says you should stop being a big wimp and you should be ashamed of yourself for forcing a child to do your dirty work."

Colin looked at Matthew in surprise, then at Janna, who was completely unreadable. He took a deep breath and stood up straight. "Okay, fine," he said and crossed the room. He went down on one knee, took her hand into his, and looked directly at her. "JannaLyn, will you marry me?"

She said nothing, didn't even move.

"Hey," he said, "I know we've been through some tough times, and I know there's healing left to do, but we can do it together, Janna. Let me be there for you, always, and—"

Janna pressed her fingers over his lips. "Stop talking and kiss me."

Colin did as she asked, surprised and confused. She reached her hands around his neck and eased off the couch, kneeling to face him.

"Does this mean yes?" he asked, pulling back briefly.

Janna smiled. Then she laughed. "Yes, it means yes."

Colin's relief was so immense he nearly collapsed. He was vaguely aware of Matthew jumping up and down with excitement as he slipped the ring on Janna's finger, then he kissed her again.

"You know," Colin said, moving to the couch and urging Janna onto his lap, "my whole family is coming for Memorial Day."

"Yes, I know. That's this weekend, isn't it?"

"It is," Colin said. "Saturday evening we're having a big barbecue thing, and if it's all right with you, I'd like to announce our plans when we're all together."

"That's fine with me," she said, "but I'm not sure I can remember all their names. Some of them I haven't even met."

"I'm not sure I can remember them all myself," he chuckled.

Colin called Matthew over and told him to calm down. The three of them decided on a tentative date in July, when they would all be sealed together in the Mt. Timpanogos Temple. Janna said she would make an appointment with her bishop to start the process of getting her sealing to Russell canceled. Even though she was attending church under an assumed name, she'd candidly told her bishop about the situation, and he had given her a great deal of help and understanding.

It was difficult for Colin to leave Janna and Matthew that evening, but he decided he'd never been so happy in his life. The future wasn't some obscure glimmer on the horizon anymore. It was only a matter of weeks before they would be the family they should have been eight years ago.

* * * * *

Karen came by Friday afternoon, and Janna felt bubbly with excitement as she repeated the way Colin—and Matthew—had proposed to her. They had a nice visit, then Karen offered to take Matthew with her, since he was planning to spend the night at

Cathy's anyway. She was just leaving when Colin arrived. He talked to Matthew out by the car for a minute, then came up the stairs.

"Hello, gorgeous," he said, giving Janna a quick kiss.

"Hello," she smiled as he turned to meet Karen's curious expression.

"I've told you about Karen," Janna said and Colin grinned.

"Of course, Karen. It's a pleasure to meet you at last."

"And you must be the infamous Colin Trevor."

"Infamous?" Colin repeated, giving Janna a sidelong glance.

She shrugged her shoulders innocently. "Karen's giving Matthew a ride to Cathy's."

"Oh, that's nice," Colin said. "If you'll excuse me, I'm going to the men's room."

He slipped into the bathroom, and Karen shook her head in apparent disbelief. "Mercy, but he's adorable. I'd say he's even a tough match for Kevin Costner."

"Oh," Janna smiled, "he's much better than Costner."

"How do you figure?"

"Colin's a Mormon."

"Good point," Karen said.

When Colin came out of the bathroom, Karen and Matthew were gone. He took Janna's hand and urged the ring close to his face.

"It really is true," he said. "You're actually engaged to the *infamous* Colin Trevor. I was wondering if I'd dreamed it."

"Oh, it's true all right," she said, pushing her arms around his neck. He lifted her right off the floor and she laughed. "And it's high time. I wonder if there's ever been a shotgun wedding like this one before."

Colin twirled her around and laughed, landing on the couch with Janna on his lap. "I don't think they let those shotguns into the temple, white or not."

Colin kissed her, wondering if life could possibly get any better, then he declared, "I think we'd be wise to go somewhere, Mrs. Trevor-almost."

"Why is that?"

"Because Matthew isn't here to chaperone, and . . . well, you know."

They went out for an early dinner and a movie. Then they drove through American Fork and up around the Mt. Timpanogos

Temple. Walking hand in hand around the perimeter of the building, Janna told Colin how she had visited with her bishop last night about the sealing cancellation. She needed to write a letter explaining her situation to the First Presidency of the Church. She expressed her feelings about it being difficult, but she'd already begun to work on it, and felt that it would be a big step in her healing.

Following a lull of silence, she added softly, "I can't wait, Colin. Maybe when we're married, I'll stop wishing that I hadn't been such a fool."

"You can stop now. That's all in the past."

"I know, but—"

"Stop talking and kiss me," he said, turning to face her.

"How about June?" she asked.

"What?"

"I don't want to wait until July. Let's make it June."

"You'll have to ask Matthew," Colin said. "If it were up to me, well . . ." He grinned. "They have a temple in Las Vegas, don't they?"

Janna laughed and hugged him tight. If not for this wretched fear of Russell Clark, her life would be almost perfect.

* * * * *

Colin called Janna the following morning and told her Cathy had some things she needed to do, and had asked if Colin would bring Matthew home. "Or do you want me to just keep him, and—"

"No," Janna interrupted. "We have to get some books back to the library, and I promised he could go with me. Do you want to come with us?"

"I'd love to," Colin laughed. "But I promised Mother I'd help her get some things cleaned up before the grand gathering begins. It's how I pay my rent."

"And when is this grand gathering?" she asked lightly.

"Oh, they should start arriving in the next few hours."

"And how many did you say are coming?"

"With Matthew, there are thirty-seven grandchildren—and their parents will be here, too, of course. I'll bring Matthew home, then I'll be back to get you around five for the barbecue."

"I'm looking forward to it . . . I think," she laughed.

"Don't worry," Colin insisted, "they'll love you."

"Even though I left with your son and—"

"Janna, it's in the past. It's between you and me. Whatever they want to think is up to them, but actually, from what Mother has said, they're getting used to the fact that their brother was a scoundrel in his youth."

Janna reminded herself to keep the past in the past. "Maybe you still are," she said lightly. "Didn't you say something last night about Las Vegas?"

Colin only stayed a minute when he brought Matthew back, but it was long enough to get a good kiss and calm Janna's nerves a little about meeting his family.

Shortly after Colin left, Janna called to Matthew, "Come along." She picked up her purse and the books that needed to be returned. "We need to hurry so we can get everything done before your dad comes back to get us."

Janna checked her face in the mirror and picked up the keys just as Matthew opened the door. She heard him scream and turned around. She had feared this moment for so long that it almost didn't seem real.

"Hello, my love." Russell's voice triggered the reality as he stepped through the door and calmly closed it behind him. "I've been meaning to have a little talk with you."

Janna dropped her purse and books and took a step backward. Hearing the bedroom door close, she knew that Matthew was safe for the moment. She finally found the voice to speak. "How did you find me?"

Russell laughed as if it was all just a silly game. "It wasn't easy, I'll grant you that. But you underestimate me, my love. As does your friend Karen. There was just something about the way she looked at me when we passed each other at church. At first I assumed it was just because she had believed all those lies you were telling about me. Then I realized it was more. It became apparent to me that she knew where you were. It didn't take long for a private investigator to track her visits here. Of course, he was discreet."

Janna tried to convince herself that he wasn't necessarily going to hurt her. Maybe he really did just want to talk to her. She felt briefly angry with him for putting her through the hell of having to live this way. But her anger was quickly squelched by that inevitable, wretched fear. She saw the rage come into his eyes—that horrible evil look she knew so well. Her heart began to beat so hard she feared that it alone would kill her.

Please, God, she prayed in her mind, *don't let him hurt Matthew.* She was contemplating a scream that might draw the neighbors' attention when the first blow came. Janna had forgotten how much it could hurt as she slumped to the floor. She tried to scramble to her feet, tried to get a sound out of her mouth, anything to get some help, to get out of here before he killed her. But in her heart she knew she'd lost the moment he'd walked through the door. Her only peace before she lost consciousness was in knowing that Colin would be coming for Matthew. He would see that her son was cared for. Nothing else mattered now. It was over.

CHAPTER FIFTEEN

*N*ancy answered the phone while Colin was dusting some cobwebs she couldn't reach.

"Is my dad there?" Matthew asked in a panicked voice.

"Just a minute," she said, pushing the phone abruptly toward Colin. "It's Matthew. He sounds hysterical."

"What?" Colin asked, fearing the worst.

"He found us, Dad," Matthew sobbed in a whisper. "He's hurting her, Dad. He's . . ." Matthew's words became undiscernible through the tears.

"Matthew," Colin tried to sound calm while everything inside him turned to knots, "I'm going to call the police, and then I'm coming to get you. Don't—"

"I already did!" Matthew managed. "I called 911. Just like Grandma taught me. I did. I did."

"Okay, I'm coming. I'm coming!"

Colin pressed the phone into Nancy's trembling hand. "Keep him on the line," he ordered and ran for the door. He ignored the speed limits and cried and prayed aloud. Two blocks from Janna's apartment, he passed an ambulance at full throttle, sirens blaring. His heart sank a little further. Was that her? Was it really that bad? There were two police cars in front of the apartment. The door was open. Colin hurried inside to see Matthew crying in the arms of an officer. Matthew looked up and hurled himself into Colin's arms, sobbing hysterically.

"You must be his father," the officer said kindly.

"Yes," Colin managed to say over Matthew's crying. He was relieved when the officer began a report, since he didn't know how to ask.

"Matthew was a very brave little boy. We got his call and hurried over. He was under the bed talking to . . . I believe it was your mother, on the phone."

Colin nodded. He wanted to ask about Janna, but Matthew was so upset it was difficult to hear what the officer said. He was relieved when the officer attempted to distract Matthew with some words of comfort.

"Hey, big guy," the officer put his hat on Matthew's head. Matthew clung to Colin but turned reluctantly and reduced his cries to an occasional whimper. "Your mother is on her way to the hospital in a very fast ambulance. And they're going to take good care of her. They have a lot of very smart doctors and nurses there who will know what to do for her. You've been very brave today, and if you promise to stay brave and take good care of your dad while your mom is in the hospital, then I have a surprise for you."

Matthew nodded firmly, and another officer passed over a stuffed teddy bear. Matthew took the bear and hugged it tightly. "You can keep that," the officer said. "And when you get a chance, you come down to the police station and visit. I'd like to introduce you to my friends there."

Matthew nodded again.

"Would you like to go with me for a minute and see my police car while my friend talks to your dad?"

Matthew looked at Colin, as if for permission. "You go ahead. I'll be right out and take you to Grandma's house."

With Matthew and his teddy bear outside, the officer kindly explained that with Matthew's accurate description of what was taking place, they were able to enter the apartment, where they caught Russell red-handed. He was arrested, and the paramedics immediately got Janna on her way to the hospital. But he had no idea how bad off she was, only that she'd been unconscious.

Colin thanked him, then added, "And thanks for the teddy bear. It did the trick."

"We keep a few in the trunk. They were donated by a local Relief Society to help traumatized kids in situations like this."

Colin nodded and tried not to get choked up. When the officers finished their report and left Colin and Matthew alone, Colin helped Matthew pack enough of his things to stay at least a few days. He kept talking to Matthew in a serene tone, hoping to keep him calm. While Colin's mind was in a panic, wondering about Janna, he reminded himself that he had to think of Matthew right now. She was in good hands, and even if he was at the hospital, they probably wouldn't let him see her at this point.

He called his mother and gave her a quick report, then he checked the lights and windows and headed for the door. Matthew was already outside with his suitcase when Colin noticed the books scattered on the floor, and Janna's purse among them. He stooped to pick them up, knowing she'd been on her way to the library. Then he noticed the blood. A quick appraisal told him there were several significant spots on the carpet. Attempting to subdue a sudden wave of nausea, Colin stood up, reminding himself that Matthew was waiting. Then he saw the blood splattered on the wall.

"Oh, dear God," he murmured, and had to sit down for a minute to keep his head from spinning.

"Are you comin', Dad?" Matthew called from the door.

Colin quickly gathered up the books and the keys, not wanting to draw Matthew's attention to this grisly mess before it was cleaned up. He locked the door and hurried Matthew out to the car.

During the short drive, Colin got Matthew to repeat what had happened. He managed to do it without getting terribly upset. Then he said, "I don't want to go to Grandma's. I want to be with Mom at the hospital."

"I know you do, buddy. But I'm afraid there are certain parts of the hospital where they won't let children in. I know it's hard for you, but I need you to keep Grandma and Grandpa company while I stay with your mother. They're very worried, and they need you there to remind them that everything is going to be all right. I need you to be brave, okay?"

"If I'm brave, does that mean I can't cry?" he asked with a shaky voice.

Colin bit his trembling lip and swallowed the lump in his throat before answering, but he still had a crack in his voice. "No, buddy, sometimes being brave means knowing it's okay to cry when you're hurt or scared."

"Are you scared?"

"Yes, Matthew, I'm scared."

"Is she going to die?" Matthew asked.

Colin didn't know how to answer. He had no idea how bad it was. "I don't know, Matthew," he answered, deciding honesty was the only option. "But I promise I'll tell you everything the doctors tell me, okay?"

Matthew nodded. "I'm going to say a prayer when I get to Grandma's house, and ask Heavenly Father to help Mom get better."

"That's an excellent idea," Colin said. "Every time you feel scared, you talk to Heavenly Father about it, and I'll do the same. Okay?"

Matthew nodded, seeming to feel a little better.

Nancy came out of the house to meet them as they pulled into the driveway. She helped Matthew out of the car and hugged him tightly. Then she took the suitcase from Colin and motioned him back into the car.

"You hurry down there and be with her. We'll take care of Matthew." Tears brimmed in her eyes. "Tell her we love her. We'll be praying."

Colin nodded and got back in the car. Now that he was alone, he couldn't hold the tears back as he drove the short distance to Utah Valley Regional Medical Center. He couldn't believe it. He just couldn't believe it. He wondered now if he'd tried to convince himself all this time that Janna's fear was blown out of proportion. He wondered if he should have been more careful, more empathetic.

Pulling into the emergency parking area, Colin wiped the tears dry and hurried inside. He inquired but was told nothing except that she was still in the emergency room, and the doctors were with her.

Doctors? his mind echoed as he paced the waiting area. Was it so bad that they needed more than one? At least she was alive, he thought. Only a few minutes later, his name was called. A doctor ushered him into a small, private room and urged him to sit down.

"Are you her husband, then?" he was asked.

"Almost," Colin said. "I'm the only family she's got beyond her son. He's with my parents now."

The doctor nodded. "Right now, our biggest concern is internal bleeding. We've been unable to get it under control. I'll be honest with you . . . it's serious."

Colin put a hand over his mouth and willed himself not to be sick as he imagined what Russell might have done to cause severe internal bleeding.

"They're prepping her for surgery right now, and I can give you a better idea of what to expect when she comes out."

Colin nodded. There were so many questions he wanted to ask, but knew this wasn't the time.

"She should be on her way to surgery any minute. You can wait there, and I'll have you notified of any significant change."

"Thank you." Colin stood when the doctor did and walked toward the long hall that led to the surgery waiting area. He was grateful to be familiar with the huge hospital. He'd been here many times, waiting for friends and family through a number of incidents—mostly stitches and broken bones. As he turned the corner into the hall, he saw a medical team and a gurney roll out of the emergency room. They were all but running, with the doctor he'd just talked to following close behind. It took every ounce of self-control to not run and catch up.

Colin called his mother and told her what he knew. He spoke to Matthew and explained that they were going to operate to try and fix some things that were bleeding inside. The boy seemed to understand and accept it. Nancy got back on the phone and told Colin that Matthew had cried some, but he was holding up pretty well. The family had begun to arrive, and she felt sure that Matthew would be distracted by some new cousins to play with.

Colin sat down uneasily on one of the many couches and looked at the ceiling. This was a weekend he'd been looking forward to. He was excited about being with family members he hadn't seen for a long time, and having Janna be a part of it. The whole family was now aware that Matthew was his son. Some had expressed varying degrees of disappointment over the discovery, but it had eventually smoothed over, and Colin had been looking forward to announcing that he and Janna would soon be married in the temple.

The thought made Colin groan and press his head into his hands. What would he do if he lost her now? After all they'd been through, could he possibly bear it? Did he have a choice? He tried to comprehend what might have happened if Matthew hadn't gone home to go to the library with Janna. Would she be dead by now if not for Matthew's call? The thought was chilling.

As the time dragged by, Colin turned his mind to prayer. He tried to tell the Lord that he would accept his will, but at the same moment he couldn't help begging for her life to be spared.

Colin called his mother again a little after ten. She reported that Matthew was sound asleep. She put his sister on the phone, and it lifted his spirits a little to hear Colette's words of encouragement. They had once been very close, but he couldn't remember the last time they'd talked.

When the doctor finally appeared a little before eleven, he looked exhausted and concerned. Colin stood to meet him. He could almost imagine him giving the news that she had not made it through. He sat down and urged Colin to do the same.

Colin's head swam while he received a detailed report of injuries and repairs that all muddled together. The only thing that stuck with clarity was the fact that she was stable now, and would be taken to the Intensive Care Unit as soon as she was out of recovery.

Colin got to ICU before Janna did. A kind nurse told him which room she would be coming to and offered him a comfortable place to wait and something to drink. She told him that after Janna was settled in the room she would come and get him, and he was welcome to stay with her. She warned him that Janna would have a respirator in her mouth, and she probably wouldn't look very good. When she left him alone, Colin turned his mind back to prayer, trying to prepare himself for this. He recalled Sean telling him that he needed to be committed to Janna, no matter what the future might bring. The way his heart was breaking, he knew there was no question about his love and commitment to her. He felt as if he would die without her.

The waiting seemed endless. It was well past one in the morning before they came to get him, but he didn't feel the least bit sleepy. As prepared as he'd tried to be, he couldn't help feeling shocked to see her. Both eyes were blackened, and her face was discolored and swollen, just as it had been when he'd first helped her get away from Russell. There were a few stitches across her right cheek-bone, and her nose was heavily bandaged, with tubes coming from beneath the dressings.

"Any questions?" The nurse who was checking her vitals asked, as if she sensed his distress.

"I don't know where to start," he admitted, trying not to sound emotional.

"Well, I don't know what they've told you already, but the discoloring of her eyes is partly because her nose was broken."

Colin briefly closed his eyes.

"They did some work on it while she was under the anesthetic." The nurse went on to explain a little about her internal injuries, including broken ribs and a punctured lung.

She pointed out a recliner near the bed and invited him to use it and make himself comfortable. "Generally our visiting times are very limited," she informed him. "But as long as she's stable and you don't get in the way, you're welcome to stay. It wouldn't hurt to hold her hand and talk to her. It's been known to help pull people through."

Colin nodded, feeling a little helpless as she left him alone, assuring him she was close by. He moved the recliner a little closer to the bed and sat on its edge. Carefully taking her hand into his, Colin tried to put his mind into a positive frame. But all he could think of was Russell Clark and what he'd done to her. He began to seethe with so much anger that he had to force himself to put it out of his mind completely. He reminded himself that Russell was behind bars now. It would be a good, long time before the man ever saw the light of day again.

The important thing now was getting Janna well. Gently rubbing her fingers between his, he talked to her as if she could hear him, telling her of the life of freedom she had ahead of her now, and all they would do together. He fingered her engagement ring and talked to her about the children they would have and the joy they would share. He cried as he talked, and he wondered if the nurse's suggestion was as much for his sake as it was for Janna's. Surely these people were used to dealing with life-and-death situations, and soothing concerned relatives.

After Janna was checked twice more, Colin fell asleep in the recliner, not waking until after five, when a different nurse came in to do a more thorough examination of Janna and everything that was attached to her. She kindly asked him to leave for a few minutes, and he took the opportunity to call his mother.

"Sorry to wake you," he said.

"I've hardly slept a wink," she admitted. "I'm glad you called. Tell me."

"She's in ICU. She's stable, but it's not good." He tried to repeat as much about her injuries as he could remember. His mother told him that following the barbecue last night, the family had begun a fast, and they would break it together this evening.

"Thank you," Colin said, feeling an immense gratitude for the family he'd been blessed with. Perhaps if Janna had had the same opportunities, she wouldn't be where she was now.

Colin returned to Janna's bedside, where nothing had changed. He counted seventeen things that were either attached to her or coming out of her body—IVs, monitors, drainage tubes, and who knew what else.

Mid-afternoon, Colin looked up to see his parents enter the room. He wondered if he'd ever been so glad to see them in his whole life. Nancy gave him a quick hug, then her attention turned to Janna as Carl put a warm hand on Colin's shoulder.

"Oh, my sweet Janna," Nancy cried, moving unsteadily to the chair near the bed. She held Janna's hand, and the tears rolled down her face. Colin couldn't hold his own tears back, and he was grateful for his father's firm embrace and willing shoulder.

When the emotion settled somewhat, Carl helped Colin give her a priesthood blessing. He was grateful this time for his father's willingness to be the mouthpiece, and he cried all over again as Carl uttered a promise that Janna would survive and eventually heal in body and spirit. And that she would live to raise a family and find much joy in her life.

When the blessing was finished, Nancy put her arms around Colin and said, "There's someone here to see you. Will you come out to the waiting room for a few minutes?"

"Matthew?" he asked.

Nancy shook her head. "We thought it best that he stay away altogether for the time being. He's doing relatively well."

Nancy took his hand and led him down the hall and around the corner. The ICU waiting room was warm and comfortable, and Colin suspected that many families had gathered here in all degrees of concern. But he wasn't prepared to come around the corner and see all seven of his siblings sitting together. Some of them he'd not seen since his younger brother had married nearly three years ago. He wondered if any grown man had ever cried so much as they rose and huddled around him, each in turn embracing him with silent understanding and support. When the greetings were finished, Colin wiped his face and managed some semblance of a chuckle. "I can't believe it," he said. "I'm not sure I even remember all your names."

They all laughed while Carl and Nancy exchanged a quick embrace and a warm glance.

"It's that 'C' thing," Cameron, the oldest brother, said.

"What's with the 'C' thing, anyway, Dad?" Cathy asked.

"That was your mother's doing," Carl stated.

"Well, we just happened to like the names Caroline, Cathy, and Cameron," Nancy explained. "By then, we couldn't name the next one Julie and make her feel like an oddball."

"I prefer Christine over Julie," Christine piped in. "Thank you very much."

"Then there was Colette and Colin," Cathy added. "I always thought it sounded like twins."

"I thank heaven we weren't," Colette chuckled.

"Me too," Nancy added.

"Then Casey and Cory," Carl said. "Although on that last one or two, we seriously considered the name 'Caboose'."

"Oh, that would have been great," Cory said with sarcasm. "Caboose Trevor on my driver's license."

"We have much to be grateful for," Casey nudged his younger brother.

There was a moment of silence as the statement seemed to strike deep.

"How is she?" Cameron asked Colin solemnly.

"Not good," Colin answered. "But I think *I'm* feeling a little better."

"Good," Caroline smiled and hugged Colin again. "Then it was worth it."

"She came the most miles," Cathy said. "Maine is a long way from Utah."

"I hope we didn't ruin your vacation," Colin said.

"Hey," Christine took Colin's hand, "maybe that's why the Lord got us all together—now. It's been too long anyway."

Colin nodded feebly, feeling his emotion rise again.

"Matthew's a wonderful boy," Colette said. "We want you to know that we're all glad to have him as a part of the family."

That did it. As every one of them made it evident that they agreed emphatically, Colin pressed a hand briefly over his mouth. "Thank you," he managed. "You can't know what that means to me. I only wish Janna were here to . . ." His voice caught, and he shook his head in frustration. "Well, you know," he added, then he cleared his throat carefully and forced the emotion back. "We were planning to tell you . . . all of you . . . since we were going to all be together . . . Janna and I . . ." He paused a moment to regain his composure. "We're getting married . . . in the Mt. Timpanogos Temple." Colin pushed a hand through his hair. "We talked about July. I don't know . . . when it will be now, but . . ."

"We'll be there," Christine said, and the others echoed her promise.

"Whenever it happens," Cameron added, "we'll find a way to get back."

Colin laughed in an effort to avoid sobbing all over again. "Thank you," he managed.

They all embraced Colin once more, and told him they would be praying for Janna—and for him, too. Nancy and Carl walked with Colin back to Janna's room, and the reality descended freshly. But as he sat alone by her bedside the remainder of the day, he had to admit that he didn't feel lonely. His family was with him in spirit, and the love of his Father in Heaven felt close.

For the next twenty-four hours, Colin kept a close vigil at Janna's bedside, nearly every minute they would allow him to be there. But her condition didn't change. She remained unconscious and stable. Colin's family members made occasional visits to the ICU waiting room. The support was appreciated, but Colin found it discouraging to realize they were all leaving again, and he'd hardly seen them at all.

On Tuesday morning, Janna developed a fever and her blood pressure went up. Colin's concern rose, but he tried not to panic, reminding himself of the blessing she'd been given. She *would* heal. He had to remember that.

Colin used the phone in Janna's room to call his office and let them know the situation. He made arrangements for his colleagues to take over the pressing matters, and put off anything that could be postponed. Then he called Sean's office, hoping to catch him between clients.

"What's up?" Sean asked after the receptionist connected them.

"Hi," Colin squeaked. "Is it possible for you to meet me for lunch?"

"I don't have an appointment until two. That shouldn't be a problem. You sound awful. Dare I ask?"

"Uh . . ." Colin began, then the nurse came in and distracted him a moment.

"Colin?" Sean asked. "Are you okay?"

"We can talk over lunch."

"Where?"

"How's the hospital cafeteria?"

"You're joking, right?"

"No, I'm not joking. I'll meet you in the tower lobby."

"Twenty minutes."

"Thank you, Sean."

Colin got out of the elevator on the main floor and immediately saw Sean. They both got back on, but so did several other people, and Colin wanted a chance to tell him what was happening before they went to the cafeteria. He got off on the second floor, and Sean followed him into the ICU waiting room.

"Intensive Care?" Sean asked.

Colin just walked into the hall with Sean at his side.

"Are you trying to torment me, or what?" Sean pressed.

"I'm trying to keep from crying again," Colin answered and pushed open the door to Janna's room.

Sean looked hesitant as he stepped inside and Colin followed. "He found her," Colin stated. Sean groaned and pushed an anguished hand through his hair as he stepped closer to the bed. "Her nose was badly broken, and you can see the stitches. She's got some broken ribs, a punctured lung, and there was severe internal bleeding from who knows what." Colin's voice deepened in anger. "How many times do you think he had to kick her to cause severe internal bleeding? Both her kidneys are bruised, and there's infection somewhere, because now she's got a fever. Her blood pressure's too high, and they can't get it to drop."

Sean turned to look at Colin and asked solemnly, "And how are you?"

Colin rubbed his eyes and admitted, "I need a friend."

"Come on." Sean put a hand on his shoulder and guided him out of the room. "I'll buy you lunch."

In a corner of the cafeteria, they talked quietly about the anger Colin felt toward Russell, and even toward himself. He speculated on all the things he might have done to prevent this, and barely touched his meal. Sean helped him understand that sometimes bad things happen to good people for reasons we can't understand. And he reminded him of two facts that gave him comfort. One was that Russell would meet justice, not only in this life, but in the life to come. And the second was that life had no room for regrets. "If you look back with regret," he said, "you'll only find bitterness. Like Lot's wife in the Bible, who looked back and turned to salt."

"And you know," Sean added, "miracles happen. May I tell you about one of mine?"

"Sure, I could use it."

"When I was nineteen, I went through the windshield of a car face first." Colin's eyes widened as Sean continued. "My hands saved my face, beyond this." He pointed out the two significant scars on his face that Colin had always wondered about. Sean then held out his hands and pointed out some subtle scars. "It took several surgeries to make them usable. But that was insignificant to the healing I went through before that. I had so many broken bones and so many surgeries that I lost track. My body has so many scars, it looks like it was put together by a mad scientist. Now, the really stupid thing is that I was stoned and drunk when I got in that car."

Colin leaned back, trying to absorb this new revelation about the Sean O'Hara he knew.

"Now, is that enough for you to know that I learned there's no room for regret? Is that enough for you to know that miracles happen? I've got some scars, but I'm whole, and I'm sane, and I'm happy. I never would have joined the Church if not for that accident, Colin. How can I regret *that?*

"What you're going through right now is tough, Colin, and I don't envy what you must be feeling. I'm here if you need me, anytime, day or night. When you get those low moments, just close your eyes and imagine the day when you look at Janna across a temple altar and make her yours forever. It'll happen, and I intend to be there."

Colin knew there were no words to express the depth of his gratitude for all that Sean O'Hara had taught him, but he tried anyway as they walked together back to the elevators. When he returned to Janna's room, he bowed his head in prayer and thanked his Father in Heaven, too.

Later that afternoon, Janna finally regained consciousness, looking frightened and miserable. The respirator was replaced by an oxygen mask that could easily be lifted if she needed to speak. The nurses cautioned Colin to be mindful of her blood pressure, and not say anything to upset her, or try to get her to talk too much.

When they were left alone, he didn't know where to begin. He took her hand in his and looked into her eyes, fighting to hold back his emotion and smile.

"I'm not dead," she said as if she was disappointed.

"I'm not letting you leave me again until you're at least ninety," he said in the lightest tone he could manage. She made no acknowledgment, and he wondered if she was too drugged with medication to care.

"Where is Matthew?" she asked hoarsely.

"He's with Mom and Dad. He's worried about you, but he's fine."

Janna nodded slightly, then seemed distracted by the pain. "Russell, he's . . . he's . . ." She seemed agitated, and Colin was concerned about her blood pressure.

"He's not going to hurt you anymore, Janna. He's in jail. Do you understand?" She calmed down but gave no response.

"JannaLyn," he said carefully, "are you with me?" She focused her eyes on him and he added with fervor, "I love you. Everything's going to be all right."

Her only response was the tears leaking out of the corners of her eyes.

With Janna conscious and not doing well, they asked Colin to stick to regular visiting hours for the time being. He felt frustrated and impatient, and decided it was a good time to go home and spend some time with Matthew.

Colin didn't realize how exhausted he really was until he pulled into the driveway and just sat there. He figured Matthew would probably be getting ready for bed by now, and he steeled himself to face the boy with a positive outlook. When he walked in the front door, Matthew looked up from the story Carl was reading him. He squealed and ran into Colin's arms, wearing the pajamas Janna had made him for Christmas.

"Did you see Mom?" he asked. "Did you see her?"

"Yes, buddy, I saw her," he said, trying to smile.

Nancy appeared in the hallway just as Carl said, "Come sit down, son, and tell us what's happening."

Colin sat on the couch and held Matthew on his lap. His mother sat close beside him. "Well," he began, "she regained consciousness this afternoon."

Nancy sighed audibly, but Matthew asked, "What does that mean?"

"Your mother woke up, Matthew. She asked about you first thing, and I told her you were worried about her, but you were doing fine. That made her feel a lot better."

Matthew smiled. Colin briefly explained the status of her condition in terms Matthew could understand, then Carl finished the story and Colin tucked his son into bed. They prayed together, then sat on the bed and talked until Matthew drifted off.

Nancy served Colin a hot meal, even though it was after ten o'clock, then she insisted he get into a hot tub before he went to bed. He cried himself to sleep, but he slept long and deep, and woke up feeling anxious to see Janna.

While he was eating a late breakfast, Matthew sat across from him, looking glum.

"Why the sad face, buddy?" Colin asked.

"I miss Mom."

"I know."

"Grandma says I can't go see her. But I should be able to go see her, because I'm her only blood relative."

Colin shook his head, freshly amazed by his son's vocabulary. While a part of him wished he could take Matthew to see her, he had to admit he was grateful for the rules. He didn't *want* Matthew to see his mother like this.

"Yes, you probably should be able to go see her. But the hospital has rules about that. When she gets a little better, they'll move her to a different part of the hospital and you can go see her. The minute they say it's okay, we'll get you there. I promise."

"Okay," he said, but he still looked glum.

"Tell you what," Nancy said. "Even though you can't see your mother, why don't we meet your dad at the hospital and have a late lunch with him."

"Could we?" Matthew beamed.

"That sounds great," Colin said. "I'll look forward to it."

Colin arrived at Janna's room to find her looking no better except for being without the oxygen mask. The monitors made it immediately evident that her temperature was still too high, as was her blood pressure. He assumed she was sleeping, but as soon as he took her hand, her eyes came slowly open.

"Hello, my love," he smiled, but she hardly acknowledged him. He stayed with her every minute they'd let him, which wasn't nearly enough in his opinion.

Nancy and Matthew met Colin for lunch, then they went to a park where Matthew played on the swings for a short while.

"Colin," Nancy said, sitting on a bench beside him, "Matthew's been upset a great deal lately; of course that's understandable. But this morning after you left, I felt inclined to try and talk to him. It took some prodding to get him to open up, but he finally admitted that . . ."

Nancy hesitated, and Colin's concern rose sharply. "That what?" he pressed.

"Do you remember how difficult it was for the counselors to get Matthew to open up about his abuse?"

"Yes," Colin drawled, hating where this was leading.

"Well, apparently Russell threatened him with . . ." Nancy hesitated again as emotion intervened. "He told Matthew that if he ever said anything to anyone about the abuse, he would hurt his mother more than he ever had before."

Colin pressed his head into his hands with a loud sigh as the picture began to take hold.

"Colin, he believes that what happened was his fault, because the abuse was talked about in court. He thinks that's the reason Russell hurt her so badly."

Colin leaned back and wiped a hand quickly over his face. "What did you tell him?"

"Of course I assured him that wasn't the case, but he didn't seem convinced. I've already made an appointment with him to see Sean tomorrow. I can take him in."

"Thank you," Colin said. Then he just shook his head, wondering if life could possibly be any more difficult than this.

When Colin returned to the hospital, he called his father at work and asked if he'd meet him later to give Janna another blessing, now that she was conscious and things were not improving. This time Colin spoke the blessing, and though it was difficult for him, he found comfort in the fresh evidence that she would get beyond this.

The following morning, Colin walked into Janna's room to find her sitting up slightly, actually looking coherent.

"Well, hello, beautiful," he said eagerly.

"You need your eyes checked, Colin," she said with a raspy voice.

"Well, at least you know who I am. And I don't care what anyone says, you're still beautiful." He gave her a careful kiss and touched her face. "How are you feeling?"

"Like I've just emerged from the depths of hell—or maybe I'm still there. It's hard to tell."

Colin tentatively pushed his fingers through her hair. "I'd say that's a fair description."

While Colin was wondering what else to say, Janna spoke solemnly. "I really didn't expect to wake up . . . at least not on this side of the veil."

"Well, I thank God about every ten minutes that you did."

She turned to him with cold eyes and asked, "Why?"

"Why?" he repeated, his voice rising a pitch. "Are you trying to tell me you would rather be dead right now?"

Janna looked away but wouldn't answer.

"JannaLyn?" He took her hand and squeezed it gently. "You have a son who needs you. *I* need you."

"I'm certain the two of you could manage together."

"What are you saying?" he asked breathily, while an uneasiness crept up the back of his neck.

Janna turned to him and gave a wan smile. "Forget it, Colin." She squeezed his hand. "They tell me you hardly left my side for days. I don't know why you're so sweet."

"I love you, Janna. I didn't want to be anywhere else."

She smiled again, then closed her eyes as if she was exhausted. "How is Matthew?" she asked.

"He misses you. He's mad because they won't let him see you." He didn't mention Matthew's other concerns.

"I don't want him to see me like this," she insisted.

"I agree. We'll bring him in when you're up to it. He'll be fine. He's tough, you know."

"Yes," she said, "like his father."

Colin carefully pressed his face into the pillow next to hers, whispering with emotion, "Maybe I'm not so tough. I've cried like a baby the last several days."

Janna turned her face to look into his eyes. Again she asked, "Why, Colin?"

The uneasiness he was trying to ignore rushed over him in torrents. "Why do you have to ask?" he questioned intently.

She turned away. "Forget it, Colin," she said, then she drifted off to sleep. But no matter how hard Colin tried, he couldn't forget it.

CHAPTER SIXTEEN

*C*olin felt all of the prayers and fasting kick in over the next few days. Janna recovered so quickly that even the doctors were saying it was incredible. She was moved to Intermediate Care on the fifth floor, where physical therapists began helping her get on her feet and walk at regular intervals. The pain was evident, but her progress remained steady.

While Colin found hope in her physical progress, a dark cloud hung over her that was downright frightening. She became deeply despondent, barely acknowledging Colin at all, and refusing to see Matthew altogether. Colin kept lying to his son, telling him that children were not allowed.

Nancy came nearly every day, but even she couldn't penetrate the invisible wall that seemed to surround Janna's spirit. Colin nearly called Sean a dozen times, but not only had he begun to feel like he was becoming a pest to Sean, Janna had gotten angry at the suggestion. It seemed that Janna had no desire to live, and no desire to heal.

Colin tried to keep up his own spirits, hoping to lighten hers. He read jokes to her out of the *Reader's Digest*, and segments from other books that were uplifting or funny. He painted her toenails while he reminisced about the reason he'd started doing this in the first place. "After we did that toenail thing at Mutual, I just always thought your feet were so . . . *cute*," he said. "This is romantic, you know," he added. "How many men would paint a woman's toenails?"

"But it's bright purple, Colin," she protested.

"Variety is nice," he replied. "We could try orange next time."

Still, with all his efforts, she hardly talked, never laughed, and rarely cracked even a hint of a smile.

When the fear of infection was past and they allowed flowers in Janna's room, Colin took her a mixed bouquet that looked like something he might have picked himself from an elaborate flower garden.

"Thank you," Janna said, "they're beautiful."

"So how are you?" he asked, but she said nothing. "Is it so difficult to answer a simple question?"

"If I answer it honestly, you'll have Sean in here examining my head."

"If you don't want me to call him, Janna, I won't." A minute later, he asked again, "So, how are you?"

"I don't want to be here, Colin."

"They said you can probably go home soon, and—"

Her cold gaze stopped him. "No, Colin. I don't want to be *here*."

As her meaning became clear, everything inside of Colin reacted. His heart raced, his stomach tightened, his breath quickened. But he steeled his expression and said in the lightest tone he could manage, "So, the prospect of life with me is that bad, eh?"

"That's not it at all, and you know it."

"How can I know *anything*, Janna, when you won't talk to me? I don't know what to say. I don't know what to think. The only thing I know for certain is that I love you, and we have a son who loves you. How long do I have to keep lying to him?"

She looked mildly surprised.

"He wants to see you, Janna. He misses you desperately. Should I just tell him the truth—that you don't care enough about him to spend some time with him? Do you want me to tell him you don't want him to see you while your face isn't perfect, when he's seen it much worse in the past? Should I tell him you don't love him enough to want to live for *his* sake?"

"You're being cruel and unfair, Colin."

"Maybe I am, but I don't know what else to do."

They stared at each other in tense silence for a long moment, then Colin changed the subject, hoping it wouldn't start a whole new argument. "Matthew wants to get the rest of his things from the apartment. He says he doesn't want to go back there to live." He hesitated and added, "Do you want me to just leave your things there, or—"

"I don't want to go back there, either."

"Okay. So what should I do with the—"

"I don't care what you do with any of it. I just don't want to go back there."

"Okay," he said and hurried out of the room, fearing he would really blow it. He'd barely walked around the corner when he literally bumped into Sean O'Hara.

"Whoa there, boy," Sean chuckled. "What's up?"

Colin leaned his head against the wall. "You are like a walking miracle, you know that?"

"How do you figure?"

"If I've ever needed you, it's now. But Janna made me promise not to call you, and—"

"Well, don't go thinking I've had some great vision or something," Sean said. "Your mother called me this morning. She said Janna's depressed."

"Yeah," Colin folded his arms and looked at the floor, "I'd say she's depressed."

"Well then," Sean took hold of Colin's arm, "let's go talk to her."

"Then you can talk to me. Because I'm depressed, too."

"I'll do what I can," Sean said with a wry smile.

They stopped at the nurse's station, where Sean told them who he was and asked if he could have some uninterrupted time with his patient. The nurse checked Janna's vitals and made certain everything was okay, then she held the door open for Sean and Colin, saying with a smile, "Good luck."

"Hello, JannaLyn," Sean said while Janna scowled at Colin.

"I *didn't* call him," Colin said. "He was . . . prompted."

Sean sat down near the bed and crossed his legs as if they were lounging on the back lawn. "Well," he said, "I must say you're looking better than the last time I saw you."

"I assume I wasn't conscious," Janna said.

"And now that you *are* conscious," Sean went on, "I assume you don't want to see *me*. Should I be offended?"

Janna was silent a long moment. "I just don't want to get into it, Sean. It feels too heavy."

"Do you think ignoring it will lighten it any?"

"I don't know," she snapped.

Colin watched with fresh amazement as Sean carefully maneuvered Janna's feelings into the open. She cried and raged, but she still came to the firm conclusion that she didn't want to live.

"Why not?" Sean asked.

Janna looked hesitant and Colin asked, "Do you want me to leave?"

"I don't care," she said, so he leaned back and crossed his arms.

"Why don't you want to live, JannaLyn?" Sean asked more firmly. "You know," he added when she still didn't answer, "there are few people who go through intensive care for *any* reason who don't have some struggle with the 'I would rather just die' thing. While human beings have a strong instinct to live, pulling through serious illness or injury sometimes just seems to take too much effort or willpower. I've been there personally. Even getting a bad flu bug can give you a temporary urge to just die and get it over with. But people usually get past it, and their living instinct takes over. What I want to know is, why aren't you getting over it?"

Still she said nothing.

"I get the impression you don't want to talk to me."

"I'm tired," she stated.

"Can I come back tomorrow?" Sean asked.

"I don't care. I'm not going anywhere."

"Promise?"

"Yes, Sean, I promise."

"Good. I'll see you tomorrow."

In the hall, Sean told Colin, "I'm going to talk to her primary physician about prescribing an antidepressant and see if that doesn't help a little. But it will take time. I'm also going to see if we can get her pain medication changed; that could make a difference. But the bottom line is that it's got to come from inside here." He put a hand to his chest. "If she doesn't want to help herself, nobody can force her to be happy." He put a hand on Colin's shoulder. "Remember, miracles happen. Keep praying."

"I am," Colin said. "And I've put her name in every temple in the state."

"That's good. Those are the best kind of prayers."

"Thank you, Sean."

"Glad I can help. And hey," he slapped Colin's shoulder lightly, "call me, whether she wants you to or not."

Colin nodded. "I don't want to make a pest of myself."

Sean looked Colin in the eye. "If you had a knee injury and the pain wasn't going away, would you not call your doctor?" He gave Colin a quick brotherly embrace. "I'm here for you. And don't forget it."

Three days showed no improvement in Janna's mental condition, and it quickly became evident that it was affecting her physical progress. Colin's frustration continued to mount until he hardly dared talk to her for fear of erupting. Out of necessity, he had to spend more time at work to keep things moving, but he was almost relieved to not have to deal with Janna's emotions so often. He felt helpless.

Sean had spent time alone with Janna, and he'd told Colin that she was just plain weary of living in fear and having to deal with the struggles of life. "She's just got to find a way to take hold of the good things in her life," he told Colin. "And nobody can do it but her."

Colin hardly slept that night as his head pounded with frustration. Janna wouldn't even talk to Matthew on the phone, and his mother had come home from her last two visits in tears. He prayed with all his heart and soul that he could find a way to appeal to Janna's will to live—that he could show her the good things in life.

By morning, Colin had made up his mind to be happy in spite of her, to show her how much he loved her, loved being with her, to remind her of the good things they'd shared in the past, and the brightness of their future. He arrived at the hospital to find Janna sitting in a chair with only a single I.V. attached to her. She'd come a long way. Even her face looked almost normal.

"Good morning," he said brightly. He let some more sun into the windows, hung up a couple of pictures of Matthew on her bulletin board, then told her they were going out.

"Out?" she questioned cynically.

"They have this great restaurant here," he said. "Actually, they call it a cafeteria, but they have a different gourmet specialty every day. I have your nurse's permission. So, we're going out."

While she argued and refused, Colin fought to hold back his temper. Instead he closed his eyes in silent prayer, and a minute later Sean walked through the door.

"Did I come at a tense moment?" he asked gingerly.

"Is there any other kind?" Colin retorted.

"What's the deal, Janna?" Sean asked.

"I'm sick of you people telling me that I need to cheer up. I don't want to—"

Colin held his breath as Sean bolted toward Janna and leaned over her, placing his hands on the arms of the chair, looking into her eyes.

"I have something I need to say to you, Janna, and I want you to listen closely, and absorb it. Because I'm not coming back—at least not until we can change the subject. I have patients who need me more than you do. I have a thirteen-year-old rape victim, a guy who just woke up paralyzed from the neck down, and a woman whose husband shook their baby to death."

Janna squeezed her eyes shut and turned away. Sean touched her chin to make her face him. "I'll be the first to admit that your life has dealt you some tough hands," he continued. "You've made some mistakes. You've done some stupid things. Who hasn't? But you've also been handed some prime blessings. Without being presumptuous, I would like to say that the very fact that Colin and I are both standing in this room at this moment is evidence that God loves you, JannaLyn, and he wants you to be happy. *But even he cannot do it for you!* Do you hear what I'm saying? No one can force you to be happy, Janna. No one can force you to live. If you are so determined to end it, then do it and get it over with. Let the people who love you have something *real* to mourn. Then they could get over it and get on with their lives."

He took a deep breath. "Do you have any idea of the message you are giving to the people you love right now? It's in blaring neon, Janna. You might as well shout it in their faces. 'I don't care enough to be there for you!'

"They're frustrated, and they're helpless. And eventually they would say 'to hell with it,' because you're giving them no choice. If you're trying to convince Colin that he's a stupid idiot for loving you, a woman with problems and complications, eventually you will. Well, *everyone* has problems and complications, JannaLyn, so buck up and get a life! Or you might just create a *real* suicidal situation, and I don't want to have anything to do with it."

Sean stood up straight and folded his arms. He looked at Janna long and hard, then added in a tender voice, "Colin is a wonderful man, Janna—one of the best. And of all the women in the world, he's chosen *you* to spend eternity with. If he didn't want you, he would have given up years ago. But he's still here. A hundred other men would have dropped out of the picture the second time you wouldn't talk. But he's a human being, too. He has needs, and he's spent a lot of time waiting around for you to heal and be willing to love him the way he deserves to be loved. Just love him, Janna. And let him love you. And I swear to you, you'll always find something worth living for."

Sean stood there a minute, then he turned and walked out of the room, nodding toward Colin on his way out. Colin watched a stray tear roll down Janna's cheek and wondered if he should leave her alone. He opened the door to go, saying only, "I'll be back later."

Colin saw Sean at the nurse's station using the phone. He waited for him and they walked down the hall together.

"I might not normally behave that way toward a suicidal patient," Sean said. "But my intuition told me it's what she needs. We can only hope and pray that it helps."

Colin said nothing and Sean added, "She's going to need a lot of love and patience, Colin. But you've got to keep it in perspective. You have to learn to recognize your boundaries, and don't let her push you too far. That's where you get into that nasty codependent thing."

"I think that makes sense."

"It'll come," Sean smiled. "Hang in there. Oh," he pointed a finger at him just as the elevator opened, "take Matthew to see her . . . maybe tomorrow, whether she wants to see him or not. Tell the kid what to expect, then go for it."

Colin nodded as the elevator door closed between them. He stood there for a minute, then pushed the button to call it again. At the moment, going to work and letting Janna absorb Sean's lecture seemed the best thing to do. He called Janna that evening to ask how she was doing, but as usual, she said little. He wondered if Sean's speech had had any effect at all.

The following morning, Colin went to work early, then he came home early afternoon. "Hey, Matthew!" Colin called as he walked through the front door.

"Dad!" Matthew came bounding up the stairs and into his arms.

"Guess what, buddy? You get to go see your mom."

"Right now?" he beamed.

"Right now. Go tell Grandma we're going."

"Grandma heard," Nancy said as she appeared. "Have a good time."

"Wish us luck," Colin said with a discreet glance toward his mother.

"I'll be praying," she said and held up crossed fingers.

Matthew chattered constantly on the way to the hospital, but when they arrived, Colin turned to him in the car and said, "I need to talk to you before we go in. Okay?"

Matthew nodded firmly. "Grandma says I have to be quiet like at church, because people are trying to rest."

"That's right. And you also need to know that your mother is having a hard time. She's doing a lot better, and she's nearly ready to leave the hospital, but she's been kind of scared and sad about what happened."

"Grandma says she's depressed."

"Grandma's right again. So you smile for her, and tell her how much you love her and miss her, but don't be disappointed if she doesn't say much. It doesn't mean she doesn't love you. She's just having a hard time, okay?"

"Okay, Dad. Can we go see her now?"

"One more thing. She's still got some places that really hurt. You need to be very careful when you hug her. Okay?"

"Okay," he said and jumped out of the car.

Before they went up to the seventh floor where Janna had been moved for the final stretch of her stay, Colin took Matthew into the ICU waiting area because he wanted to see the aquarium that Colin had told him about. They walked into the hall and looked beyond the sign that Matthew read aloud, saying that no one under twelve was admitted.

"I'm glad she's not in there anymore," Matthew said as they were getting back on the elevator.

"Me too," Colin said. "Push the seven."

On the seventh floor, Colin impulsively sat Matthew down beside him on a couch. "There's one more thing I want to say before we go in. I want you to know that what happened to your mother is not your fault, Matthew. *Nothing* Russell did to her had anything to do with you. Do you understand that?"

Matthew nodded firmly. "I thought it did at first, but I talked to Sean about it. He told me that Russell lied to me. He said he was just saying that to keep me from telling anybody that he had hurt me, too."

"That's exactly right, Matthew, and I don't want you to ever forget it. If you ever have bad thoughts about it, or there's something you don't understand, all you have to do is come and talk to me, and if we need to, we'll have Sean help us understand it. All right?"

Matthew nodded again. "Can we go see Mom now?"

"We sure can." Colin smiled and took his hand.

As they approached Janna's room, Colin felt nervous. "She doesn't know you're coming, so it's a surprise."

Matthew nodded, grinning as if it was Christmas.

Janna was sitting in the chair, as she had been for hours, confused and distraught over the things Sean had said. She heard the door opening and looked up. Every thought fled before the reality of seeing Matthew timidly enter the room.

Colin held his breath. Janna hesitated only a moment before she opened her arms and Matthew ran to her. Tears blurred his vision, and he could almost literally feel some hope surging into her from the way she clung to her son.

Colin sat down and observed the innocent way Matthew reminded Janna of life's beauty through a child's eyes. He told her about butterflies and flowers, swimming lessons, and the new slide at the park. He talked on and on about the old bike in the garage Grandpa had fixed up for him to ride, and how Grandma had taught him to make chocolate chip cookies all by himself. He promised to make her some when she came home, and he made her promise to take him to the mall and the park and the library.

When Matthew had explored the room and asked questions about everything in it, Colin finally intervened. "Take a look at this, buddy," he said, lifting him onto the edge of the bed. Colin pushed the button and the bed went up.

"Wow, that's cool," he said, and Janna actually smiled.

Matthew tried all the buttons himself, then Colin said, "Hey, your mom needs to get some rest. We'll come back again tomorrow."

"Promise?" he asked.

"I promise," Colin said.

Matthew hugged his mother again and reluctantly opened the door. Colin moved to follow him and Janna said, "Hey there, handsome, I thought we were going *out*."

Colin resisted the urge to cross the room and pull her into his arms. Instead he just smiled and said, "You get some rest, gorgeous, and I'll be back before you know it."

"I'll be here," she said.

When Colin returned later that day, Janna was wearing a clean hospital gown, and a nurse was brushing through her damp hair.

"Look at you," he said.

"All dressed up and nowhere to go," the nurse said.

"That's not true," Colin said, "we're going *out*. Well," he added in response to her concerned look, "out of this room, at least."

Janna got into the wheelchair on her own without much trouble, and Colin wheeled her into the hall. Instead of going to the cafeteria, they went to the snack bar and had a hamburger and a malt. Janna didn't talk much, but she seemed less tense than she had since this whole thing started. It gave Colin hope, and he decided that hope could go a long way in such matters.

They went up the elevator in the old section of the hospital, and down the long hall on the third floor into the new section.

"Wait," Janna said as they passed a long glass window. "Go back."

Colin turned the wheelchair around and realized they were at the infant nursery. A baby girl was being examined by a nurse, and Colin was amazed at how tiny she was. He wanted to ask if Matthew had been that small, but he feared bringing up anything that might remind her of past struggles.

Janna surprised him when she asked, "Do you think we'll be able to have more children?"

"Yes," he said without hesitation. She looked dubious and he added, "Do you remember the blessing you got when you were miscarrying?"

"I'm afraid I don't," she said, her focus shifting to the baby.

"You were told that Matthew would have brothers and sisters."

She looked thoughtful, then admitted, "I'm not sure if I believe in priesthood blessings, Colin. Is that wrong?"

"If you feel it, it's valid. Do you want to tell me why?"

"After the divorce, I was told I would be protected. I understood why God couldn't help me when I left you. I lied to you, and I withdrew myself from the Spirit. But why . . ." Her voice cracked with emotion. "Why did he let Russell find me, when . . ."

Colin was grateful for his clear memory of that blessing while he was searching for the best way to answer her concerns. "Janna," he said quietly, "God is bound by natural laws. We each have our own free agency, and our own struggles to overcome."

"Maybe I should have gone further away. Maybe I should have—"

"Hey," he interrupted, "as I see it, such things are irrelevant. You did what you thought was best, but . . . well, I'm paraphrasing, but in that blessing you were admonished to lean on the people who love you. And you were told to make your choices according to faith, not fear."

Colin feared she might get defensive or upset. But she looked up at him with wide eyes. "It would seem I forgot that, too. Or maybe I just wasn't listening." She closed her eyes and shook her head. "I ran like a scared rabbit."

"Your fear was understandable, Janna. And that time was good for all of us, in a way."

"But . . ." she began but couldn't finish.

"We live and learn."

Janna said nothing, but as her eyes focused again on the baby through the glass, a smile touched the corners of her lips. And Colin felt hope.

As they moved on down the hall, Colin was surprised to hear Janna giggle.

"What's so funny?" he asked.

"Why do I feel like we're doing something we shouldn't be?"

Colin chuckled. "Maybe it's because you have a guilty conscience about the time we took Myrtle Simpson's extra wheelchair and had races up and down the street with Billy, that paralyzed kid who lived around the corner from you for about a year."

Janna actually laughed. "I'd forgotten. But wasn't it Richard Lowery who took the wheelchair?"

"I believe it was."

"And if I recall correctly, Myrtle Simpson was sitting on her porch cheering us on."

"And we were good," Colin said, breaking into a careful run down the long hall.

"Colin!" she protested quietly, then laughed.

"Remember how smooth we took the corners?" he said and swerved into the lobby by the tower elevators.

Janna attempted to stifle her laughter when an older woman looked up from a magazine with apparent disdain. They got on the elevator and the door closed.

"That was embarrassing," she said when they were alone, but she laughed again.

"Nah," Colin said, "that woman could just take a lesson from Myrtle Simpson. After Billy won the races hands down, she invited us in and let us use her kitchen to make brownies and hot chocolate. There must have been ten of us."

"She let us do just about anything for the sake of having some company."

"She was a sweet old woman."

"Whatever happened to her?" Janna asked.

"She died while I was on my mission. Mom said her son told that wheelchair story at her funeral."

Janna said nothing more as Colin wheeled her back into her room. Without her permission, he scooped her into his arms and laid her carefully on the bed.

"Are you tired?" he asked.

"No."

"Do you want me to leave you alone?"

"No."

"Well, what *do* you want?" he asked, sitting on the edge of the bed. "Name it."

Janna took his hand. "I want to reminisce some more."

"I can do that." He lifted his brows quickly, then began rambling about the ball games, the dances, the Mutual activities. She'd been there when he got his Eagle Scout award. He'd been there when she'd received her Young Womanhood Recognition award. She'd gone to his family reunions. He'd taken her and her mother out to dinner twice a month once he got a good job. Following a long silence, Janna said wistfully, "I'll never forget the first time I saw you."

"Tell me about it," he said.

"I remember hearing the girls whispering in Young Women's meeting one Sunday about this family that had just moved into our ward from another ward in the stake. 'Three gorgeous boys,' they said, 'and the oldest of them is Colin.' We went into Sunday School after that, and our classes were doubled up because the teacher was sick. When you walked in, they were all practically drooling."

"Oh, please," Colin said with embarrassment.

"It's true. And I remember actually thinking: Which one of them is he going to be interested in? They were practically making wagers for the next two weeks about who you would ask out first. And I can tell you, I was not one of their guesses."

"Well," he smiled, "we certainly fooled them."

"And I'll never forget that first time you turned to look at me. We were in Mutual opening exercises. I was watching this note go back and forth between Tammy Warr and Linda Roberts." Janna's eyes became distant. "I remember wondering what on earth could be so important, then I looked up, and you were watching me. You didn't turn away or act embarrassed. You just smiled."

"I remember," Colin said. "I kept thinking you looked familiar; but then I knew that if I'd seen you before I'd moved there, I never would have forgotten it." He touched her hair and lowered his voice. "I remember how my heart beat faster when you looked at me . . . the same way it did the first time I kissed you."

Janna chuckled. "We were sitting on the couch at my house, and my mother walked in on us." She looked into his eyes. "I remember wondering why, of all the girls in that neighborhood, you were kissing *me*."

Colin tried to absorb the implication beneath her words, and something began to jell in his mind. "Why was it always so difficult to believe that I loved you—that I wanted *you?*"

Janna began to wring her hands, and her eyes moved away from his. He laughed softly in an effort to ease the tension. "I took one look at you and thought you were the most beautiful thing I'd ever seen. And the more I got to know you, the more beautiful you became. But you never believed me, did you." It was not a question. "Right from the start, you always questioned me when I told you that you were beautiful, that I loved you. Why, Janna?"

"I don't know," she said, but Colin's instincts told him differently.

"I'm guessing that you *do* know," he said, hoping this would do more good than harm. "I'm guessing that you just don't want to say it."

Her nervousness seemed to intensify, but still she said nothing.

"Janna," he said close to her ear, pushing her hair back off her face with a gentle hand, "help me understand."

"You're right," she admitted tersely, "I don't want to say it."

"Why not?"

"I've never told *anyone*. There are things I've never even told Sean. Maybe I believed that holding it inside would make it go away."

"Obviously it hasn't."

Janna was grateful for the silence that allowed her to gather her thoughts. Her mind quickly tallied every rotten thing in her life, and she wondered, as Sean had once suggested, if it all hinged on that experience with her father. The very thought made her sick to her stomach. Then Sean's speech from yesterday hurtled into her mind. He'd taught her that she needed to talk, to deal with her fears and feelings head on. He'd reminded her that she had much to live for, but it was up to her to face up to the things still smoldering inside her. And here sat Colin. Since the day he'd first taken notice of her, he had always been there for her. Their separations had been *her* doing. He was offering her a life of love and security, and she was trying to convince him that she wasn't worthy of it. And now he sensed the truth—that something had been wrong long before he met her. It wasn't going to go away by itself; the years had proven that. Colin was offering her the chance to unburden herself—if only a little. And in her heart, she knew he wouldn't throw harsh judgments back at her.

Muttering a quick prayer for courage and help, she turned to face him. His expression alone was so filled with love and acceptance that she felt tempted to just break down and cry.

"Are you sure you want to know?" she asked to test him.

"I wouldn't ask if I didn't." Colin's heart began to pound when it became evident that she was contemplating a deep confession. Seeing the look in her eyes, he wondered if he *did* want to know.

"Every time you told me you loved me, I would remember my father saying that I was a simple-headed . . . *bitch* . . . like my mother."

Colin winced as she said it, cringing inwardly at the thought of how the intensity of such a thing might have affected her.

"And just like my mother," she went on, "once he got through with me, no man would ever want me."

Colin swallowed hard. "And you believed *him*."

"Apparently I did." Janna's eyes became hollow as she finished. "Maybe it was the way he had me pinned to the floor with his hands beneath my clothes when he said it."

Colin cringed visibly and felt a little queasy. Janna turned toward him and said with an emotionless voice, "You know, my mother married him because he got her pregnant."

Colin took in a sharp breath. Though he could never explain it aloud, he felt a whole new layer of understanding fall into place. Did this have something to do with Janna's reluctance to marry a man because she was pregnant? Carefully he eased her into his arms and buried his face in her hair. "Oh, Janna," he murmured, "I'm so sorry. I never dreamed it would be so hard for you. I just wanted you so badly, that I—"

"I wanted you, too, Colin." She pushed a hand into his hair and he looked into her eyes. "I don't think either of us had any comprehension of the pain it would bring into our lives."

"Janna, when it happened . . . was . . . was your father there . . . in your head?"

She hesitated a long moment. "At first, but then . . . it was just you and me." She closed her eyes as if to remember more clearly. "And nothing else mattered. I remember wanting my whole life to be that way—to be in your arms, knowing beyond any doubt that I was the most important thing in the world to you."

"You *are* the most important thing in the world to me, Janna. I should have been man enough to let you know that by respecting your virtue. You were always important to me. You always will be."

By the way he looked into her eyes, she could almost believe him. "But . . ." she protested softly, "after all that's happened, how can you—"

"JannaLyn," he interrupted, "I love you. Why can't you believe me?"

She turned away. "It's difficult to comprehend that you can look at me and see a woman worth loving, when I look at myself in the mirror and see . . ."

"What?" he pressed when she didn't finish. "What do you see, Janna?"

How could Janna possibly explain to him the way her own reflection was so disturbing? Technically it was the same woman, but she had a memory of what her face was supposed to look like. And this wasn't it. The subtle changes in her appearance were only a stark reminder of the turmoil going on inside her. Not wanting to get into it, she simply said, "This is not the face of the girl you fell in love with, Colin."

"No," he said, tilting her chin toward him, "this is the face of the woman I love now." He kissed her warmly. "The woman I will love forever."

Janna looked up and saw tears in Colin's eyes. His love for her truly put everything else into perspective. "I want to go home, Colin."

Colin released a little sob as something akin to pure joy burned in his chest. "If those tests tomorrow morning turn out okay, they'll release you the day after."

She nodded and eased her head to his shoulder.

"Does this mean you're feeling better?" he asked.

"I believe I am," she answered, nuzzling a little closer. "Last night I couldn't sleep. I kept thinking about everything Sean had said. I was angry with him at first, but I could see that he was right." She laughed softly. "He always is." Her voice became severe, and she pushed her arms around Colin, holding to him tightly. "I prayed for what seemed like hours, to just be able to make it through this, to have the will to go on. I don't know when I finally fell asleep, but when the nurse came in at five this morning, I realized I'd been dreaming. And for some reason, I felt better. It was like this darkness that had been around me was gone."

"What were you dreaming?" he asked, stroking her hair. "Do you remember?"

"Very well, actually. I doubt I'll ever forget it."

"Tell me," he whispered.

Janna sighed audibly. "It was like a battle scene out of a war movie. I was sitting in the middle of this field, with shells exploding all around me. I was terrified. I knew I had to get out of there, but every time I tried to move, there was another explosion that held me back. And then you appeared out of nowhere. You pulled me up in your arms." Janna's voice cracked and she tightened her embrace. "And you ran. There were explosions and fire all around us, but you held me tight against you, and you just kept running. You fell a couple of times, and your hands got burned. But you didn't let go of me until we were safe, and everything became still and peaceful. Then I bandaged your hands. And I woke up."

Colin eased her closer still, and his heart quickened the same way it had when he'd first stopped to really look at JannaLyn Hayne.

"I love you, Janna," he said, "and I will always be here for you."

"I know," she murmured. Then she fell asleep in his arms.

When Colin told Matthew that his mother's tests had showed that she was healed enough to come home, the child nearly flew through the roof with excitement. While Colin went to the hospital to pick Janna up, Nancy and Matthew organized a few welcome-home surprises. He arrived to find Janna sitting on the edge of the bed, wearing jeans and a button-up shirt, struggling to put on her shoes.

"Would you mind?" she sighed. "I'm still too sore in the middle to bend very far."

"It would be a pleasure," Colin said, going down on one knee. He tickled the bottom of her foot quickly and she gave him a comical scowl. He smiled to see evidence of the Janna he loved.

"I have one question," he asked while he was tying her shoes. "Why are your toenails orange?"

Janna laughed and messed up his hair. Colin grabbed her hand and kissed it.

Colin pushed the wheelchair to where the car was waiting, while a nurse carried everything she was supposed to take home with her. As they turned a corner into a long hall, he leaned over and whispered, "Do you want me to run?"

"No," she giggled.

When they were settled in the car she said, "We can't go yet."

"Why not?" he asked, wondering if he'd forgotten to sign a paper or something.

"I have an urge to feel the wind in my hair, and you haven't put the top down on the car."

Colin grinned and watched her look skyward as the roof of the convertible opened up. As they pulled out of the hospital parking lot, he said, "I'm not coming back here until we have another baby."

Janna smiled but said nothing.

When the silence grew too long, Colin said, "I cleaned out the apartment. All of your personal things are home waiting for you; Mom took care of that part. I took care of the rent and utilities and stuff. And the furniture's in a storage unit . . . until we decide where we want to live."

She nodded, but still she said nothing. Colin could see evidence of much healing, and he was grateful for how far she'd come—both physically and emotionally. But nothing had been said about the wedding, and a part of him feared she would want to put it off. *One day at a time*, he reminded himself.

"Where is Russell?" she asked as they started up the hill toward the house.

"He's in jail, waiting for a trial," Colin answered tonelessly. "And he'll be behind bars for a long time beyond that. There's no question about it this time." He glanced over at her and added, "You seem . . . upset."

"I was just wondering what I'll do when he gets out."

"You have some time to think that through, Janna."

"But it's inevitable."

"Yes, it's inevitable." He took her hand and added, "Hey, one day at a time, okay?"

Janna forced a smile and nodded in agreement. Her thoughts quickly shifted as they pulled into the driveway, and she laughed to see what seemed like hundreds of yellow ribbons tied all over the yard.

"It would seem you were missed," Colin said as he helped her out of the car and Matthew came running.

Janna felt good to be *home*, and it wasn't difficult for her to settle in and feel comfortable. Each day she felt a little better, and as she sorted things through in her head, she came to a firm conclusion. She knew there were things still ahead that would have to be faced, and she likely had many layers of healing yet to discover—according to Sean. But one thing was clear: she needed Colin to help her through those things. She felt anxious to get on with her life, and to share that life with him. The trick was in letting him know she was ready.

CHAPTER SEVENTEEN

A few minutes after Colin finished with a client, he looked up to see Matthew coming into his office.

"Hey there, buddy," Colin grinned. "What are you doing here?"

"There's something I need to ask you," he said as Janna came through the door, wearing a white linen dress and sandals. Colin winked at her as she closed the door and leaned against it.

"Okay, I'm listening," Colin said.

Matthew quickly went down on one knee and said, "Mom wants to know if you'll marry her."

Colin quickly looked to Janna, and he felt warmed by the serenity in her eyes. Colin pulled Matthew up on his lap and whispered something in his ear. Matthew marched over to his mother and said firmly, "He says you should be ashamed of yourself for asking a child to do your dirty work."

"Somehow I knew he was going to say that," Janna said. She ruffled Matthew's hair a little, then sauntered slowly toward Colin. He stood to meet her, and she took both his hands into hers.

"Will you marry me, Colin?" she asked in little more than a whisper.

Colin fingered the ring she wore and brought her hand to his lips. "Only if it's forever."

Janna smiled and he pulled her into his arms, hugging her tightly, grateful to know that it didn't hurt her. They'd come a long way.

"Soon," she whispered in his ear at the same time she pressed a hand into his hair.

"How soon?" he asked.

"Well, I've sent off that letter to the First Presidency. The bishop said if everything goes well, the sealing could be canceled in a few weeks." She smiled, and her eyes glowed with mischief. "You'd better call the temple and then get a marriage license, Mr. Trevor. This is a shotgun wedding."

"So it is," he chuckled and kissed her. Then the happiness erupted in a peal of laughter as he lifted her off the floor.

That evening after dinner, they sat at the kitchen table, compromising with Nancy on a date, so that she could at least get some invitations out.

"Who do we need to invite that we can't call on the phone?" Colin asked.

"Well, your brothers and sisters want to be here, and they need a little warning. And even if you don't *invite* anyone but them, we need to send out *announcements*. Friends and relatives need to know you're getting married."

"How's this?" Janna asked, sliding a notebook toward Colin. He read her draft of an announcement, then started crossing things out and changing it.

"How's this?" he repeated, sliding it back to her.

Janna chuckled. "You're joking, right?"

"No, I'm quite serious."

"You want to announce to the whole world that we have a son?"

"That's right."

"Read it to me," Nancy said.

Colin cleared his throat elaborately and said, "Matthew Colin Hayne is pleased and happy to announce the marriage of his parents, JannaLyn Hayne and Colin Matthew Trevor." He pointed out a line at the bottom of the page to Janna. "I like this part best. Marriage solemnized in the Mt. Timpanogos Temple."

"I like that part, too," she smiled.

"I think it's perfect," Nancy insisted.

Colin leaned across the table to kiss Janna. "It's perfect," he echoed.

* * * * *

Janna was amazed at how quickly everything came together.

The cancellation of her sealing to Russell went through miraculously fast. By the time their wedding day arrived, Colin and Matthew were settled into an apartment with most of Janna's things there, waiting for her to move in. Nancy had managed to put together a simple open house to be held in their backyard, and Colin's family members had flown in from all over the country.

The sun was just peeking over the top of Mt. Timpanogos when Colin and Janna walked into the temple together. She'd never been happier. And when Colin met her eyes, she knew he felt the same way.

While Nancy was adjusting Janna's dress in the bride's room, Janna felt a strong impression that her own mother was there with her. The thought was accompanied by a mixture of emotions that hovered with her as they met in one of the largest sealing rooms available, in order to accommodate Colin's family. Sean and his wife, Tara, were also present.

As Janna and Colin were seated close together, he whispered discreetly, "Is something wrong?"

She shook her head. "I just feel as if . . . my mother's here."

Colin pressed her hand over his arm and smiled. "I know," he said. "I feel it, too."

Janna had no thoughts of abuse or heartache as she knelt across the altar from Colin to be married and sealed. Her mind and spirit were consumed with Colin and the happiness that lay before them. She felt blessed and full of life.

As Colin looked at Janna across the altar, he felt hard pressed to keep the emotion back. There was no visible sign of her ordeal beyond a light scar across her cheekbone where the stitches had been removed before she'd left the hospital. As she slipped her hand into his, he realized that he'd not felt this kind of peace since Janna's mother had passed away. Perhaps that was the reason he seemed to feel Diane Hayne's presence with them now. He could almost imagine her saying, "It's high time, Colin Trevor. You take good care of my girl now." Just the way she would have said it if he'd been late to pick Janna up for a date.

After the rings were exchanged, Colin leaned close to Janna's ear and whispered, "Better late than never."

Matthew was then sealed to his parents, and a short while later the entire family filled the banquet room of a nearby restaurant. In the middle of dessert, Colin stood and the room became still.

"First of all," he said, "I want to thank you all for your effort in coming so far to share this day with us. It is truly a pleasure to have you share in our joy, as you shared in our suffering not so long ago. I wonder if any man has ever come from a better family, and I'm truly grateful." He nodded toward his parents, who were holding hands. "I want to thank you, Mom and Dad, for your love and acceptance . . . through these difficult months, especially. We never could have done it without you."

He smiled toward Sean. "And on behalf of Janna and myself, I want to thank you, Sean, for your knowledge and commitment to helping us through this. And for your friendship. And to you, Tara," Colin added, "for sharing him with us."

Colin motioned for Matthew to come stand beside him. "I want to tell my son how much I love him, and how grateful I am for his very existence—and to know that he will be with us forever."

He felt briefly at a loss for words and said, "I feel like I'm bearing my testimony."

Everyone chuckled, then became silent again as Colin took Janna's hand and she stood at his other side. "I've learned a great deal about life and love since the Lord led me back to JannaLyn. I've seen a lot of evidence of the cruelty and heartache in this world. And I've felt the agony of sin, many years after the fact. But far more importantly, I have felt much evidence of the love our Father in Heaven has for us. I've seen miracles and blessings in abundance. Still, as I sat in that sealing room and looked around, I learned something that I hadn't expected. I think for the first time in my life, I truly understood, if just for a moment, what the atonement of Jesus Christ really means. I made a mistake in my youth—a big one. And I did my best to make it right. But there were wounds caused that I never comprehended at the time—things that I could never fix. Because our Savior died for us," emotion teased his voice and he urged Janna closer, "I was able to stand within temple walls, knowing that I will be with those I love forever, and the future is as pure as we make it." He looked at Janna and added firmly, "May the mistakes of the future turn out so well."

Colin kissed Janna and hugged Matthew close to him. Then he chuckled to ease the tense silence in the room. Lifting his glass of water high, he said lightly, "Better late than never."

As they were leaving the restaurant, Nancy took Matthew's hand, saying, "Why don't the two of you go back to the apartment and get some rest before the open house? We'll take Matthew and see you later."

Colin was stunned to silence as his mother winked and walked away with Matthew. He turned to look at Janna, who appeared as taken aback by the reality as he felt. *They were married.*

In the car, he took Janna's hand and kissed it, fingering her wedding ring. "You're awfully quiet, Mrs. Trevor."

Janna laughed softly. "I'm just trying to convince myself that it's real . . . that I truly am Mrs. Trevor."

"I think we'll get used to the idea," he chuckled.

Colin carried Janna over the threshold of the apartment and kicked the door closed. "So, what now?" he asked, setting her on her feet.

"Well," Janna feigned innocence, "we might have time to watch a video, or I could clean the bathroom, or—"

She laughed as he pulled her into his arms. "Stop talking and kiss me, Mrs. Trevor."

She kissed him warmly, then went on, "We could take a nap or—"

"You're getting closer," he whispered and kissed her again. And with their kiss, everything changed. They were husband and wife now. "Janna," he murmured, kissing her face, her throat, her face again. "It's been so long. Do you think we can remember what to do?"

"I don't think that's a problem," she whispered, pressing her hands into his hair.

Colin lifted her into his arms again and carried her to the bed. He paused a moment to just absorb how beautiful she was, and then he let out a long, slow breath—as if he'd been holding it since the last time he'd shared this with her. He marveled at the experience as memories of the past merged with the present, and it all became right. He could see now that what they had shared before was shallow and trite in comparison with this moment. There was no guilt or shame tainting the love they shared, and the rightness of their union brought everything together in an experience that he could only describe as complete. Being with Janna now fulfilled his every expectation. And they'd done it right this time.

As he lay quietly, holding Janna close to him, Colin couldn't help wondering if the experience had been clouded for her by the memories of her abuse. Wanting nothing to come between them, he leaned up on one elbow and looked down at her.

"Forgive me," he whispered, "but I have to know. Were they there, Janna? In your head? Russell, your father. Did they—"

Janna pressed a finger to his lips. "There are *no* similarities, Colin. All of that is in the past."

Colin appreciated her attitude, but he wondered if it was complete. "Janna, I just have to know if—"

"It was only you, Colin," she said serenely, and peace enveloped him. "Now stop talking and kiss me."

"You don't have to ask me twice," he smiled, and with their kiss his peace deepened—a peace that hovered with him through the remainder of the day as they returned to his parents' home for pictures and the open house. Little was said by their guests concerning the unusual circumstances of the marriage, and Colin wondered what it might have been like if they'd married eight years ago, with everyone as good as knowing that Janna was pregnant. Then he realized that it just didn't matter what anyone thought. They were at peace with each other and with the Lord. And it only took one look at Janna to know that life could get no better than this.

Janna had made Colin promise that when they cut the wedding cake and fed it to each other, he wouldn't push it in her face. He promised adamantly, but as she urged him to eat his piece of cake, she laughed and pushed it just enough to get it all around his mouth.

"That's not fair," he laughed.

"Sure it is," she said in a voice so full of happiness it was difficult to comprehend that she had ever been any other way. "You didn't make *me* promise not to do it."

He laughed again and pulled her into his arms, kissing her long and hard, leaving cake and frosting all over her mouth, while family and friends cheered and whistled. They had just wiped each other's faces off with napkins when Colin turned to see Judge Beckett extending a hand.

"Well, hello," Colin said, shaking the judge's hand firmly.

"It would seem you're busy," the judge said. "I'm a little late, but I didn't want to miss the opportunity to congratulate you."

"Thank you," Colin said, feeling a little in awe that this man would actually come to his wedding reception. "This is my wife, JannaLyn." Just saying it warmed Colin through.

"Ah, yes." The judge took both of Janna's hands into his as Colin finished the introduction.

"Janna, this is Judge Beckett."

"Of course," Janna smiled. "I remember."

There was a hint of sadness in her eyes as she said it, and the judge apparently noticed. "Yes, I'm certain you do, young lady," he said. "And that's part of the reason I'm here. First of all, I wanted to tell you that this is a fine young attorney you've married. It's not an easy business to be in, and I don't want you to ever let him forget that his reasons for doing it are noble."

Janna nodded firmly toward the judge. Colin glanced down, too moved to speak.

"And secondly," the judge said, "I have a little wedding gift for you. It's not something I can wrap up and put a bow on, but I wanted to deliver it personally. I found it ironic that the case of a certain Russell Clark came before me just this morning. I threw the book at him, Mrs. Trevor. I gave him the maximum penalty allowable by law. It's not nearly enough in my opinion, but my hope is that it will give you the time to make a new life for yourself." He grinned toward Colin. "And it would seem you've made a marvelous beginning here."

Colin saw the tears in Janna's eyes just before she put her arms around the judge and hugged him tightly. "Thank you," she said.

A moment later, Matthew appeared, tugging on Colin's arm. "You gotta come see your car, Dad. Come see."

"Oh, I can hardly wait," he muttered with light sarcasm, and the judge chuckled.

Colin introduced Matthew to the judge, who said with an easy smile, "So, young man, you've finally got your parents married."

"Yeah," Matthew grinned, remembering his father's earlier declaration. "Better late than never."

Photo by Nathan Barney

About the Author

Anita Stansfield is an imaginative and prolific writer whose stories of love and romance have captivated the LDS market. *Return to Love* is her sixth novel to be published by Covenant; her other best-selling titles include *First Love and Forever* (winner of the 1994-95 Best Fiction Award from the Independent LDS Booksellers), *First Love, Second Chances, Now and Forever, By Love and Grace,* and *A Promise of Forever.*

Anita has been writing since she was in high school, and her work has appeared in *Cosmopolitan* and other publications. She is an active member of the League of Utah Writers.

Anita and her husband, Vince, live with their four children and a cat named "Ivan the Terrible" in Alpine, Utah.